NAVAL ACADEMY ★

5

REINA MERCEDES

DATE			

SEW

SHIP 31

EE BASIN

MAST OF THE
U.S.S. *MAINE*

COOPER ROAD

FARRAGUT FIELD

SHERWOOD
HALL

VILLE GRIFFIN SAM

ECATUR ROAD

BALCH ROAD

PARKER RD.

MAI

MAIN

OMPSON
TADIUM

GATE 4

JAN 07 1994

ATHLETIC FIELD

ANNAPOLIS

THE OBSTACLE COURSE

The *O*bstacle Course

J. F. FREEDMAN

VIKING

VIKING
Published by the Penguin Group
Penguin Books USA Inc., 375 Hudson Street,
New York, New York 10014, U.S.A.
Penguin Books Ltd, 27 Wrights Lane,
London W8 5TZ, England
Penguin Books Australia Ltd, Ringwood,
Victoria, Australia
Penguin Books Canada Ltd, 10 Alcorn Avenue,
Toronto, Ontario, Canada M4V 3B2
Penguin Books (N.Z.) Ltd, 182–190 Wairau Road,
Auckland 10, New Zealand

Penguin Books Ltd, Registered Offices:
Harmondsworth, Middlesex, England

First published in 1994 by Viking Penguin,
a division of Penguin Books USA Inc.

1 3 5 7 9 10 8 6 4 2

PUBLISHER'S NOTE
This is a work of fiction. Names, characters, places, and incidents
either are the product of the author's imagination or are used fictitiously,
and any resemblance to actual persons, living or dead, events, or locales
is entirely coincidental.

Grateful acknowledgment is made for permission to reprint an excerpt
from "The Boy" by Rainer Maria Rilke from *The Best of Rilke*, translated
by Walter Arndt. © 1989 by Walter Arndt. By permission of
University Press of New England.

LIBRARY OF CONGRESS CATALOGING IN PUBLICATION DATA
Freedman, J. F.
The obstacle course: a novel / J. F. Freedman.
p.   cm.
ISBN 0-670-85346-1
1. Teenage boys—Maryland—Annapolis region—Fiction.   I. Title.
PS3556.R3833O27   1994
813'.54—dc20   93-22915

Printed in the United States of America
Set in Postscript Plantin
Designed by Ann Gold

TO RENDY

I want to be like one of those who race
With bolting steeds across the night-black air,
With flaming torches like unfastened hair
Aflutter in the stormwind of their chase.
Rainer Maria Rilke, "The Boy"
(translated by Walter Arndt)

ACKNOWLEDGMENTS

Bob Lescher and Al Silverman have been steadfast
in their unflagging encouragement and support.

This story takes place in southern Maryland,
from January to June, 1957.

January

ONE

The reason I got here so early, here being the U.S. Naval Academy in Annapolis, Maryland, was 'cause my old man came home around one-thirty in the morning drunker'n shit and woke the whole damn house up, staggering around, bumping into every stick of furniture in the damn house and swearing to beat the band. He and my old lady got into it real hot and heavy like they always do when he comes home in the bag, which is at least once a week, usually more. My sister Ruthie, who's in the eleventh grade and has a set on her like Cadillac bumpers—36DD, I swear to God, I know 'cause she's always hanging her bras and stockings in the bathroom, there's no way I couldn't see how big they were even if I was a blind man—she got into it and tried to separate them, which did a lot of good, all that happened was he got on her case worse'n my mom's, they all wound up yelling and cussing out each other.

I laid in bed and watched the snow come down. I need that kind of shit like I need another asshole.

They all went back to bed, but I couldn't fall asleep again. I hate that, people getting drunk and yelling and cursing each other. I don't know why my mom doesn't leave my dad, she hates his guts, she tells him "I hate your goddamn guts, you sonofabitch," she'll get right in his face, even though she knows he might coldcock her, even though she is a woman. That fucker gets drunk he's liable to do anything.

More than anything, what I want, except to come to the Naval Academy and be a midshipman, is to get out of my house. I'm going to, too. The day I turn sixteen and get my own wheels I'm out of here, I shit you not.

I jacked off again to try to get back to sleep but that didn't do any good, I was too worked up from all that commotion, they could wake up a goddamn graveyard the way they yell and bitch at each other, so I got dressed and went downstairs. My old man was laid out on the sofa, cold as a fish, pukey drunk-dribble coming out of his mouth, I could've shot off a shotgun in his ear he wouldn't have moved. He's a pretty tall guy, when he was my age he was skinny like me, but now he's got a beer-gut on him like he's got his bowling bag stuffed inside his shirt. He's pretty good-looking, actually, he's still got all his hair and teeth, he's always had this kind of mean-nasty truck-stop look about him that a lot of women seem to like, although his act wore out with my old lady a long time ago. I lifted a couple of bucks out of his wallet; he wouldn't know if he had five dollars or fifty in there, condition he was in. I figured he owed me. I didn't give a shit anyway—better his own son borrowing a few bucks than having him throw it at some barmaid down at the Dixie Bar & Grill.

Practically as soon as I stuck my thumb out I got a ride

straight to Annapolis, a bunch of good ol' boys going over to the Eastern Shore to duck hunt, happy as hell even though it was four-thirty in the morning. I went duck hunting once, last year, with Burt Kellogg and his brother and old man and a bunch of their friends. I didn't feature it all that much—you sit around colder and wetter than shit waiting for a bunch of dumb birds to fly close enough so you can blow their asses off. Burt's dad, he eats it on a stick—drinking coffee and booze with your buddies, getting away from everything. He's a cool guy. He gets drinking, everything's real easy. Like these hunters. Some guys they start drinking, they get real funny and mellow. Other guys get mean and fucked-up. I got lucky—I got the mean, fucked-up kind.

I folded my jacket carefully, wrapping it up in newspapers to keep it from getting wet from the snow, and laid it on one of the wooden benches. It's not that good a jacket, actually it's pretty ratty, but it's the only one I've got and my old man would tar my ass something fierce if I lost it, so I take real good care of it. I lost a jacket two years ago, I put it down and somebody walked off with it—a nigger probably although I couldn't prove it for sure—and my old man just about had a hemorrhage. I had to go without a jacket for a month until my mom talked him into getting me this one. It was wintertime, too, colder'n shit, I liked to freeze my cookies off walking to school. It'll make you a man, was the way my old man put it. Like he knows what the hell it takes to make anyone a man.

It was still snowing, falling down easy, the flakes large and wet, laying a smooth blanket a foot deep.

The campus was quiet. Nothing was moving except the boats moored on the water, the Severn River. The sky was gray-white with the snow. No one was awake. Dawn and the sun were still an hour away.

It's an old campus in an old town. The buildings are stone and wood. A place for serious business; a place to become a man. That's what I've always thought, ever since I started coming up here as a little boy, first with my family, then by myself.

This is where I'd learn to be a man. That's why I come all the time.

The athletic fields were beautiful under the snow. Icicles hung from the metal basketball nets and the wire-mesh batting cages.

All the way at the back was the obstacle course. It's this great big area, a good two and a half times larger than a football field. It can be murder running this thing, I've seen midshipmen who thought they were in good shape puke after running it just one time. It has thirty-six separate obstacles, and not one of them a piece of cake. Twenty-five-foot rope ladders, twelve-foot-high walls of brick with intricate footholds, water-jumps fifteen feet across, all kinds of tough barriers, forming a circled track inside its fenced-in space.

I stood at the starting line.

Before I go any further I should probably tell you something about myself. Just the facts, like Jack Webb says. Okay; I'm fourteen years old, soon to turn fifteen, in the ninth grade, taller than average, and strong for my age. Well-coordinated, too—I've been playing Boys Club football and baseball since I was ten and I'm one of the best ones on the team, especially football. I play quarterback, and center field in baseball.

One thing about the way I look—I'm always surprised when I see myself in a mirror, because my face has this stubborn expression, like I'm pissed off at something, even when I'm not. My teachers call it my sullen look; they say I look like I'm never happy about anything, that I look on the world as my enemy, as if something's always out there to beat me down, fuck me over.

A lot of boys I know have this look—most of my friends, in fact.

But when I'm doing something I enjoy, like running the obstacle course, my look changes. I don't have to look in a mirror, either; I just know. Everything relaxes, my face, my body, it's like I'm weightless. Then I look like somebody about to fly, to really fly up into the clouds. I really have my head in the clouds here; but no one sees it.

It wasn't all that cold out. I was wearing my jeans and sneakers and a sweatshirt over my T-shirt and I wasn't hardly cold at all, when it's snowing it doesn't get so cold, something about the air and the moisture, we learned about that stuff in science class, but I didn't remember it, if I need to know a fact for some reason, which I will when I go here, I'll look it up in the encyclopedia. I like reading the *Encyclopaedia Britannica*—I've read it all the way through a bunch of times, because when I was in the third grade and my teacher, Mrs. Witcomb, would keep me in at recess for doing something bad like talking out of turn or carving my initials in my desk, I'd read from the encyclopedia. By the time I was finished third grade I'd read the whole thing, cover to cover, all eighteen volumes. The encyclopedia's pretty neat; you can learn a lot from books.

One thing about knowing things, though: you have to be careful where and how you use them. In Ravensburg, the town I live in, it's not cool to be too smart. People think you're putting on airs, too good for them, that kind of shit.

Actually, when I was in grade school, I was a good student; in grade school you could be a good student and still be cool. One term in fifth grade I got four A's and two B's. Even my parents had been impressed. In junior high, though, that stopped, almost from the day I walked in. One of the first things I learned was not only is it uncool to be smart as far as kids are concerned, teachers don't like it, either. Not the kind of smart where you think for yourself and say so. What they want is conformity, and above all, no hassles. Don't fuck with them, do your homework, be part of the crowd, and you're a solid B student, easy. I could never go along with that shit, so right out of the box I was branded as a troublemaker, which is the same thing in their puny little minds as a bad student, to the point where, even though I don't deep-down believe it, I acknowledge it. Anyway, fuck 'em if they can't take a joke, that's one of my mottos.

I took some slow, deep breaths, clenching and unclenching my hands, shaking my fingers, rocking back and forth a few times.

Doing that stuff gets you loose, I learned it from watching these track guys, broad-jumpers, here and at the University of Maryland. It's cool-looking, too.

Then I started running.

I ran at a fast, steady pace, concentrating on nothing except the obstacle in front of me, and then the one after that. I took each easily and with assurance, landing lightly on the balls of my feet after each jump. This is what I'm best at, where I can lose myself in the dreams that career around in my head, away from the bullshit that forces itself on me in ways beyond my control, ways I can't handle. When I run here there's nothing in the world to stop me, to tell me I'm less than perfect, which is how things go usually.

The thing I like the most about the obstacle course is that it's just me and it; you can't bullshit it, you can't fake it out with lies or promises. You run it, that's all. If you put in the effort you get rewarded, and if you slough it you know it. No one has to tell you.

There was no one around to watch, to applaud. That was fine; I prefer being on my own, in my solitary world, hearing the cheers inside my head, the roar of winning, with the snow ahead of me, clear and crusty, breaking under my stride.

I came to the end and stopped for a moment, deep-breathing, bent over, hands on thighs. Scooping up a chunk of snow, I made a couple of snowballs, hard ones, packing them tight as baseballs, and threw them at the nearest obstacle. They hit with a good hard thud, the sound echoing faintly in the quiet.

I took a deep breath and started to run the course again.

I ran the course five times. That isn't so many, I can do that many pretty easy, I'm faster on it than most of the midshipmen. I've got a lot of stamina for a kid my age. I ran it once twelve times in a row without stopping. That was last summer, when it was light out until nine-thirty. There were some midshipmen hanging around, working out, and they started watching me when I got going, then they started cheering for me, rooting me on, "come on, kid, keep going," they were yelling, counting the laps, one would join me for a lap and then he'd drop out and another one would take a lap with me. A whole bunch of them came over to watch, it was like a big party, they were laughing and yelling and really having a good time. I was, too.

Later on they took me over to Bancroft Hall and let me eat with them. It was really neat, they have good food there and plenty of it. Actually, it was one of the best days of my life. Probably the best day.

The sun came out while I was running. It looked like a slice of lemon, real pale yellow. It didn't get any warmer, though, actually it got colder, because the snow stopped falling. The day was really clear like it gets sometimes after it stops snowing, this kind of real hard, pale, metal-blue-looking kind of sky. All the big soft clouds drifted off, leaving these little finger clouds, real high in the sky.

Five times is about average for me. I could always come back and run more if I felt like it. I had sweated clear through my T-shirt and sweatshirt both; I was warm now, comfortable even without my jacket. My shirts were sticking to my chest so I plucked them away from my skin, the steam from my sweat rising up over my body, like it does after you take a real hot shower, the kind where the needles sting real good and your body gets as red as a lobster. I walked over to a patch of clean snow and fell straight back, keeping stiff so as not to spoil it, and then I moved my arms and legs to make an angel.

I just lay there for a while. Way off in the distance the bells of the Academy started chiming church carols. They do that every Sunday, it's really beautiful. I like getting up here early to hear them. I don't actually like going to church but I like hearing the bells. If you listen carefully you can hear the bells coming from town as well, they've got churches all over Annapolis, it's a really old town, the oldest state capital in the U.S., I learned that from the encyclopedia, too. In sixth-grade geography class we studied Maryland state history, I used to be able to name every county in Maryland. There's twenty-three of them. I know just about everything there is about Annapolis and the Naval Academy, I can be really smart when something interests me, I could be the smartest kid in my class if I felt like it.

I don't remember all twenty-three counties by heart anymore. If I need to know them again I'll look them up.

I was sitting under Tecumseh, a famous old statue of an Indian chief which is like a symbol of the Academy. It's outside Bancroft Hall, the main building where all the midshipmen live and eat. They can serve four thousand people at the same time, it's the biggest dining room I've ever seen—probably one of the biggest ones in the whole country, I'll bet.

The midshipmen were coming by in groups on their way to breakfast. On Sundays they can come to meals when they want. The rest of the week they march to meals in formation, the whole brigade. It's one of the coolest things you can see, all of them marching like one man, ramrod-straight in uniform.

One thing I love about the Academy is the uniforms. They're really neat-looking, summer and winter both. What's good is that they're all wearing the same thing. You don't have to worry about whether you're a cool dresser or not, or if you have enough money to buy all the right clothes or not. Some kids, just because they can't afford new clothes, are treated like shit. There's some kids in my class who've probably never had new clothes in their life, not even shoes. They have to wear their older brothers' or sisters' hand-me-downs. One girl in elementary school had to wear her older brother's clothes, even his shoes, which were big black brogans—clodhoppers, they're called. I really felt sorry for that girl, Clara Wilson. Her parents were sharecroppers and when the farm they shared on got sold they had to move. She was a nice girl, too, pretty and smart both, but all the other girls treated her like a leper. It wasn't her fault her folks were poor. If she was still around I'd probably be wanting to take her out. She really was pretty, even in fifth grade.

I was hungry as hell. You get hungry running the obstacle course as many times as I did. I could've gone into town and bought some breakfast, but I wanted to eat here, with all these guys. Sometimes I pretend I'm somebody's kid brother, visiting for the weekend. The problem is I don't have a brother, and if I did he sure wouldn't be here, not the way my family operates. That's another reason I want to get out when I'm old enough, because if the people here ever found out what kind of family I've got I could kiss my chances of getting in goodbye.

"Had your breakfast yet?"

I jumped up and fell in step with this midshipman. He was second-year, what they call a youngster, walking along all by his lonesome. I could tell his rank by the stripes on his uniform, I know all that shit, I've memorized it.

"Breakfast," I repeated. "Had yours yet?"

"On my way," he answered, glancing over at me.

"Take me in with you, will you?" I asked, trying to keep the whine out of my voice. Sometimes when I want something real bad my voice goes up so I sound like I'm about ten years old. I hate it when that happens. "You can bring guests in on the weekend," I told him, in case he didn't know.

"Only family." He knew.

"So tell 'em I'm your brother." He was walking fast, the way they do, but I kept up, matching him step for step.

"Don't have a brother," he told me.

"Bet you always wanted one."

"Not today, kid. Take off."

I waited near the entrance, biding my time. You've got to be patient when you're trying something like this. A few minutes later three first-classmen headed towards me. They had officers' epaulets on their uniforms, which meant they were very big deals. They were laughing and talking, real confident laughs and booming voices, like they owned the world.

I stopped one as he passed by me. He was a big guy, pleasant-looking, kind of like a hick with a coat of polish on him. A lot of these guys are just hicks from the sticks when they come here, but they're men of the world when they leave. This one looked like a pretty easy mark, one of those nice big guys who's everybody's friend.

"Don't I know you from somewhere?" I asked him, talking fast.

He looked at me for a second.

"You talking to me, kid?"

"You're on the football team, right? I saw you play against Maryland last year, didn't I?"

You always ask a big guy if he's on the football team. Even if he isn't it makes him feel good, like he's this big stud jock.

"No," he answered, like the question embarrassed him almost. Maybe he'd tried out and hadn't made it.

"You look like a football player to me," I told him. "A good one." A little flattery never hurts, I learned that early on.

"I play lacrosse," he said, trying to come on real modest-like.

"Bet you're good, too," I said.

"Good enough. I start."

He was smiling. Everybody likes to brag on himself.

"I knew it," I crowed triumphantly. "I saw you play against Hopkins last year, didn't I? You probably scored a mess of goals."

Wrong move. His face clouded up right away.

"I missed the Hopkins game," he said. I could hear the anger rising in his voice. "Lousy demerits. Cost me my letter."

"Hey, you'll get it this year, no sweat," I told him. I was getting nervous—we were almost at the front door.

"Shake it, Maguire," one of the other ones said to my mark, "the bus for the Colts game leaves in half an hour."

"Take me in with you," I pressed, hearing the begging tone

in my voice. Maybe he'd take pity on me, as long as he got me inside I didn't give a shit how.

"No." He walked faster, trying to get away.

"Listen, I'm not kidding, it's simple, just tell the checker at the door I'm your brother, I do it all the time, nobody cares."

"Forget it." He pushed me away as he walked through the door.

It was that damn Hopkins game. I've got to learn to keep my stupid mouth shut once I'm ahead.

"Fuck off, lardass," I yelled after him, "the only team you'll ever get a letter from is the beat-your-meat team."

He spun on his heel like he was going to chase me, but I was already gone. He couldn't have caught me if he'd chased me clear to Baltimore. He really did have a fat ass, he was probably called lardass all the time, he didn't want some kid reminding his friends about it.

The morning was slipping by. I should've gone into town and eaten, but I wanted to eat here, it was like something inside of me had to have it. I could smell the hot cakes and bacon and sausage aromas drifting out from inside. I was so hungry I could've eaten a horse, tail and all.

Then I saw him—the mark of all time, this skinny little guy wearing glasses that looked like Coke-bottle bottoms, they were so thick. I didn't know you could get into the Naval Academy if your eyes were that bad. Maybe they hadn't been as bad when he came, maybe they got bad from all the studying you have to do. You have to work your ass off to get through four years here. You've got to work your ass off and really be smart at the same time.

He was a complete wet-shit, that's the only honest description you could give him. No way this pussy was a jock. The only sport he'd be good for would be tiddlywinks. I could run rings around him on the obstacle course, I knew that for sure. This poor guy probably didn't have a friend in the world. He'd be happy to have company for breakfast.

I strolled up to him, synchronized my steps with his.

"Today's take-a-buddy-to-breakfast day, okay?" I told him in a low voice, talking fast out of the side of my mouth.

He looked at me kind of strangely but didn't say anything; he probably hadn't ever had anyone want to eat breakfast with him before. I was going to do him a favor, to tell you the truth.

"Just tell the guy checking the door I'm your brother," I explained, "they don't give a shit on Sundays, I'll shine your brass for you if you bring me in, that's a good deal."

The guy cracked a smile. I had him, I knew it. I fell in lockstep with him as we hit the door together.

"I'm your brother, got it?" I instructed him under my breath. You've got to be patient with these guys sometimes, they've got their heads way up in the clouds, all the studying they do.

We passed through the door into King's Hall, which is the actual dining room. This asshole nodded to the checker without saying a word, he just kept going. The checker leaned over and grabbed me by the collar.

"I'm his brother!" I called to the dumb bastard's back: "Hey, tell him!"

The checker was this stout, happy-go-lucky-looking plebe. He smiled kind of sympathetically to me.

"Sorry, kid." He pushed me away.

I looked inside. The mark was standing in the hallway, talking to another midshipman, another loser from the looks of him. They must've been charter members in the Annapolis loser's club.

"Asshole," I muttered under my breath. I was pissed off, no way I was going to let him get away with treating me like that, so I grabbed a handful of snow, made a hard ball out of it, and threw a Johnny Unitas spiral into the doorway, right at his scalped head.

"Hey!" he yelled, startled and angry.

I took off, running across the quad. He was a wet shit but he was still bigger and stronger than me. Stupid asshole—served him right. Like another order of pancakes and sausage would hurt anyone. When I'm a midshipman I'll take in any kid that asks. I'll go *find* kids and bring them in. I'll be the best friend here a kid could ever have.

The Severn River was choppy, big dark-green waves slamming against the breakwater. There was another storm coming in tonight, I can tell when the weather's going to turn shitty, it's usually when I'm out on the road. I'd have to make sure I hit the highway early enough to hitch a ride while it was still light out, otherwise I could be standing there with my thumb hanging out all night long.

I walked along the embankment, hunched over against the wind. My jacket isn't all that warm, it's just a car coat for the fall, I don't have a real winter jacket. The one I lost was a good one, but my old man didn't feel like throwing good money away after bad, was how he saw it, meaning I'd lose another one. That's one of the things I really like about my old man, how much he believes in me.

The boats on the river were drifting in the water, their mooring lines straining tight against the piers, the masts bare. It was quiet—the only sounds were the windblown whitecaps moving across the water, slapping against the sides of the hulls. One halyard had got unfastened, snapping back and forth against itself like a bullwhip.

I bought a couple of hot dogs off a stand down by where the Academy keeps their racing sailboats: high-masted yawls, brought up out of the water, dry-docked for the winter. The rolls were stale—the vendor must've been hanging onto them since last weekend, waiting for some hungry sucker like me to take them off his hands. I ate the hot dogs and threw most of the rolls away for the seagulls.

The sun finally came out around midafternoon, but the clouds were still hovering. The snow was half-melted, turning to slush. I hate it when snow melts like that. Somehow all the dog shit in the world surfaces under the slush, it's like one big carpet of dog crap. I drifted around the campus, looking at the families that had come down to be with their sons. Some of the families had kids my age. They always look like they belong here, like they fit in. I think that's part of my problem—I don't look like I fit in.

For a while I played in a pickup basketball game with some boys my age. They didn't want me to, I could tell, but they were too chickenshit to keep me out. They played this finesse game, fancy dribbling and stuff like that. My style is to put my head down and go for the basket and everybody get the hell out of my way. I call a lot of fouls, too. Needless to say they weren't real happy with my coming in and upsetting their little applecart. We played one game of twenty-one, then they picked up their ball and left. I didn't have a ball of my own, so there wasn't much point in sticking around there.

By the time I wound up back at the obstacle course the sun was fading fast. It didn't matter—I could run it blindfolded if I wanted to. I ran it hard, really attacking it, punishing it, running as hard and fast as I could until I ran out of gas and had to finally stop, bent over double, sucking in the air, my hands on my knees. It feels good, running hard like that, sucking in air so hard it feels like your lungs are burning.

I ran it one more time. I didn't much feel like it, but I did it anyway.

TWO

It was colder than shit out and snowing again. I couldn't get a lift to save my life. I felt like some stray dog left out in the rain to fend for itself, like those dogs you see whose owners don't want them anymore and just leave them by the side of the road, chuck them out of the car without even looking back. They come up to you with this begging kind of look, their tails between their raggedy legs, all dirty and matted up, kind of whimpering and whining, expecting you to kick them. That's about how I felt right then.

I don't get rides as easy as I used to. I hit my growth spurt last year and put on a good four inches. I grew so fast I outgrew all my clothes; I looked like the scarecrow from *The Wizard of Oz*. It's especially bad at night, when you're standing out there in the dark on Defense Highway, 'cause the only light is when a headlight hits you from a car going by and by then it's too late for them to stop. I don't look like a kid anymore, that's the problem. When I was a little kid, even last year, rides would come real easy, not only men drivers but women, too, they'd see this kid standing out there with his thumb sticking out, looking all forlorn like Little Orphan Annie, and they'd get feeling guilty and motherly and they'd pull over and take a look at me to make sure I wasn't some midget ax murderer or something and then once I was in the car they'd ask where I was going and where I lived and did my parents know I was out by myself at night and all that other motherly shit. I'd make up some story for them, whatever popped into my head. It was usually a good one. One time this woman started crying, I laid such a load of pathetic shit on her.

Finally I got a ride from some guy driving this raggedy-ass milk tanker heading into D.C. from the Eastern Shore. It was an old Mack in serious need of a ring job, the smoke was coming out the exhaust so black you couldn't hardly see out the little back window of the cab. Not only that but the guy had a serious case of the farts—I had to crack my window, the fart smell was so putrid. The funny thing was, I don't think he even knew he was doing it. He was a real farmer, this guy.

"Ravensburg," he said when I told him where I was going, "I can drop you there, night like this rides're gonna be hard to come by." He had one of those super-thick Eastern Shore accents, the kind even people from other parts of Maryland can't hardly understand. The only reason I can is because my mother's people came from Tilghman Island originally, which is this real neat little island over on the Eastern Shore where they do oyster fishing in these old sailboats called skipjacks. Her people weren't oyster fishers, though; my mom gets seasick just looking at a boat.

Anyway, big fucking deal, he can drop me there. Defense

Highway, the road we were on, which is the only road between Annapolis and Washington, goes through Ravensburg. Splits it right down the center, in fact. The way he put it, it was like he was doing me a big favor, going out of his way for me. I hate it when people act like they're doing you a big favor when they aren't doing jack-shit. Beggars can't be choosers, though, not when you're out there thumbing in a snowstorm.

"Bum one of your smokes?" I asked. He had a pack of Chesterfields sitting up on the dash. I personally can't stand Chesterfields, but I needed a smoke to calm my nerves and to cut the fart odor.

He gave me a funny look, like he didn't want to, but he did. It's funny how people are, they won't want to do something like let you bum one of their cigs but they won't come out and say no, they'll just give you one of these looks that's supposed to do it for them. And then you're supposed to know that the look means "I don't want to" and not bum one, or whatever it is you asked for they didn't want to give you. But I don't go for that, not if I really wanted it, and I really wanted that Chesterfield, although normally I wouldn't touch one with a ten-foot pole, so I just pretended like I didn't understand the "look" routine, and slid one out of his pack.

"Where you been?" he asked after I fired it up and blew a smoke ring. I blow the best smoke rings of any kid in my class, it's one of my specialties.

"Annapolis," I told him. "The Naval Academy."

"Uh huh," he said, like the Naval Academy was no big deal.

"My brother's a midshipman," I elaborated.

"Oh, yeah?" That impressed him—kind of. Like I said, he was a real farmer, having a midshipman for a brother had to impress someone like him.

"He's a middie second-class," I continued, "he graduates next year."

He didn't comment on that. Probably still worrying about that one pathetic Chesterfield.

"He's captain of his company. Actually of his whole brigade. He's on the football team, too. Halfback."

That got his attention. The funny thing was, if he'd known anything at all about the Naval Academy he'd have busted me there and then, because you don't get to be a brigade commander until your senior year. But he was so stupid he didn't even know that.

"I must've seen him play last year," he said. "I went to the Maryland game."

"Right," I answered, getting into it, "that was him. He had a real good game, even though he was only a sophomore."

"Maryland creamed 'em," the driver said, real pissed-off, "nobody from Navy had a good game the Maryland game." He said it like it was my fault Maryland creamed Navy last year.

"He had a better game than anyone else," I said, quick to defend my "brother," "anyway, they're gonna be good this year. He might make All-American."

The driver looked over at me kind of suspicious, like he thought I was bullshitting him but wasn't sure.

"What did you say his name was?" he asked. "Your brother?"

"Tolliver," I lied. It slid right off my tongue. "Peter Tolliver."

"Oh, sure. I've heard of him. Everybody's heard of him. There was a big article in the *Sun*'s sports section about him last fall." His tone of voice was suddenly a lot more respectful.

"I ride the team bus when they've got a game in Baltimore," I continued, really into my own bullshit now, when I get on a roll I can talk your ears off and make you believe it. "They eat breakfast early Saturday morning and then they get on the team bus up to Baltimore. I eat breakfast with them and ride up on the bus."

"Like the team mascot," he chipped in. I had him eating out of my hand.

We drove a little ways without talking. It was snowing good, he had to pay attention to the road.

"It ain't none of my bidness," he said, looking at me again, at my raggedy jacket and all, "but this is lousy weather for a kid to be hitchhiking in. How come your parents didn't come up with you?"

I fidgeted around in my seat like I was embarrassed, which I was, kind of, but not because of the reason he thought.

"My father's dead," I said real low, like I didn't want to, "he got killed in Korea. He was a fighter pilot in the Marines. He got shot down over North Korea."

"Jesus," he muttered.

"My mother has to work weekends," I went on. When I get going on a story I'm like a runaway freight train, I can't stop even if I want to. "She sews clothes. She's never seen my brother play."

"Damn."

"That's why it's real important for me to go. So I can come home and tell her all about it. She listens on the radio, though."

"It's a shame she can't get one weekend off to see him," he said, real sympathetic-like, "especially since you live so close. Not many mothers have a son who's starting halfback for one of the best teams in the country."

"It wouldn't make any difference," I told him, my voice getting real quiet. "She's blind. She's been blind ever since my father died. It's in her head is what the doctors say. Like once he died there wasn't anything for her to want to see anymore."

He had to jerk the steering wheel real hard then, because he'd practically driven off the road when he heard that.

"Jesus."

I thought he was going to cry, he sounded so sad.

"The doctors hope someday she might be able to see again," I told him. "If she can ever get over my father's dying."

He let me off in front of the elementary school. It was snowing to beat the band, I felt cold as soon as I opened the door.

This car coat of mine just doesn't do the job, not when it's snowing and freezing like this.

"Thanks for the ride, sir," I told him politely. I actually did appreciate it, I could still be standing in Annapolis with my thumb out, freezing my cookies off.

"That's okay, kid."

A sudden gust of wind blew under my jacket, making me shiver. I pulled it tight. My mom had wanted to get me a decent jacket at the beginning of the school year but my old man nixed it, next year would be soon enough, he'd said, times are tough and money doesn't grow on trees, he's always saying stupid shit like that, plus of course I'd lost my other jacket. "He's a regular absent-minded professor," he'll say, "except he ain't no professor, not with his piss-poor grades." Then he'll go on about how after the bare necessities, like the house payment, there's never anything left, which is a crock of shit, he has a steady job at the Government Printing Office and makes good money. "There's always money for Four Roses," my mother rags on him. Her voice is hoarse, deep as a man's, more from the constant ragging on him she does than the two packs of Kents she smokes a day, "there's always money for Jim Beam, how come there's always money for whatever you can pour down your goddamned throat but the kids got to walk around looking like we're on tobacco road." That's an exaggeration, of course, there's plenty of kids in my school who actually are from tobacco road and we don't look anything like them. My parents fight all the time, he'll knock her upside her head and she'll throw a frying pan or something at him and then she'll start crying. She hates looking poor. My old man doesn't give a shit, though, he'll tell her if she don't like it she can lump it. That's one of his favorite expressions—it's about the best he can do, he doesn't have a real good vocabulary, I know twice as much as he does already and I'm only in the ninth grade.

My hair was turning white from the snow. It was covering my head and shoulders, too.

"You get inside where it's warm," the driver said.

"I'm going straight home," I promised him.

He crunched the gears and pulled away, heading for Washington. I stood there and watched him go, feeling the snow falling on my head.

Even though it was cold out I took my time walking home. It was past seven, so I was already late for dinner; no sense rushing a bad thing. I looked in some of the windows as I walked down the street. People were eating dinner or watching television. Some were doing both at the same time. I know everybody in the neighborhood, practically. Ravensburg's one of these real old towns going back to the 1600's, there're stones in the graveyards going back to 1640. I like the graveyard, it's quiet there, not scary at all. I have friends whose people go clear back to the 1600's in Ravensburg, you can see their family names on some of the old markers. There's no real reason to stay here but hardly anybody ever leaves. Not me, though. When the time comes I'm leaving in a cloud of dust and a hearty "Hi, ho, Silver, away."

The lights were on in our kitchen. I peeked through the window. My family was eating dinner. Even from outside I knew what it was: Swiss steak, kale, potatoes, and bread to dip in the gravy. None of those things are my favorites, but beggars can't be choosers. My old man, as usual, was washing his down with a jelly-jar glass of booze—probably Four Roses, his everyday poison.

I was jittery—being late for dinner is a sure way to piss my old man off. Just about everything I do pisses him off. He's pissed off with me about something almost every day.

I counted from twenty backwards three times, took a deep breath, and ran inside, huffing and puffing like I'd been running a mile.

"I couldn't help it!" I immediately started improvising like mad, you never know, someday someone might believe you. "I swear to God I'd've been home an hour ago but this old lady got a flat tire and I had to help her fix it 'cause she was going to Prince Georges Hospital 'cause her husband's got cancer. He could die any minute.''

My old man didn't even bother to look up from his plate.

"Tell me another one."

I threw my coat on the couch, sat down at the table.

"It's true, I swear to God." I blew on my hands to get them warm. "Boy, I'm starving, what's for dinner, mom?"

She shuffled over to the oven, took out my plate (which she'd kept warm, like always), and put it in front of me without saying a word. She's been doing this for years.

Ruthie glanced over at me.

"I liked the story about the kid whose dog got run over better," she said, real snide.

"Up yours," I told her under my breath. Like her shit don't stink.

"You can do the dishes tonight," my mother told me.

That was okay, it beats the shit out of getting your ass tanned any day. Her and Ruthie got up to go in the living room for a smoke. She looked tired—she usually looks tired. Even though I don't favor women coloring their hair unless they're old and gray, my mom's one woman who ought to. It's this kind of dishwater-blond that doesn't look pretty no matter how she styles it. She doesn't wear makeup around the house, so the lines around her mouth and eyes are starting to show pretty strong. She's only thirty-six but she's aging fast. Living in my family'll do that to you.

Ruthie was wearing one of her extra-tight Orlon sweaters, the kind where her bra shows through. She doesn't hide them, that's for sure. By the time she's twenty-five she'll have an ass as wide as two ax handles, the way she chows down. She's built good now, though—once in a while I'll sneak a look at her while she's getting undressed. She's got a set on her like Jayne Mansfield, I swear to God. All my buddies're always trying to get me to let them sneak a look, but I never do. She's my sister, after all, and anyway my old man would whip my ass from here to Hyattsville if he ever caught us.

My dad polished off the last of his drink, belched like a car backfiring, and went in to watch television. My plate looked like something the dog would've thrown up, but I ate it all anyway.

"Hits or cracks?"

"Cracks."

Burt peeled the stamp off the back of the Camels pack. There was an H 1 written underneath.

"It's always hits," Joe complained.

"So say hits," Burt answered.

Joe pulled his left arm out of his jacket and rolled up his shirtsleeve. Burt pinched some skin behind his biceps, and gave Joe a mean-looking frog with the first knuckle of his middle finger.

"Shit!" Joe flinched.

They hurt, especially when someone who knows how to give them does it. Joe's arm'll be black and blue all day from that one frog.

We've been playing this game since third grade, when we started smoking. All packs of Camels have either the letter H or the letter K behind the tobacco stamp. The H always has the number one after it, while the K can have any number, usually ten or more, up to fifty. Almost all packs have an H, but if you ever get a K, you can frog a guy to death, which is why people will choose K, even if it almost never comes up.

Me, Joe Matthews and Burt Kellogg, the Three Musketeers we call ourselves, were hunched down between cars in the teachers' parking lot, near where the teachers' lounge is located. They're my best friends, true asshole buddies, one for all and all for one. We've been tight as brothers since seventh grade when Burt moved to Ravensburg from Brookland, in D.C.

Clarence Kane was with us, also. He's okay, but he's not close, he's just another kid.

We were sharing a butt, our jackets tight around our necks to keep warm. I was wearing my new Ravensburg High jacket, which I'd just gotten at the high school bookstore. I finally couldn't stand that raggedy-ass old jacket of mine anymore, so I bought this new one with some money from my secret stash. It was totally cherry—midnight-blue with white trim, and lined inside, so it was extra-warm. My parents probably figured I'd bought it out of last summer's lawnmowing earnings. They don't give a shit as long as it doesn't come out of their pockets, my old man especially.

"Nice jacket, Roy," Burt said. He fingered the material.

"Hands off the merchandise," I told him. "I don't want your goddamn cooties."

"Touchy touchy touchy."

Before I could stop myself, this humongous belch rolled up my throat and out my mouth. My mom had made Spam and eggs for breakfast; Spam'll make me belch every time.

"Shit, man," Burt complained. "Ain't you got no couth?"

"Saves wear and tear on the asshole," I informed him.

It was cold out, dry-cold. We were early, we had time to kill before we had to be inside for homeroom. Clarence passed the crumpled-up Camel to me. We usually smoke Camels 'cause they're a cent cheaper than Luckies and you can play hits or cracks with them. I took it carefully between my thumb and forefinger and took a hard drag, making sure my lips were drawn back tight against my gums.

A piece of tobacco stuck to my lip anyway. I spat it out.

"Don't nigger-lip it, Roy, goddamnit," Clarence hissed.

I French-inhaled like I've seen my sister do. She learned that from the movies. I passed the butt left, to Burt.

"Don't get your bowels in an uproar," I told Clarence.

Burt took a drag and passed the butt to Joe.

"You know what Danny Detweiler told me?" Joe asked, taking a deep drag. "He said he finger-fucked Darlene Mast at the movies Saturday night." He passed the cig over to Clarence.

My breath froze in my throat. The idea that anybody would've touched Darlene Mast gave me a hard knot in my stomach; that it was Danny Detweiler, the one kid in the whole school I hate with a purple passion, made the thought especially shitty.

"Who told you that crap?" Burt asked skeptically.

"Danny. He said he had her so hot he almost came in his Jockeys."

Burt turned to me. "You believe that?"

I shrugged like I could give a shit either way. No one knows how I feel about Darlene, not even my best buddies. But my asshole was so tight you couldn't have forced a BB up it with an air gun.

"Well, I don't," Clarence said, " 'cause I saw Darlene at the skating rink Saturday night and Danny wasn't even there."

"Darlene's the worst cockteaser that ever lived," Burt added. "That girl's gonna cause more cases of blue balls in history before she's through."

"Aw, come on, man, she is not," I countered as casually as I could, wanting to defend her without giving myself away. "You're probably jealous because she never pays you any attention," I said, pretending like I was kidding him.

"She's a little cockteaser," Burt assured me, "take it from the pro. She'll tell a guy she likes him just to get another guy jealous. She did it to Kevin Rooney last fall—remember how he thought she was all hot for him? She didn't give a flying fuck for Kevin, she just wanted to make some DeMatha creep jealous. Broke poor ol' Kevin's heart for at least two, three days. I feel for the poor bastard ever gets involved with her," he added with finality, dismissing any yearnings towards her on his part, which was fine with me, I don't like being in competition with my buddies. It's an unwritten code between us, if one of us likes a girl and declares it, the others keep hands off, even if they like her, too.

"I *knew* Danny was full of it," Joe said, pissed off at himself for having been taken in. "Lying motherfucker."

Even though I didn't care for Burt calling Darlene a cock-teaser, I can't tell you how relieved I felt. I was lightheaded, it had shook me up so bad—the thought of Darlene and Danny together. The thought of Darlene and *anybody* together.

Nobody knows that Darlene is the love of my life and the constant object of my most personal sexual dreams. Especially her—she barely knows I exist, even though we've been in the same grade, the same homeroom even, for two and a half years. That's not true, I mean literally, she certainly knows I exist, everybody in the school knows I exist, but it's like it doesn't matter to her, she ignores me so bad. Sometimes I think she ignores me just because she's aware of me and wants to show me that she isn't.

I remember the first time I saw Darlene naked. It was in seventh grade, more than two years ago. Me and Joe and Burt had finished gym class and were hanging around. It was winter and gym was held inside. The girls were down at the other end of the gym playing volleyball, jumping around and squealing. After the bell had rung to signal it was time to go change, Joe whistled me over.

"Hey, Poole," he'd commanded, "get your ass up here."

I'd followed him and Burt up onto the stage, which is at the end of the gym. (It's a combination gym and auditorium, we have assemblies in there as well as sports.) While the other boys in our class went to take their showers we'd hid behind the curtains on the side of the stage next to the girls' locker room.

"Take a look," Joe had told us.

He pulled aside a loose piece of beaverboard that exposed the stairs leading from the girls' locker room down to their shower, which was a flight below.

"How'd you find out about this?" Burt had asked, real wide-eyed. We were young and hairless boys still, but old enough to know how important this knowledge was.

"My brother told me," Joe had boasted. "Old family tradition." *Joe's brother's in senior high, a real rock.*

We had watched in silence as the girls ran out of their locker room, down the stairs to the showers. Most of them were still flat, since they were only seventh-graders, but a few were starting to get real titties. Nancy Calhoun and Sonja Swarrel and Carrie Bestrow passed in front of our eyes, girls we'd known all our lives, from before first grade even.

Then Darlene had emerged. I had never seen her before. Until this summer she lived in Landover, which is two towns over from Ravens-burg, and went to elementary school there. Now she bussed in here, like most of the kids.

She ran down the stairs on her tiptoes, almost like she was dancing. Her titties were just starting to come out—not like now, which are perfect, not huge like my sister's but just right, the size of oranges and perfectly shaped. Her long dark hair fell down her shoulders like a cloud almost. I knew I was in love the second I saw her.

I've never asked her out. Not once. She'd say "no" anyway so why make myself miserable? I hear she has a boyfriend at DeMatha, which is this Catholic high school in Hyattsville specializing in basketball—some junior hotshot who has his own wheels. If he goes to DeMatha he probably has an IQ in the high teens at least. That's okay—in a little more than a year I'll be sixteen, with wheels of my own. Then she'll see how cool I am.

"Shit." Burt looked up suddenly, interrupting my reverie. "Here comes Duffy."

Joe stomped the butt out and flipped it under the nearest car. Horace Duffy is the principal. He used to be a gym teacher, that tells you how good a school it is, when the gym teacher becomes the principal. He's bald as a cue ball and getting fat, but he's still tough as hell. Here it was the middle of winter and this guy's walking around in a short-sleeve shirt and a bow tie. It could be colder than a brass toilet seat in the Yukon and Duffy'll be walking around without his coat on. He really is tougher than shit. We don't like to admit that he's tougher than us, but he definitely is.

We stood up, acting real nonchalant, like we were going to

pull one over on him. This guy's probably seen more shit than all of us have put together.

"What're you boys doing out here?" he asked pleasantly. That's his style, one moment he's real buddy-buddy, the next he's an inch away from ripping you a new asshole. You never know when, either, it's part of what makes him so scary.

"Nothing, Mr. Duffy," I said.

"How's about moving it inside? I'm getting tired of seeing y'all in detention hall." He laid a heavy hand on my shoulder—it was not a comforting gesture, to say the least. "Especially you, Mr. Poole," he told me with this evil smile.

"Yes, sir."

"Didn't you have any homework last night?" he asked me. He could see I didn't have any of my schoolbooks with me. None of the other guys did, either, but he'd picked me out this morning to rag on. He gets on me a lot, I'll bet he gets on me as much as any kid in the whole school.

"I already left them in my locker, Mr. Duffy."

"Glad to hear it. I've noticed your grades haven't been the best this year."

"They'll get better, I promise."

"I'm going to hold you to it, Roy. All of you," he said, looking at everyone. "You're smart boys, there's no reason you shouldn't be doing better."

We nodded our heads and shuffled our feet. We get this all the time from teachers, how we're really smart and just don't apply ourselves. I've been hearing that shit from first grade. Actually, it's true. At least I am, I don't know about these other guys, but I can be smart when I want to be. The thing is, who cares about being smart in such a dumb school? The other thing is I don't look like a brain or act like one so my teachers treat me like I'm dogshit, which is how they treat most of the kids here. It's not exactly the best way to get somebody to do better. Anyway, I'll buckle down when I get to high school, 'cause I'll have to get good grades to get into Annapolis.

Satisfied that he'd gotten our attention, Duffy turned on his heel and strolled away. Burt kissed his middle finger and shot him the bird.

"Detention hall next week, Kellogg," Duffy sang out, not even turning around to look at us. The guy's got eyes in the back of his head, I swear to God.

"Hey Sarkie babe," I whispered under my breath, "you do the math homework?"

In the whole time I've been in this school I've never cracked a book. Hardly anybody I know ever does. The only ones that do are the brains, who are so weird they actually like studying, and the dipshits, who are too scared not to.

Of course, that can present problems, like if you've got a math assignment due and you haven't done it, which was the case this morning.

Sarkind is the uncoolest kid in my class. He's this short, fat wet-shit. His name is Lewis but no one ever calls him that except the teachers. He's one of the "brains" in the class, always studying and getting straight A's. Guys like Duffy love his ass, but I'll bet he doesn't have one friend in the school. I kind of feel sorry for him, actually. He can't help it if he's a jerk. I could get straight A's too if all I wanted to do was study all night long, but I've got better things to do with my time.

He didn't answer. He was too busy strapping his slide rule onto his belt. He's one of these kids who wears his belt about six inches under his armpits, and always has his slide rule on it. He's probably the only kid in the whole school who knows how to use the damn thing. Actually, I'm going to have to learn how because you do a lot of math at Annapolis. Maybe I can get Sarkie to teach me. He'd love to have me as his friend. In his whole life he's probably never dreamed he could have a friend like me.

"Lend it to me, will you?" I asked. "I had to take my mother out shopping last night and ran out of time."

"Shut up down there!" Mr. Archibald, one of the teachers monitoring the halls, called out in our direction. We're not allowed to talk in the halls. It's one of the millions of rules we have.

Sarkie pretended like he didn't hear me, so I grabbed his arm and twisted it to get his attention. I didn't twist it hard, I just wanted to get his attention.

"Come on, be a good guy."

He didn't say anything so I twisted it a little harder, just so he'd know I was serious.

"Hey, cut it out, Poole, that hurts," he said in this real whimpering voice, like I was really doing him harm.

"I don't want to hurt you, man," I reassured him, "just let me . . ."

Suddenly I was grabbed by the neck and lifted straight up in the air by Mr. Boyle, the vice principal. He's real tall, probably 6'6" at least, and skinny as a stringbean, but he's got a grip on him like Charles Atlas. He stood there dangling me by the neck.

"Who gave you permission to talk in the hall?" he asked.

I didn't answer him. The first thing you learn in this school, like the first week of seventh grade, is not to answer questions like that. You answer a question like that and they'll eat your lunch.

"Why don't you pick on someone your own size, Poole?" he went on, smiling at me. He's got these huge teeth, they look like horse teeth. He looks like this huge horse and he's about as smart.

He was dangling me in the air. Some of the kids were watching and snickering. My neck hurt like hell.

"You want a fight?"

"No, sir," I answered. My teeth were clenched, I was squirming around. This was pissing me off royally, not only because it really did hurt, but also because this shithead was making a laughingstock out of me. If there's one thing I can't stand it's people laughing at me. I'll kill some fucker he laughs at me the wrong way.

Boyle slammed me into a locker.

"I'm getting tired of your shenanigans, Poole, you understand me?"

"Yes, sir." My voice came out like a squeak. I hate it when that happens, when some teacher pulls that kind of shit on you.

He released his grip. I slumped down onto the floor. Goddamn, my neck ached. The bastard might've broken it. I'll sue him for a million dollars if he did.

"Get your ass in homeroom," he commanded me. "Now."

I grabbed my books and slammed my locker shut. Sarkind was watching with this stupid smirk on his face.

"You'll get yours later," I warned him. You ask some wetshit for a simple favor, you're willing to be his friend, and look what happens to you.

Mrs. Fletcher, our homeroom teacher, took the roll. She's got a seating chart and if you're not in your assigned seat when the bell rings you get a tardy slip and have to go to the principal's office and get a note signed by your parents and all that bullshit. I learned to forge my mother's name one month after I started seventh grade.

I had the hots for Mrs. Fletcher. I know that's weird 'cause she's flat as a board, what you'd call a carpenter's dream, but she's got good legs she likes to show off—she's always crossing them and showing some thigh. This is her first year teaching, she just got out of teachers' college up at Towson State and her husband's in the army in Ft. Jackson, South Carolina. She hasn't seen him since Christmas. She's complained to some of the girls, her little brown-noser favorites, about her lack of nookie. I mean she didn't say it like that, not to a bunch of ninth-grade girls, but that's what she meant. What she didn't know was that news gets broadcast all over the school in about ten seconds flat, you tell one of these girls a secret you might as well put it on "Ed Sullivan."

She's a horny lady schoolteacher, no question, sitting up there crossing and uncrossing her legs, dangling her shoes off her toes. I could see a couple of fresh pimples on her chin, even though she'd tried to cover them with makeup. She must've been on the rag. Between my mother and sister there's always used Kotex in the bathroom wastebasket. I hate living in a house with only one bathroom. Someday I'll have my own private bathroom and I won't have to put up with that gross shit.

Vernice Oglethorpe was sitting in front of me. She's this tall, skinny girl, plain as cardboard.

"Vernice, you do the math?" I whispered. I had to have that math homework.

She tried to ignore me, which was pretty difficult, since my lips were about two inches from her ear.

"I know you did. Lend it to me."

"No," she said, her back all rigid.

"Come on, Vernice," I practically begged, "Swindel'll murdelize me if I don't have it today."

"You should've thought about that before now," Vernice whispered back.

I leaned closer to her, so Mrs. Fletcher wouldn't hear us. Vernice's hair smelled nice. She must've washed it last night. It wasn't her fault she was a skag.

"Vernice," I coaxed, singing her name softly.

"Roy, leave me alone," she pleaded, her voice kind of shaking. She's never had a date in her life, she's scared to death of boys.

I reached under her arm and started tickling her. She jerked like a puppet, trying to squirm away.

"Don't!"

"C'mon, Vernice." I kept tickling her. She was biting her wrist to keep from laughing out loud.

"Goddamn you, Roy," she hissed, as she angrily handed her notebook back to me.

"Admit it, Vernice, you love me." I smiled at her as I started copying her work into my book as fast as I could.

The morning announcements came over the P.A. You're supposed to stop what you're doing and listen up, but I kept copying her math into my book. I managed to finish just before we had to stand for the Lord's Prayer and Pledge of Allegiance.

"Thanks, my dear," I told her as I passed the work back.

"You're not welcome," she said, trying to act like she was real pissed off.

"Don't forget, Vernice, you love me," I teased her. The sad thing is, deep down that's true. Even skags have feelings, that's why I knew she wasn't as pissed off as she wanted me to believe. If I ever actually liked her it would be the greatest thrill of her young life.

I got through the first part of the morning easily enough. Most teachers, if you keep your mouth shut and lay low, they'll leave you alone. They don't want a hassle any more than you do—life's tough enough being a junior-high teacher in a shitty school like Ravensburg Junior High without going out looking for trouble.

The last class before lunch was math. I was sweating bullets, praying that Swindel wouldn't call on me to put a problem up on the board. I just wanted to turn in the homework and get out alive. Usually she starts with the A's and goes alphabetically and I can finesse it, since my name starts with a P, but this time she pulled a fast one and started with the last name, Bonnie Yates, and went backwards.

"Roy Poole," she called.

"Present and accounted for, Miz Swindel, ma'am," I sang out. Sometimes that'll get a laugh and she'll pass me by.

"I can see that, Roy," she answered. "Now if it wouldn't tax your energy too much would you please go to the board and put up number nine." She looked around the room like she was an actress in a play and we were the audience, which is how she often does shit like that. "That is, if you did number nine. Or any of the assignment."

She expected me to come up empty, as usual, so she could embarrass me for about two minutes.

"Yes, ma'am, I did the assignment," I answered, fighting real hard to keep a shit-eating grin off my face. I could see from her look at me that I'd hoisted her by her own petard, as the Three Musketeers would say. "I did all of 'em, took me half the night but I got 'em all done. Didn't make my mom too happy," I embellished, "me staying up that late, what with my dad being sick with double pneumonia like he's been."

Sometimes this shit'll come out of my mouth when I least expect it. It's a part of me I can't control, like an evil twin. I glanced across the room. Vernice was staring like she wanted to kill me, she was so pissed. I smiled at her real sweet, like we were boyfriend-girlfriend. In her dreams.

Miss Swindel, forgetting that I'm one of the world's greatest bullshit artists, turned white as a ghost.

"I didn't know there was an illness in your family," she told me. "I'm sorry."

"He'll recover," I answered. I should be so lucky my old man would ever be laid up seriously. Be the only time we'd ever have any peace and quiet around our house.

"I am glad you did the assignment for once," she said.

I walked to the front of the room with my math homework and joined the other kids who were beavering away at the board. I took my time, making sure I had the right piece of chalk, that I had a good area on the board to put the problem on. I looked at it for a while, squinting like I was puzzled, the way these contestants do on "The $64,000 Question" on TV, they'll go into all these stupid contortions when everybody knows they have the answer right on the tip of their tongue.

Finally, when I'd delayed as long as I could, I copied the problem out of my book onto the board, alongside the others. Then I walked back to my seat in the rear and slid down, real low. I'd showed her—now she wouldn't call on me for the rest of the month.

When everyone was finished Swindel checked the work. If it wasn't right she had the student come up and work with her so they'd see where they had fucked up. The few that got them right she just checked off. I was praying Vernice had gotten this problem right. She's pretty smart in math.

Swindel came to my problem last. She looked at it for a long time, double-checking the equation—she was having a hard time believing what she was seeing.

"Very good, Roy," she said, unable to keep the surprise out of her voice.

I let out a big sigh of relief, silent of course. Thank God for Vernice, I had to do something nice for her to make up for helping me, even though she hadn't wanted to.

"Thank you, Miz Swindel. That one was pretty hard."

Why the hell couldn't I have kept my goddamn mouth shut? That's all I had to do, shut the fuck up. She would've gone on to something else and I'd've been home free. But I didn't. Story of my life.

"You're finally getting a grasp of the work."

"Yes, ma'am, I'm trying to." Now we were in a damn conversation.

"I've always felt you had it in you, if you'd only try."

Like I said, they've been singing that tune my whole life.

"Yes, ma'am."

She started to move on—then she turned back to me.

"Would you mind explaining it to the class, step by step?" she asked, extending her hand out to me. "Come up here to the board so we can all see you."

Shit on a goddamn stick.

"I'd rather not, ma'am," I said, thinking as fast as I could, "I'm not real good at talking in front of people."

That got a good laugh. I got a mouth on me like a goddamn preacher, that's how come I get in trouble so much.

"Front and center, Roy. Now."

I walked to the front of the room like a man on his way to the gallows and stood at the board.

"Go ahead, Roy," she decreed.

I looked at the problem carefully. I'm pretty good at math, actually, if I'd studied up on this stuff I might've been able to bullshit my way through, but I didn't know dick about this, not word one. But I had to say something.

"Okay," I said, real slow, "you've got your denominator . . ."

"That's fractions, Roy," she interrupted, "this is algebra."

"Right, right. I mean your sine . . ."

"Geometry. Stick to algebra, Roy. Geometry was last semester."

"Right, that's right, Miz Swindel, what I meant was . . ."

I stared at the problem again, wrinkling my brow like those brains on TV do, like if I wrinkled it hard enough the answer would just pop into my head.

"I'm having a hard time explaining it this morning," I told her, "on account of how I didn't get much sleep last night staying up so late and all."

"That's a pretty feeble excuse, Roy," she told me. Her voice was getting shrill. "I don't see how you managed to do this problem if you can't explain it now."

She'd caught me. Big fucking deal.

"Maybe you had some help. Is that possible?" She was laying the sarcasm on pretty thick.

"Anything's possible."

Some titters and laughs slipped out from the class. She quieted them with a blistering look. Fucking with her was not a cool thing to do, I knew that from experience.

"Who did this work?"

"A friend of mine helped me. I admit it."

"A friend. What is this friend's name, pray tell?"

Out of the corner of my eye I caught Vernice smirking. She stuck her tongue out at me. For a second I got this brilliant idea—I'd say it was her, that I'd gone over to her house last night and spent the time with her in her room, just the two of us alone, while she helped me. She'd crawl under her desk and die if I did that.

I couldn't do it. It would've been like taking candy from a baby. There's no point in hurting somebody just 'cause you've fucked up.

"Your friend, Roy," Miss Swindel commanded.

"Albert Einstein," I told her.

The class erupted in laughter. Swindel glared at me for a moment, then turned her back. I was going to pay for this, that I knew. Not the lying and messing up, everyone expected that from me. For showing her up, she hated that more than anything.

"Return to your seat, Roy." Her voice was flat. I was definitely going to pay for this.

As I walked back to my desk I caught Vernice and Sarkind smiling at me in triumph. I didn't even think about plotting revenge on them—I deserved it, for being such a wiseass and not keeping my dumb mouth shut.

"So Earl and Lloyd, they had this one-truck garbage business, you know," Burt was saying, telling this joke, me and Joe and Clarence and a couple other boys huddled around him, "just this old stake-bed, and they're hauling trash and garbage, all kinds of shit, rotten eggs and coffee grinds and rubbers . . ."

"Kotex," Clarence chimed in.

"The bloodier the better," Burt assured us, "all kinds of good shit, of course they don't handle that shit their own selves, they got a couple of niggers doing the heavy lifting for 'em . . ."

"Leroy and Rastas," Clarence kicked in again.

"Who the fuck's telling this joke, me or you?" Burt complained.

"All right, already."

"So anyway," Burt continued, "as a matter of fact those were the niggers' names, so one day they're driving down the road and it's windier than shit and the tarp blows off that's covering the load? So all this garbage starts blowing around, all over the road and shit, so Lloyd tells Leroy, 'Boy, climb on up the back of the truck and lie down on top of that pile so's it won't blow away.' So ol' Leroy climbs up on the pile of garbage, I mean it was all kinds of ugly shit, you couldn't pay a white man a million dollars to lie down on that shit, but ol' Leroy he's a good worker so he gets on top of it and it's blowing like a motherfucker so he's got to spread-eagle on it to keep it down, you know?, so they're driving on down to the dump and they drive under this bridge and there's these two little kids standing on the bridge, just hanging around, and one of them sees the truck driving by and he turns to the other kid and says, 'Will you look at that, somebody's throwed away a perfectly good nigger.' "

We all cracked up, laughing so hard the tears came to our eyes.

"I've got to remember that one," Joe said, still laughing. "Somebody throwed away a perfectly good nigger. That is funnier'n shit."

There was no more sun in the sky than there had been at seven in the morning. We all milled around on the hard clay ground behind the school, boys on one side of the yard and girls on the other, our breath coming out in puffs of vapor, like when we were little kids with these bubble-gum cigarettes and pretended we were really exhaling, holding our hands against our armpits to keep them from numbing. The few ugly trees at the edge of the playground were small and bent and bare. It was too cold to be outside, but it was recess, we had to be.

We checked out the snatch.

"Helen does."

"My ass. She never has."

"I heard she did once last summer."

"You heard wrong."

"She does." Somebody pointed at another one. "Sally."

"I heard that too."

"I'll believe it when I see it."

Burt was the most skeptical. As far as he was concerned, they were all virgins until he'd checked them out personally.

"Sandy Weise for sure."

"Bullfuckingshit."

"She's got to. Look at those knockers."

"Just 'cause a girl's got big titties doesn't mean she fucks. I guarantee Sandy Weise does not fuck."

"You made a move on her and she turned you down?"

"Take it from the pro. I know."

I hung on the edge, listening to the banter but not joining in much. I didn't think hardly any of the girls in our class had lost their cherries yet, just like none of my buddies have, even though they all carry a Trojan in their wallets, the roll making a commonly recognizable impression in the leather. Only a couple of the girls had, and everybody knew who they were, because they let everyone know. Like it was a big deal losing your cherry while you were still in junior high. My sister hadn't lost hers until this summer and she was faster than any of them.

Darlene was standing across the yard with a group of her girlfriends. She was a virgin, that was for sure, I knew that like I knew my own heartbeat; she had to be, it would kill me if she wasn't. She probably wouldn't even do it in high school, she was that kind of girl. Saving it for her husband. Sometimes I would dream about what it would be like being married to Darlene. We'd live in Cheverly in a split-level house and have a new car every other year. I'd be in the Navy, commanding a boat or something, and we'd go up to Annapolis on the weekends and go sailing with our kids.

Then Danny Detweiler, the world's biggest shithead, walked over to Darlene and her friends. He said something I couldn't hear, but it must have been funny, because all the girls laughed, especially Darlene.

Danny and me have been mortal enemies since first grade. We were both big kids when we were little, good athletes even as

grade-schoolers, we'd always be the first ones picked when somebody was choosing up sides. Danny's pretty smart—not as smart
as he thinks, but he gets good grades and I never have, so the
teachers always liked him and never liked me. Danny's family
lives good, too. His father's a roofing contractor and they have a
nice big house in Cheverly. Danny's father gets a new Oldsmobile
Super 88 every other year—he'd just got a brand-new one last
month, a cherry two-tone green job, the chrome dripping off it,
I'd seen it when Danny's mother came by after school one day
to pick Danny up to take him to his piano lesson. Danny's always
had the neatest clothes, too, not raggedy old shit like I have to
wear.

Darlene was smiling up at Danny. Motherfucker. I felt like
walking over and punching Danny in his fucking mouth, knock
half his teeth out.

Burt nudged me out of my fantasy, pointing across the yard.

"Hey, Ginger," Burt called out.

Ginger Huntwell, who is this short slutty girl with pointy little
titties, separated from some other girls and sashayed over to us.

"She does," Burt told us.

"Says who?"

"Take it from the pro."

We'd heard the rumors—that Ginger did it on a mattress
down in the basement of an apartment building in Kent Village
with grown men. The joke was if you lent your jacket to Ginger
Huntwell it would be returned with come stains in the lining.

"Hi, Burt."

"Hi, Ginger."

"Hi, Ginger," I kicked in. Doesn't hurt to be friendly with a
girl who puts out.

"Hi, Roy."

She smiled at me. I've been told that she likes me. I didn't
know—I liked her okay but I was saving myself for Darlene.

"Hey Ginger, is that a new coat?" Burt asked.

" 'Course not, silly." She giggled, her voice real high-pitched.

How come girls with slutty reputations always have high squeaky voices? Nothing personal but she really is dumb. It all must have gone into her cunt, nothing left for brains.

"It fits so tight I thought you might've got it new for Christmas," Burt said.

He was bullshitting her like a champ and fingering the material at the same time, his hand sliding underneath to her titties, feeling her up right in front of everybody. She smiled this kind of goofy smile and squirmed a little when he hit a particularly sensitive spot, which must've been her nipple. Feeling up a girl's nipple right out in the open, Burt's pretty cool.

"Didn't your mother never teach you no manners?" she said, like she was all out of breath, finally removing his hand, but not before letting him cop her up good. She sounded to me like she was trying to act like Marilyn Monroe. She held Burt's hand for a moment longer, then turned and walked back to her girlfriends, her low-slung ass pivoting in her tight wool skirt like two bowling balls trying to make a seven-ten split.

"I mean to have a piece of that before I die," Burt gasped.

"He died with his boots on," I drawled. "Ride 'em cowboy." I could feel my own hard-on, even though Ginger didn't mean anything to me. I've never jacked off to her, not one time. She's too slutty for me. You've got to draw the line somewhere.

School was over for the day. Finally. Sometimes a day in this school feels like a week. A week, if it's the wrong week, can seem like a year, an eternity. Everything's a hassle, a challenge. It can wear you down.

I shuffled down the empty corridors, the taps on the heels of my Flagg Brothers clip-toe blue suede bombers echoing loudly on the scuffed-up tile floors.

This is the only time I actually like school, when it's empty and quiet like this. You don't have all the teachers and dumb kids pestering you and getting in your face all the time. If it was this quiet I could probably be a good student. I don't know how anyone can work in all that racket the way it is during the regular day.

I entered the library, walked down the row of stacks, and took down one of the books from the set called *History of the United States Naval Operations in World War II*. The books are old and dog-eared, with pictures and descriptions of all the ships in the U.S. Navy used in the war, destroyers and aircraft carriers and battleships and everything. I know them like the back of my hand, I've read them all so many times.

I sat down at an empty table and started reading. Mr. Pitaro, who was the teacher in charge of detention hall this week, walked over to me.

"I don't have your name down here, Roy," he said, checking his list of detainees. The way it works is, if you screw up you get assigned to detention hall, which means you have to stay after school in the library. Nobody ever stays in the library after school unless they've pulled detention, not even the brains. I'm probably the only one who actually ever comes in here after school because he feels like it.

"I don't have detention, Mr. Pitaro," I explained to him. "I just wanted to read where it's quiet. That's okay, isn't it?"

He was kind of taken aback, I could tell. It's his first time running detention hall, that's how come he didn't know I come here just because I feel like it.

"Sure, yeah, I guess so," he said. Like it was against the law to use the library or something. That's the way this school is, even when you want to actually learn something they think you're weird.

I got lost in the book. It really is a neat book, it's kind of a bible for learning about Navy ships, which is real important to me. I must've been there longer than I realized because when I looked up for a minute to clear my head the room was empty except for me and the librarian, Miss Hughes, this ancient spinster who's got three hairy moles on her chin. She's pretty nice, actually, she lets me take out books and never charges me if I bring them back late. We're often the only two people in the whole library, I think that's one of the reasons she likes me, because I keep her company. It must get pretty boring, sitting in a library all by yourself.

The light was fading fast in the windows. Miss Hughes pointed to the clock on the wall. It was four-thirty, closing time. I put my book back on the shelf real carefully. I'd hate it if anything ever happened to those books.

Kresge's five-and-dime is down the hill from the junior high. It's a typical Ravensburg low-rent place, same as every other store in this hick town, selling cheap crap that's either used up fast and thrown away, lipstick and stuff women use, or crap people don't really want but wind up buying anyway because it costs practically nothing, like a new Speidel watchband.

I wandered around the aisles, aimlessly drifting. I like to do that sometimes, check out the cheap shit they're selling. The customers were mostly housewives. Some had their hair up in curlers even though it was past four-thirty in the afternoon, sundown practically. A woman walking around in curlers out in public is about as tacky as it gets. They were doing women things, like testing the atomizers of toilet water or buying stockings or maybe having a soda at the counter. Hardly any boys ever come in here, it's not a man's kind of store, except for cigarettes and pipe tobacco and stuff like that.

I flipped through the small collection of 45's they had in the record bin. It was my parents' kind of stuff—no rock 'n' roll at all, not even Elvis, Chuck Berry, or the Crickets. Tells you what kind of piss-poor store it was; about ten years behind the times.

"Can I help you?" This horse-faced saleslady stuck her face in front of mine. I could smell her breath she was so close. She had crappy breath, I almost felt like puking in her stupid face.

"Just looking," I told her, playing real innocent-like.

"No loitering, boy." She pointed to the sign.

"Yes, ma'am. I won't be long."

I moved away from her. She probably thought I was going to swipe something. As soon as any salesperson sees a teenage boy in a store that's the first thing that comes into their feeble minds. Like every boy's a common thief. I know plenty of girls that steal like bandits, they'll come out of this store or Doc Goldberg's drugstore and their pockets and purses'll be bulging with nylons, makeup, lipsticks, anything they can stuff in. They'll take stuff they don't want, like pipe tobacco. Some even put stuff up their girdles, because they know no salesman would dare check under their skirts.

I knew I had to go home but it was cold out and I wanted to postpone the inevitable, so I drifted over to the notions counter where odds and ends are sold, stuff that doesn't fit in any particular department. At one end of the counter were these stretch-band identification bracelets with a snap-open compartment that holds a photograph. They're real popular in my school, they sell for a buck and everybody always wants one, you can insert your girlfriend's or boyfriend's picture and think you're hot shit.

The nearest saleswoman was all the way at the far end of the counter, ringing up a sale. I nonchalantly strolled by the counter, took one more quick look to double-check that I wasn't being watched, and without even breaking stride stuffed a handful of bracelets into the pocket of my new Ravensburg High jacket. That's one of the good things about these jackets, they have real deep pockets. I was out of there in no time flat, and nobody even took a second look at me, that's how shifty I was at doing it.

Once in a while I'll hook a few of these. It's like taking candy from a baby and anyway they're not going to miss a few crappy bracelets. I'll give them to my friends or sell them half-price. It's not like I'm taking something valuable, they'd just sit there until they rusted out if I didn't take them.

As I passed the school on my way home two girls came out of the gym and crossed the street, heading in my direction. They were wearing cheerleader uniforms under their jackets because there had been a pep rally after lunch for the basketball team. Then after school, they stay and practice.

One of the girls was Darlene. She's co-captain of the cheerleading squad, which has all the neatest girls in the school. It's like if a girl thinks she's neat, but she isn't a cheerleader, then she really isn't.

I slowed down so we'd have to cross paths, hoping her and the other girl, Joan Jackson, who's real stuck-up even though she's flat as a board, would split up and I could talk to the woman of my dreams.

They passed me by, giggling and pretending like they didn't barely see me. I knew they did, though. I've got this feeling Darlene secretly likes me, but she'd never show it because I'm such a fuckup in school. Darlene's a nice girl, she comes from a nice home, nice parents, probably has a nice dog that doesn't jump on your leg and try to hump you.

I turned and watched them until they faded into the gloom. Then I put my head down against the wind and walked real slow up the street towards my house. You've got to go home sooner or later, even if you don't much feel like it.

February

THREE

|sat at my desk, my new model spread out in front of me. It was a Revolutionary War–era frigate, thousands of little pieces, some so tiny I have to fit them together with tweezers and a magnifying glass—the kind of model only a serious builder will tackle, and I ain't patting myself on the back saying that, it's the truth. It's about three-quarters done—I've been working on it every night for almost a month.

My room is like a miniature nautical museum, filled with ships and boats of various sizes and displacements, all of which I've made myself. I've been making models seriously for two years now and I'm damn good at it if I do say so myself, although normally I'm not the type who goes around bragging on himself. Other people say it, too, people who know what they're talking about, like the guys who run the hobby shop where I buy my models. They tell me I'm as good as any of their adult customers, and they're not blowing smoke up my ass, either. They appreciate a good builder no matter how old he is.

Besides all the ships I've got Navy posters and pictures plastered all over the walls as well. If I ever brought a four-star admiral in here he'd go apeshit.

The rest of the room is pretty bare. I like it that way—easier to clean, which I do myself, all of it, plus my own ironing (I guarantee you I'm the only boy in Ravensburg Junior High who irons his own shirts), I even vacuum twice a week, to make sure the models are free of dust. No one ever comes in. My old man could give a shit less, and my mom's happy that she's got one less set of chores to do. The only time anyone even sticks their head in is when my old man gets drunk and wants to give me a ration of shit, or when mom or Ruthie absolutely have to talk to me. They never come all the way in, they know I want my privacy. I've even got a padlock for it when I'm not here.

The phone rang downstairs. Ruthie answered it, of course. She thinks she owns the damn thing, anyone else gets a call she acts like they're invading her privacy. If she really wanted privacy she wouldn't hang her stockings and undies all over the house where anyone could see them.

"Roy!" She called out after a minute. "For you."

I shut the door firmly and boogied down the stairs.

"Don't take forever," she glared as she handed it over to me.

"Don't get your bowels in an uproar," I told her. "You don't pay the bills, Daddy does." I turned away from her, cradling the phone on my shoulder. "Hello." It was Burt. I listened for a moment. "Just a sec."

I ran up to my room, grabbed the first book I could lay my hands on, and ran back down to the phone, leafing through it like I was looking for something specific.

"Here it is," I told him over the phone, "page forty-three, numbers one through ten." I listened a minute. "Yeah." I turned around carefully, checking to see if my nosy sister was eaves-dropping. She's low enough that she would if I gave her half a chance. But she'd gone back into the kitchen to gossip with my mom, so she was safely out of earshot.

"Okay," I whispered, "'bye." I hung up.

"Who was that?" my mom asked as she passed through on her way to her bedroom.

"Burt. He forgot the history assignment."

"Someone's calling you to ask about homework?" Ruthie butted in. "That's a first."

I ignored her. With her, that's usually the best tactic.

"I'm pretty tired," I announced. "I'm going to bed."

"Okay, sweetie," my mom told me. She still treats me like a little kid sometimes, like she wishes I was, not back-talking and being a general pain in the ass. She gave me a peck on the cheek. "See you in the morning."

"See you." I stuck my head into the living room. " 'Night, dad."

My old man grunted a response. He was watching TV, "Strike It Rich," one of his favorite shows. He's always on the outlook for a get-rich-quick scheme. If some asshole can win all that money for doing nothing except come out with some sob story on television, he'll say, why can't I?

"Jesus, look at it," he bitched. "That is pathetic. How can people be so stupid?"

He wasn't talking to me, he was just bitching, probably his favorite thing in the world after drinking and screwing. He never talks to me. As far as he's concerned, I'm not even there. We don't have any real conversations, about the best we ever do is exchange information, like pass the salt. About the only time we're ever actually talking to each other is when we're fighting with each other, which is a hell of a lot more than I wish it was. I can't remember me and my old man ever having a normal father-son relationship. We probably never did, even when I was little. He's never come to one Boys Club baseball or football game I've ever played, even though I'm one of the stars. He's never heard me sing in the choir at school, never looked over my schoolwork. Not once. He pays the bills, that's about it for him as far as being a family man goes.

I put on my pajamas and brushed my teeth, leaving the bathroom door open so everyone could see and hear me. I called out "good night" one more time for good measure, closed and locked my door behind me, and turned off the light.

After waiting a couple minutes to make sure they all thought I was asleep, I slithered out of my pajamas, pulled my clothes back on, and slid open my bedroom window. The incoming air was cold and clean. I took a deep drag. It was frosty but it felt good, jolting me awake after the hot, still air inside my room had half knocked me out.

I put on my new jacket, slipped a long-necked screwdriver into a pocket, and climbed out the window, quietly sliding it shut behind me. I oil it regularly to keep it from squeaking. My parents don't know I do this—my old man would blister my ass into ribbons if he ever found out. There are a lot of things my parents don't know about me, a whole other life.

I worked my way to the edge of the roof, dropped like a cat to the ground, tiptoed around to the side of the house, and snuck a look in one of the windows. No one had heard anything, they were all zombied out in front of the TV. Silent as an Indian warrior, I moved through our yard and took off down the street, sliding down the fresh ice, grinning like a nut. Sometimes something simple like sliding down fresh-frozen ice can be the most fun in the world.

Burt and Joe met me at the bottom of the hill. I met Joe the first day of first grade, back in Ravensburg Elementary School. Burt made it a trio when he moved here two years ago, when the

D.C. schools integrated and the niggers took over. His older brother and sister had graduated Eastern High and Burt had always dreamed of it—his older brother's a really cool guy. But after Washington integrated, Eastern, like every other white school (except in northwest D.C., where the rich people live) went from one-hundred-percent white to about ninety-percent colored overnight. That's when everybody moved out.

Ravensburg is totally segregated, like every other school in this county. It's redneck to the core, always has been and always will be and proud of it. No niggers are ever going to come to our school, not unless they feature getting their brains beaten out.

It isn't like we hate niggers or anything. It's just that they're one thing and we're another, and mixing us doesn't do nothing but cause trouble. Actually, I've never hardly had any contact with colored people, except for maids and shit like that, garbage collectors. There's an area south of town, the Heights, where they live, but I've never been to it. No one I know has. There's all these stories about how they practice voodoo and all kinds of weird stuff, like drinking chicken blood and grisly shit like that.

Of all of us, Burt's the one who really hates coloreds, because they ran his family out of their own neighborhood. All his old stomping grounds are full of black faces now. It would be as if all of a sudden I woke up one morning and I was the only white kid in Ravensburg Junior High. I don't know what I'd do if that ever happened but I wouldn't stick around long, that is for shit-sure. That's what Burt's older brother must've felt—he went back to Eastern one time after it was desegregated, to get an old trophy or something, and the halls were filled with colored students, it made him so sick he almost puked on the spot. He drove over to the Anacostia River, took off his class ring, and threw it in. Then he went out and got royally shitfaced.

We crossed the highway and went down the hill to Quincy Arms, these cheap two-story brick apartment buildings that were built ten years ago after the war for the returning vets who needed a place they could afford to live and start up their families in before they could buy regular houses. They were the first apartments built in Ravensburg—now there's three other developments scattered around the town. Quincy Arms is only ten years old and already looks like it's about to fall down, it's so dirty and grimy and putrid. Ravensburg's still a small town full of hicks for the most part, but it's no longer the little out-of-touch farming community it was when I was born.

A few apartments were lit, but it was pretty still. They don't allow dogs here, so you can pretty much come and go as you please and no one ever knows.

We approached the buildings from the back, waiting near the playground to see if there was any activity. Satisfied we hadn't been spotted, we carefully picked our way down the icy sidewalk and went in through one of the unlocked basement doors.

The basement was like a labyrinth, stretching under several adjoining buildings. It was dim, even in daytime, just some naked bulbs hanging down. There are dozens of entrances and exits and crawlspaces and doors leading upstairs to apartments.

We're always wary when we come in. Better safe than sorry, that's my motto. After we were sure no one else was around we moved through a bunch of corridors until we came to the laundry room.

The laundry room is a big square white-tiled room with four coin-operated washing machines and four dryers set against the walls. Each machine has slots for dimes and nickels. The first thing we always do is check to make sure nobody has a load going, because we don't want somebody coming down to take out their dirty underwear and find us there. We've found some really funny stuff in those machines. It's amazing what people'll put in the wash.

All the machines were empty. We had it made in the shade.

"Helloooo down there," Joe mooed in this real low voice, which echoed off the walls like at the Grand Canyon. He's a real clown sometimes, most usually when it's the wrong time.

"Shut the fuck up, you asshole," Burt whispered. "You want

some dumb-shit housewife to come down here and start screaming her lungs out?''

"I got her lungs," Joe laughed, grabbing his balls through his
pants.

"You got jack-shit," Burt said. "Now shut the fuck up."

There were two entrances, the one we'd come in and another
one at the far end, about fifty feet further down. Joe stood guard
at one and Burt watched the other. I took the long-necked screwdriver out of my jacket pocket and pried it into the coin box of
the nearest washing machine. I've got this down to a science; a
few good thrusts, and the box popped open. I scooped the coins
into a bookbag Joe'd brought and went to work on the next one.

I checked Burt and Joe. They were bouncing on the balls of
their feet, ready to run. I was the cool one—I just went from box
to box, doing my work. I'm pretty cool under pressure, I guess
it comes from having to dodge my old man all the time.

The whole operation took less than three minutes. I scooped
the last of the coins into the bookbag and carefully reattached the
coin boxes to the machines; until they were opened by the guy
that services them nobody could tell they'd been fucked with.

We ran out the way we'd come in and up the hill clear of the
apartments, resting behind the Mobil station.

"I thought sure somebody was coming down that time," Joe
said, gulping for air, "it was so quiet I couldn't hardly stand it."

"Somebody should've come down the way you were mouth-
ing off," Burt said.

"Oh, fuck you," Joe said.

"Fuck you, too," Burt came back.

We're always talking to each other like that. It's like somebody else saying 'how you doing.'

"I've been through every corner of that place," I told them.
"I've got ways in and out of there you ain't never seen yet." I'm
good at planning strategy for shit like that, that's how come I
know I'll do good at the Naval Academy.

"Count up and let's get out of here. I'm freezing my cookies off," Burt said, shivering as much from the danger as the cold.

"You ain't got enough cookies to freeze off," I told him.

"Ask Carolyn Hill how much cookies I got," Burt fired back.

"You getting any off her?" Joe asked.

"Bare titty and more to come," Burt said, strutting his achievement like a goddamn rooster in a barnyard.

"You wouldn't know what to do with it if you got it, which you never will," I jibed at him.

"Fuck I wouldn't."

"Come on, count up," Joe said. It really was cold out, our breath was condensing in front of our faces.

I laid the change out on the ground, making three equal piles. The take came to almost three dollars each.

"Not bad for a night's work," I stated, feeling proud. Three dollars is good money any way you look at it.

"Let's adios the hell out of here," Burt said, scooping his share into his pockets.

"We've already done the deed," I told him, "so don't get your bowels in an uproar."

I silently climbed through the window into my room, crossed the dark floor, and opened my closet door, where I took out a Mason jar that I've hidden behind some old football pads, way in the back. I opened the lid and put my night's work inside. The jar was three-quarters filled with nickels and dimes. That's where I get the money to buy stuff like my models and the new Ravensburg High jacket.

I hid the jar away and got back into my pajamas. Then I cracked my door, checking things out. There weren't any lights except the glow from the television set.

My old man was sleeping in front of the test pattern. He woke up with a start when he heard me come into the room.

"Got hungry," I explained, making sure to stay upwind from him, because his breath, a combination of booze and mouth-open sleeping, was truly vicious. He could get a job steaming wallpaper off walls, I swear to God.

He grunted with a loud belch. If he lit a match he'd blow up the whole goddamn house. Finally he forced himself up from the couch and staggered upstairs, shedding his clothes as he went for my mom to pick up in the morning.

There was the usual stack of unwashed dishes in the sink along with a bunch of greasy glasses, some smeared with lipstick. I got out a fry pan and fixed myself three western-omelette sandwiches and washed them down with a couple glasses of chocolate milk. I'm a growing boy, since I was about six years old everyone's been saying I've got a hollow leg. My old man's always threatening to charge me room and board because I eat so much. Someday he will, he's such a bastard.

The kitchen was clean when I went back upstairs. I hate a dirty kitchen.

I lay on my bed looking up at the ceiling for a long time, playing with my cock, thinking of Darlene, Ginger Huntwell, Mrs. Fletcher. My ceiling is papered in swirls and patterns, an old job that's faded over the years. As I lay there thoughts of pussy faded away, and just before I fell asleep I saw the patterns above my head come alive and start to move.

I was running the obstacle course in my dream. I was in slow motion, flowing like the wind to the cheers of the spectators who were lined up to watch. I ran effortlessly, smoothly, all power and grace, every muscle working in harmony.

I came to the last hurdle, the highest one. Springing at it, I cleared the top with ease, soaring into the air, up and up and up, flying like a young god towards the sky.

FOUR

MacGregor's Hobby Shop is the most complete model shop in the Washington area. It's way over on Georgia Avenue, in Silver Spring, which is in a different county, but it's the only place to buy your models if you're a serious builder. I take the bus near my house down to the Mt. Rainier depot and transfer to another bus that goes to Montgomery County, which takes more than an hour, or I hitchhike, which can take a lot of time, too, depending on the rides. Even so, I mostly hitch unless the weather is bad, because I'll put my money into a model over bus fare every time.

I was checking out this frigate, a Confederate model from the Civil War. I like frigates; I like older boats in general, they come from a time I wish I'd lived in, such as when Tom Sawyer and Huckleberry Finn and those guys lived. I've built a couple frigates, one from scratch even; I found these old drawings and diagrams in this book I checked out from the library in Hyattsville, it took me three months and it didn't come out exactly the way I'd wanted it to, but it was a good ship, I had a lot of fun making it. Building ships is fun, especially sailing ships. Someday when I'm old and retired from the Navy I want to be a ship's architect and builder.

One thing I've got to do first is learn how to sail. I've never actually been on a boat, I mean I've been on them but they were always tied up at the dock, not counting boats like canoes and rowboats, I've been on those of course, just not a real sailing boat. This summer I'm going to learn, I'm going to go up to Annapolis and find somebody that owns one and volunteer to help out in exchange for lessons. I've seen these ads posted around the harbor looking for people to crew, I could be good at that, I'll be old enough to be away from home on my own, it'll probably be a relief for my folks to have me out of the house for a while—the feeling would be mutual on my part, too. I've been looking forward to it for months, actually, I've even figured out how many weeks it'll be before school's over.

Besides the frigate there was also this battleship that interested me. It was a World War Two model, really big. It would be the biggest model I've ever built. It isn't graceful like a sailing ship, it's more just raw power, meant for hunting and destroying. It's the kind of ship I'll be in command of someday.

I really like frigates but I'd already built a bunch of them. It was time to build a battleship. I started looking at the plans.

There were a couple other kids in the store besides me, but they were with their dads. These professional-quality models take too much time for a kid, plus they cost real money, a kid would have to be pretty rich to be able to afford them. I've tried to get a conversation going with a couple of these kids but we don't talk the same language. Like I said, I'm a serious builder.

"Now that is a ship." Bill, a man about my dad's age who's one of the owners of the shop, came over and looked at the plans with me. "You're going to have your hands full with that one, Roy." Bill's a really neat guy, we talk about models all the time, he doesn't talk to me like I'm some dumb kid, like my teachers do. If some of my teachers could see me in here with these complicated models they'd be pretty impressed.

"I know," I said. "I've never built one this big."

"I guess your dad'll be helping you, huh?"

What guys like Bill don't know won't hurt them.

"He likes 'em, but I do most of the work. He just kind of tells me how great they are. He's real proud of me."

My old man's never seen one of my models, not up close. The times he's looked in my room he was usually drunk and ragging on me, he wouldn't know if there was a full-size boat in there, the shape he's in those times. If he ever did check them out for real he'd think they were junk I'd wasted my money on.

"I want to try a new kind of glue," I told Bill, moving the conversation off my family, "that kind you were telling me about that dries slower but holds better."

"These are what the old pros use," Bill told me, reaching up on the shelf for a handful of bottles. "You have to be very careful with them. I usually don't recommend them to fellows your age but I think you can handle these, the sophistication level of models you've been building."

He glanced up at a man who was waiting to pay for some brushes.

"What do you think, Admiral," Bill asked, "isn't this the brand you like?"

I turned around. This older man was standing behind me. He picked up one of the bottles and examined it with a practiced eye.

The man had salt-and-pepper hair, wore these old-fashioned rimless glasses, and stood erect, like he had a coat hanger in his shirt, except he was relaxed, too, like the way the midshipmen at the Academy stand. I felt myself standing up straighter without thinking about it. He was an old guy, definitely older than my old man, maybe as old as fifty, the kind of man you felt you had to respect just because of the way he looked, like Admiral Halsey, who I've seen in the old war newsreels they show at the movies, or MacArthur. MacArthur's in the Army, not the Navy, but he's a neat-looking guy, with the aviator sunglasses and the corncob pipe you always see between his teeth. I've got this corncob pipe which I hooked from the dime store after I saw this movie about Huckleberry Finn, the one with Mickey Rooney. Once in a while me and my friends go out in this abandoned field near our houses and lie on top of the tall grass and smoke cigarette tobacco in our corncob pipes. It's nice out there in the fields, it's like we're not in Ravensburg at all.

"Yes, I use this brand," the old guy said, turning to me. "What model are you planning to build?"

"This one," I said, showing him the battleship kit.

"That's a large undertaking. You must be an experienced model builder."

"Roy's as capable as any of my adult customers," Bill told him, gushing all over me. Usually I hate it when people do shit like that but when Bill does it it's okay, because he means it, he isn't trying to snow me like my teachers do when they're talking about my so-called wasted potential.

"You should see some of the frigates and cutters he's completed," he went on. "He brought one in last month, I swear you would have thought it was crafted by someone who's been building these things for a lifetime."

This was getting to be too much, this bragging on me that he was doing. I'm more used to being told how crummy I am at things, not how good.

"You like building ships, do you?" this old guy asked.

"Yes, sir. Someday I want to have a full collection, every ship that's ever been commissioned by the U.S. Navy."

"You must have salt water in your blood," he said, smiling at me.

"Yes, sir." There was something about him that made it natural to call him "sir," it wasn't phony or anything, I didn't feel like a brown-noser doing it. "I love it, when I graduate high school I'm going to Annapolis."

I've never told anybody that before, not even my best friends. They'd mock me for it is why. This old guy, though, he didn't look the type who'd mock anyone.

He stared at me for a minute, this unblinking stare.

"I'm a graduate of the Naval Academy myself," he informed me, not bragging or anything, just stating a fact.

"You are . . . were . . . ?" I felt dumb saying it like that. He didn't seem to notice, fortunately, or I'd have really felt stupid.

"Class of '23."

"I'll bet you've been all over the world." This was a real Navy man standing in front of me, the first one I'd ever actually had a normal conversation with.

"I've seen my share."

"I guess you were in World War Two."

"Yes, I was."

"Which theatre?" I asked.

"Pacific."

"The big one." I nodded. I've studied all the battles of World War Two. I pretend I'm in them, commanding a battleship or a destroyer. "Did you know Admiral Halsey?" I asked.

"Yes, we knew each other."

"Nimitz?"

"I knew him as well."

"The admiral's being modest," Bill cut in, from behind the counter, "he was Nimitz's right-hand man before he retired."

"You were?" I was in awe, I shit you not. He was just this little guy, he kind of looked like old President Truman, who was a little guy too, although he was a tough motherfucker from what my teachers have said. Here I was standing at a counter in this rinky-dink hobby shop talking with a guy who'd been a real Navy admiral, who'd worn stars on his collar.

"For a time."

"During the war?"

"Yes."

For one of the few times in my life I was speechless.

"Where are you from, son?" he asked me, it was like he could tell how I was feeling.

"Ravensburg, sir. Over to Prince Georges." It was pretty obvious since I was wearing my Ravensburg High jacket, but he was the kind of polite guy who would ask you where you were from even if it was obvious.

"A town I know," he said.

"You do?" Ravensburg's a hick town, how could a man like this know it? Heard of it, maybe, but *know* it?

"The British burned it on their way to the capital during the War of 1812," he informed me.

"Oh yeah, that." Big fucking deal, it's Ravensburg's one claim to fame, something that happened a hundred and forty years ago. Nothing else has ever happened since, that's the kind of town it is.

"And it's on the road to the Academy," he added. "Have you ever been there?"

"I go every weekend practically," I said. "I practically live there weekends."

"Really?" He seemed impressed at that.

"Oh, yeah, I really like it up there, I hang around, eat with some of the midshipmen, run the obstacle course and stuff with them . . ." I trailed off—something told me this wasn't a guy to throw a load of bullshit at.

"And you want to be one of us," he said. "An Annapolis man."

"It's my dream, sir."

That made him smile, although I felt self-conscious about saying it, since I never do.

There wasn't much more to talk about after that. A fourteen-year-old kid and a retired admiral in the Navy—except for liking models and the Navy we didn't have a lot in common, if you know what I mean. Anyway, I was pretty tongue-tied, from who he was and what he'd done.

"Good luck on your model," he told me, offering his hand, which I shook.

"Thank you, sir."

"Perhaps we'll meet again. Continue our discussion."

"Sure," I said. "Okay." I felt like a complete moron, even though he was trying hard to be nice and make me feel easy. I couldn't help it; he had too much class for me to be comfortable with him, not right away anyway.

He paid for his purchases and walked out. I watched him go. An admiral—a Naval Academy admiral. I'd actually talked to one.

"Hell of a nice guy, the old admiral," Bill said, bringing me back to earth. "Good model builder, too," he added, "he's in here almost as much as you are. You'll probably run into him again sometime. You can compare notes."

Sure, I thought. Like some Navy admiral wants to talk to a kid like me. He'd been polite, that's all. But we had talked. From now on, any time I worked on a model, I'd remember that.

We were cruising around, me and Burt. Not really cruising, you need wheels for that, just kind of bopping here and there, fucking off, trying to keep from being bored out of our gourds, which is pretty easy to do in a chickenshit town like Ravensburg. Be bored, I mean. First we hit Doc Goldberg's drugstore and read through about half the comic books before Doc came over and told us "library's closed, boys." That's his favorite expression. I've been reading comic books in there since first grade, which is how I learned to read, sitting on a pile of ladies' magazines and working my way through the comic books in Doc's drugstore. He's a pretty good guy, just don't swipe nothing from him, Dickie Chast stole a comic once, one measly comic, and Doc called the cops on him. Dickie had to go to jail all night long until his old man bailed him out, for a dime *Plastic Man.*

Just about everything was closed, seeing's how it was a weeknight. Everything closes real early around here during the week, except the places that sell booze. There ain't no clock on drinking, as my old man likes to say.

Finally we wound up down at the bowling alley, which is this low-slung unpainted cinderblock job connected to the skating rink, which is where I spend quite a few of my Saturday afternoons when I'm not up at Annapolis. Everybody hangs out at the rink, you can see all your buddies there, plus all the girls in town go, all the neat ones anyway. It's got a big parking lot in front. There ain't a hell of a lot of money in Ravensburg but what there is goes into wheels. You catch some cherry vehicles cruising around this town, best cars in the whole D.C. area.

The alley and rink are in the south part of town, the real white-trash section, about as far south as any sober white man wants to go at night. Any farther you're looking to get your head bashed in by one of the hobos living in the jungle down by the railroad tracks, or by some nigger voodoo doctor wanting some white blood for one of their sacrifices. The niggers live past the railroad tracks on the other side of the Anacostia River. Nobody's crazy enough to go down there, that is for shit-sure. I don't know anybody who's actually had his veins opened up by any of the coloreds, but I've heard the stories since I was a kid, and I don't want to ever find out if they're true or false.

I didn't really want to go in the bowling alley, but it's about the only place open at night where kids can go in, and they've got a whole lot of great pinball machines, which Burt likes playing with a purple passion. That boy is one mean pinball player, he could win contests if they ever had any.

The reason I didn't want to go in was because my old man was inside. Tuesday night's his league's bowling night. He's on

the Lions Club team, the Ravensburg Lions. Not exactly an ex-
clusive club, not with my old man being a member. They're a
motley crew, they can't bowl worth a shit except for my old man,
they're always down at the bottom of the standings. Not that they
give a shit—they just want a night out so's they can drink and
check out the women bowlers. Nobody ever comes with their wife
or husband, it's like an unwritten law, nobody wants their style
cramped.

"Your old man here tonight?" Burt asked. We were standing
outside, freezing our buns off.

"More'n likely."

"I bet he don't feature you coming in here."

"He doesn't give a shit." Which is a lie, he's telling me all
the time not to come down the alley when it's his league night,
he doesn't like the distractions. I think it's 'cause he doesn't like
me seeing him checking out the pussy. My old man's a legend in
his own time when it comes to pussy, he's had more ass than a
toilet bowl. I'm not supposed to know anything about that but
you hear so many damn stories you know some of them have to
be true.

"So are we going in or not?" Burt asked, shifting from one
foot to the other, blowing on his hands. "I'm freezing my cookies
off out here."

"I'm thinking, I'm thinking," I said. That's one of my favorite
lines, I got it from Jack Benny, that guy cracks me up, he's funnier
than Amos and Andy even.

"You're chickenshit 'cause you don't want your old man seeing you."

"Fuck I am."

"Fuck you're not."

We still weren't going anywhere. I didn't want to go in 'cause
my old man would be royally pissed if I did, but I don't ever let
Burt tell me what I'm chickenshit about. Not Burt, not anybody.

"I just want to avoid him in case he's in a bad mood," I said.
Which is about the only mood he's ever in.

"We'll sneak in and go right to the back and play the machines," Burt offered. "No one'll even see us."

"Yeah, that's probably best." Me and Burt're real good at sneaking around, with any luck my old man wouldn't spot us at all.

It was crowded inside and smoky as hell. The noise was so deafening with the crash of the bowling and the yelling back and forth you couldn't hardly hear yourself think. All twenty-four lanes were taken and everybody in the place had a drink in their hands, including the women.

"There's your dad," Burt said, pointing at a lane in the center of the alley.

My old man was standing at the head of the lane, intently looking down at the six-eight split. They bowl duckpins around here, the little balls. Anybody carrying an average over one-twenty is a major bowler. My dad's average is 127, up in the top ten, a good twenty points higher than anyone else on his team.

"Hey Steve, you convert this, son, I'm buying you any drink you want," Fred Gash called out in this deep southern-Maryland accent of his. He was laughing as he tilted a brown paper sack up to his mouth and took a good Adam's-apple-bobbing swig.

"You're buying me a drink anyways, motor-mouth," my old man answered over his shoulder, "so shut up a minute here and let me concentrate on this miserable spare I left myself."

He powdered his hands and picked up one of his own purple-pearlescent Brunswick duckpin balls—he's one of the only guys in the league who owns his own balls, along with his own mono-grammed ball bag—crouched down real low with his ass pointing up in the air, and took careful aim. He took his four smooth steps, right-left-right-glide, and threw a Brooklyn fade that caught the six ball and sent it skidding ever so sweetly into the eight for his spare.

I love watching my old man bowl. It's like he's another person almost.

"Way to go, big Steve," Fred yelled admiringly. Fred has this habit of talking like Norton on "The Honeymooners," another one of my favorite shows. I love it when Kramden says "one of these days, Alice, one of these days, pow, right in the kisser!" It's like my folks, except Kramden never hits his wife.

"Make it a double," my dad told Fred, feeling cocky. He pulled his comb out of his back pocket and rearranged his hair. He spends as much time on his hair as a girl, especially now that Elvis is popular, that's how my old man wears his hair; one of the few personal things we have in common, a good thick head of hair and the style we wear it in. He likes to look cool, in case one of the cooze is eyeballing him, which has been known to happen.

"Daniels," he specified, "none of that lowdown shit you're drinking out of that sack of yours." He lifted a Pall Mall out of the pack in Fred's shirt pocket—the Ravensburg Lions Club bowling shirt they all wear, it's purple and yellow sateen with their names embroidered on the pocket—fired it up, and blew a smoke ring at the ceiling. That's where I get being good at smoke rings, I'll bet.

"Your old man's rolling good," Burt observed.

"He's okay. Let's go play some pinball." I didn't like standing around there.

We went back to the pinball machines. Burt stuck a nickel in the Wizard, the hardest machine in the place. You need a million points for one free game. Burt's about the only guy who ever wins games on the Wizard. I dumped a nickel in Roller Derby, one of my own favorites that's not too hard, and had just put the first ball in play when out of the corner of my eye I saw my old man walking across the alley to where the women leagues were bowling. He reached over the seats and pulled at the ponytail of some bleached blonde wearing a shirt from Ledo's Pizza, over in the Adelphi shopping center. She's one of the waitresses there. They've got about the best pizza in the whole area; my old man takes Ruthie and me there once in a while. He leaves my mom at home, he says he likes to spend a little time alone with his kids, which is a crock of shit. This waitress, her name is Peg, she's always the one waits on us and he doesn't want my mom to see, that's what I think. She's kind of tall and stringy but she's got what're called bedroom eyes. I think she's got the hots for my old man.

They started talking; I couldn't hear what since I was too far away, but they seemed pretty friendly.

Then Roger Coffey happened to look back, and caught my eye. He was sitting next to Fred, sharing his bottle. He smiled at me and waved. I waved back, kind of feebly. I like Roger, he's a nice guy, but I didn't feature getting spotted. It was too late, though, he'd nabbed me.

"Hey, Steve," Roger called across the alley.

My old man looked up and Roger jerked his thumb over to me. My old man turned with this annoyed expression on his face. I know that look. I kind of waved at him. He said something to Peg and walked back over to his lane. He was pissed I was there, I knew that for sure.

That was the end of my pinball playing for the night. I tilted out and gave the damn machine a good hard whack. What the hell, here we were, might as well join the party. You never know with my old man, he can be a lot of fun sometimes, especially if he's bowling good.

I walked over and plopped down between Fred and Roger. Fred rumpled up my hair. He knows I hate it when he does that, that's how come he does it. These guys, it's like if they fuck with you it means they like you.

"How's it going, ace?" Fred asked.

"Could be better, could be worse," I replied. I dug out my comb and redid my hair, sneaking a look over at my dad.

"How're you doing tonight?" I asked him, checking out the score sheet. "One thirty-seven, damn, Dad, you might be high man tonight!"

He looked at me quick, drained his drink, got into position to bowl. Fred offered his bottle to me.

"You want something to warm you up?" he teased me.

"What you got?" I asked, playing along. Like I'm going to actually drink in front of my old man.

"V.O."

I shook my head.

"Naw. I only drink Four Buds."

"Your old man was wondering how come his whiskey tasted like it was watered," Roger said. "Hey Steve," he called out to my dad, who was on the line getting into position, "it ain't your old lady's been watering your whiskey after all."

They laughed. My old man paid them no mind. He was intent on finishing up good.

One, two, three steps and start the glide.

"Hit it clean, Dad," I called, just as the ball was leaving his hand.

The ball hooked like a son of a bitch, leaving most of the pins standing.

"Thanks for the help," my old man said sarcastically. He was pissed, I could tell, but he was trying to keep the cork in the bottle on account of his friends being there. A few lousy pins, who gives a shit?

"Anytime, dad," I answered. Once we get going it's hard to stop.

"How's about you two pretending you like each other?" Fred asked. "I mean you are related, ain't you?"

"Didn't you ever hear the story about how I was left on his doorstep?" I asked. "He thought I was a basketful of Four Roses is how come he took me in."

"If you wasn't a mixup at the hospital you should've been," my old man shot back.

The other men shifted around uneasily.

"You better go on home, Roy," Fred suggested.

I'd outstayed my welcome, I knew that, if I'd ever had one to begin with, which was doubtful. It always turns out like this, and I'm always hoping it won't.

"I'll see you horny old bunch of buzzards later," I told the men on the bench. I reached into Roger's shirt pocket and snatched a cigarette.

"Anybody got a match?" I asked, just as Burt joined the party. He'd either gotten tired of winning all those pinball games or wanted to see if there were going to be any fireworks between my old man and me. More likely the latter.

"I got a match," Burt sang out, trying to be cool and fit in, "your ass and my face."

The men liked to fall off the bench they all laughed so hard at that.

"I meant the other way, vice versa," Burt said quickly, turning red as a beet. That was the end of him being cool for the night. Served him right, you never get in a pissing match with my old man and his buddies, that's what they do all night long, they're masters at it.

"You were right the first time," I told him.

My old man was out of patience with the both of us.

"I want you out of here, goddamnit," he told me, real hot.

"Hey Steve," Roger said, "loosen up, boy, Christ almighty a stranger'd think you two was mortal enemies the way you carry on."

My old man didn't want to be pacified.

"He's my kid and I'll talk to him like I feel. You don't give a damn, do you?" he asked me. I could tell he was feeling guilty, trying to find a way to back out. "Anyways," he went on, "what're you doing out here this time of night? I told you you were grounded this week."

He's always grounding me on some petty shit or other, to show me he's the boss and can run my life any way he pleases. What he doesn't know won't hurt him, and that's a hell of a lot.

"Me and Burt had to go to the library to do our homework. You want me to do my homework, don't you?"

"I didn't see you doing no homework over by them pinballs."

"I stopped off to see you."

"Okay. Now you've seen me. Now go on home."

I walked away, but didn't leave completely. I stood near the door, watching him.

"Come on, man!" Burt hissed. He knew what my old man was like when he was mad.

"In a minute," I told him. "Don't get your bowels in an uproar."

"I'm leaving," Burt said. "See you tomorrow."

"Not if I see you first."

He took off. I should've too, but like the dumb ass I can be, I didn't. Sure enough, my old man spotted me lingering.

"Go on home!" he called out over the noise. "I don't want you hanging 'round here. It's a bad atmosphere for kids."

I almost laughed out loud at that one. He glared at me. There was nothing I could do, so I turned and walked out, trying to be as cool as I could.

The bowlers emerged from the lanes, their jackets held tight against their bodies. It was cold as hell out and coming from inside where it was like an oven made it seem colder. People said their good-nights, stumbled to their cars.

My old man saw me. I was standing alongside the building, hunched up against the wind.

"Boy, I'm about out of patience with you," he told me, his voice letting me know just how angry he was, "did I not tell you to haul your ass home?"

"I figured I'd wait and ride back with you being's how you were almost finished."

We eyeballed each other.

"I appreciate that, Roy, believe me I do," he said, his voice quieter now, like he actually understood how I felt for once, "but we're going on down the Dixie for a couple brews, so you mosey on home and I'll catch up with you in a bit."

"Why don't I come with you? I ain't tired anyways." I really wanted to come.

" 'Cause they don't let minors in that's why and I don't want you in that place, you'll be old enough soon enough, now go on, you're going to catch cold out here."

He started to turn away, then turned back.

"And tell your mama not to wait up for me."

I started walking away as the men piled into their cars and headed out to continue their drinking, no doubt—anything to keep from going home to the ball and chain. As soon as I heard them leaving I stopped, watching from the shadows so my old man couldn't see me, in case he was checking up. Then I followed the men the way they had gone.

The Dixie Bar & Grill, where my old man and his pals prefer to do their serious social drinking, is this beat-to-shit old dive about a block from the Peace Cross, which is a huge concrete cross at least twenty feet high stuck right in the middle of the street where Defense Highway crosses Edmonston Road, that was put up after World War Two to honor all the dead soldiers from Prince Georges County. It's kind of famous, at least that's what every teacher I've ever had tells us, it's about the only thing Ravensburg's ever been famous for, I'll bet. Nothing ever happens around here worth a shit, it's like a bus stop on the road to nowheresville living around here. Anybody wants excitement they go down to the District, which is about as different from Ravensburg as any two places can be, even though they're only twenty miles apart. It's like they're a million miles apart, though, in the way they are.

Anyway, I was standing out there under the Peace Cross, freezing my cookies off, looking down the road at the pink neon sign that blinks "Dixie Bar" on and off. I knew my old man was inside and I wanted to be in there with him, where it would be warm and there would be friendly people, like the guys he bowls with. They all treat me fine, he's the only one I've got a problem with. The funny thing is, despite all the ass-whippings and hollerings-at and putdowns he's always laying on me, I still have this feeling that we ought to be good buddies. One of these days I've got this feeling I'm going to do something that'll really make him sit up and notice me and then he'll start treating me good. When I get into the Academy he'll start noticing me, that's for sure.

There are plenty of times when I want to be with my old man, but this time was different. It was like I knew something was happening but I didn't know what. Sometimes I get this feeling I can predict the future, like looking into a crystal ball or something, and then change it, which would be a good thing to be able to do, 'cause most of the time when I look into the future it doesn't look all that good, to be honest about it.

I was going in. I never had before, but this time I was going to. I counted backwards from thirty, then I did it again, then I counted ten cars going from Ravensburg to Hyattsville, then five people coming out of the bar.

The Dixie is your typical small-town rum mill. Not that I've been in that many, actually I've never been in a real bar, I've been in plenty of restaurants that serve booze but I've never been in a bar that specializes in it, but it looked like what a typical bar would look like, you don't have to spend your life in them to know what they're like. There was an empty bandstand set low on one end with an old drum kit sitting up on it, a space in front of it for dancing, tables and booths for eating and drinking, mostly drinking. The bar was against one wall. It had a bunch of dumb slogans on the mirror behind it. The two waitresses were dressed the same, wore their hair the same—real tacky—and even wore the same makeup. They're probably like the girls in my school who call each other at night to check out what each one's wearing the next day. It's like they're a bunch of sheep. They were kind of sexy-looking, the waitresses, especially the way they were dressed in these pushup bras and low-cut blouses and high heels, until I got a better look at them up close and realized how old they were, as old as my mom or maybe even older. Burt says some of them are hookers on the side, his brother had a piece off one of them once, he said she was pretty good for an older woman. A lot of them are divorced with kids and they probably don't make enough money working at a dive like this to pay the bills. Just because they're part time whores doesn't mean they aren't nice people. It's not their fault.

Considering it was a cold weekday night, business wasn't bad. Places like this, business is probably never bad. Not when there's people around who like to put it away like my old man does. Like my mom says, he ought to own his own distillery, probably save a shitload of money. There were twice as many men as women, best I could see. You've got to wonder about the kind of woman would come in a place like this, probably somebody married to someone like my old man, trying to do better, even if it's just temporary.

The jukebox had Jim Reeves singing "Four Walls." Two or three couples were out on the floor slow-dancing, feeling each other up good with one hand while the other held a drink.

I stood just inside the door, squinting to see against the smoke. I couldn't make anybody out, the light was too low and the smoke was real thick, like a curtain almost. Real slow, so's I wouldn't get spotted, I moved further into the room.

"Hey, you. Boy." I'd been spotted: the bartender. "You ain't allowed in here."

I looked over at him. He was glaring at me, his hands pressed against the bar. He was short and stocky, like one of his own kegs. He didn't have what you'd call a laugh-a-minute face, either.

"What you doing in here this time of night?"

I looked for my old man but I couldn't see him. I couldn't see any of his friends, either, but I knew they had to be in here, I hadn't been that far behind them.

"Hey, I'm talking to you. Get your ass out of here now."

A few people turned our way to see what the hell he was going on about. I walked over to him so he wouldn't have to shout.

"I'm looking for my dad," I explained. "Steve Poole? You seen him in here?"

He shook his head. "Come on now, haul ass or I'll throw your butt out."

Just then I spotted Fred and Roger at a table on the other side of the room. Roger waved his beer bottle at me. I walked over to them, working around the dancers. There were some women at the table with them but I didn't know who they were —it wasn't their wives, I know their wives. Bowler ladies, still in their sateen bowling shirts. One smiled at me but I didn't pay her any attention, she was old enough to be my mom, who I don't need any reminders of, not in this place.

"Where's my dad gone to?" I felt better—at least I was talking to some friendly, familiar faces. I kept looking around 'cause I knew my old man had to be here if his friends were.

The jukebox switched to Ferlin Husky: "Gone."

"Hey, Roy, what're you doing in here?" Roger asked me. He was juiced but good, acting real friendly-like. "Steve know you're in here, son? You ain't supposed to be in here, don't you know that?"

"Where's he at, you know?" I figured maybe he was taking a leak.

"He ain't here, Roy," Fred informed me. He was talking like Norton again, but it wasn't funny this time. Something weird was going on. I didn't understand what it was but I could feel it.

"I thought y'all came together," I said.

Roger sighted me over the lip of his National Bohemian.

"He done cut out of here a little while ago." He grinned this big shit-eating grin like him and me were asshole buddies, and kicked out a vacant chair. "Sit down and have a brew, long's you're here." He called over to a waitress. "A beer here for my buddy."

The bartender came around the bar like a shot and stood over our table.

"He ain't drinking beer in this establishment," he told Roger. He reached over and grabbed me by the collar. "I done told you once, and I don't like repeating myself. Now get on out of here." He started pushing me towards the front door.

"I wouldn't be messing with that boy, I was you," Fred warned the bartender. He was talking like himself now. "His daddy liable to walk in here and stomp your ass."

The bartender turned back to him, still holding me in this death grip he had.

"His daddy ain't about to walk in here right now."

One of the women laughed, nudged her companion.

"If junior's cut out of the same cloth, I want some," she said, looking at me right in the face. She was pretty drunk.

"Shut the fuck up," Roger told her.

"Well, excuse me." She really was drunk, her and the other woman, drunker than the men by a long shot.

"And you shut your goddamn mouth," Roger warned the bartender. He turned to me. "He's gone, Roy. You've got to go on home, son."

I looked from one face to another. There was something going on they weren't telling me.

"Go on."

I walked out slowly, looking in the shadows, thinking maybe my old man would suddenly show up, but he didn't.

I walked across the dark parking lot, scuffing the gravel with my feet. Maybe he'd got in trouble with somebody there and they didn't want me to know about it.

Out of the corner of my eye I saw a light kick on for a second. I looked over before it went off.

My old man's car was all the way on the edge of the lot, half-hidden under some low oak trees. It's a '53 Merc, red and silver two-tone, real cherried out. He'd just bought it two months before on a repossession, a real good deal, some nigger had got behind on his payments and there was good old Steve to snatch it up. He had deniggerized it, of course, the mud flaps and shit like that, and it was looking fine. He'd even cleaned out the garage so he could overnight it inside.

I walked across the lot towards it. I'd known there was something weird going on, something the men inside hadn't wanted to tell me.

A woman was laughing from inside the car. The window had been cracked a hair so it wouldn't get all steamed up inside.

"Jesus! Oh no, no!" She was talking and laughing at the same time. "Oh God, oh God, no!"

That stopped me dead in my tracks. I was pretty close to the car, ten or fifteen feet away. I waited a minute, then I heard some more laughing coming from her. It had a cheap sound to it, like the cheap perfume they sell at the dime store.

Now I was angry. Scared, too, but more pissed off. I'd been lied to, by my old man's friends inside and by my old man out here.

Quietly, I approached the car. The woman laughed again, and moaned, too. Then I heard a man's voice. My dad's.

"Not so loud, goddamnit," he was telling her, trying to hush her up, "you'll wake them up clear down to the District."

"I can't help it, the places you're touching me. Anyway, I'm freezing to death out here."

It was Peg, the woman from the bowling alley. The pizza waitress. I know her voice, she's asked what we want on our pizza enough times.

"You ain't gonna be freezing for long, lady."

There was a moment of silence, then she started laughing and moaning again. I wanted to cover my ears so I wouldn't have to hear it, but I couldn't.

"Steve, stop it," Peg was saying. "Stop! Right now!"

"Are you shitting me?" my old man said. This time they both laughed.

Real carefully, putting one foot in front of the other, I crept up. Bracing myself on the trunk, I looked in the rear window.

Peg and my old man were in the back seat, all tangled up with each other. Her bowling shirt and bra were off, showing her little titties. I watched my old man pawing at them. They were groping at each other, mouth to mouth with their eyes closed, my old man's pants down around his knees, Peg's hand pulling at the waistband of his drawers.

Her nipples were standing up real erect. They were long and thin, as long as the first joint of my pinkie. In spite of myself I was getting a hard-on looking at them, how could you not, seeing her nipples standing up like that? Their technique was lousy— I've got better technique with the girls in my class I've made out with. My mom's much better-looking than this skinny skag, what the hell was wrong with my old man, what could he see in her?

A sudden chill took over my body. I backed away, not wanting to be seen, and then I was running down Defense Highway past the Peace Cross, running blindly, my feet felt like they were on fire as they pounded the street, there was nothing there, no cars this time of night, nothing moving except me, everything was all asleep, my breath was scalding as I ran with my head down, vaulting the railroad tracks, my eyes blinded with tears from the cold, that's what the tears were coming from, it was colder'n a witch's tit out there.

Believe it or not, I had taken a wrong turn. Maybe it was accidentally on purpose, I sure as hell didn't want to go home. I was on the road that snakes its way through the junkyards, next to where the railroad tracks cut through.

I wished I had a cig. A smoke would've been relaxing. It's always that way, you never have a cigarette when you really need one.

It's peaceful there amongst all the junk. You can lie up on this huge mountain of rubber and look out over the tracks and the river and think about things without someone getting on your ass. I come here often, sometimes alone, sometimes with my buddies. We roam around the yards, making sure to check that the dogs are caged up, which they usually are during the day, 'cause people come in and out buying and selling junk and you can't have a bunch of crazy dogs roaming around biting the customers. You still have to look out for the watchman, this crazy nigger that carries a gun and would just as soon shoot you as ask you to get out. I've never been shot at personally but I know guys who have, Joe has a cousin, this older guy, who's got a purple splotch permanent on the back of his right thigh from getting hit with a load of double-aught buckshot in this very yard, ten years ago.

"Shit."

I heard a dog. It was coming from back in the yard, its feet splattering through the slop.

I looked up. The dog was above me, up on a pile of crates, about twenty, thirty yards away, looking down, its eyes red and wet. He was a big sonofabitch, black as night, part Doberman, part Great Dane it looked like. All the dogs in this yard look like they come from the same bastard litter; big black suckers, the kind of dogs whose balls always seem to be hanging about a foot down, their coats all matted and flea-ridden, drool coming off their teeth which are the size of dominoes. The kind of dogs that're trained to tear the veins right out of your neck. It didn't bark like a normal dog would—instead, a low snarl came from deep down inside its chest. It wasn't warning me, like if I took off it would leave me alone—it was announcing that it was coming for me.

I took off like a bat out of hell, the opposite direction I'd come from, 'cause he had that way covered. Behind me I heard the fucker leap down, landing hard on its big padded feet. I didn't dare look back but I knew it would be closing on me real fast.

The train tracks were slippery, covered with a thin sheet of ice. I ran down the middle, sliding like a motherfucker on the rotting ties. I could hear the dog coming fast, gaining on me by the second.

Ahead was the high trestle that crosses the Anacostia River, connecting two flat sections of low swampy marsh, a rickety wooden structure that sways any time there's the least bit of wind, especially in winter. It's at least a hundred feet high and twice as long. There's no guardrail; from the ground it looks scary as hell, but me and my friends have been tightrope-walking the tracks for years, not thinking twice about it. We play games up here—who can run across the fastest or who'll stay on the longest when a train's coming.

Chicken's the main game we play. You go out on the track about halfway when there's a train coming. First you can hear it, from a long ways off, then you see it, a freight train it'll be, a long-hauler usually, hundreds of cars. The trains have to slow to a crawl when they hit this old trestle because it's got a big curve in it plus it hasn't been buttressed in years. It's a miracle a train's never gone over the side.

At some point you start running, because you have to make sure you're off the trestle before the train reaches it, since there's no escape hatch. It's way too high to jump off, you'd kill yourself if you tried, and the curve is blind, so the engineer would never have the time to put on his brakes, not with all those heavy freight cars behind him.

I am a master at the art of playing chicken. This is no lie, ask anyone. No matter how much guts another kid has, I can outwait him. I'm fast, one of the fastest kids in my grade, and I've got a lot of guts myself, but the most important thing is I'm not afraid of heights, I have no fear of them at all. Some kids, they get up there and realize where they are, one look down and they're scared shitless, they start shaking and sweating and they have to crawl back off, they're so scared. This one kid, Jimmy Hauser, he froze completely, it was last summer, he'd never tried it before, he got out to the middle and he couldn't get back, he sat down and he flat-out couldn't move. I was with him and we could hear the train coming and he still couldn't move. I liked to shit my pants, I couldn't leave the dumb asshole and I couldn't budge him either, Jimmy's this big fat kid, he must weigh a good fifty pounds more than me at least, he just sat there in the middle of the tracks, crying like a baby.

We got off—barely. I don't know to this day how I did it, I had to carry him practically, half-carrying half-pushing him, calling him every name in the book, somehow I got his fat ass off there just as the train was rounding the curve. I remember the look on the engineer's face, sheer panic is what it was, which I'm sure was the same look I had on my own face as we dove off the end of the trestle and hit the ground.

The funniest thing was that old Jimmy was so scared he actually pissed his pants, clear through. He had to pay me three bucks bribe so I wouldn't blab it all over school. I figured it was okay taking it from him—I did save his life, no question.

I reached the trestle, looking back over my shoulder to see how close the dog was. He was right behind me, about to sink those fangs of his into my hide.

But he didn't get me. I ran out on the trestle, onto the bare ties that didn't have dirt under them. The dog skidded to a stop like one of these dogs in a Bugs Bunny cartoon.

"Fuck you, asshole," I said. I was standing on the track above the river, about fifteen feet from the dog, looking back at it, my heart pounding in my chest like a kettledrum. That had been too damn close.

"Come on, asshole," I taunted the dog, "come get me."

The dog stood on the edge, growling, his tongue hanging out the side of his mouth with the drool dripping off it, panting like he was hungry. He was—for me. I hated this dog with a purple passion.

"Fuck you, motherfucker," I told the dog, walking a few feet closer. The dog rose up on its hind legs, barking.

"Come on, asshole, come on out here. I'll flip your ass clear off this fucker," I taunted him.

The dog was too smart for that. He wasn't putting one foot on the trestle.

"Nice doggie," I said in this real soothing voice, "nice motherfucker."

The dog was snarling low in its throat. I took a couple more steps towards him. We were only about ten feet apart. I could see the hair standing up on the back of his neck, the black crud on his pointed yellow teeth that looked as sharp as razor blades, even smell his rotten breath.

"Come on, asshole. One time."

Real slow-like I reached my hand out towards its face. The dumb shit couldn't resist—it threw caution to the wind and lunged at me.

I jerked my hand back as the teeth snapped down like a vise, the dog leaping at me and missing and landing on the slippery ties. It pawed wildly, trying to secure a footing, its feet slipping through the spaces between the ties.

"Die, motherfucker." I watched the dog slipping. It was going to slide right across and through and fall a hundred feet to its death.

Except it didn't. Somehow it got lucky and braced itself, managing to work back to dirt where it was secure. It stood there shaking, panting with fear and relief, staring at me fifteen feet away. So near and yet so far.

Now what the hell was I going to do? I was royally fucked. That dog was never going to move, it would stand guard there all night, as long as I was in sight of it. I was going to have to cross the trestle and find my way home from the other side. I'd never been over there in my whole life, that was no-man's-land.

Shit on a stick. I took one last look at that stupid dog and took off walking in the opposite direction, across the rotting, slippery ties.

There was some kind of town up ahead, about a quarter-mile the other side of the river from where I'd crossed it. Lights were flickering here and there. I'd never known there was anything down this way, this far past the junkyards. Exeter, the town closest to them, is way the other side, by a good mile or more.

I had some money on me, a couple bucks in washing machine nickels and dimes. Maybe there'd be a store open where I could buy a pack of butts and something hot to drink, like hot chocolate. I struck out towards the lights with my head scrunched down and my hands in my pockets to fight off the cold, which was getting worse by the minute.

It was a dirt road, hard-packed, hardly wide enough for one car to ride on. I had a sour taste in my mouth from all that had gone on tonight, seeing my father with Peg from the bowling alley plus that shit-eating dog. A cigarette and a cup of hot chocolate would burn that taste right away.

The lights were getting closer. Sounds drifted my way, voices, men's and women's, and music, too. It meant people were still awake. Up ahead I saw some houses, real ramshackle jobs, the old wood falling apart and the paint peeling so's you could see the cracks in the wood. I don't know anybody lives in houses this poor, even out by Lanham, which is twenty miles out in the country, where the real poor kids I know live, the ones who get their milk and lunches free, the houses aren't this piss-poor.

A sudden gust of wind came up, bringing a powerful smell to my nose. Somebody's plumbing must've frozen up and busted, it was that bad. That happens once in a while with people who build their houses above the ground and leave the plumbing exposed underneath.

Then I saw this little building next to a nearby house, a half-moon cut into the door. I couldn't believe my eyes—an honest-to-God outhouse. I haven't seen one of them for a hell of a long time, I didn't know they even existed in Prince Georges County anymore. My grandparents' old farm over in Talbot County had one a long time ago when I was a little kid but even they have indoor fixtures now, and they're about as country as you can get.

It was freezing out. I needed that hot chocolate something fierce, so I moved closer to the lights.

The place was some kind of bar or restaurant but it didn't have any sign on it, just one bare light bulb hanging over the open door. The sounds of music were coming from inside, some shouting and laughing, too. I'd never heard that kind of music, it was like Chuck Berry or one of those colored singers but more down and dirty, like sex almost, I could feel it down to my balls. It didn't feel like the kind of place would serve hot chocolate, but they'd have smokes. I'm not a coffee drinker but it was cold enough that I could force down a cup, put in enough milk and sugar you can make that work.

Two men and a woman stumbled out, the woman sandwiched between the men. A blind man could've seen they were drunk, drunker even than my old man's friends and their women companions had been back at the Dixie. Something was seriously wrong with my destiny all around, every encounter I'd had tonight was fucked: my old man, the junkyard dog, everybody else I laid eyes on was shit-faced out of their gourds—I was fated to spend this night around drunks, fornicators, and killer dogs.

All three were leaning on each other, the woman especially, she had the ol' drunk jelly-leg. They were poor country-looking people, their coats patched here and there, their shoes cracked and dirty. The thing that stopped me in my tracks, though, was that they were colored, as black as the sky over my head, all three of them.

"Hey, sweet thing, pass me that schnapps, would you?" one of the men called out. He had a real deep voice like the colored singer in that movie *Showboat*, the one who sings "Ol' Man River."

"Be my guest," the woman laughed, handing over a pint bottle which she almost dropped, her coordination was so bad from being drunk. Her voice was deep for a woman, it didn't have that whiny sound to it like most of the women I know, such as my mother.

My breath died in my throat. I was paralyzed, right where I stood. The only thing in my favor was they hadn't spotted me.

After all these years I'd wound up in The Heights, on the coldest night of the year. I knew where the regular road that led into The Heights was and I knew how to steer clear of it, too. But I'd stumbled in the back way, thanks to that goddamn shit-eating dog. Now I had to figure how to get out in one piece.

They walked away from me, more weaving than walking, disappearing around the corner of the closest house. I looked down the path they'd taken, then back at the roadhouse they'd come from. Forget the cigs and the coffee, I needed to find the way out of here without anybody noticing me. Even though I knew, deep down, that most of the stories I'd heard about The Heights were bullshit, I didn't want to get caught and have to test them.

I've lived my whole life near colored people and I don't know the first thing about them. Ravensburg is totally segregated, always has been, just like all of southern Maryland. The only colored people I know to say hello to are the cleaning women who work in some of my friends' houses, the richer ones that live in places like Cheverly. I've never been in school with a colored kid, never been in a movie house with one, or ate in a restaurant that served coloreds. It's like there's this wall between us, solid and absolute.

I had to move. If I was caught standing here I was done for. I was scared totally shitless, I kid you not.

Sticking to the shadows, I stayed on the edge of the dirt road, creeping past the little houses. It was late out, close to midnight by now, most of the places were dark, people would be sleeping in their houses, which is where I wished I was. One time I heard a dog barking off in the distance and I picked up a big stick. I like dogs, I wish I had one of my own, but any dog came at me now I'd bust the motherfucker's head open. My old man won't let me have a dog, no pets at all. He doesn't want to be bothered is his excuse, plus they smell bad when it rains, track in dirt, cost money.

If I want something, my old man doesn't. That's the way it's always been.

Up in front of me a couple hundred yards I could see the entrance to the place. I walked as fast as I could alongside the road towards it. I was starting to finally relax—I'd made it out, safe.

Then I saw something that stopped me dead in my tracks.

Up ahead a little ways a man was working on his car. What he'd done was, he'd rigged his front yard with a bunch of lights strung up on poles, a real rinky-dink job, so that the yard was lit up like a goddamn plastic Christmas tree. He was wearing an old car coat, wool gloves with the fingers cut out, and a seaman's watch cap pulled down over his ears. A smoking cigarette dangled from his thick purple lips.

The car, this Ford coupe, a '47 or '48, was up on blocks. It was factory-painted, the original plain black, with one side window cracked from a rock or something. That's about my favorite car—it comes with a straight eight, you can catch rubber in first and second both. One thing everybody knows about niggers is they like hot cars. I'm planning on getting myself one as soon as I turn sixteen. Once I have wheels I'll be free.

There was no way I could sneak past the man. I'd have to wait until he finished and went inside, which was a real bitch because it was getting colder by the minute, it had to be way below freezing by now, I could feel my toes turning to ice.

The man flicked his butt across the yard, pulled some makings from inside his coat, and rolled himself a fresh one. He did it like the experts, one-handed, dribbling just the right amount of loose tobacco from his Bull Durham pouch, licking the edge of the paper like a cat, sticking the thin homemade in his mouth and striking a safety match on the sole of his shoe. He just stood there in his yard like a bird in its nest, enjoying his smoke and fucking with his machine.

Man, what I'd have given for a smoke right then, even a homemade job like that. I've tried it a couple times but it's too hard. I'd like to learn how, though, it's neat, John Wayne does it in the movies.

I was about one inch away from freezing. Come on, man, I was begging to myself, go in already.

Instead, this woman came out. She had an old flimsy robe pulled tight around her and carpet slippers on her feet. She wasn't bad-looking for a colored woman, I thought, as I checked her out. About my mom's age, although I don't know how colored people look at whatever age.

"You coming in soon, honey?" she asked the man, leaning down close to him, her head under the hood next to his. He gave her a kiss on the mouth, a nice one.

"Soon's I finish torquing this head gasket," he told her. "Lookit them stars," he said, pulling his head out from under the car and pointing up at the sky, "peaceful out tonight." He wiped his hands on a rag and wrapped his arms around her. "Ain't you cold out here?"

"Not now I ain't," she answered him.

They snuggled up to each other.

I felt kind of embarrassed, like I was watching something I shouldn't be, but there wasn't anything I could do *but* watch.

"How you doin', honey?" he asked.

"Tired."

"How many houses you done cleaned today?"

"Three. One was Miz Witt's."

"That big ol' house? No wonder you tired, baby." He tossed his half-finished cigarette. "Car can wait. Come on inside, I'll give you a good foot massage."

"Yeah." Her voice was sleepy, a sexy kind of sleepy. "I'd like that."

They went in. My old man's never massaged my mom's feet, no matter how tired she was, I know that for sure. I can't remember how long it's been since I've seen my folks do anything close like that, something simple like hug each other.

The light went out inside their house. I left the shadows and started down the road. Then I stopped and took a quick look around.

No one was in sight. I ran into their yard and grabbed the cig he'd thrown away. That drag tasted about as good as any ever has, even if a nigger had put his mouth on it.

All the lights were out inside my house. My old man's Merc was parked out in front. He hadn't put it in the garage—too distracted by his latest conquest, no doubt.

I went over to the car and checked the front door. Unlocked. Jesus, my old man had to have been seriously fucked up in the brain to leave his pride and joy unlocked on the street like that.

It was warm inside the car, the windows still steamed up. He must've not been home that long. I could smell woman, the smell of pussy, I've never actually smelled a woman's pussy but I know that's what it must smell like. The horny bastard would have to drive around with the windows rolled down tomorrow freezing his buns off to get rid of it.

I closed my eyes and thought about Peg, her little titties standing up, about Darlene, about Mrs. Fletcher. Thinking about all that good pussy got me hard as a rod so I whipped out the old tool and went to town, it felt like my whole body was exploding out the end of my pecker as I left a thick wet calling card all over the back seat of my old man's pride and joy.

March

FIVE

"Hello, again."

I turned with a start. The admiral, that little guy I'd met last month who'd served with Nimitz and all that good shit, was standing behind me with a couple of bottles of dope in his hand. Just standing there like any old regular model builder, not like some famous Navy legend. I knew he wasn't exactly a legend, but he was close; close enough for me.

"How's your battleship model coming along?" he asked real pleasantly, like we were two regular guys sitting around shooting the breeze. He was dressed like a regular guy—flannel shirt under an old windbreaker, khakis, plain old shoes. Nothing fancy or important, although his khakis had a crease ironed in them you could've cut your finger on, it was that sharp.

"Pretty good," I told him, "it's taking a lot of time, but it's fun. I love building models." I was kind of flattered that he'd remembered what type of ship I was working on.

"Good. That's the point, particularly at your age. What are you in for today?" he asked.

"Dope and brushes." I held up my purchases for him to see.

"Small world; so am I." He showed me his. We'd selected almost identical stuff.

He paused for a moment, staring at me with this Navy look he had, where you look hard at someone without blinking. "I was hoping I'd find you in here again."

You could've knocked me over with a feather. "You were?"

He nodded. "I enjoy meeting fellow model builders. You're the first one I've met who seems to take it seriously. The first young one, I mean; teenager-size."

"They're too hard for most kids," I agreed, knowing that would impress him—my ability to make grownup models. "Usually their dads wind up doing all the work." I knew that because Bill had told me, but I said it because I wanted to blow my own horn, impress him; besides, it's true, I know what my friends are like, none of them have the patience to stick with anything as complicated and time-consuming as building professional-looking models. I do it because I like starting a job and finishing it, especially when it takes hard work and concentration and is something I can do by myself without anybody's help or interference; and because building models is part of my Annapolis goal, like in my head I think if I build miniature ships, someday I can sail real ones.

"You build them all by yourself? No help?"

"Pretty much. It's not something my old . . . my father's interested in."

"Sometimes it's fun to work with someone, though."

Admiral Wells lived in Washington, on Kalorama Road, which is one of the classiest areas in the whole D.C. area. I've never in my whole life seen a house as big and fancy as this one was, let alone been in one; it made the houses in Cheverly, which I'd always thought were the hottest shit there was, look like matchboxes. This house was huge, three stories, all brick and stone, with a big front lawn overhung with oak and maple and birch trees, plus a separate three-car garage.

Only millionaires live in houses like this, I was thinking to myself as the admiral and me drove up and parked in his driveway. Admiral Wells drove this old-time Packard which was shined like burnished leather, inside and out. He's probably the kind of guy who hand-waxes his car every month. That's one of the things they teach you in the Navy.

As we walked towards the front door I saw another car parked in the garage, which had the doors open. It was this 1956 Lincoln Mark II, one of the cherriest cars in history, painted a metallic turquoise-blue. My old man would cream in his jeans to get a ride in a set of wheels like that. There's hardly any around, they're all made special-order. I've never seen one for real, only in magazines like *Life*, with a movie star behind the wheel, Cary Grant or one of those guys.

"You're noticing the Lincoln," Admiral Wells said.

"Yes, sir." I was gawking, my mouth wide open.

"I'll show it to you later." He paused for a minute. "It's my wife's automobile. She has an eye for fine things and fortunately the pocketbook to pay for them."

A colored maid wearing a starched uniform took my jacket. I followed the admiral through the house to the study, which was in the back, on the ground floor. I couldn't believe what I was seeing, one incredible thing after another, rooms filled with fancy furniture, none of it with plastic or slipcovers on them, and paintings on the walls that I could tell were real, not paintings-by-the-

number like Burt's mother does. Some of them looked like
Revolutionary War art, like you see in museums. Pictures of Admiral Wells's great-grandparents, I figured.

"My wife's people," Admiral Wells commented as he saw me
looking at the paintings. "She's a long-standing member of the
D.A.R., almost before the Pilgrims."

He was kind of grinning when he said that, like we were sharing a secret. I don't know who the D.A.R. is, but they must be
important, the way he said it.

The study was a real man's study, like a duke or an earl in
England would have, all wood and leather like you'd expect
from an old Navy man, they don't go in for any of this modern
shit. There was a large picture window overlooking the back
yard. The grass was brown now and the trees were all bare, but
come spring it would be pretty. Lots of flowers, tulips and roses,
the kind of yard my mom would kill for; when she was growing
up her family always had gardens, flowers and vegetables both.
She misses flowers, growing things, our yard's too small to grow
anything.

My mom's never been in a house this nice. No one in my
family ever has.

The thing that really knocked me for a loop was the models.
There must've been three or four dozen all over the room, ships
and boats of all types from every period of Navy history in America, sitting up on side tables, bookshelves, some even on stands
that were just for them to sit on.

"Whoa!" I couldn't help myself. They were beautiful, I'd
never seen so many fantastic models in my life. On one of the
shelves I saw a Confederate Civil War cutter that was the same
as one I'd built. It looked to me that mine was about as nice, no
bragging intended, but I bet if I took it down and looked at it
carefully I'd see little things Admiral Wells had done to really fit
it out perfectly.

"Take a look around, pick up anything that catches your

fancy, I can tell a connoisseur when I see one," the admiral offered.

"You sure it's okay?" I asked. I was nervous, that's all I needed was to drop one of them.

"I built them, so I guess it is," he said, like I was this old friend of his that he trusted with his best stuff.

"Are your grades good, Roy?"

"Pretty good." I squirmed, feeling uneasy about answering that question, because I had to lie, and I didn't want to. "They're okay, I mean they could be better."

"Pretty good won't cut it, Roy, not if you want to go to Annapolis. You have to be at the top of your class."

"Yes, sir. I know that."

We were sitting in the admiral's study. The admiral was sipping sherry and I was drinking a Coke, the two of us resting after finishing off working on models all day long.

The admiral's workshop was in his basement. He had the neatest tools I'd ever seen, from England, Czechoslovakia, Germany, places like that, you couldn't buy tools this good in Washington even if you could afford to. He knew everything about every tool, what specialty it was used for, where he'd bought it, he'd even in some cases tell a little story about the toolmaker. It was like talking to a living encyclopedia of tools.

He made most of his models from scratch, not kits, using all these exotic woods, cherry and teak, stuff like that, some of them I'd never even heard of, wood from Hawaii, all kinds of places he'd been to in his travels in the Navy, all over the world. I would be, too, he said, if I went to Annapolis.

What was really great was he'd let me use these expensive tools of his—made me, in fact. I was pretty nervous, all I needed was to ruin one, but he was real cool about it, tools are for using, he'd say, and he'd handed me one, like it was no big deal.

"Is it a good school, Ravensburg High School?" the admiral asked, taking a sip of sherry.

"I'm in junior high actually," I corrected him, "high school doesn't start till tenth grade around here, but it's okay, I guess, I mean it's not great or anything, there's a lot of vocational training, shop and stuff like that."

"But they do have an academic program?" He was pressing me, like he was worried about how good the school was, whether it was good enough. "A college preparatory curriculum?"

"Oh yeah, sure, plenty of kids from Ravensburg go to college." That was a crock of shit, hardly any kids from Ravensburg High ever go to college. What it's good at is teaching auto mechanics, practical stuff. That's what all the older brothers of my buddies take. None of them have even given a thought about going to college. I'll bet I'm the only one, and I don't talk about it. I don't mean I'm embarrassed about it, it's just they wouldn't get it, especially about me.

"Good." The admiral took a sip of his sherry. "That's good. A first-rate school, especially if it's a public one, is essential." He paused for a moment. "One more thing, Roy: about your grades . . ."

"Yes?" I felt my stomach knot up.

"You said they were . . . pretty good?"

"Yes, sir."

"I don't mean to harp on this, Roy. But pretty good doesn't cut it. They have to be excellent. The very best."

"Yes, sir. I know."

"Can you get them up?"

This guy knew me. He had me nailed.

"I'll try, sir."

He looked at me sharply, like he was looking straight through me.

"I mean yes, sure, absolutely."

"*I* know you can," he said, smiling at me again. "I'm counting on you, Roy."

I was moving restlessly in my chair, a high-backed leather armchair, extra-soft leather. I didn't like the direction the conversation was taking—my schoolwork was crummy and there was no getting around it, I'd never cared about school and my teachers had never cared about me, as long as I kept my mouth shut that's all they wanted. The truth was I gave up on school a long time ago—even when I knew the answer to a question, which was actually more frequent than my teachers realize, I wouldn't speak up in class. I'd been labeled as a poor student, a loser, and once that happens it's about impossible to turn it around. Teachers talk to each other, they know who the smart kids are and the dumb ones, and they especially pass on who the troublemakers are. I've been in the troublemaker category since the first week of junior high, when me and Bobby Londale and Alex Dappa had been caught out in the hall without a pass, because we'd been kicked out of class for wising off, and had gotten the paddle for the first time. Maybe I'll be able to turn things around in high school, but junior high's been a complete waste.

"What's that picture?" I asked, pointing to a small framed newspaper photograph that hung on the wall opposite where I was sitting. I wanted to change the subject, but it also interested me for real.

"That was taken during the war," the admiral told me, turning to look at it.

"Is that you on the left?"

"That's me, all right." He smiled. "I looked a lot younger then, didn't I?"

I got up to take a closer look. The picture was from the *New York Times*, 1942, fifteen years ago. No wonder the admiral looked younger.

"I was a captain then," he said, "I didn't get my star until a year later. During that part of the war I was a commodore," he explained, "a rank that no longer exists."

"Who's the other guy?" I asked.

"Nimitz."

"Wow." I looked back at the admiral, who was sitting in his chair by the fire, smiling at me looking at his picture. It was true, all that stuff Bill from the hobby shop had told me. This little guy—who couldn't be more than 5'6" when he was standing ramrod-straight like Annapolis men do, he was sitting here, working with me on my models, and talking to me like I was a regular person, not some dumb kid—had been an admiral in the war. Probably a hero, but I'll bet you'd never catch him bragging on himself.

"You must've seen a lot of action," I said.

"Enough to last a lifetime," he said tensely.

I was tongue-tied, which is certainly not my normal way.

"Mrs. Wells put those pictures up," the admiral said. He stood up and came over to me. "Ancient history as far as I'm concerned, but they mean something to her, I suppose." He took my glass. "You could use a fill-up." That was him being polite about not wanting to talk about himself anymore.

A woman came to the door. She was in the shadows, all I could see of her was the way she held herself erect, as straight as the admiral did.

"A new friend?" Her voice was low and husky, like that movie actress who's married to Humphrey Bogart. She took a deep drag from her cigarette, and when she exhaled the smoke curled up around her head.

The admiral stood up. I did, too. I'd been feeling comfortable in this house, but suddenly I felt like an intruder.

"Come in, darling," he said to her.

The woman took a few steps into the study, far enough so I could see her. She was small and thin, with one of those drawn-tight faces that have strong cheekbones, like a model's face. Her hair, which she was wearing twisted in a long braid on top of her head, was very black.

"I met this young fellow at the model shop," the admiral told her, introducing me, "he's quite the experienced shipwright for someone so young."

He put a hand on my shoulder. It wasn't like when someone in school does it, a teacher or a principal, it felt friendly.

"Roy, I'd like you to meet my wife. Beatrice, this is Roy Poole."

"Pleased to meet you, ma'am," I said in a quieter voice than usual. She wasn't the kind of woman you talk loud around, something about her told me that.

She stepped closer. She was older than I realized, almost as old as the admiral was, probably, which figured since they were married. Her eyes were the greenest I've ever seen. She was wearing a black dress that was pretty tight across her hips and breasts, I couldn't help noticing—she had quite a good figure actually, it looked better than my mom's even though my mom was much younger. She was kind of an old woman, I realized, but she sure was beautiful. I didn't want to stare at her but it was hard not to.

"It's nice to meet you, Roy," she said, holding out her hand to me.

I was careful shaking it, the way you'd hold a bird that was hurt. She wasn't like any woman I'd ever known before.

"I don't want to break up your little soiree," she said, smiling first at me and then at the admiral, "but we do have the Morrises in forty-five minutes, James, and you'll want to change."

Admiral Wells rapped his knuckles on his forehead. "I'd completely forgotten about that," he said, "I had thought we would invite Roy to have dinner here with us."

Boy, did that startle me. I just stared at him.

"If you had mentioned that earlier we might have made accommodations . . ." Her voice trailed off. She glanced at me, checking me out more carefully.

"I've got to get home," I told them real quickly, "my old . . . my parents don't like me being out too late." I was scared, I admit it, eating dinner with people like them was definitely more than I could handle, my first day at their house and all. Besides, something about Mrs. Wells told me I wasn't welcome eating with them, not tonight anyway.

"We'll do it next time," the admiral said, taking a glance at her. She didn't seem to react one way or the other.

I did, though. He'd said "next time." I was going to come here again; he wanted me to.

"That would be lovely," Mrs. Wells said finally, like she had to think about it. "We haven't had a young person in the house for a long time."

Then she smiled at me. She had this dazzling smile. She had very full lips, actually her mouth was pretty sexy-looking like the rest of her. It felt weird thinking that, because she really was old and besides she was married to the admiral.

At the same time, though, it shook me up, that smile. Something about her scared me—it was like she could see right through me, and she didn't like what she saw, smile or no smile.

"It was nice to meet you, Roy," she said. "I'm sure I'll be seeing you again. Don't be late, darling," she cautioned her husband.

"I'll run Roy down to the bus stop," he told her.

She left the room. We both watched her without saying anything.

It was dark. The evening cold was settling in as the admiral pulled his old Packard to the curb by the bus stop.

"Does the bus go directly to Ravensburg?" he asked.

"They all go through Mt. Rainier, but it's an easy transfer."

He frowned. "You'll be late for your supper."

"It's pretty casual at my house, they won't mind."

"Take a taxi." He pulled a money clip from his pocket—it was real silver, I could see that, he's the kind of man who would only have a real silver one—and peeled off a five.

"Will this be enough?" he asked.

"Oh, sure," I told him, "that's plenty, but listen, Admiral Wells, I can take the bus." Normally I would've grabbed the bill but I didn't want his money, not after this afternoon and the way we'd spent it together.

"I don't want you out on the streets at night," the admiral told me. "Take it. Please."

The way he'd put it I didn't have a choice. I took the money and stuffed it in my pocket.

"I'll wait until we see a cab coming, then you can jump out and hail it."

"Oh no, sir, you don't have to do that, you don't want to be late for your wife, I'm fine, really." I didn't want him being late for his wife, that's one thing for sure.

"All right." He patted my shoulder. "It was a pleasure."

"Thank you, sir. Me, too."

Right out of the blue, then, the admiral asked me, "Would you like to come over next weekend? We could work on a ship together. Although I'm sure a boy your age has many activities," he added hastily.

I swallowed. The question had caught me unawares, I wasn't prepared for it.

"Only if your parents approved," he said, he must've thought I was thinking something else, like figuring all those activities he thought I had, "and you're available, of course."

"No, it'll be fine with them." No way my parents were ever going to find out about this. "I'm totally free weekends."

"Good." He smiled, like I'd done him this big favor. "I could drive over and pick you up at your house. It's a long bus ride, I imagine."

"You don't have to do that," I told him lickety-split. If he ever saw where I lived he'd never want me near him again. "I can take the bus, I do it all the time, going to MacGregor's and places like that."

That satisfied him. We shook hands and I got out of his car. He waved goodbye to me and drove off.

After I was sure he was gone I stepped off the curb and stuck out my thumb. I could use that five dollars a lot more than some dumb cab driver.

My math homework kept me up until two o'clock in the morning. It was a bitch, especially since I've never cracked a book in my life. Okay, that's an exaggeration, but not all that much, I'll bet you could count the times on the fingers of one hand. It's not like I *can't* do the work—I'm pretty good at schoolwork, it's that I never put my mind to it. Math is one subject I actually kind of like; it's logical, one step leads to another, if you study on them you can come out all right at the end. Any good model builder, of which I am one, has got to be good at math, at least in his head, because there's a lot of math in building, figuring out how things go together. I can look at a thousand parts of a model lying on my desk and see the completed ship, even without a drawing or sketch. Math's like that, I think—you see the problem solved, and then figure how to get there.

No way was I going to make up nine years of lost time in one semester, but I had to start sometime; if I knew the admiral he'd be wanting to check my work out sooner or later, and there's no way I could bullshit him, even if I wanted to, which I don't.

I studied in the library until Miss Hughes had to close up, then I went straight home, no dicking around at the dime store or with my buddies or anything—just straight home, up to my room, and except for dinner, which I inhaled in about thirty seconds flat, that's where I was all night.

"Roy, are you okay in there?" my mom asked about ten-thirty, before she went to bed, opening the door a crack to poke her nose in—she hardly ever does it, she knows I hate having my privacy violated—and looking at me anxiously, like I was sick or something.

"Yeah, Mom, I'm fine," I said, not bothering to look up from my book.

"Do you have a test or something?"

"Just homework."

"Oh." She closed the door quietly so as not to disturb me, like I was a scientist working on important research. Maybe she thought I did homework all the time, but I doubt it. I can pull the wool over her eyes some of the time but she didn't fall out of the tree this morning, if you know what I mean.

"You're doing homework?" Ruthie asked in this totally stunned voice about ten minutes later.

"Good news travels fast." I said it under my breath, hoping she'd take the hint and leave me alone.

She came in, though, right into my room. I don't mind that so much, she's the only one I can tolerate at all in my room, she is my sister after all and I go in hers, too, which sometimes pisses her off, especially if she isn't dressed. Like I want to spy on my own sister naked.

Some of my work was scattered over the floor, the problems I'd fucked up and had to do over, which was most of them.

"This is a first. Roy Poole with his nose in a book. A schoolbook."

"Go to hell." I stared at her with the angriest stare I could. What a family—you try to improve yourself and they shoot you down for it.

"Well, I am so sorry, mister genius." She pouted, checking herself out in the mirror to see how she looked. She thinks she looks like Justine Carillo, on "American Bandstand." That's her life's goal, to get on "Bandstand." She's saving up to go to Philadelphia. "You got a new girlfriend who likes brains or something? Come on, you can tell your sister."

She's always trying to get me to tell her about my love life. It's just an excuse, so she can tell me about hers. She loves to gossip. She even told me one of her friends has the hots for me. Like I'm interested in some girl two years older than me.

"I'm just studying, that's all," I explained, trying to be patient with her so she'd leave. "Don't you ever just study?"

She looked at me like I was crazy.

"What's got into you?" she asked.

"I want to get decent grades for a change. Is that a crime?"

Around midnight I took a milk-and-cookies break. As I was walking back upstairs I heard my old man's car pull up. I ran the rest of the way before the front door opened, turned off the lights in my room, and waited for him to stagger his way through the house. No telling what would happen if he saw the light on under my door—better to let sleeping dogs lie, that's my motto.

As usual, my mom had to come to his rescue. They bickered, the usual arguments. It's the only thing that keeps them together, I was thinking as I sat there in the dark, if they didn't have this shit to fight about they wouldn't have anything. What a life— what a crappy life.

It was after two when I finally finished the assignment. I was dog-tired, I was practically propping my eyes open with tooth-picks I was so tired, I didn't even know if I'd actually gotten any of them right, but I felt really good, which was a first, since I haven't felt good about school in years.

"Can't anyone explain this?" Miss Swindel asked. "Lewis, what about you?"

"I didn't get that far, Miss Swindel," Sarkind the brain said from his seat, which of course was in the front row, where all the brown-nosers sit.

"No one?"

They all sat there like bumps on a log, even the good students who always get it done.

"I thought this class had more on the ball." She was pissed, you could tell. "It'll have to be tonight's work, then."

She started to go to the blackboard but turned as a hand was raised in the back of the room. It was mine.

"Yes, Roy, what is it? Do you need a hall pass for the bathroom?"

She doesn't mind giving me a hall pass, even though she knows I'm probably going to sneak a smoke. It keeps me out of her hair for a while.

"I got that far."

"Excuse me?"

"I said I got that far. With the homework."

"Are you sure?"

I could see the gears turning inside her puny brain—I'd never done a lick of homework in this class the whole year, and from what she'd heard from the other teachers, I'd never done any in their classes, either.

"Yes, ma'am."

She had to figure something was up, like I was setting a trap that would embarrass and humiliate her.

"Come up here."

As I stood and walked to the front of the room she backed off behind her desk, checking her hemline to make sure her slip wasn't showing, something I'd pointed out to her in the past. It wasn't, so at least I couldn't get her that way.

She put her hand out for the work, looked it over, kind of just glancing at it at first, like it would be a dirty doodle or something stupid. Then she looked at it more carefully, like she couldn't believe her eyes. Finally, she handed it back to me.

"Did your friend Mr. Einstein help you with this?" she asked in this sarcastic tone of voice. Some of the kids giggled, which made her smile. I could give a shit less about those morons.

"I couldn't get ahold of him," I told her, "seeing how he's dead, so I had to do it my own self."

That shut her up fast.

"Put it up on the board, please. Explain it to the class as you go, step by step."

She still didn't believe me, like I'd gotten some grownup to do it or something, and would make an ass of myself.

This particular problem was really a bitch. It had taken me almost an hour to do it, and like I said, I didn't know if I had it right. I copied it up on the board, racking my brain, trying to remember how I'd figured it out in the first place.

"What about this?" she asked, pointing to the center of the equation. "Shouldn't this sign be squared?"

"Oh, yeah, I forgot that"; meaning putting it in the right place, not doing it. I was sweating like a bandit, I shit you not. My knees were actually shaking—but I finished, and stepped aside.

The classroom was still. I glanced at Joe out of the corner of my eye. He was staring at me with his mouth wide open.

Swindel looked at the problem real carefully, going over it herself, actually talking to herself under her breath.

"Darn it," she said, almost to herself. To me: "This sign should be a positive, not a negative," pointing out where I'd fucked up. "What do you have when you multiply a negative by a negative?" she prompted.

Son of a fucking bitch—the simplest part of the whole damn thing, and I'd blown it. My body sagged; all the air had gone out of my balloon. I turned to go back to my seat.

"Not so fast, buster," Swindel called. "Come back here. Come on," she coaxed, walking over and taking me by the hand, actually holding mine in hers. "Let's work it out together," she said, leading me back to the board. "Here, where you goofed. Although it's the kind of mistake we all make," she added quickly, "I can't tell you how many times I've made that exact same mistake."

Damn. For the first time in my whole life, a teacher was on my side.

I corrected my mistake, made the corresponding changes, stood back from the board.

"Now it's right. Excellent, Roy, excellent." She glanced at my paper again. "And you did this all by yourself? No one helped you?"

"Who would've helped me?" I threw back at her, offended.

I'd done the goddamn work, she'd seen me do it right, there at the board; I wanted to get credit for it. They give it to you, then they want to take it away. "Nobody else got that far."

"You're absolutely right. I apologize." She meant it; I could tell. That felt good.

I started back to my seat. I was playing it pretty cool, but I felt good, I couldn't deny it.

"Roy?" she called, before I could sit down.

"Yes, Miz Swindel?" I said, turning to her.

"This is an A paper. I don't even have to look at the rest of it; the fact that you did the work is enough for me." She smiled. "I wanted you to know that. Congratulations."

"Thank you, ma'am." I felt kind of self-conscious, not being used to this kind of praise, not for schoolwork.

She still wasn't finished; she turned to the class. "This is a wonderful example of how a student can do well when he puts his mind to it." She looked around the class, stopping her gaze on several of my friends—the ones, like me, who never do any work. "Roy should be an inspiration to you all."

Before, the praise had felt good, but now it was getting embarrassing. Doing the work was one thing, because of my promise to the admiral, but being gushed all over for it was something else; something I wasn't all that keen on. Being a good student at Ravensburg Junior High is not very cool, to put it mildly. Swindel was talking about me like I was one of the grinds, a first-class brown-noser. That's the kind of praise I can definitely do without.

Everybody was staring at me: Joe, Burt; even Danny Detweiler, that moron. Served him right—I was king shit in the class for once, instead of him.

"Perhaps you could stay after school and explain to some of your classmates how you were able to get this work done when they weren't," Swindel added, digging them good.

What the hell—in for a dime, in for a dollar.

"Sure," I said, giving off a shit-eating grin like I was an innocent little church choirboy. "Especially Vernice, 'cause she's helped me out so much."

I looked over at Vernice. She was blushing so bad she looked like she was sunburned.

"I'm sure Vernice would appreciate that."

"I'm busy after school today," Vernice managed to choke out.

"Anytime, Vernice," I said, winking at her, "just let me know. Anytime, anyplace."

That was the wrong thing to say, which I knew as soon as it came out of my mouth, she was the wrong person to joke with like that, especially in front of other people. Some of the boys laughed, which made it extra-bad. She turned away when I looked at her again—I really felt bad then, it was a cruel thing to do, it isn't her fault she's a skag, it doesn't make her a bad person, she's like me in some ways, she just shows it differently. Being an ugly girl can be a real bitch—even worse than being the class joke.

I'll be nicer to her, sit next to her at lunch or something. After all, she loves me.

SIX

We were down in the boys' shower room, showering off after gym, which had been wrestling, since it was raining out and we had to stay indoors. You have to shower after gym whether you're sweaty or not, it's another one of the stupid rules they have at this stupid school.

Like always, it was a complete clusterfuck. Try taking a decent shower when there's six rusted-out showerheads for twenty guys and the water pressure goes down every time a toilet gets flushed anywhere in the school, it's like standing under an elephant pissing. The walls are cracked and the plumbing looks like it's going to fall apart any second, it's worse than the goddamn county jail, I shit you not. It's like something out of *Tales from the Crypt*. The room gets all steamed up and the floor's slippery as hell, you can't hardly see across the place it's so steamy, someday one of us is going to slip and break his neck and sue the school, which they deserve for making us shower in this dump.

"Hey," a voice called out from somewhere in the steam, "lend me your twelve-inch raping tool, Stovall, I got me a hot date with Ginger Huntwell tonight."

All the guys in my class call their dicks "raping tools." That's because of this book in the library, *The Southpaw*. It was put in the sports section by accident because technically it's about a baseball player, but what it's actually about is fucking chicks and talking about guys' cocks and stuff like that. If Miss Hughes knew what it really was about she'd have a hemorrhage, because a junior high isn't supposed to have books like that in its library. Every guy in the class has read it, even the ones who can't read.

The boy that got called out, Stovall, is this retard in our class. He's flunked about three times, he's older than my sister I'll bet, he shaves every day and has his driver's license already. He's extra-dumb, he's by far the dumbest kid in the class, which he should be, since he really is a retard, but he's got the biggest tool anyone's ever laid eyes on, it's as big as my forearm, practically.

"You wouldn't know what to do with it if he lent it to you, you three-inch wonder," somebody else called out in answer.

All that talk is ninety-nine percent bullshit. Everybody in here was a virgin, except Stovall and maybe Burt, who talks about how he gets it but never offers up any proof, because you're not supposed to talk about who the girl is, according to him, like it's a code of honor: you can fuck a girl, but you can't say her name. Maybe Burt has gotten laid, he sure talks about it enough; but deep down that's all I think it is—talk.

Everybody's ready, though, that is for shit-sure. Even the few poor bastards who don't have any hair on their balls yet and are always trying to hide what little they've got, even they talk about getting a piece. It's like until you get laid you're not a man, which is true in a way, although you can get laid and still not be a man. You can be old enough to be one but not be one if you know what I mean, there are guys who live their whole lives and never grow up. Most of the guys in this sorry town, for example. That's another reason I want to go to Annapolis—you've *got* to be a man there, they make you whether you like it or not.

The most stupid thing about this shower room is there's only ten towels, which means half the kids have to use a wet one somebody else already used. The school does it deliberately just to piss us off, I'm convinced of it. The way it actually works is the tougher you are the more often you get a clean one. For instance, I haven't gotten a soiled one this year. It's kind of cruel but when it comes to towels it's a dog-eat-dog world.

Out of the corner of my eye I noticed Lewis Sarkind, who definitely fits in the used-towel category, sneak a clean one off the pile and start drying off, hoping to get done and out before anyone caught him, since the rest of us were still fighting for water to rinse off with, and horsing around in general. He froze for a second when he caught my eye but I just turned away. Who gives a shit about a crummy towel, I'll snag a dry one anyways, and if I had to have a wet one one time what difference would it make?

"Sarkie, what the fuck're you doing?" It was Danny numbnuts Detweiler. He'd caught the poor bastard in the act.

Sarkind froze. He held the towel up against his pudgy little stomach for protection, not that he has much to protect.

"You ain't finished showering yet, Sarkie," Danny yelled.

That got everybody's attention, him yelling real loud like that, sound bounces off these concrete walls like an echo chamber. The horsing around stopped as the other boys turned to see what was causing the ruckus.

"Yes, I have," Sarkind answered weakly.

"Who says?"

"Leave him alone, Danny, for Chrissakes," Joe called from inside the steam.

"Why should I?" Danny demanded. "He doesn't even take a decent shower, then he takes a clean towel and wipes all his dirt off on it."

He moved closer to Sarkind, who hunched up behind his towel.

"That's *my* towel, you bastard," Danny said, "and you've got your cooties all over it."

He pushed Sarkind against the shower-room wall; the little jerk hit hard against the concrete, his body's as soft as a bowl of mashed potatoes.

"I ain't gonna dry myself off with that scum-rag towel you used," Danny told him, hovering over the poor, pathetic, frightened kid, raising his fist to throw a punch.

That's when my wet balled-up jockstrap smacked Danny hard on the back of his head. It sounded like a baseball hitting, it hit him so hard, it practically knocked him over.

Danny spun around. Man, was he furious!

"There's your towel." I stepped out of the steam so he could see me clearly. I didn't want to fight him, but I'd had it with his whole bullshit attitude.

Joe, Burt, some of the others laughed. They hated Danny's guts, too.

"Nobody asked for your opinion, Poole," Danny said, rubbing the back of his head where the jock hit him. One thing I can do good is throw hard, baseball's one of my best sports.

"That's okay, I'm giving it free of charge."

"When I want advice from you, fart-breath, I'll ask for it," Danny said back. One thing you can say about him, he's original as hell on the comeback.

"Okay," I grinned, "if that's the way you want it."

I bent over, spread my cheeks, and laid a real loud one in his face. Everybody was howling with laughter, even Sarkind, who'd been down on his knees in the fetal position to protect himself from Danny.

Like the coward he is, Danny turned to Sarkind.

"You think that's funny?"

"Yeah," Sarkind answered, finding bravery in numbers.

"You little asshole. I'm gonna give you something you can really laugh about, you turdbrain."

He started kicking Sarkie, kicking him up against the wall.

I'd been wanting a chance to put that prick in his place and this was it. I grabbed Danny from behind and spun him around.

"How's about trying me instead?" I challenged him. I was dripping from head to toe, bouncing on the balls of my feet like Sugar Ray Robinson, ready to move in any direction.

"I don't want to fight you, Poole, this ain't none of your damn business."

"I'm making it my business. What do you want to do about it?"

Danny backed away. "Nothing," he muttered.

"Nothing is exactly right."

He couldn't let that go; he had to come back on me, or be a pussy. We've got an unwritten rule in our school: don't let your mouth make promises your fists can't deliver. Danny had broken that rule.

"I don't fight brown-nosers, anyway," he spat out, trying to salvage some small part of his bruised manhood; the part between his ears, not the part between his legs.

When he said that, it burned my ass something fierce. "Who the fuck're you, calling me a brown-noser, you asshole?" I really was getting pissed—if he was going to make this personal, he could kiss his sorry ass goodbye, because I wasn't about to cut him any slack, not one inch.

"You," he spat out. "In math. You had your nose so far up Swindel's fat butt she probably thought it was your dick."

We stared at each other. The room was quiet.

"Chickenshit," I threw in his face. "Like you never have?" That was Danny every time; assholing out on somebody for something he does all the time himself.

He stared daggers at me. He was burning inside, you could almost see the smoke coming out of his ears.

"Fuck this shit," I said. Dismissing him: "And fuck you."

With that I deliberately turned my back on him, like I was going to finish showering off, and as soon as I did, the prick tackled me from behind, thinking he could catch me unawares. He hit me like he wanted to drive my head right into the tiles on the floor, but I twisted away, because I'd figured he might try some petty shit like that. We got into it tooth and nail, swinging at each other and twisting on the floor, banging up against the walls, slipping and sliding from the water beating down on our bodies.

The rest of the guys immediately formed a circle around us, yelling and egging us on. Everybody likes a good fight. We slid and fell as we tried to pound the shit out of each other. This was a real fight, because we hated each other's guts, we weren't going to fight for a few minutes and then give it up, there was going to be a winner and a loser.

Then in one sudden moment the room became quiet, but Danny and me didn't stop, because we were too busy trying to kill each other. Finally we realized it, but it was too late, way too late.

Mr. Henry, the gym teacher, was standing in the doorway. He's one of those short, bald men who're built like a keg of beer and have hair all over their bodies except on their heads. We call him Knobby Walsh behind his back. Sometimes he'll take his shirt off when he's teaching wrestling, it's like he's wearing a rug. One thing everybody knows about him is his temper, it's legendary.

We struggled to our feet. The others were pressed up against the walls, as far from Mr. Henry as they could get.

"Which one of you started this?" he asked Danny and me.

We looked at each other; neither of us spoke out.

He turned to the others. "Who started it?" he demanded.

Everyone was dead silent.

"Nobody saw it start, huh?"

Everybody kept quiet. You can hate another kid's guts but against a teacher you stick together.

"Fine by me," he told us. "I'm going to give you all a chance to improve your sorry memories. I'll be back later . . . maybe."

He went out and closed the door behind him. We heard the lock click.

"The bastard's locked us in!" Joe cried in amazement.

"What'd you expect, flowers?" Burt asked, pissed to shit.

"That's really great," Danny said disgustedly, "we're going to freeze our asses off in here. Way to go, Poole."

"Hey, shut your fucking mouth," I shot back, "you're the asshole started it."

Danny turned to the others.

"Let's take a vote on who turns himself in. I vote Sarkind started it."

"You're full of it!" the small boy screamed, outraged.

"I vote to kick your teeth in after school," I told Danny.

Danny glowered at me, but didn't make a move. "Someday you'll get yours, Poole," he said, like he was going to scare me or something.

"Maybe I will, but not from you."

I turned my back on him and took a leak down the drain.

We milled around, half-dry. The showerheads leaked rusty water. Overhead, the bare bulbs flickered in their wire cages.

"Motherfucker! It's colder'n shit in here," Burt complained.

"Get your friend Poole to admit the blame and we can get out," Danny told him.

"Fuck you," Burt responded.

We heard the door unlocking. Mr. Henry came back into the

room, smiling at how we looked as sorry as dogs left out in the rain.

"You can get dressed now, ladies."

We started trudging out. As I passed him he put up a hairy arm to block me.

"Report to the office after you're dressed, Poole."

"I didn't start it!" I yelled. Goddamn, that burned my ass! If I'd started the fight I'd have copped to it, everybody knows me. I'm willing to take my punishment when I deserve it, but this one wasn't my fault.

Mr. Henry pushed me against the wall. He may be a short fucker but he's strong as hell.

"Don't give me any mouth, fellow." His veins were bulging in his neck he was so angry.

"What about Danny?"

"I said move it, boy!"

"How come I'm always the one gets singled out?" I moaned. All the teachers are like this, they love to show you how tough they are.

" 'Cause whenever's there's trouble, Poole," Mr. Henry said, "you're in the middle of it. Now move your ass."

"It isn't fair." I could hear the whine in my voice but I didn't give a shit. This was totally unfair. I'd been trying to help some-body who was too weak to take care of himself and look what happened.

"I don't mean maybe," he growled in a low threatening voice. He locked eyes with me before he walked away.

We walked the stairs to the locker room. Danny was laughing, the prick, but I shut his sorry face with a withering look.

Sarkind came up to me. "I'm sorry, Roy."

"It's okay," I said. "But you owe me the math homework for the rest of the year."

"Fine," Sarkind said gratefully. "I mean . . ."

"Forget it," I cut him off. "I was kidding, I can do my own homework." I'm the one who's going to the Naval Academy, not

Lewis Sarkind, the little weenie. I've got to do my homework on my own.

I hung around the locker room until everybody had left. Whatever would happen to me in the office wasn't good, there was no sense rushing it. Finally, with my hair still wet, I trudged across the gym floor.

The girls were finishing up playing volleyball. They rushed past me into their locker room, giggling and carrying on. I looked at Darlene as she ran by, but as usual she wasn't paying me any attention.

No one else was on the floor. I double-checked to make sure, then I jumped up onto the stage and slipped behind the drawn curtains, hidden from view. Real carefully, I moved the old backing on the wall that gave me a glimpse of the stairs leading from the girls' locker room to their showers, the trick Joe had showed me and Burt back in seventh grade.

The girls came running out of the locker room and down the stairs. They were naked as jaybirds. I watched like a hawk, my mouth going dry. My cock instantly got as hard as a stalactite, if somebody had flicked it it would've shattered like an icicle.

"JesusMaryJoseph," I whispered to myself: Darlene had appeared in the locker-room door. She stood for a minute at the head of the stairs like she was waiting to get into a swimming pool—then she skipped down the steps on her tiptoes like a ballerina.

My heart was pounding in my chest, watching her. Halfway down she hesitated, and turned. She was looking right at me, right where I was hidden. I flinched, even though I knew she couldn't see me, couldn't know I was hiding behind that wall.

Maybe she sensed someone was there, I thought. Maybe she sensed it was me.

She was perfection. Whatever I'd dreamed or imagined couldn't compare to the real thing, right in front of my face.

I felt like she was looking right at me, *through* me. It was only a split second but it seemed much longer, it was like she was suspended there in slow motion with my eyes stuck to her young and lovely body.

Then she turned and ran the rest of the way down the stairs.

I waited until I was sure all the girls were gone. Then I moved away slowly, feeling my body tingling with excitement and desire.

I could hear the *whoosh* of the paddle even before it stung my bare ass, dozens of tiny welts rising like wasp bites with the first crack of laminated wood on my skin. My pants were down around my knees as I straddled a chair in the vice principal's office. Mr. Boyle, his jacket off and shirtsleeves rolled up, was administering the painful medicine. The weapon was his old fraternity paddle from college, worn from years of use on the asses of kids like me. He'd drilled dozens of tiny holes into the meat end, the better to sweep through the air and draw blood. Up and down his arm went, ten times in all, whacking my raw butt until there was a thin line of blood on each cheek from hip to crease.

He handed me a roll of toilet paper to stem the flow.

"Pull up your drawers," he said. He was panting from the ass-whipping he'd given me, like he was the one suffering.

I dabbed at my sore rear. It hurt like a motherfucker now and it was going to hurt even more tomorrow, I knew that from past experience. I've had the paddle more times than I care to remember. For most kids once is enough to make a lasting impression, but somehow I haven't mastered that yet, not even after several times. Sometimes I think they manufacture ways to have an excuse to whip my ass, like in the locker room just now.

"Sit down," Mr. Boyle commanded me. "I called your mother, she'll come fetch you after a while, she said to tell you. She must be getting tired of hauling down here after your sorry hide. You know what I don't understand?" he added, rolling down his shirtsleeves.

"What?" I could barely talk, it hurt so bad.

"I've been hearing good things about you lately," Boyle said. He slipped into his jacket. "You've been attentive in class, you're doing your homework, you're a real student." He shook his head. "Then you go and pull a stunt like this. I guess you can't ask the leopard to change his spots."

I *had* changed, that was the thing. But no one would ever believe me.

I waited in his outer office, standing because my butt hurt too much to sit. It was quiet, the only sound that of the telephones ringing.

School ended. Burt and Joe stuck their heads in the office and grinned at me. I grimaced back—I wasn't about to let those jokers know how much my ass hurt.

My mother came rushing into the office, her face still pink from the cold, a scarf wrapped over her head covering a cluster of bobby pins to hold in her curl. It had stopped raining but she had her umbrella, just in case. It's a good thing we don't live that far from the school, she can walk it in about ten minutes. It's a walk she's had to make more times than I care to remember.

She'd made herself up, even to putting on stockings and heels. The heels made her legs look good. She ought to wear them more often but she probably figures she doesn't have a reason to. My old man never takes her anywhere—they don't even go to the movies together anymore. The only time she ever gets out is with one of her girlfriends, and you don't have to dress up for that.

She pulled the bobby pins from her hair and shook it loose with her fingers. She looked pretty nice, except she was angry as hell.

"You just don't know how to stay out of trouble, do you?"

she asked me, practically spitting out the words. She was truly pissed off, I hadn't seen her this mad in a long time. She shook her head again, fluffing her hair, checking herself out in the mirror.

"It wasn't my fault this time, Mom."

She glared at me like she'd stare at a pile of fresh dog shit on her living-room carpet.

"Just can't ever do it."

Mr. Boyle stuck his head out from his inner office. "Sorry to have to see you again under such circumstances, Mrs. Poole," he said, smiling at her.

She smiled back, exactly like the girls at school do when they're trying to let a boy know they like him.

She was flirting with him, I realized. Sonofabitch! Then I thought, well, why not? She's still good-looking, for an older woman that is, and my old man doesn't pay her the time of day. A woman wants a man to look at her like he likes what he's seeing, I'm still not a man yet but I know that much.

"I know," she answered him, giving me another dark look. Then her face changed into a smile for him: "It gives me an excuse to get out of the house, anyway."

"You certainly don't need an excuse for that," Mr. Boyle assured her. "You're welcome to come and talk about Roy's behavior and progress anytime."

"Thank you."

"Come in, please."

She turned to me. "Wait here for me."

Mr. Boyle's hand was on her elbow as he escorted her into his office, closing the door behind them.

I pulled myself over the last barrier on the obstacle course, landing on the ground with a thump. It was almost dark out. I'd walked out of school as soon as my mom and Boyle started their meeting—all she would do was give me another ration of shit, so why stick around? As soon as I stuck out my thumb this guy pulled over for me, right in front of the school, if Mr. Boyle and my mom had been looking out the window they'd have seen me, but I knew they weren't looking for me, not out there. My ride took me right to the gate of the Academy, I guess he took pity on me because the weather was so shitty—even though it had stopped raining it was still cold and wet out.

I went right to the course and ran it a bunch of times, trying to run myself ragged. My ass hurt from the whipping I'd gotten but once I started running I forgot about that. It just felt good to run, it felt clean, away from all the bullshit.

The low overhead clouds changed form and grew darker; with a burst of lightning and a loud clap of thunder the sky opened, and it began to pour again.

It was still raining cats and dogs when I got out of my last ride and started walking down the dark streets towards my house. It was late, the rides had been shitty—short and far between.

All the lights were off except one in the kitchen. I was dripping wet as I walked in the back door. My mom was sitting by herself at the kitchen table having a coffee and a smoke with her shoes off, her stockinged feet propped up on another chair. In the soft light she seemed fragile and worn-out. I sat down at the table and pulled my wet shoes and socks off, leaving them in a heap on the floor.

"Where'd you go?" She had changed back into her house clothes—she didn't look so young and sexy anymore.

"What's the difference?"

"If that's your attitude, none I guess."

"Even when I'm not wrong I get accused!" I blurted out, angry. My ass was starting to numb up, by morning it would be solid black and blue. "What's the point of hanging around? I didn't do anything this time, but who would ever believe me?"

"*Who* is a good question." Obviously, she didn't.

"Where's Dad?" I asked, changing the subject. I wanted to avoid him tonight at all costs.

"He's out tonight . . . with his friends. The boys." She said it like she was saying "the turds."

Out with his "covers," I thought, his so-called "partners in crime." What my mom doesn't know won't hurt her—but she is my mother, she shouldn't have to put up with that kind of shit, even if she doesn't know. She probably does, though, she has to suspect something, maybe that's why she came on to a jerk like Mr. Boyle.

"Ruthie's spending the night with some friends." She took a long drag off her cigarette. I wanted one pretty bad but I didn't dare bum one of hers. She doesn't know I smoke yet, it would be one more thing to get on my case about.

"Mr. Boyle told me he thought about suspending you for a week," she continued, "he said if they did you might flunk this year. He said you've been doing good, too, doing all your home-work and being good in class." She dropped the cig in her coffee cup. "You just can't be good for two minutes, can you?" she moaned. "You've got to pull a stupid stunt."

I've been in trouble before but I've never come close to flunk-ing. Just the thought of it started me shivering, I couldn't help it, it was mostly from being wet and cold but still . . . I leaned over and buried my face in my hands. I can't flunk, my whole life would be ruined.

"I didn't tell your father about today. He'd skin you alive."

I nodded thanks but didn't say anything. I was too shook up.

"Anyway," she went on, "I talked Mr. Boyle out of suspend-ing you. He's not going to, not this time. He's giving you one more chance—because you've been improving." She glanced at me sharply, then looked away, firing up a fresh smoke.

I stared at the back of her head. What went on in that office? She wouldn't lay him, not there certainly, but who knows? Any-way, she'd saved my bacon, that's all that mattered.

"Thanks, Mom. I really mean it. And I'll be good, I promise." I leaned over to kiss her. She looked up at me, shaking her head sadly.

"I don't know what to do with you much longer, Roy," she said, her voice real sad, "I can't understand you anymore."

"I'll do good, I promise." I have to, the admiral's counting on me. I can't flunk, I can't even just do average anymore.

"Go on upstairs," my mom said. "Get out of those wet clothes before you catch your death."

I picked up my soggy shoes and socks and climbed the stairs to my room. There were pieces of a model on my desk, a Spanish-American War cutter I've been working on. It's a real neat model, the admiral has one just like it, he helped me pick it out.

I took one look at it, stripped off my wet clothes, and crawled into bed.

SEVEN

Joe stood guard in one entrance in the apartment house basement, Burt watched the other. I moved swiftly and surely like a veteran, uncoupling the coin boxes from the gleaming white washing machines. Four down and four to go, like a well-oiled watch.

"Anybody got a weed?" I asked.

"Yeah, I got one," Burt answered. He walked over, stuck it in my mouth and lit it as I kept working, squinting my eye against the smoke.

Five down, three to go. The boxes were full tonight, it was going to be a nice payday.

Somewhere in the distance a door slammed. We both froze, looking over at the entrance Burt had been guarding. I put my finger to my lips, then motioned to him with my hand. He snuck back to where he'd been and looked around the corner.

"Shit!" he mouthed. He took off in the opposite direction, towards me.

"Come on!" he yelled.

He barrel-assed for the far exit as I scooped up the coins into the bookbag and ran after him and Joe. They were heading towards the nearest stairway but I whistled them away. If you go up into the building and anyone's there, you're dead.

"This way," I called out softly.

They followed me down the maze of corridors that connects each building to the next, like in one of these underground Egyptian tombs with all the secret passages. We disappeared around the corner just as this fat old housewife came waddling into the laundry room carrying a basketful of washing.

"Hey, you, stop!" we heard her shriek as she saw the disconnected coin boxes, "somebody stop him!" She hadn't actually seen any of us but she was screaming at the top of her lungs, she could've been heard clear down to the District.

We raced through several corridors, careening around the bends, running for our lives. If we ever got caught it was reform school for sure, we'd done those machines so many times. Joe and Burt followed me as I led them down a side corridor they hadn't been in before, a dark old passageway with one light bulb burnt out that had a trap-door panel set in the wall, about five feet off the floor. I could feel the blood pumping in my heart and I knew they could, too. We'd never been caught, never even had a close call, but we knew it was only a matter of time before this happened. The fact it actually had, though, was scaring the living shit out of us.

I quickly pried the trap door open and boosted Burt up, him being the smallest. Joe followed right behind him, with me bringing up the rear. In the distance, down one of the corridors, we could hear people running, calling out. If they ever did catch us they'd tear us limb from limb, no question. As soon as I was inside I reached down and pulled the door panel back into place. From the other side, no one would ever know we'd been there.

The crawlspace was low and dusty. It had been built so that workmen could get underneath to fix the pipes and supports, but it didn't look like anybody'd been in here since day one. There were cobwebs and rat turds all over the place. I led the way as we scrambled along the dirt floor on all fours.

"How the hell'd you learn about this?" Burt coughed. "Jesus, there must be a million rats live in here."

We could hear their little voices squeaking around us. For all I knew they were an inch away. I didn't even want to look, you could see their beady eyes glistening in the dark.

"Checked it out," I answered, moving right along, "in case something like this ever happened. Gotta be prepared."

"You'd make a great goddamn Boy Scout, Poole," Joe said, the sarcastic bastard.

"Better than getting your ass shipped up to Lockraven," I told him. Lockraven's the state reform school, north of Baltimore. There's plenty of dumb jokes about Lockraven and Ravensburg, the names being so similar, how they're almost the same, which is a load of shit. I've known older guys, like Victor Gallegly in my sister's class, who've gone there and returned to tell the tale. It isn't pretty.

We came to a grate in the foundation wall. Pushing at it until it came loose in my hands, I exposed a small opening to the outside, less than a yard square. I slithered through first, leading the way.

"God-fucking-damnit!" I'd torn my shirt on a jagged piece of molding.

I pushed the rest of the way out. Burt handed me the money satchel, then followed. Joe brought up the rear.

"Son of a fucking bitch." I stuck a finger through the rent in my shirt. "I'm going to have to charge y'all for a new shirt for getting your sorry asses out alive."

We were outside the apartment complex, a couple hundred yards from where we'd entered. We set the grate back in place and stood silently for a moment, listening to make sure we hadn't been spotted. Then we disappeared into the night.

I bought a sweatshirt for a buck, which I made Burt and Joe pay out of their share of the loot, seeing's how I'd saved their bacon back there. They bitched and moaned but they paid up. Let's face it, without me leading them by the hand they wouldn't have gotten out of there alive, let alone have plenty of coins rattling around in their jeans. It was my idea to do those boxes anyway, way back last year. I'm the brains in this group, I deserve a little tribute now and then.

We were in Kresge's, hiding out. It was late; the place was almost deserted. Except for guys like my old man who're out drinking and whoring, this town rolls the sidewalks up when the sun goes down; before, practically. It really is a hick town, I shit you not. I pulled the sweatshirt over my head to cover the tear in my shirt. At least I hadn't been wearing my new Ravensburg High jacket, that would've frosted my ass something severe.

Burt and Joe were wandering around like drunk sailors, still shook up from our narrow escape, buying all kinds of goofy shit, trivial worthless items like key chains and yo-yos. We had plenty of money, it had been a good night even though we'd missed the last three boxes.

"Lookit who's here," Burt winked, nudging Joe.

I glanced up, unaware of what had caught their eye.

Darlene Mast was directly across the counter from me, shopping with her mother. She caught my look and smiled at me.

I smiled back. I was frozen; I couldn't move a muscle.

"Hi, Roy," she called.

"Hi . . . Darlene," I managed to say.

She smiled at me for a moment like she was expecting me to do something. I couldn't—I was rooted to the spot, a block of stone. Her mom looked over at me with this puzzled look on her puss, like "who's he," since I've never met Darlene's parents before. She's a nice-looking woman, kind of looks like Darlene, but real prissy. She moved on down the aisle.

Darlene stared at me a moment longer, like she was waiting for me to do something, but I didn't, I was still frozen there, so she caught up to her mom, turning once to look back and make sure I was still there, looking at her.

"Hi, Roy," Burt sang out in this stupid falsetto voice.

"Fuck you."

"You know something, Roy?" Joe asked.

I wasn't even with them—I was watching Darlene from across the store, hoping she'd turn back and look my way again.

"I think old Darlene likes you," Joe went on, "I definitely think she does."

"Up yours."

"Lots of guys wouldn't mind Darlene liking 'em," he said, "especially Danny Detweiler."

I glared at them. They got the hint and backed off, moving down the aisle, looking for more junk to spend their booty on.

I moved in Darlene's direction, playing it real casual, bird-dogging her from aisle to aisle. Out of the corner of my eye I saw Joe and Burt, those stupid twerps, pick up on what I was doing. They started following me following her, like in one of those Marx Brothers movies, big shit-eating grins plastered across their faces.

She looked back towards me. I turned away like I wasn't looking at her at all.

"Oh lover boy," Burt whispered.

"I'm gonna kill your ass, man," I warned him.

"Oh lover boy," he sang back.

Darlene and her mother had finished what they'd come for.

They headed for the checkout stand. I could tell by the way Darlene paused, her hand on her hip, that she was stalling.

It was now or never. I counted down from ten, then did it again.

"Would you like a sundae with me? Can I buy one for you?" I'd come up in front of her, blocking her path. It startled her but she smiled, quickly turning to her mother for approval.

"Mom, can I?"

Her mom gave me a real good up-and-down appraisal. I felt like a specimen under a microscope in biology class—this was a no-nonsense woman.

"This is Roy Poole, Mom. From my class." She smiled at her mom like they were sharing a secret. "He's *really* nice."

Mrs. Mast nodded her approval. "I'll wait for you in the car. Don't take forever." She gave me another look-see, collected her change, and left us.

I expelled my breath, which I didn't even know I'd been holding.

"Come on, then," Darlene said, taking my arm.

We sat at the counter, eating hot-fudge sundaes with the works. She ate like a lady, holding her pinkie away from her spoon and dabbing her napkin at her lips between bites. She was putting it away in style, though, I noticed. I myself was having a hard time getting the spoon to my mouth, let alone eat.

Joe and Burt slid onto the stools on either side of us.

"Hi, Darlene," they sang out in unison.

"Hi Burt, hi Joe," she answered, favoring each one with a dazzling smile.

I looked straight ahead, spooning in the ice cream. I was going to kick some serious butt later on, they could make book on that.

"What'cha eating?" Burt asked, like he couldn't see, it was right there in front of him.

"Hot-fudge sundae," Darlene told him, playing right along, even holding up a spoonful for him to see.

"Looks good," Joe kicked in, "I think I'll have me one."

"Yeah, me too," Burt chimed in.

"I thought y'all had to get home early," I said, making sure they heard the pissed-off in my voice.

"No, I don't have to," Burt said.

"Me, neither," Joe added. He called down the counter: "Hey, can we get some service down here?" then he spun around to face Darlene. "How've you been, Darlene?"

"I've been fine." She spooned in a dainty mouthful, and smiled at me. She could tell this was bugging the shit out of me, but she wasn't going to do anything to stop it. That was my job.

I sat there, silent. The pimply-faced counter girl, whose feet were killing her, you could tell by the way she walked, came down the duckboards.

"What do you brats want?"

"I want one of them hot-fudge sundaes. With nuts on top," Joe informed her.

"That's what I want, too," Burt seconded.

The counter girl started working on their sundaes. I sat stiff as a board, shoveling ice cream down my mouth like it was my last supper.

Burt glanced over at me. "So Darlene . . . how's Danny been these days?"

"Danny who?" she asked, glancing at me.

"How many Dannys are there? Detweiler. I heard you and him were going steady."

I almost choked on my ice cream. Man, that sucker was cruising for a bruising.

Darlene faced Burt squarely. "I am not going with anyone. *Especially* not that stuck-up Danny Detweiler."

"Somebody told me you were," Burt said, innocent as an altar boy.

"Well, somebody was wrong."

The counter girl put Joe's and Burt's sundaes in front of them.

"That'll be a quarter apiece."

They fished handfuls of nickels out, plunked them down on the counter.

"These look great," Burt said. "I'm starving."

"Me, too," Joe kicked in.

They started scarfing down the sundaes.

Darlene stole a look at me, put her spoon down. "This is an awfully big sundae, Roy," she said, "I can't eat another bite."

I seized the opportunity. "Me neither."

"Why don't you walk me out?"

"Okay," I told her. "Sure."

We stood up. I looked down at the chumps.

"You can finish ours if you're still hungry. No charge."

I followed her out, leaving Burt and Joe stuck. Served them right, the assholes.

"I'll bet they didn't even want them," she giggled in my ear.

Boy, that got me tingling. Her lips had been an inch away from touching me.

We went outside. She turned to me before we got to where her mom was waiting. "Do you want to walk me home?" she asked shyly.

"Yeah." I swallowed. "I mean sure. Yes."

Mrs. Mast was waiting in their Buick. "All set?" She was impatient and wasn't trying to hide it.

"Can Roy walk me home, Mom?" Darlene asked, leaning in the window. "I want to talk to him about our history assignment. Roy's real good in history."

Mrs. Mast looked me over again. I could read her mind— this boy doesn't look like any good student I've ever seen, was what she was thinking.

"I don't know. It's getting late, I want you home." This was a tough cookie, all right.

"We won't stop anywhere, Mrs. Mast," I hurriedly assured her, "I'll walk Darlene straight home." I said a silent prayer.

"Straight home," she finally allowed, "no dawdling."

"My mom's pretty good, all things considered," Darlene told me as we watched the big Buick ease into traffic, "but she can be so strict. Sometimes she treats me like I'm still in sixth grade."

"My mom, too," I lied. I didn't know what else to say, but I felt I had to say something.

She put on her earmuffs. They were pink, like bunny's ears. "Let's walk," she said. "I'm cold."

We walked along side by side. Darlene lived in Rolling Rock, a new development of solid houses and nice lawns, up the road a mile or so from the older part of town. Rolling Rock isn't as nice as Cheverly, but it's a lot nicer than where I live.

I was nervous and happy at the same time. I glanced over at her. She seemed completely at ease. She was a girl, girls know stuff boys never will, I knew that for sure. Boys talk about things, but girls have the knowledge. I don't know how I know that, but I know it's true.

"I've been wondering when you were going to say something to me," Darlene said, turning to me.

"You have?" I stammered. Jesus, what a dummy I can be. She didn't seem to notice, though. That's because it was pretty dark, and there wasn't much of a moon out.

"I mean . . . I noticed you watching me sometimes."

"Well," I admitted, "I guess I have. Sometimes."

"Well, I'm sure glad you finally said something to me."

"You are?" I was absolutely astonished. I could've kicked myself I felt so stupid. I've got this big reputation, the rock who never takes any shit from anyone, not even a teacher, someone who's gotten bare titty from plenty of girls, and here I was as tongue-tied as an imbecile, unable to say three words to her without tripping over myself. I stole another look at her — she didn't seem to notice any of my dumbness.

"I know there's lots of girls that like you, Roy." She was looking forward, not at me.

"Not that many." Sometimes you've got to be modest, especially around a girl like this. The truth is, there are several girls that I know like me, but I don't want Darlene to think I've been with every girl in the school, just with enough to let her know I'm worth it.

"I mean . . . do you like *me?*" she asked.

She was nervous, too. Goddamn! I had to play this really cool.

"Sure I do."

"I mean . . . you know . . ."

"Yeah . . ."

"I do, too."

"You do?"

"Can't you tell?" She took my arm. "I'm cold," she said, pressing up against me.

We walked for a minute. I was counting my breaths. She giggled.

"Now I'm not."

Her porch light was on. We stood off to the side so it wouldn't shine on us. She had made me walk real quiet up the stairs, so her mom wouldn't hear us.

"Well . . . good night, Roy."

"Good night, Darlene."

"See you tomorrow?"

"Sure."

We stared awkwardly at each other.

"Darlene, would you like to go steady with me?" I heard myself blurt out. I hadn't meant to say it, it just came out.

She was taken aback.

"I mean . . . I know it's like . . ." What the fuck did I mean? I didn't know myself. I did want to, I'd been wanting to since the day I laid eyes on her, but you don't ask a girl to go with you when you haven't even had one real date.

"I . . . my mother doesn't let me."

"Oh . . . okay . . . sure . . ."

"But if she did . . . I would like to go out with you whenever you can . . . when you want to . . . if you do . . . is that okay?"

"Sure, yeah. That's great." Is that *okay?* Is the pope Catholic?

"That's good." She smiled.

I'd run out of gas. This was more than I could handle for one night.

"Well, I'll see you tomorrow, I guess." I turned to go.

"Roy?"

"Yeah?"

"Don't you want to kiss me good night?"

Whoa, Nellie. "Sure."

She came to me. I held her, awkwardly, bending down and giving her a nice kiss, a kiss that wouldn't offend her, since it was our first time.

A nice kiss was not what this girl had in mind. She Frenched me so deep down my throat I almost felt her tongue touching my tonsils.

That was all I needed. We made out like fiends, right there on her mother's front porch. Even though she was wearing a heavy coat I could feel her titties pressed up against me. I had to shift my leg slightly so she wouldn't feel my boner. She shifted with me, pressing her thigh right between my legs.

She took a deep breath when we finally came up for air. Then she leaned forward and bit my lip.

My leg started jitterbugging on its own. Damn, she was wild! Darlene Mast, who everybody thought was untouchable.

"Boy, Roy, you sure do kiss great."

"So do you, Darlene."

"I'll bet you've had lots of practice," she teased, "a lot more than me."

I wasn't sure about that, not after the way she'd just kissed me, but I wasn't going to say so. You've got to act like a gentleman sometimes, even if it means not saying everything that's on your mind.

"I don't want to anymore," I told her, "only with you."

This was the truth. If I didn't kiss another girl the rest of my life I wouldn't care.

She leaned against me one more time before pulling away.

"My mother knows we're out here," she whispered. "I'd better say good night, so she'll let me see you again."

"Good night," I said back to her.

She touched my cheek with her mittened hand one time, then darted inside. A moment later, the porch light went off.

I stood without moving for a long time, until I forced myself to walk down the stairs. I could've slept on their porch all night, except they'd have thought I was crazy.

I was floating on air as I walked home. This was definitely one of the great days of my life. Probably the greatest.

EIGHT

"That's a nice-looking blazer, Roy," Admiral Wells said, squinting at me as I stood in front of the full-length mirror. "Blue looks good on you, which is fortunate for someone who aspires to Annapolis." He has this real dry sense of humor, the admiral, half the time I don't know if he's kidding or not. He turned to the salesman, who was holding another sports coat. "Let's try on the tweed now, shall we?"

We were in this very fancy men's store in Washington, Louis and Thomas Saltz, where the admiral buys his own clothes. Everybody in here knew him—as soon as we walked in all the salesmen started falling over themselves trying to help.

"We need a jacket for my young friend here," he'd told the salesman, "a sports coat he can wear with anything. We'll also be wanting a couple of shirts, a tie, and a pair of slacks. Cords should do the trick, I think." He glanced down at my shoes. I was wearing my clip-toe bombers, which have a two-inch thick sole. "We'll worry about shoes next time, if that's all right with you," he said to me.

I shrugged, too intimidated to answer. I felt like a chump, not only because of the clothes—which if any of my friends ever saw me in would be the end of my being thought of as cool—but the fact that he was going to pay for it all.

"And some socks, too," he added, "something that covers the calf. A gray should work."

We'd been down in his basement earlier in the day, working on a model. I'd been over his house the last three weekends, since that first time he'd brought me there. It was great: we'd work on stuff together, and then talk about Annapolis and the Navy. The admiral talked to me like a regular person, not the way I'm used to being talked to by a grownup. Like two friends talking.

He'd turned to me, down there, and said, "By the way, you'll be staying for dinner tonight. Mrs. Wells is having some people over and we want them to meet you." Then he'd looked me up and down. I was wearing my usual, jeans and a sports shirt. "We'll have to get you some clothes," he'd said, "we dress for dinner."

"I don't have any money," I'd stammered, scared to death. He must've thought I was rolling in dough, the way I was always buying models and stuff. "I mean on me."

"This will be my treat," he'd informed me, in this particular tone of voice he has. When he talks that way you don't argue with him, you just do it. It's the way he talked to the men in his command, I'll bet. He never yells or anything, but you know that's the way it's going to be.

"That one looks better, I think," he said now, confirming his choice with the salesman, who obviously agreed to anything the admiral wanted—meaning the tweed jacket, which I had put on. "How do you feel, Roy?"

I looked at myself in the mirror. It was a cool-looking sports coat, I had to admit. The only sports jacket I've ever owned was one my mom got me a couple years ago when we had to go to her baby sister's wedding. It was from Robert Hall and didn't fit very well. This one fit me like a glove.

"Yeah, I like it," I kind of mumbled.

"That's the one, then," he said, smiling his approval. He smoothed the back of it. "It's a good fit, don't you think, Arnold?" he asked the salesman. "Even the sleeves."

"Like it was tailored," the salesman agreed. He was the kind of salesman who would agree with whatever the admiral said, I could tell that right away.

"It's a good thing," the admiral said, "because we don't have time to have it altered. All right, then, shirts. Button-down. A white and a blue, I think." He turned to me. "The blue one will be good for a more casual occasion. You'll wear the white tonight, of course."

I didn't know what he was talking about, but I nodded in agreement. It was his money; I was just along for the ride.

We waited while the tailor cuffed the pants. When they were finished, the salesman handed the admiral the bill. Admiral Wells signed it without even looking at the amount.

"Now we've got you properly attired," he smiled, winking at me. "You'll knock all the ladies dead tonight."

"You'll be sitting two places to Mrs. Wells's right," the admiral told me, "you'll pull her chair out for her when we enter the dining room, and after she's seated you will seat yourself. Are you clear on that?"

"Yes, sir." We were upstairs in his private dressing room, getting dressed for dinner. Admiral Wells and Mrs. Wells both had their own dressing rooms. They had their own separate bathrooms, too. It was like being in a Cary Grant movie.

At least I wasn't wearing one of those monkey suits. The admiral was all gussied up in a tuxedo, with a starched white shirt, gold cuff links, and shoes that were made out of patent leather, real shiny. They looked like ballerina shoes, I swear to God. He looked at me watching him getting dressed, and smiled.

"Do I look foolish enough?" he asked.

"No . . . I mean . . ." He did look pretty silly, but I wasn't about to say so.

"I feel like a trained ape," he said, "but once in a blue moon I have to do this, to please Mrs. Wells. Going formal is her idea of a good time, don't ask me why. Generations of inbreeding, I suppose." He looked me over. I was wearing all my new clothes. The only old stuff I had on was my underpants and shoes.

"We should have done something about your footwear," he said, grimacing at them, "but your feet will be under the table most of the time. All in all, I'd say you look damn good. Damn good." He winked at me like he'd done in the store, like we were sharing a private joke.

I was pretty nervous, but I was excited, too. I'd never had dinner with Admiral and Mrs. Wells before. Whenever he would bring it up it would turn out they had to be somewhere else, some fancy party or something. Mrs. Wells was always nice to me, but I had a strong feeling that eating dinner with me was not at the top of her list of have-to-do's. That's why I was really surprised when the admiral had told me, earlier that afternoon, that I was going to be one of the dinner guests tonight, and that it was Mrs. Wells's idea. Mrs. Wells was with us in the study when he'd said that. I'd looked at her to make sure that this was for real. She'd smiled at me and said, "I hope you like your prime rib rare, Roy."

"Yes, ma'am," I'd told her, "that's my favorite way." I didn't know what she was talking about, but if that's what they ate, it was fine with me.

We went downstairs. I followed the admiral around as he poked his head in the kitchen for a minute, talking to the colored cook about the dinner plans. She was wearing one of those gray-and-black uniforms like in *Gone With the Wind*.

"That smells fabulous," he remarked as he opened the oven door and stuck his head close. That's what prime rib was, I realized—roast beef. It smelled great. I've only had roast beef a couple times in my life, it's too expensive for us.

"Get that nose of yours out of my cooking," the cook, whose name was Mary, scolded at him, laughing like they were the best of friends. "You'll get your supper soon enough."

"Not soon enough for me. I've got to do my dog-and-pony show first." From the tone of his voice it sounded like they were sharing a joke, in a way that he'd never do with his own wife.

Mary looked over at me.

"This the boy you been telling me 'bout?" she asked him.

"Yep. Roy, come over here and say hello to the best darn cook in all of Washington, and Maryland and Virginia, too."

"Oh, get on with you."

"It's the truth," he told her. "Why would all of our friends be trying to steal you away otherwise?"

"Get on with you, Admiral Wells." She was practically giggling like a schoolgirl, she was so tickled by his flattery. It was obvious they liked each other a lot.

It was the first time I'd ever seen a white person have a normal conversation with a colored person. I know that sounds weird, being raised in Maryland and all, but it's the truth. It wasn't the way I'd thought it would be, being in the same room with one and talking regular-like.

She caught me staring at her.

"Hello, there, Roy," she said. She wiped her hand on her apron and held it out to me. I shook it. It was soft and hot, from being in the kitchen. "I hope you like old-fashioned southern cooking," she said.

"He'll love your cooking," the admiral said.

"Yes, ma'am, I like it fine," I said. I don't know why I called her "ma'am," since she was a colored person, but she was older than me, older than my mom probably, it seemed the right thing to do. Nobody I knew was there, they'd never know.

The guests started arriving. They were as old as Admiral Wells, some even older. The men were all dressed up in tuxedos like he was, or else in full-dress military uniform. The ones in uniform were all admirals or generals: each one had enough fruit salad on his chest to fill a trunk, while the women were all dolled up in fancy dresses, fancy hairdos, and tons of makeup. They wore jewelry, too; real stuff, diamonds and pearls. Nobody told me it was real, but I could tell.

"You look sensational, Sadie," the admiral said to one of the women, "a picture of beauty." He took her hand and kissed the fingers, like she was a queen.

"You're the last real gentleman, James," the woman answered, "even if it is absolute malarkey." Talk about a thick southern accent! She must've been from Mississippi or someplace like that. "Your wife is the only beauty left. The rest of us make do with camouflage and girdles."

He laughed at that, and introduced me.

"This is Roy Poole," he told the woman and her husband, "a recent and valued acquaintance of mine. Roy is going to be joining us for dinner tonight. Roy, General and Mrs. McClain."

I shook his hand and then hers—there's no way I was going to kiss it, she wouldn't have expected it anyway, not from a kid. She was wearing enough perfume to overpower a skunk—there's no way I'd ever explain that smell on me to my folks. I'd lied like a rug already, calling them up to tell them I was spending the night at Joe's, then having to call Joe to make sure and cover for me in case they called over, like if somebody died or something.

"Pleased to meet you, ma'am," I said.

She smiled at me, kind of a blank smile, like she hadn't actually said hello to a kid my age in twenty years.

The admiral greeted each couple as they arrived. They were

all ex-military and their wives, all important people. He introduced me to one and all, like I was his new best friend.

"Why aren't you in uniform, Jim?" joshed one of the men, who was himself in the full-dress uniform of a two-star Army general. "You like Ike, don't you? You're not a closet Stevenson supporter, for God's sakes?"

"I like Ike fine," the admiral answered, "but I'm retired now. I wore the uniform long enough. Let the men doing the fighting wear it. I'll save mine for Armistice Day."

The man who'd asked the question looked put off by that. Admiral Wells saw he'd embarrassed the guy and quickly changed the subject.

"Let me get you one of my Manhattans," he said. "I know you love them."

He led me back into the kitchen, where he pulled a gallon jug out from under the sink. It was filled to the brim with whiskey.

"Saves me from having to fix up a fresh batch every ten minutes," he explained. "This crowd loves their bourbon."

He lined up a bunch of cocktail glasses on the sink, filled a cocktail shaker with ice, and stirred a bunch of the whiskey and sweet vermouth up in it. He poured the drinks into the glasses, and dropped a cherry in each one.

"Juanita," he called to the other uniformed colored maid in the kitchen, who was helping Mary with the cooking, "would you put these on a tray and serve them? We have a bunch of thirsty guests out there."

"Yes, sir."

"A southern military crowd," the admiral informed me. "Best drinkers in the world—to hear them tell it."

I went back into the living room—and saw why the admiral and Mrs. Wells had wanted me to be at their dinner tonight. This old guy and his wife were coming in the door. They were a lot older than the others, from the looks of them, both all gussied up, the woman in a dress that came down to the floor, dripping with jewelry around her arms and neck, the man in an admiral's uniform. I almost shit a brick when I saw the epaulets on his shoulders—the guy was a bona fide four-star admiral. He was obviously too old to still be on active duty, but he was a heavy-weight, no question, heavier even than Admiral Wells.

Meeting up with some four-star admiral wasn't why I was there, though. They had a girl with them about my age, dressed up like a teenage version of the older woman, long fancy dress and all.

That's why Mrs. Wells had asked me to dinner, I realized; not because she was dying for my company, but so this girl wouldn't be the only kid there.

I watched the girl from across the room as she hung onto the old woman's arm. I don't know who was leaning on the other more, her or the old woman, but I could tell she was feeling pretty uncomfortable, being the only kid in a group of old folks. So she thought, anyway.

Then she saw me. Her face changed real fast: from surprise, to not knowing what was going on, to being shy; all in about three seconds. Even though I'd been the only kid there until then I hadn't been feeling all that weird, because the admiral always made me feel comfortable, like a regular person, not a dumb kid.

For a second, though, I did feel kind of shy, seeing her seeing me, but I got over that fast. For one thing, I'm not very shy, not usually. For another, I could tell by looking at her that I was cooler than her. She might have more money than me—if she was with these people she had to—but I knew more things, I'd been around a lot more.

She turned away. I kept looking at her. For one thing, she was kind of cute, in the face anyway. She wasn't some raving beauty or anything, but she was definitely okay in the face. She didn't have any makeup on, and all the girls in my school, all the cute ones anyway, wear makeup. This girl wore her hair in long ringlets like out of *Little Women* or something, and she was a bit of a porker, to tell the truth. I don't mean she was a sow or anything gross like that, but she definitely had packed away her share of groceries. Kind of like a big farm girl who happened to be rich.

What she had that kept my eyes glued on her, though, was not her face or her old-fashioned hair or any of that other stuff. This girl had big tits—really big. Darlene's were great, but these titties were definitely bigger, monsters practically, even bigger than my sister's.

"Here's someone I'm sure you will enjoy meeting." Admiral Wells was suddenly next to me, his hand on my elbow guiding me across the room towards the old four-star admiral and his wife and the girl.

"Sherman and Helene, let me introduce Roy Poole, the young man I've mentioned to you. Roy, this is Admiral Sherman Prescott and Mrs. Prescott."

"Pleased to meet you, sir," I said, "it's a real honor. You, too, ma'am," I added hastily, shaking in my boots.

Admiral Sherman Prescott was famous, I'd read about him in lots of history books about the Navy, he was one of the most important admirals in the entire Atlantic fleet, almost as important as Nimitz or Halsey.

"It's a pleasure to meet *you*, Roy," Mrs. Prescott said, holding on to my hand for dear life. Her hand was bony and dry, the way old people's hands get. My grandma's hand is like that. You can practically feel all the individual bones in these old ladies' hands. "Your mentor has told us *so* many lovely things about you, I feel like we already know you," she added. She sounded like a little bird, she practically sang when she talked.

By "mentor" I knew she meant the admiral. I glanced back at him. He was smiling like the cat who ate the canary. It was kind of strange-feeling, that he'd been talking about me to people. I didn't know how to take that, even though it was a compliment. Still, it gave me a funny feeling.

"Yes, a pleasure," old Admiral Prescott kicked in. He had a

deep voice, the kind that makes you sit up and listen. A good voice for an admiral.

"And this is Melanie Prescott," Mrs. Prescott said, pulling the girl forward, towards me. "Our granddaughter."

"Hi," she said. She blushed a little.

"Hi," I said back to her, forcing myself to look at her face, because if I looked at her tits she'd probably blush so hard she'd break a blood vessel, and besides I was already getting a boner. That was all I needed, a boner in front of this girl and the admiral and all his guests.

"Melanie is in the ninth grade," her grandmother told me. She said it like she was trying to fix us up or something. I had the distinct impression, in fact, that Admiral Wells and her had talked about this girl and me. Not fixing us up directly or anything, but getting us together and seeing what happened.

"What grade are you in, Roy?" Mrs. Prescott jumped in right away. She wasn't shy about sticking her nose into other people's business, that was obvious.

"I'm in the ninth, too."

"Isn't that interesting," she said, with a tone in her voice like I'd said something real clever and witty.

As she prattled on I couldn't help but take a peek at Melanie's tits pushing against her dress. Man, was that a mistake! My cock immediately sprung to life. I put my hand in my pants pocket to try and cover it up. If anybody looked down, I was dead meat.

Strictly by accident, Mrs. Wells saved me.

"Ah, here's Beatrice at last, making the grand entrance," Mrs. Prescott exclaimed, looking towards the staircase. "As usual, the belle of the ball."

Everybody turned and looked as Mrs. Wells walked down the staircase. Unlike the other women, who were all dressed like they were going to a big formal affair, she was wearing a simple black dress that came just below her knees. She had hardly any makeup on, and the only jewelry she wore was one string of pearls. But she was the prettiest woman there, by far. My throat got dry just looking at her.

Mrs. Wells moved around the room, kissing everybody, getting kissed back in return; just on the cheek, not on the mouth, men and women both. I'd seen that kind of stuff in the movies but I didn't know people actually did it in real life. There were a lot of things about people like this I didn't know anything about. It made me feel sort of clumsy, knowing I wasn't like them. Actually, it scared the shit out of me, if I thought about it. What was I doing here, really? I was a fish out of water, a dumb hick from Ravensburg, and I knew it showed. I figured the best thing to do was keep my mouth shut as much as possible and watch how these people acted.

"Hello, darling," Mrs. Wells said to her husband as she finally got around to where we were standing. The kiss she gave him was different from the ones she gave everyone else, more like a nuzzle on his neck. "Sorry I'm late, it takes me longer to get ready than it used to," she said with a smile. She turned to Admiral Prescott and Mrs. Prescott and gave them each kisses. "Helene. Sherman." Mrs. Prescott kissed her back. The admiral shook her hand.

"I see you two have met," Mrs. Wells said to me then, looking from me to Melanie.

"Yes, ma'am," I told her. "Just now."

"Melanie's a special favorite of ours," Mrs. Wells told me, as if Melanie was invisible, instead of standing right next to her.

I looked over at Melanie. She was blushing up a storm.

"I'm sure you two young people will have a lot in common," Mrs. Wells went on. "You're both so . . . creative."

I looked at her like she was a Martian or something. Where the hell'd she come up with that? She hardly ever gave me the time of day, normally, she didn't know jack-shit about me, unless she meant the model building. For some reason, though, she was trying to make me look good to Melanie and her grandparents.

"How charming," Mrs. Prescott said, in her singing tone of voice.

Admiral Wells had his hand on my back, like a father does when he's proud of a son—not that my old man's ever done it with me, but I know how it would feel. He looked at me, and although he didn't actually wink like he'd done earlier—he couldn't with all these other people around—I felt like we were sharing a secret. It was a good feeling.

"Let's get you good people a drink," the admiral said to the Prescotts. "I'm sure the youth contingent will find things to talk about," he added, giving me a good hard look. Then he and Mrs. Wells led the Prescotts to another part of the house, and suddenly there I was, standing alone with Melanie.

I looked at her. She looked away, blushing again. I kept on looking at her. There wasn't anything else I could do to help her out except walk away, and I couldn't do that.

She forced herself to turn back to look at me. As I watched her I started feeling sorry for her. I mean, okay, her grandfather was a famous war hero, and she was probably rich as hell and all that good shit, but I knew as sure as God made little green apples that this girl had never had a date in her life—not with a boy who really liked her for herself, instead of having to because his parents knew her parents. She was standing here in front of this strange boy, who I'm sure didn't look like any boy she knew, not with my hair, which is cut modified Elvis-style, its shape held firmly in place with a healthy dollop of Brylcreem ("a little dab'll do you"), my Flagg Brothers bombers, and all the rest. I was dressed in nice clothes and everything, but she had to know I was not her style, like I knew she wasn't like the girls in my school.

It took some of the edge off my inner worry, knowing that she was as nervous as I was, as out of place and scared.

"That's a pretty dress," I told her, giving her a smile. One of us had to say something, and I knew she'd never be the one to talk first.

She blushed again. "Thank you."

"Pretty fancy," I said.

"It was my grandmother's choice." She wet her lips. She had nice, full lips. "I don't usually dress like this," she added, like she was apologizing for it.

"Me neither." My eyes drifted back down again—I couldn't help it. This time she caught me, and did she ever blush then! I forced my look back up. "I mean I'd look pretty silly in a dress, don't you think?"

She giggled out loud, covering her mouth so nobody would hear. "That's funny," she said, giggling again.

"Yeah, I'm a regular Jackie Gleason," I told her. "Hey, Ralphie babe," I said, imitating my dad's buddy Fred Gash imitating Ed Norton.

Man, that about cracked her up. She started giggling like crazy, burying her face in her hands so she wouldn't be embarrassed. She embarrassed easily, that was obvious, with all the blushing she'd been doing.

"That is *funny*," she said, when she'd finally gotten the giggles under control. "*Really* funny."

"Ralphie babe," I said again, in my Norton voice.

She grabbed hold of my wrist as she laughed again.

"Don't," she begged, "people are watching."

I glanced around. No one was paying us any attention at all.

"No, they're not," I assured her. "Anyway, what if they were? What's wrong with laughing?"

"I don't like people looking at me," she said. "It makes me self-conscious."

"Okay, then. I'll quit." I liked that, that she admitted she didn't like being looked at. One thing that was nice about this girl, she didn't know it was uncool not to be cool.

She looked up at me without blushing this time.

"Are you from around here?" she asked. "I haven't seen you before."

"No, I'm not from around here."

"Oh." She paused, like she didn't know what to say next. "How do you know the Wellses?"

"Me and the admiral . . ." I corrected myself: "the admiral and me . . . and I . . . we build models together. Ship models. I met him in a model shop."

That threw her. She wouldn't know anything about models, so she didn't know what else to say.

"What about you?" I asked, keeping it going. "Do you live near here?"

"Around the corner. On California Street."

I was right—she was rich. California Street was one block over, with houses as big and fancy as the Wellses'.

"Pretty fancy," I said.

She blushed again and stared down at her feet, which gave me another chance to steal a quick look at her tits.

"It's just a house," she said. She had this habit of apologizing for everything. Maybe it was because of me—she had to know I didn't come from any place like California Street, not even close. "Where *do* you live?" she asked. The way she asked, it was like she didn't want to because it wasn't polite, but she was too curious not to.

"Ravensburg," I said, fast and low.

"Oh." Like, where the hell is that?

"It's in Prince Georges County."

"I know where Ravensburg is. Do you have a farm?"

I'd have bet a million dollars she'd say that. That's what people think when they think about Ravensburg, if they ever do think about it. Years ago it was farms, before World War Two, but there aren't hardly any farms around anymore; the ones that're left are pretty small places, not big enough to make a living from. If you want to farm now you have to move farther out, Bowie and Largo and places like that. But she wouldn't know that, all she knows about Ravensburg is if you're from there you're a farmer. This girl has probably never even been in Prince Georges County in her life, except to drive through it on the way to Annapolis or the Eastern Shore.

"No, we just have a plain old house."

"Oh," she said again. Then she smiled. She had a nice smile, it lit up her whole face. "I've always thought it would be fun to live on a farm. I love animals."

"Me, too." Of course, I've never had any. She looked like a farm girl. I could see her out there in the barn, milking the cows and shit. I knew one set of tits I wouldn't mind milking, I thought, looking at her. That's what Burt would've said if he'd been here.

We stood there for a minute without talking. I'd been doing it all and I didn't feel like it right then. I felt like the first time I'd come here with the admiral; that I didn't belong. That people could look right through me and see that I didn't.

"I'm glad you're here, Roy," Melanie said suddenly, looking at me right in the face. "I was afraid I'd be the only person here under fifty."

"Yeah," I said, surprised that she'd said something on her own, "I know the feeling."

"Sometimes I feel like a fifth wheel," she went on, "being at these parties with all these old people. I like the people, don't get me wrong, but I don't spend very much time with my friends, except when I'm in school."

"Don't you have other kids living on your block?"

"None my age." She hesitated. "My parents are divorced. I live with my mother but most of the time my grandmother takes care of me. My dad lives in New Orleans. I hardly ever see him."

Shit, I thought, that's a bitch. Not that I'm all that crazy about living with my own parents, but the way she said it, it sounded so sad. She really was a poor little rich girl, like in the stories.

"I'll bet it's fun where you live," she said. "Do you go to public school?"

"Ravensburg Junior High. Next year I'll be in high school."

"I wish I went to public school," she said. "I hate where I go."

"Where?" I asked.

"National Cathedral School. It's an all-girls school."

That explained part of it, the part about being shy around boys; although she'd be shy anywhere, it's who she was.

"Do you have a girlfriend?" she asked me then, out of the blue.

"Um . . ." Damn, she sure was getting forward all of a sudden!

"I'll bet you do," she said real fast, not waiting for me to answer. "A boy who looks like you has to beat the girls off with a stick."

"Sure," I laughed. "Millions of them."

"Do you have a steady?"

"Well . . ." I thought about Darlene. I'd asked her to go with me, but she couldn't because of her mother; but I knew I wasn't going to date any other girls, not seriously, anyway.

"It's none of my business, is it?" she said, before I could come up with an acceptable answer, one that wasn't an out-and-out lie but didn't hurt her feelings, either. "I don't know why I even asked, it's rude."

"No, it's okay."

"You don't have to answer."

"Well, I don't," I told her.

"Oh. I thought you would."

"Nope." I could tell that she liked that I wasn't going steady with anyone. "How about you?"

"No," she said. "I don't date. My grandparents wouldn't like it. They think I'm too young to date."

Talk about different worlds. I've been dating girls since sixth grade. Everybody does where I come from.

"It's hard at an all-girls school," she explained.

"Yeah, I'll bet."

"Anyway," she said, her voice dropping down to a whisper, "you can't date if you're not asked."

Talk about feeling like shit. I'd been feeling sorry for myself and here was Melanie with a lot more to feel sorry about than I did, even if she was rich and had a set of knockers as big as Kathryn Grayson, that actress in *Showboat*.

I was about to tell her I knew plenty of guys who wouldn't mind taking her out, which wouldn't have been a lie, not with those knockers, but Mrs. Wells came back into the room from wherever she'd been and called out: "Dinner, everyone."

I made sure Mrs. Wells was seated, the way Admiral Wells had instructed me. She smiled at me as I pushed her chair in.

"Are you enjoying yourself, Roy?" she asked.

What was I going to say? "Yes, ma'am."

"Isn't Melanie nice?"

"Yes, ma'am."

"Her grandparents are our closest friends. We think of her almost like a daughter."

I didn't know what kind of answer to make to that, so I just sat down with the other guests.

Dinner was served in several courses, starting with soup made out of carrots, which sounds crummy but which was actually very good. The table was real long—there were twenty people sitting at it, counting Melanie and me, tall candles were burning in silver candlesticks, and dozens of flowers stuck out of big vases. I was nervous, eating with all these fancy people. There were more knives and forks at my individual place setting than my whole family all put together has at our meals.

Mary the cook and the other colored girl waited on us, starting with Mrs. Wells. They would stand next to you and you'd serve yourself out of the bowl or plate. I watched Mrs. Wells like a hawk and imitated everything she did, how to serve and what knife and fork to use. The food was really delicious, the prime rib especially, which was by far the best roast beef I'd ever eaten, but I was so nervous about not fucking up that I didn't enjoy it as much as I would have liked. The only good thing was that because I was a kid, nobody paid any attention to me.

I looked across the table from time to time at Melanie, who was seated at the other end, near the admiral. She talked to some of the people around her a little bit, but mostly she just ate, like me.

I got through the meal without making a total ass of myself, meaning I didn't spill anything or burp out loud. After dessert, which was this incredible ice-cream dish that was set on fire before it was served, Admiral Wells stood up and raised his wineglass.

"To good friends," he said.

All the other people raised their wineglasses. I looked over at Melanie, who was picking her glass up. We had the same kind of glasses, except we had grape juice in ours instead of wine.

"Hear, hear," some of the men said. I swear to God, the whole thing was like out of a movie.

"Cigars and brandy in my study, gentlemen," Admiral Wells announced.

Mrs. Wells looked at me, so I got up fast and pulled her chair out to let her stand up without knocking it over.

"Sherry in the living room for the ladies," she said.

Everyone started moving out of the dining room. Mrs. Wells turned to me.

"Did you enjoy dinner, Roy?"

"Yes, ma'am," I told her, "it was delicious."

"Good, I'm glad." She smiled. "Your table manners were exemplary."

That's a word I haven't gotten around to learning yet, but it sounded like I'd passed muster.

"It's a lovely evening tonight," she continued. "Perhaps you and Melanie would like to take a walk, instead of listening to the old fogeys prattle on."

It was more than a suggestion, the way she put it.

"Yes, ma'am, that's a good idea."

"Take your time. You can let yourselves in when you return." She put her hand on mine. "She's a lovely girl."

It was warm outside. Melanie and I walked along the quiet streets. I didn't know whether to hold her hand or not. She probably would've liked it, but it might've scared her, so I didn't.

"This is my house."

We were standing in front of a big old stone-and-brick house, all dark inside.

"It looks nice," I told her. It was pretty awesome, to tell you the truth, as awesome as the admiral's.

"My mother's in New York," she said. "I'm staying with my grandparents. That's why there's no lights on inside."

"Must be nice, living in a house . . . living here," I said. I didn't want to come on too much like a hick, gawking in front of a big old house. Like a farmer, the way she'd thought of me when I first met her.

"It is nice. My mother travels quite a bit, so I'm not here all the time. But it's nice."

How's about if you show me inside, I thought. You could show me your bedroom and you could whip off that stupid-looking old-lady's dress and you could show me your titties and I could show you the best time of your young life.

"I'd like to show you the inside," she said. For a minute I thought she was reading my mind—"but there's nobody there, we don't keep live-in servants since it's just my mother and me."

"Do you ever see your father?" I asked. As soon as the words came out I wanted to bite my tongue off. She'd already told me he didn't live around here, maybe she never saw him. Maybe he was dead, not just divorced.

"Hardly at all," she said in this sad voice. "He's a lawyer, sometimes he has business up here. He's argued before the Supreme Court." She looked up at the empty house. "He doesn't get along with my grandparents, his mother and father. Ever since he walked out on my mother and me they've disowned him. He left my mother for his secretary," she continued in a low voice. "My grandfather hates him."

I really didn't want to hear this. Why can't you keep your big yap shut, you dumb shit, I said to myself. I could tell she was feeling bad about it, the way she was talking low and looking up at the dark house, her own house she couldn't even go into. So without even thinking about it, I took her hand.

Her hand felt nice. It wasn't sweaty or mushy the way some girls' hands are, it was soft but firm. She immediately held on tight. I knew she'd wanted me to do it.

"Do you live with both your parents?" she asked. She was looking me right in the face. She really was pretty in the face, with the moon shining on it and everything.

"Oh, sure. And my sister."

"Is she younger than you?"

"Older. Two years. She's in eleventh."

"That must be nice, having a sister. And living with both your parents."

"Yeah, it's fine," I said, lying like a rug. If she ever met my family she'd have a hemorrhage.

"What does your dad do?"

"He's a printer . . . he owns a printing shop, a printing press actually, it's the biggest printing press in Prince Georges County. That's why we live there, because that's where his business is," I went on, piling one lie on top of the other. I didn't want to, the way she was looking at me she wouldn't have given a shit if I'd said they were bank robbers, but I couldn't help myself. I was a fish out of water around her and her grandparents and the admiral and Mrs. Wells and I was ashamed of it, I was ashamed of my parents who fought all the time and my old man who got drunk and fucked around and beat up on my old lady and everything about my family.

"You sound like you have a great life," she said.

I wanted to crawl under a rock somewhere. This girl had it knocked—okay, so her parents were divorced—but still, she was the one with all the money and everything, and here she was envying *me*.

She squeezed my hand. "I like you, Roy. I like you a lot."

I swallowed. "I like you, too, Melanie."

"I mean I *really* like you."

Jesus, she sounded like Darlene. The funny thing was, I believed Melanie more.

"That's really . . . that's good, that we like each other." Shit, I'd gotten in this too deep.

"I've been looking forward to meeting you," she said.

"What?"

"I've heard Admiral Wells talking about you, to my grandparents. He says you're going to Annapolis, that he's going to sponsor you."

My head went light when I heard that. I swayed on my feet, holding onto her hand.

"He's a great guy, the admiral," I managed to say.

We started walking again. I needed to let my head clear. This whole evening was happening too fast.

"Roy?"

"Yeah, Melanie?"

"Where did you get your shoes?"

"My shoes?" How could I think about shoes? I looked down at them. "Flagg Brothers. On New York Avenue."

"They're neat-looking. I don't know any boys that wear shoes like them."

"It's what guys in my school wear."

"All the boys I know are jerks," she said. "All they care about is who has the most expensive car or what prep school they're going to." She squeezed my hand. "I like you better than any boy I know. Much better."

"I like you, too, Melanie," I gulped. I knew what she

wanted—for me to say I liked her better than any girl I knew, but I couldn't because it would be a lie, I was in love with Darlene. I'd already lied too much to her tonight, I didn't want to do it again, especially something as important as that.

We were almost back to Admiral Wells's house. Through the windows we could see the people inside.

"Roy," Melanie said, stopping me out on the sidewalk where we couldn't be seen.

"Yeah?"

"I'm having a piano recital in a few weeks. Would you . . . would you come?" It was pretty dark out, but I could see she was blushing again.

It had to be tough on her, asking me. She'd probably never asked a boy to go anywhere with her in her life. Not a boy she liked.

"Sure," I said. What the hell, she was a nice girl, why not?

My answer must've thrown her for a loop, because she swallowed hard, looked at me, and said, "will you . . . be my escort?"

"You mean like your date?"

"Yes." She was trembling inside, she had to be. I've known the feeling.

"Sure. I'd like to."

She squeezed my hand.

"Thank you."

I looked up at the house. "We'd better go inside," I said.

"I guess so." She didn't want to, not yet.

I felt good. She was a nice girl, she had huge ones, she was rich, and she liked me.

"I'm really glad you were here tonight," she said.

"Me, too."

We stood there for a minute, looking at each other. What she wanted was for me to kiss her. She wanted to grab ahold of me and kiss me as hard as she could and press those monster knockers of hers up against my body.

I wanted to, too. I could imagine those titties pressing up

against me. It would've really felt good, I definitely would've gotten a raging boner.

But I didn't. It would've been taking advantage of her, because I was in love with Darlene.

"We better go in," I told her.

"Do we have to?" she said. She was feeling bad, like she wasn't good enough for me or something like that. But I couldn't tell her about Darlene, it would've made her feel twice as bad.

"Somebody might see us."

We started walking towards the door. We were still holding hands but I let go—I didn't want Admiral Wells or Mrs. Wells to see us holding hands. They'd wanted me to be nice to her, but that would've been too much.

"Hey, Melanie," I said just before we went back in.

"Yes?"

"I'm glad you asked me to your recital."

That made her happy. It didn't make up for my not kissing her, but it helped.

As soon as we went inside she ran to her grandparents and started talking to them, her face all flushed and excited. From the way they looked in my direction it must've been about me. I felt pretty self-conscious, standing there with all those rich old people in the room and this girl talking about me to her people, one who was a famous war hero on top of everything else, so I headed for the can to take a leak. I really had to piss, I'd been holding it the whole time we were outside.

I pissed against the sides of the commode, so no one outside the room would hear me. That would've embarrassed the shit out of me, opening the bathroom door and finding some old biddy waiting to go, knowing she'd been listening to me. I'll bet I went for three minutes, pissing a rope as thick as a horse's.

On the way back I passed by what Mrs. Wells calls her drawing room. It's the room with the paintings of people from the Revolutionary War and times like that. The room was dark, but there was enough light filtering in that I could see a woman standing there. The woman had her back to me, so she didn't know I was watching. Then she turned, and I saw enough of her face to recognize her. It was Mrs. Prescott, Melanie's grandmother.

She was holding something in her hand. It looked like a silver statue, a little one. Mrs. Wells had a lot of real expensive stuff in the house, silver and gold cups and picture frames and little statues.

Old Mrs. Prescott kind of glanced around, like she was checking to see if anyone was watching her. I know that look—it's the same look I have when I'm in the dime store about to steal an ID bracelet or something. She didn't see me, though, because it was dark and I wasn't in the room, I was in the hall outside, and the curtains on the glass doors to the room blocked me out.

She looked at the statue for a minute more, then she put it down on the table and picked up another one. I don't know why, but I felt weird, like I was watching something I shouldn't be seeing, so as quietly as I could I turned away and walked back into the living room, where all the other guests were standing around, talking and socializing.

The party broke up pretty soon after. Melanie stood in the foyer with her grandparents, who were talking to the Wellses. Her grandmother was laughing and talking in that singing voice of hers like she didn't have a care in the world.

I felt weird looking at Mrs. Prescott, because I'd been spying on her in the drawing room. Melanie caught me looking and thought I was looking at her, because she blushed again. It was kind of cute, the way she blushed so much. As she followed her grandparents out the door she turned and blew me a secret kiss.

I was going to have to figure out a way to let her know I wasn't going to be her boyfriend—she was a nice girl, but we came from different worlds, if she ever found out about the real me . . . I didn't want to think about that. She was a nice girl who was lonely. And she had the best goddamn tits I'd ever seen, even though I'd been stupid enough to be a gentleman for one time in my life and not touch them.

Admiral Wells and I sat in his study, drinking hot chocolate. We were alone—all the guests had left and Mrs. Wells had gone up to bed. He was wearing pajamas and a silk dressing gown over them, like you see in the movies. I was in my jeans and T-shirt.

I was staying overnight in their guest room, because it was too late to go home. The admiral had insisted, so I'd called my mom and told her the usual lie, I lie more to my folks than I tell them the truth. What they don't know won't hurt them, that's my motto.

"Did you have fun tonight?" Admiral Wells asked me.

"Yes, sir, it was neat."

He nodded, looking at me over the rim of his mug.

"Melanie Prescott and you got along?"

"Sure. She's nice."

"Yes. She is." He paused a moment. "It would be a good thing if you and she became friends. She lives too much the cloistered life, she needs a teenager's excitement."

"I think we'll be friends," I told him. I knew he wanted to hear that, and anyway it was the truth.

"I'd like that."

We sipped our hot chocolates without talking. One thing I like about Admiral Wells, you don't have to talk to him all the time. It's okay not to say anything, to just be there.

"I've got something to show you," he said in this offhanded way, like he'd just remembered whatever it was. He walked over to his desk and picked up a catalogue, then came back and sat down next to me. "Have you heard of Admiral Farrington Academy, Roy?"

"No, sir."

"It's a military preparatory school." He held the catalogue on his lap so I could see it. It had a slick cover with a picture of some kind of Army or Navy cadet standing at attention. On top of the picture it said "Admiral Farrington Military Academy," and underneath, "Turning Boys Into Men For Over One Hundred Years."

He handed me the catalogue.

"Farrington is one of the finest military schools in the country," he told me. "They specialize in training boys to go to the Naval Academy, and from what I understand they send more boys to Annapolis than any other school in the country, by a factor of three, maybe more."

I hefted the catalogue in my hand. It was pretty heavy, with a lot of pages.

"It's something you should consider, Roy," the admiral said, turning to me.

Boy, that hit me like a ton of bricks. I didn't know what to say, so for once I was smart and didn't say anything.

"This is all preliminary, of course," he continued. "I know you live with your mother and father and sister and that you're happy at home and with your school. At the same time, I know how important going to Annapolis is to you. And I want to help you achieve that goal if I can."

"Yes, sir." I was numb, as if this was all a dream.

"I want you to take this catalogue home with you and look it over," Admiral Wells said. "I'm sure you'll find it interesting, maybe even exciting. If I were a young man considering a military career, a Navy career, I'd want to look long and hard at a school like Farrington, because it would help me reach my goal."

He sat back then and gave me a good, hard look.

"Going to a school like this would be very different from the life you live now, Roy. It would be different from the school you go to, and from any public school you will attend in the future, be it in Ravensburg or anywhere. It would even be different from a normal private school, like St. Alban's here in Washington. To begin with, you would live there. You would come home for holidays, of course, and in the summer, but for the most part you would be moving out of your home and making Farrington your new home. And you might have to repeat the ninth grade, because their standards are higher than a public school's."

I kind of squirmed around when he said that. Even though I'd been wanting to get out, for years it seemed, facing it suddenly was hard to do. What about my friends? What about Darlene? And to do ninth grade over—I was already tired of this year.

He thought I was squirming for a different reason: "I can understand your reluctance to leave home," he told me. "It's one of the most difficult decisions a young person has to make."

"Yes, sir," I said. "Other guys do it, though, so I guess I could." I wasn't sure why I'd said that, it just popped out, but it seemed okay. I *could* leave home if it was the right thing.

"Yes, you could. You're a mature young man. I think you could handle just about anything."

"Thank you." I hoped I wasn't turning red—getting compliments like that doesn't happen to me very much.

"I mean it. I've observed you long enough to know your mettle, Roy. You're first-rate. You'll make a terrific midshipman someday."

"Yes, sir," I said again, "thank you."

"It isn't easy, going to Farrington. The discipline is difficult. It is, after all, a military academy. You'll pull plenty of duty your first year; all boys do. The classwork will be hard, much harder than what you're used to. You'll be studying three or four hours a night, just to keep up."

Three or four hours every single night? Except for that time I'd busted my balls to get my math homework done, I hadn't studied three or four hours a month, ever.

"That's a lot," I said.

"Everyone does it at Farrington," he told me, "or they don't make it; they wash out." He put his hand on my shoulder. "I know you, Roy. You won't wash out."

"Yes, sir." Shit—he was talking like I was already going there. And even if I wanted to, even if I got in by some miracle, there's no way my old man would ever pay for anything like that. He'd think I was crazy, and he'd probably make me stop seeing Admiral Wells to boot, if he ever got wind of any of this stuff.

"One thing I should mention before I pursue this any further," he said. "This is an expensive school. It costs as much as a good university."

That was it. He'd told me what I'd already suspected.

"But you mustn't let that concern you," he continued. "Farrington wants the best there is. If you qualify, they'll find a way to make it work." He paused. "And if there's anything outstanding, Mrs. Wells and I will help you out."

I didn't know whether to shit or go blind. First he's telling me about this great school, then he's telling me I can get in, then he's telling me I'll make it through, and then he tells me he'll pay for it.

"I . . . I don't think I could do that, Admiral Wells," I said, feeling like I was going to barf I was so nervous. "My folks . . . they wouldn't go for someone else paying for me." Shit, my old man would skin me alive if this ever came up.

"I can appreciate that, Roy. But if and when it happens, we'll see it right. I'm sure your parents want the best for you."

Don't be so sure, I thought.

"As I said, it will be a completely new life-style. You will wear a uniform to school every day, and you'll have to be spic-and-span, just like at Annapolis." He looked at my hair. "You won't be able to wear your hair in that style."

I reached up to my hair. It was pretty long, the front in a pompadour, the sides and back combed in a modified DA. You can't wear real DAs at RJH, you have to comb the back down, but still it's a hoody hairstyle. I'd have to wear a flattop, and no sidecars, either. Roy Poole with a dorky haircut; who'd have ever thought that could happen.

"And it isn't coed," he went on. "No girls."

Now that would really be a bitch, particularly the way things were starting to go for me.

"Of course, there aren't any girls at Annapolis, either," he reminded me.

"I know that." That was okay, those were the rules. Rules are fine, as long as they're the same for everybody. That's what I hate the most about my school—they don't make everybody play by the same rules.

"Do they have a code of conduct, sir?" I wanted to know if everybody played by the same rules.

"As a matter of fact, they do," he said, his eyes smiling behind his eyeglasses.

"One set for everybody? No playing favorites?"

"Absolutely." Now he was really smiling.

"Like the one they have at the Naval Academy?"

"Identical." He waited. "Is that important to you?"

"Everybody getting treated the same is important," I told him. To be treated by what you do, not who you are or how much brown-nosing you do.

"That's how it is," the admiral assured me. He looked at me over his eyeglasses, like one of those headmasters you see in those English movies. "It's a wonderful star to mark your compass by," he said. "I've been living by that standard since my first year at the Academy. If you can handle that kind of discipline, that self-discipline, you'll do fine."

"I hope I can, sir. I want to try."

More than anything, that's what I wanted. To be judged just for me, not all the other bullshit.

He patted me on the shoulder again. "Take this catalogue up to bed with you and look it over. We'll talk about it in the morning." He stood up. "I'm bushed. These society parties wipe me out. By the way, you handled yourself quite capably this evening. Mrs. Wells said you were an absolute gentleman."

"Thank you." When he'd said he was getting tired it made me realize how beat I was. It had been a real strain, getting through this whole day and night.

"Sleep tight, Roy. See you in the morning."

"Good night, sir."

I didn't fall asleep for hours. I read the catalogue cover to cover. It looked pretty neat, even the uniforms. If everyone else is wearing one, you don't feel like a jerk.

It didn't *seem* real, though. I come from a crappy family in a crappy town, go to a crappy school, and I'm a crappy student. There's no way I could go to a place like that. I mean I wanted to go to the Naval Academy, and I knew I could make it if somebody would give me a chance, which is more than anyone ever had done about anything up to this point in my life. So that got me to thinking: if I could go to Annapolis, why couldn't I go to this military school, especially if Admiral Wells thought I could? If anybody knew what it took, he did.

It was a good feeling, that Admiral Wells thought I could do it.

Before I fell asleep, I thought about Melanie. She really was kind of sorry, compared to the girls I knew. On the other hand, she was fairly pretty in the face and she was nice as hell, not stuck-up or anything. She was rich. And she was stacked, that was maybe the most important thing about her, after being nice. Thinking about those titties got my pecker hard as a piston. It wouldn't be any big deal to be nice to her. I could even make out with her, Darlene would never know. I'd be doing Melanie a favor, and making Admiral Wells and Mrs. Wells happy as well.

I shot a mighty load into a wad of Kleenex, thinking about Melanie's tits. Then I fell asleep, dreaming about Farrington Academy, about Annapolis, about everything. About my life—about what was happening to it.

I was coming down the back stairs for breakfast when I heard Mrs. Wells and the admiral arguing, their voices coming from the breakfast nook. The guest room where I'd slept is over the kitchen, so it's easier to take the back stairs than the front ones, which are what everyone normally uses.

I stopped dead in my tracks on the staircase so they wouldn't hear me. The stairs are carpeted, so they don't creak like wooden ones.

"You're being foolish in pursuing this, James."

"Most certainly I'm not."

"You don't know a thing about this boy. Nothing."

"I know enough about him to know he's worth the effort."

"What in the world is the hurry?"

"I'm not hurrying anything." He sounded defensive. "All right, maybe I am. So what? Boys like Roy don't get many chances. You have to take them when they come, or you lose them. Him."

"You don't know his background, his people. He could have been in prison for all we know."

"He's fourteen."

"He's trash."

I could feel my balls sucking right up inside my body when I heard her say that.

"Beatrice, that is an awful thing to say about anyone, especially a young boy who has done nothing at all to offend you."

"I'm sorry. It's nothing personal, James, but he is."

"Why?" the admiral asked.

"You know perfectly well why."

"Because he comes from Ravensburg instead of Chevy Chase?"

I strained my ears to hear but she didn't answer.

"Or goes to a public school, instead of St. Alban's or Exeter or some other place for spoiled children of privilege?"

"He's a little hoodlum," she said. "Just look at him, the way he dresses, his hair—everything about him. And those are excellent schools, all our friends' children go to them and so would have ours, if we'd had any. I was happy to have him as a party guest so poor Melanie could have company, but after that I draw the line."

"He's a kid, for crying out loud!"

They were really into it. I could hear their voices rising. Right at that moment I wanted to be anywhere but where I was.

"He is vulgar. He has no class. It's not a question of . . . background or money or anything of the sort, you know me better than that, James. He's simply *not of quality.*"

That fucking tore it. I could forget Admiral Farrington Academy and all the other good shit.

Except Admiral Wells wasn't buying what she was selling.

"No," he said forcefully. "I will not ratify that. In case you've forgotten, Beatrice, since you didn't know me when I was Roy's age, I didn't attend those schools, either. My origins are similar to his, more than you care to acknowledge. I'm an old sea dog no matter how much spit and polish you lather over me. You're upset about your figurine, and you're taking it out on Roy."

"It's not about that at all," she cried. "I'm not accusing him of that. It's about who he is . . . the inner man."

"That's a crock of . . . he's a boy, for pity's sake. He's still forming."

"I beg to differ. The die has been cast with him."

"Fine," the admiral said. "Think what you will, it won't affect my friendship with him. He's a bright kid who wants to make it, and I for one admire that. I admire it enormously. And I'm going to help him any way I can."

"He'll disappoint you," she told him. Her voice rose. "He will disappoint you in ways you cannot begin to imagine."

"I doubt it. And even if he should, I'd disappoint myself more if I didn't make the effort."

"James, James, James. What is the godawful hurry?"

I could hear the demand in her voice.

"Desire can't wait," the admiral answered her. "If I wait on this boy I might lose him forever. This is a chance for him, and he's not going to have too many. That's the hurry."

My face was burning.

"What if he doesn't get into Farrington?" she asked then. "You're building up such expectations in him."

"He'll get in." I could hear the steel in his voice.

"He'd better," she said. "Otherwise he'll crash and burn, and it will be on your conscience. Can you handle that? Can he?"

My heart was pounding. What if she was right?

"He'll get in." The way he said it, there was no room for argument.

After a pause I heard her say, "You should have had a son, James. I should have given you one. It was selfish on my part not to."

"That's water under the bridge, Beatrice. And we both agreed. I as much as you."

"You went along with me. Like you always do, even when it hurts."

They stopped talking then. I sat on the stairs, shaking like a leaf. I was grateful to Admiral Wells for sticking up for me, but hearing all that stuff from Mrs. Wells had me all shook up. The worst part was that I knew that even though she didn't like me all that much, she didn't hate me, either. She thought this was how I was. And the worst part was, most of it was true.

Real carefully, so they wouldn't hear me, I climbed back up, walked the length of the hallway on the second floor, and came down the front staircase.

"Good morning, Roy," Admiral Wells greeted me, looking up from the Sunday Washington *Post.* "Did you sleep well?" He was wearing khakis and a sports shirt, like a regular guy.

"Like a log," I said, stretching and yawning, "I just this minute got up."

Mrs. Wells smiled at me. It was a thin smile, but still, it was a smile. She was already dressed up.

"Good morning, Roy," she said in a friendly-as-hell voice, like she hadn't been putting me down one minute before. She took a sip from her coffee. "I'm on my way to church," she told us. "You boys enjoy yourselves. I'll say a prayer for you."

"You do that," Admiral Wells said.

She gave him a kiss on the forehead, gathered up her purse and gloves and coat that had been sitting on the side counter, and went out. A moment later I heard her Lincoln start up and roll down the driveway.

The admiral gave me a sideways look.

"So," he said, "you just woke up?"

He was trying to be casual, but I knew he was checking to see if I'd heard them arguing about me.

"A couple minutes ago," I lied. "Then I was in the bathroom."

"Good, good." He hesitated. "Did you have a chance to look at the material I gave you?"

"Yes, sir. It looks like a real neat place. Hard, but fair."

I didn't have any idea if Farrington Academy was fair or not, but I knew people like the admiral appreciate hearing stuff like that. After what they'd been saying about me, I needed to make sure I did everything right, as much as I could.

"It is," he said. "That's exactly what it is." He paused for a minute. "So . . . do you think it's worth looking into?"

"Oh, yes, sir. Definitely."

"Good." He rubbed his hands together. A big smile broke out on his face. "Here's what we'll do. I have an application form in my study; I had the school forward one in case you were interested, because the deadline for applications is in a few weeks. If you can take an hour or so after you eat your breakfast, we'll fill it out together. It isn't difficult. Then we'll need to get a copy of your transcript from your school."

I guess I frowned or something when he said that, because he put his hand over mine.

"I've already assumed that your marks at Ravensburg are . . . shall we say a bit iffy?"

I shrugged. That was an understatement.

"It's okay, it's all right. You need more of a challenge than you're getting there, I can see that. We'll dress them up a bit, and everything will be fine. Besides, the two most important details will be your eagerness to attend, and the recommendations you'll be submitting. They require two: I'll write one, of course, and Admiral Prescott will tender the other."

As low as I'd been ten minutes before, I was higher now. Admiral Wells and Admiral Prescott writing my recommendations! Farrington would be falling all over themselves to want me.

Mary put a plate of fried eggs, potatoes, bacon, and toast in front of me.

"Good morning!" she sang out.

"Good morning!" I answered her back. The day had started out shitty, but it was definitely a good morning now.

Admiral Wells stopped me as I was putting on my Ravensburg jacket, about to leave.

"By the way, Roy," he said, "we had a slight misfortune last night. One of Mrs. Wells's silver statuettes, the ones she keeps in the drawing room, has turned up missing."

That froze me in my tracks. Old Mrs. Prescott. She'd been in there, all by herself with the lights out, checking them out.

"You weren't in the drawing room by any chance last night, were you?" he asked.

"No, sir." Technically, I wasn't lying.

"Of course not, you would have had no reason. Nor would anyone else, for that matter, not that the room is under lock and key."

He frowned. Maybe they had been thinking I'd taken it. But since I hadn't I didn't feel guilty, not about that.

"You didn't by any chance happen to see anyone in the drawing room, did you?"

Old Mrs. Prescott. I'd seen her. In the drawing room, holding some of the silver statues.

"No. No, sir."

"No." He frowned again. "It must have been misplaced by the cleaning woman. Everyone here last night is a close personal friend. Beatrice must've been mistaken, thinking she had seen it yesterday afternoon."

He was talking more to himself than to me, trying to figure out what was going on. I wanted to tell him what I'd seen, but I didn't dare to; it would've been accusing old Mrs. Prescott of taking it, and I hadn't seen her do that. She was probably just looking at them and admiring them. More likely, if anyone did take it, it would've been the other colored girl, the one who was helping Mary with the party. She didn't work there full-time, she just helped out on special occasions.

Except I'd seen that look on old Mrs. Prescott's face. I knew that look.

"It'll turn up sooner or later," he said darkly. "It better; it's an heirloom, it's priceless to my wife."

"Yes, sir," I said. "I'm sure it will."

I wanted out of there. If I didn't leave soon I was afraid I'd say the wrong thing. Admiral Wells handed me the hanger with my new sports coat and pants, and the box with my shirts. Mary had washed and ironed the one I'd worn last night.

"Don't forget these."

"No, sir. Thank you again."

We shook hands, like two men. I'd hide the clothes at the back of my closet—if my folks saw them I'd be all day explaining where I'd got them, and then they'd find out about the admiral and Farrington Academy and everything else. I'd already decided I'd spring the whole thing on them when all the pieces were in place and it was too late for anyone to stop me.

It was pretty out, warm springlike weather carried over from last night. The cherry trees were blooming, smelling stronger than a woman's perfume. I thought about going down to the Tidal Basin and checking them out. It's beautiful down there when springtime comes, acres of cherry blossoms spread around the Jefferson Memorial. Maybe I'd take my mom with me, we could take the bus together, she'd love it. We never do anything together except meet in the principal's office at school. I want to show her there's a good part of me as well—she knows there is, she's my mom, but she never gets to see it. It would've been nice if she could've been with me at dinner last night, seeing me with all those fancy rich people, holding my own. She might've been jealous, I don't know, she definitely would've been nervous, she'd probably be more comfortable with Mary and the other colored servant than with the admiral and his guests, but she would've been proud, too.

I thought back to last night, and to the conversation I'd just had with the admiral. I wish I could have told him about old Mrs. Prescott and the little silver statue, and I had a shitload of work to do on Mrs. Wells so she'd like me, instead of smiling to my face and then ragging on me to the admiral behind my back about how I wasn't good enough for them. But I was doing good; I was on a roll, and I wasn't going to let that one thing stop me from enjoying all the great changes that were starting to happen for me.

APRIL

NINE

Waking up fifteen didn't feel any different from fourteen: I was still a whole year away from getting my driver's license. Even so, fifteen *sounded* different. Fourteen's a kid; that's how people see you, even if you're growing like a weed, have hair on your balls, smoke cigarettes, and jack off twice a day. Out in the grownup world, fourteen's still a kid, no way around it. Fifteen is between being a kid, and freedom.

Darlene had a surprise present for me. It was a surprise because I didn't even know she knew it was my birthday. She gave it to me at recess, out on the field.

"How'd you know it was today?" I asked.

"A little bird told me," she teased.

"What did the little bird say?"

"That I should give you this," she said. We were standing on the side of the building, away from everybody else. She'd come up to me at lunch and told me to meet her there and make sure not to let anyone know. She pulled me up against the wall so nobody could see us, put her arms around me, and gave me a big kiss on the mouth, full tongue and everything.

"Jesus, girl, don't you got no shame?" I asked, teasing her back, looking around to make sure we weren't being watched. I wouldn't have minded someone seeing us, except for a teacher, of course, because that would've been detention for sure, and I was too close to the edge with that shit. But if a kid had seen us, like one of her girlfriends, the whole school would've known she was my girl, and that would've been a great birthday present.

No one did, though. Darlene's the kind of girl who can go crazy in private, but out in public it's like her shit don't stink. That's okay with me, I don't like a girl fawning all over a guy with people watching. It's like they're more showing off for their friends than being a straight-up girlfriend.

"Here." She pulled a little package out of her purse. It was wrapped up in tissue paper and had a pink bow tied around it.

"Open it," she said, real jittery.

"Pink's for girls," I teased.

"Just open it, silly."

I pulled the paper off. It was one of those plastic photo books, the kind that accordions out. This one had about a dozen pictures in it, and they were all of Darlene. Her class picture, a picture of her in her cheerleader's costume, all kinds of pictures. There was even one of her in a two-piece bathing suit.

Naturally, I got a hard-on looking at her in the bathing suit. I couldn't wait for summer, when we could go swimming together, so I could see the real thing, most of it anyway. Of course,

I already had seen the whole real thing, but she didn't know that, and I sure as hell wasn't going to tell her.

"Do you like it?"

"It's great," I said.

"I did it so you can always be thinking of me, even when I'm not with you."

"I do think of you," I told her. "Even when you're not around." Like when I'm lying in bed with my tool in my hand.

"So do I," she said. "Think of you."

She kissed me again and we walked back to where everybody else was hanging around. I really felt great—anybody could look at us and tell we were going together even though we couldn't officially, because of her mother.

We'd had two dates, two Friday nights in a row. The first time we went to the Cheverly movies, which is where everybody goes on Friday night—there or the Ravensburg Fire House, which has a sock hop.

We'd sat in the back row and made out like bandits. Even though it was our first official date she let me have a good feel through her bra. We made out for at least a half-hour straight, and I had my hand on her almost the whole time, even the nipple. She wouldn't let me have bare tit, though. It was our first date and she didn't want me to think she was a slut or anything. That was okay, I wasn't in a hurry.

The following Friday afternoon we took the Greyhound down to the District and saw *Trapeze* at the Capitol, which is a great old movie theatre. We sat way up in the balcony. It was a pretty good movie, what I saw of it. Most of the time we made out, and this time I got bare tit, although Darlene made a big deal out of trying to stop me and finally "not being able to help myself, you get me so hot, Roy."

Of course, that was a crock of shit. This girl was a firecracker under that goody-goody pose she put on for the public. It was just a matter of time before we went all the way. I knew she was a virgin, and I was glad I'd stayed one for her, even though it hadn't been my choice.

"I won't be able to go out with you next week," she'd said as we were walking up to her front door that night.

"Because of your mother's rule." Her mother had a rule that Darlene couldn't date any boy more than twice in a row—one of her many stupid rules.

Darlene nodded. "But I want to," she assured me.

"Who're you going to go with?" I asked. I was nervous, wondering who it would be.

"I don't know." She giggled. "Do you think Lewis Sarkind would go out with me?"

That about cracked me up. I could just see the two of them together.

"You want me to fix you up?" I volunteered. That would've been great. There's plenty of guys out there I wouldn't want Darlene going out with, but Lewis was definitely safe.

"I can get my own dates, thank you," she told me. "Don't worry," she'd continued, seeing the nervous look on my face, "it won't matter who it is. You're the only one I care about."

I stayed late at school, studying in the library until closing time. When I got home, there was a birthday cake waiting for me on the kitchen table, baked by my mom—a chocolate cake with orange frosting, my favorite. My mom's a great baker when she wants to be.

I made a wish and blew out all the candles. My first thought about a wish had been to fuck Darlene within the month, but I changed it to getting into Farrington Academy. I knew that sooner or later Darlene would do the dirty deed with me. Getting into Farrington was more important in the big scheme of things, and it wasn't as much a sure thing.

"Happy birthday, sweetheart."

My mom handed me a package. I ripped off the wrapping. It was a model, a plastic aircraft carrier.

"Thanks, Mom."

"I hope you like it. The man at the store said it was their most popular one."

"Yeah," I lied, "it's great."

I gave her a big hug. She really is a good mother—she does her best, and it isn't always easy. It's not her fault she doesn't know anything about models. This was the kind of model a ten-year-old kid could build. They don't know anything about models in this hick town, but she didn't know that. She thought she was getting me something special.

"Do you really like it?" she asked anxiously.

"Oh, yeah, it's great." I put the box down on the table.

"Ta-da." Ruthie handed me a big package, all wrapped up. "Happy birthday, baby brother."

"I'm taller now than you are, Ruthie."

"You'll always be my baby brother, Roy," she said.

I almost creamed my jeans when I saw what she'd given me. It was this incredible sweater that she'd hand-knitted, every stitch. She'd been working on it since the beginning of the school year, and all winter long she'd been telling me she was making it for some boy she was hot for in her class. All that time she'd been doing it for me.

"You sure pulled the wool over my eyes," I kidded.

She groaned. "Try it on."

I pulled it over my shirt. It was a little big, which was good, because I could get a lot of wear out of it. It was a V-neck in white and blue, Ravensburg High colors. I could wear it under my jacket, it would be a great combination.

"Thanks, Ruthie. This is really nice." Then I gave her a big hug, too. I almost felt like crying, I hadn't expected anything.

"We'll have the cake for dessert," my mom said. "I cooked your favorite dinner—stuffed pork chops. Go on upstairs and wash, dinner'll be on the table in a minute."

I started up the stairs.

"I almost forgot," she said, calling me back. She rooted around in her wallet, pulled out a five-dollar bill.

"This is from your father," she said.

"Isn't he coming home for dinner?" I asked. I knew things would be calmer if he wasn't, but I wanted him here for my birthday anyway.

"It's his bowling night," my mom reminded me, her voice taking on an embarrassed tone. "Normally he would've bagged it, but if they do good tonight they have a chance to get in-to the playoffs. He didn't feel he could let the other fellows down."

"That would be great if they could make the playoffs," I said. They've never made the playoffs in all the years my dad's been bowling with them. I didn't see how they could this year, either. They suck, plain and simple.

"He said he knew you'd understand."

"You can't let your friends down," I told her, turning away in case my face had a look on it I didn't want her to see. "I'm going up and wash, I'll be right back."

I took the stairs three at a time. Make the playoffs—that was the biggest laugh I'd had all year.

My favorite room in the Smithsonian is the Hall of Dinosaurs. It's filled with skeletons of practically every dinosaur that's ever lived, including the huge suckers like *Tyrannosaurus rex* and *Brontosaurus*. Next to it is the room with all the Ice Age shit, mastodons and mammoths and saber-toothed tigers, all rebuilt to look real, complete with skins and furs. They look pretty authentic—whoever makes them over does a good job. Most kids like the main building, with the *Spirit of St. Louis* hanging in the front hallway and all the other old planes, trains, and cars. I like it too, I like everything about the Smithsonian, it's my favorite building in Washington—it's just that I like the dinosaurs best of all. There's something about going way back in time that's exciting to me. If I didn't want to go to Annapolis and have a career in the Navy I'd become an archaeologist, digging up old bones all over the world. You could see some incredibly neat shit doing that.

We were on our field trip. Once a year every class in our school gets a field trip. That's one of the good things about living near Washington—there's a ton of great places to visit on field trips. We've been to the White House, the Washington Monument, the Capitol building, the Lincoln and Jefferson memorials, all those places. Mt. Vernon, where Washington lived. One of the things I vividly remembered about Mt. Vernon was that there were quarters for about sixty slaves. We went there in fourth grade. It must've been hotter than shit down in those slave quarters in the middle of summer. Living in Washington in the middle of summer's like living in a steam bath, and those places didn't even have windows.

"Isn't that interesting, class?" Mrs. Fletcher was trying to get us to respond to this old guide who was giving us the tour. He looked as old as one of the skeletons, like he needed to be propped up, too. Mrs. Fletcher was trying in a half-assed way to get us to pay attention, but she wasn't having too much luck; it was almost lunchtime and the natives were getting restless. The old guy was as bored as we were. What he was mostly interested in was checking out the girls, who were dressed up for the occasion, wearing stockings and high heels and girdles and all the rest. There's some righteous pussy in our class, I shit you not—not just Darlene, lots of the girls are sexy. They work hard at it.

"Does anyone have any questions before we move on?" Mrs. F. continued.

Half the class didn't even hear her. Old Burt was standing near her, though, and he raised his hand.

"I have a question, Miz Fletcher."

"Yes, Burt, what is it?"

Me and Joe were already cracking up. If Burt ever had a serious question about anything in his entire life I'd shit a gold-plated brick.

"What's black, has six legs, and catches flies?" he asked, in this super-serious voice.

We actually did crack up. So did about half the other kids. He's a natural-born comedian, that kid. Somebody ought to put him on "The Ed Sullivan Show."

Mrs. Fletcher tried to keep things under control: "I fail to see what that has to do with what we've been talking about."

"Well, it doesn't, but I was wondering if you knew," he said.

"No, I don't," she said, pissed off. "Let's move on, please."

"The New York Giants outfield."

We'd all heard it before, but we laughed anyway.

"If you care to sit on the bus for the remainder of the day you're more than welcome to," she told him. Then she turned on her heel and marched off down the hall. You know she won't be teaching when she's an old lady, she hates us all already. If she lasts another year past this one it'll be a miracle.

All the time we'd been there I had hung with my buddies, but at the same time I was trying to bird-dog Darlene, who was in the middle of a bunch of her giggling girlfriends. Everything's funny to the girls in ninth grade this year, it must have something to do with their tits growing out. She'd catch my eye and smile, but she stayed with the other girls.

When we moved into the Ice Age room I managed to get next to her for a moment, and accidentally-on-purpose brushed my hand against her left tit.

"Don't, Roy," she whispered, looking around to see if anyone'd seen it.

"It was an accident."

"It was not and you know it."

I pretended like I was sulking. I wasn't actually, I just wanted her to think I was.

It worked: "You can't do that in front of everyone, Roy," she said, sweet-talking me, "now just wait until we're alone."

"Jesus, it already feels like I've been waiting my whole life practically." I really was horny for her—if I hadn't jacked off every night, usually more than once, I'd have a case of blue balls like you couldn't believe, that's how hot I was for her.

"Listen, Roy, I don't even kiss every boy I go out with, let alone make out like we do."

"I know you don't, but ain't I special?"

"I like you, Roy, really I do, it just scares me is all."

"That's okay," I said. Anything to make her come around.

"I know how you feel," she said. "I do, too." She thought for a minute. "Why don't you take me to the movies Friday night?"

"Friday night?"

"I mean if you're not busy or anything," she said, trying to act hurt.

"No, I ain't busy. But what about your mother?"

"I'll lie to her."

"How?"

"I'll say I'm going out with a friend. Joan. I'll even have Joan come pick me up, then I can meet you at the movies." She looked around to see if anyone was spying on us. They weren't. "You aren't mad, are you? That I'm not being with you today?"

"No." But I was. Not mad, actually, just pissed off that we couldn't be together all the time, especially in a place like this, away from school.

"Listen," she whispered, like we were concocting up a plot, "I've got an idea. We could get together by that fountain outside if we finish our lunches early. Okay?"

"Sure," I whispered back, sucked right in.

"We'd better not let anyone see us too friendly now," she said. "Nobody even knows I'm going with you." Then she drifted away to rejoin her circle of friends.

I was floating, not knowing whether to shit or go blind. She'd said "going with you." From her lips right into my ear.

Like the idiot I am, I was the last student out of the museum cafeteria line. Everybody else had gone through by the time I'd woke up that it was lunchtime, because I'd been in my own world, mooning about Darlene. My girl, true love, all that stupid bullshit only girls are supposed to think about. I didn't give a flying fuck, though—when the other boys in my class saw her on my arm next week, I would be king shit of Ravensburg Junior High.

I found a seat at a table which was occupied by three ladies, real old-fashioned southern types, the kind that keep their hats on inside and carry lace handkerchiefs in their sleeves and have pale white skin with liver spots all over their veiny hands. They were eating sandwiches with the crusts cut off, and drinking iced tea. My plate was piled so high I could hardly see over it—not really, but there was enough food on it for three ordinary people. The old ladies looked at me like I was a dog turd somebody'd dropped in their laps. I wasn't that keen on sitting with them, either, but it was the only seat I could find—lots of people, like government workers, eat here because the food's good and it's cheap.

Across the room I could see the kids from my class. Most were almost finished. I started digging in, forking the food in my face as fast as I could. I really was hungry, and I was in a hurry, too, because I wanted to be with Darlene.

"Have you ever been given instructions in the proper use of a knife and fork, young man?" one of the old biddies asked.

"Yeah, lady," I told her, my mouth stuffed with food, "I use them all the time." I held them up in front of me like in a jailhouse movie. "See?"

I wasn't being rude intentionally—I knew how to eat properly, I'd done fine at the admiral's house, but I wanted to finish quickly, so I wouldn't lose track of Darlene. I could see her across the room, sitting at a table with three other girls.

The old lady turned away in disgust, ignoring me.

"Riffraff," she said under her breath, but loud enough so I'd hear.

"That's me, lady," wiping my mouth, "the best white trash you'll ever come across." Fuck 'em if they can't take a joke, that's one of my mottos.

My classmates were drifting out of the room in twos and threes. Darlene and the other girls at her table got up. She was looking around for me, but she couldn't see me because I was hidden from view by the hats of the three old ladies. She stood there for a minute, but then one of the girls said something to her and she left with them.

I raced through my meal, even leaving half a piece of cherry pie. When I jumped up to go my chair tipped over, hitting the floor with a bang. The old ladies practically had a hemorrhage from the sound.

"Sorry," I apologized. They were nice old ladies, it wasn't their fault they'd had to eat lunch with a crazy man.

Outside the cafeteria there was another long corridor that led from one part of the building to another. As I came out into it I could see Darlene all the way down at the other end, walking slowly away from me. She was by herself—something she'd obviously arranged. As I watched, she turned the corner, out of sight.

I took off down the corridor after her. It was near the end of our lunch break; we were supposed to meet up in about ten minutes. That would give Darlene and me ten minutes to be alone. You can get a lot done in ten minutes.

I rounded the corner where I'd seen her disappear. At the far end I spied the door leading outside, where the fountain where Darlene had said she'd meet me was. I started towards it, my cock rising in my pants I was so hot-to-trot.

There were several small rooms off this corridor, housing different exhibits. As I passed by one of the rooms, I heard this noise from behind the door. Even though I was hauling ass to catch up to Darlene, something about the sounds made me stop.

There were two voices coming out of the room: a boy's and a girl's. The boy said something low that I couldn't make out and the girl laughed, like he'd told her a joke, or, more likely, had said something sexy that had turned her on. Then they were quiet.

I knew I shouldn't eavesdrop, because Darlene was waiting outside for me and we didn't have much time, but I couldn't help myself, I had to know who it was. Everybody always wants to know who's going with who, what girl likes what boy and vice versa. I have a big nose, I always have to know what's going on behind closed doors. So as quietly as I could, making sure they couldn't hear me, I snuck up to the partly opened door and peeked inside.

The girl in the room was Darlene, and the boy was Danny Detweiler. They were locked in a feverish kiss, her arms around him, her hands pulling at his hair, like she was trying to pull him right inside of her mouth. One of her legs was twisted up around his, her skirt was riding almost up to her pussy. I could see where her stocking was fastened to her girdle, even see a flash of white panties. One of his hands was moving around her ass to her front, like he was about to finger-fuck her.

I couldn't do anything but watch. Danny put his other hand inside Darlene's sweater and started massaging her left tit like crazy, squeezing it so hard it looked like the damn thing would come off in his hand. She was groaning and panting like a bitch-dog in heat.

Burt had been right. Darlene was a cocktease, plain and simple. Only a blind man wouldn't have seen it. She'd been using me to make Danny jealous, and it had worked—he was all over her, before long she'd have a ring through his nose. I'd been a goddamn dupe for her.

For what felt like forever I was a piece of petrified wood, locked there. Then I snapped out of it, looking around to see if anyone was watching me watching them—watching the horns grow on me, the horns that motherfucker and the girl I'd thought loved me had put on me.

No one was there. I was alone.

Without making a sound, I turned and left the building.

I hung around outside, trying to get my heart to stop pounding. I'd completely lost track of the time. The last thing I wanted was to go back and look at Darlene. I didn't know what she'd say to me, what lie she'd make up, but it would be a beaut, that I knew. Lying cunt. Even worse would be having to face Danny pussyface Detweiler, who had successfully bird-dogged me.

After a while I went into the main building, where I knew the class wouldn't be, since that had been our first stop, and checked out the old trains and planes and cars, like the Wright Brothers' plane, the one that flew at Kitty Hawk, even though I've seen it a million times and didn't at that particular minute give a rat's ass about it, anyway. Near it was the *Spirit of St. Louis*. Sometimes I think I'd like to become a Navy pilot instead of a ship's commander, landing on an aircraft carrier late at night in the North Atlantic. I love it when the newsreels have scenes of that happening.

But I didn't feel any of that. My mind was on other things: one other thing. First, how to get her to want me back worse than anything she'd ever wanted in her young life. Then, after that, to shit all over her, worse than she had shit on me.

I kept wandering aimlessly, but finally I knew I had to face the music. I went outside to the parking lot, where the school bus was parked.

Except the bus wasn't there. I ran over to the attendant in the parking booth.

"Hey, what happened to that bus that was here?" I asked. "The school bus."

"It left," he said, almost hitting my shoes with a big squirt of snuff juice.

"Left?"

"About a half-hour ago."

I panicked. "What time is it?"

He looked at his watch. "Close to four."

"Sonofabitch!"

"That your bus?" he asked.

Stupid asshole. Like what the fuck am I asking for? I cursed again under my breath, mad as hell at myself. How could I have been so stupid that I missed the goddamn bus? That would be another one I'd owe Darlene.

I took off running down the street.

"You ain't gonna catch it," the attendant called after me, laughing like it was a goddamn joke. "She's long gone."

I don't know how long I moped around. Longer than I should have. I didn't feel like being back in Ravensburg, that I knew, so I cruised around the streets, making my way down E Street, where all the pawnshops and hillbilly bars are clustered. I had money in my pocket, because I'd taken ten bucks from my washing-machine stash the day before and changed it into dollars at the Mobil station down the block from my house, in case I wanted to buy something at the Smithsonian. A souvenir for Darlene was what I'd had in mind, something she'd always have to remember the day by. Mr. Big Shot, showing off for her, showing her how much money I had, like the older high school guys she dated. Now the money sat in my wallet like burnt ashes. One thing for sure, I wouldn't spend a dime on her again if my life depended on it.

It was dark by the time I walked up 12th Street to the Greyhound station.

"One way to Ravensburg," I told the cashier, pushing a buck under the ticket window. The bus costs eighty-five cents, I've taken it a million times.

He shook his head. "Last bus to Ravensburg left. Twenty

minutes ago." He pointed behind me, to the schedule posted on the large board in the middle of the room.

"I've taken that bus a million times!" I yelled in disbelief, "the last bus doesn't leave till eight!"

"That's weekends," he matter-of-fact informed me. "Weekdays it's six-thirty."

I thought I'd drop dead right there on the floor.

"There's an overnight bus to the Eastern Shore," he said sympathetically—he could see how lousy I felt. "It could drop you off. It doesn't leave till midnight, though."

First Darlene with Danny, then missing the school bus, now this. I felt like throwing up. Now I'd have to hitchhike home. The way my luck had been running today, if I wasn't careful I'd get hit by a truck.

It was raining like a motherfucker. I stood under the awning of a DGS store, watching it come down in buckets. I'd jumped under the awning as soon as I'd spotted shelter, but I was still soaked clear through.

I was on Florida Avenue. In case you don't know, Florida Avenue, at least in this area, is one-hundred-percent colored. You could walk for twenty blocks in any direction and you wouldn't see one white face, except for the people who own the stores. Most of the stores around here are owned by white people, especially the liquor stores.

I don't know how I wound up in this neighborhood in the first place. After I got over having missed the Greyhound and realizing there wasn't a damn thing I could do about it, I kind of bummed around, walking the streets, major pissed-off and giving not a shit who knew it, it was like I had this black cloud over my head like that guy in *Li'l Abner*, Joe Whateverthefuck.

What had really pissed me off, like putting the capper on the whole sorry affair, was that when I'd walked out of the Greyhound station I'd jammed my hands in the pockets of my jacket, because it was getting cold. Guess what I found in one of the pockets? The very same accordion photo-book Darlene had given me for my birthday, crammed full of pictures of her. Talk about adding insult to injury! I looked at each picture, feeling sorrier and sorrier for myself, hating her, hating Danny motherfucking Detweiler, hating the whole world. Then slowly and methodically I ripped each picture up into a million tiny pieces and ground them into the sidewalk with my heel.

After that childish but satisfying act I tried hitchhiking, on different street corners, but I couldn't get a ride to save my life. It was dark out by now, cold as a witch's tit already and getting colder, you couldn't even see me standing on a corner trying to thumb a ride. I shifted from one foot to the other to try and stay warm and keep my circulation going while standing in the gutter, but the traffic was a blur—with all the lights, and pedestrians coming and going, a driver couldn't even see me to stop if he wanted to, which nobody did. I've learned over the years that hitchhiking in the middle of Washington during rush hour is the worst time to try and get a ride. What you have to do is wait until rush hour's over.

The only problem with that was, the rain killed that possibility. Nobody stops for you in the rain, especially when you're as wet as a mongrel dog, and probably smell as bad as one, the rain creating steam as it came off the wool and leather of my jacket.

And the worst part was, by wandering around and moping and feeling sorry for myself like a crybaby, I'd wound up on Florida fucking Avenue, in the heart of enemy territory. A white kid wearing a Ravensburg High jacket in the middle of Africa. Talk about being fucked up! All the cars around here would be full of colored people. I was really going to get into a car at night with a mess of them. For one thing, everybody knows all colored guys carry straight razors and drink Thunderbird straight out of the bottle. I might be a sorry asshole, standing out in the rain, but like they say, my mama didn't raise no simpletons. I was not hitchhiking in this neighborhood, plain and simple.

The rain let up for a minute and I stepped out from under the awning, trying to get my bearings so I'd know how far I'd have to walk until I could start hitching without fear of getting my throat slit.

Believe it or not, I was right across the street from Griffith Stadium, behind the right-field wall. I've been going to Senators games since I was a kid, nine or ten. It's easy to sneak into Griffith Stadium, it's a rickety old ballpark and the guards never pay any attention. They probably don't care, because nobody goes anyway. They are without a doubt the sorriest team in baseball. They're in last place every year. Not only are the Senators a shitty team, they're dumb as hell, too. Every time they get a good player, like Irv Noren or Jackie Jensen, they trade him.

My favorite team is the Brooklyn Dodgers. I know that's pretty weird, since they're from New York, and in the National League to boot, but they are. When I was a little kid, just starting to like baseball, Walt Kowalski, an FBI agent who lived on our block, gave me a junior Brooklyn Dodgers uniform. I think he came from Brooklyn originally and got it from a relative. As soon as I put it on, presto, I was a Dodgers fan for life. My first favorite player was Jackie Robinson. I liked Roy Campanella and Gil Hodges, too. Now my favorite's Willie Mays, although I also like Mickey Mantle a lot as well. About the only good player Washington has ever had on their team for more than a couple years was Mickey Vernon. I like him good enough, I just like the other guys more.

Speaking of Mickey Mantle, a few years ago I saw him hit the longest home run in the history of baseball. It was a Senators game, of course. He hit it off Chuck Stobbs, and it went clear over the left-field fence, just nicking the big scoreboard there that sits on top of the bleachers. It's the only home run ever hit over the left-field bleachers. The reason I saw it happen was that it was Patrol Boys day, when every safety-patrol boy in the D.C. area gets into the game for free. I was in fifth grade then, and I was probably the shittiest patrol boy in the history of Ravensburg

Elementary School. I never paid any attention if cars were coming or not when there were kids crossing the street. Usually me and Howie Klinger, who was my patrol partner that year, would both stand on the same side of the street, Defense Highway, which is the most dangerous street in the whole county. We'd be sneaking a weed or playing hits and cracks, never paying attention. It's a miracle a kid wasn't killed crossing that road. In fact, about a week after that Senators game, Howie and me were kicked off patrol, because some parent snitched on us.

What's strange, when I think about it, is that almost all my favorite ballplayers are colored guys. It's kind of liking Chuck Berry or Fats Domino more than Elvis and Buddy Holly. But they are, I don't know why.

Being outside Griffith Stadium wasn't helping me now, though. The Senators were on the road this week, the old stadium a dark hulk looming over me. If there had been a game I might've snuck in and watched. Then I might've been able to grab a ride home with someone. Like they say, if wishes were dollars, I'd be a millionaire, and if a frog had wings, he wouldn't bump his ass on the ground all the time, either.

I t started raining again. The only place on the block that was open was this raunchy-looking bar & grill across the street, down under an old brownstone at basement level. Twenty or thirty years ago this was probably a real nice neighborhood, all these big old brownstone houses sitting side by side. Now it was all trashy little apartments for coloreds. I figured there wasn't much point in going in, because I'm underage and they'd have to kick me out like they did that time at the Dixie, but beggars can't be choosers and I was cold and wet and tired of standing outside with my thumb up my ass. Maybe things were different in colored bars in the District, maybe they let kids in. And if they did kick me out, big deal, you never know till you try, that's my motto.

It was as dark as a tomb in there, the light so low I thought maybe nobody would see me if I stayed close to the door, in the shadows. The place was one long, narrow, low-ceilinged room, with a bar that ran the length of most of one side while the other side was red fake-leather booths. Over in one corner was a juke-box, playing jazz music. I don't know anything about that kind of music, I've only heard it a couple times. It's neat music, a different beat than rock 'n' roll, music that sounds pretty hard to dance to—more for listening. Some Negro woman who sounded like she'd smoked a million cigarettes was singing about how her man was always treating her like shit but she stuck with him anyway because he was her man. My mom would've liked that song, what it was about. The story of her life.

I stood there in the shadows, checking things out. It was nice and warm—just being out of the cold and rain was a plus. There were maybe a dozen people in here besides the bartender. Some were sitting in the booths, the rest at the bar, mostly men, a few women, all of them drinking boilermakers, shots and beer. Hard drinkers, people serious about their whiskey.

A couple of people in one of the booths were eating fried chicken and biscuits. It smelled good—rich and heavy. My mouth started watering, as hungry as I was by now, since my normal dinnertime had come and gone hours ago. I had money; maybe they'd serve me some food if I could muster up the nerve to ask.

At the near end of the bar, closest to where I was standing, two women were sitting together. Both were smoking cigarettes, sipping their drinks, and nodding their heads in time to the music. They were dressed in flashy dresses and high-heeled toeless shoes, although even from where I stood in the dark, observing them, I could tell their wardrobes were cheap jobs that wouldn't hold up; the satin fake, the imitation-fur coats folded on the empty barstool next to them nappy and matted, all of it discount-store quality. The women had a lot of makeup on, and their hair was slicked down and covered with some kind of shiny pomade you see in ads for colored-women's hair, Dixie Peach, or something like it. Major conks on both their heads, like Chuck Berry's, except theirs was women's hair, longer, shiny hair reflecting blue light that came from behind the back bar. They looked pretty old to me, almost as old as my mother.

"This rain is a stone bitch," one of them complained to the air.

"A bitch," the other one answered.

"Gonna cost me some *serious* money," said number one.

"*Serious* money," came from her friend, like she was the first one's echo.

"And I got rent due," said the first one. She raised one finger towards the bartender, and he started fixing her a fresh drink. She was drinking a martini from a cocktail glass, I could tell by the clear color of it and the fact it had an olive in it, not a shot and a chaser like the others were having. She was classier than the others somehow. It was hard to tell, the room being so dark, but she looked prettier than her friend, sexier, although both were fairly sexy, in a lowdown kind of way.

The bartender placed the drink in front of her and she sucked the olive off the toothpick, her dark red tongue curling around it. It was a sexy move; I could tell she was one of those women who are naturally sexy from the time they're born, everything they do has a sexy ring to it, even eating an olive out of a martini glass.

She closed her eyes as she took a sip from her drink, then lit a cigarette from a pack that was sitting on the bar between them, and inhaled half the length in one drag.

I couldn't keep from staring at her.

She must have felt my presence, because suddenly she turned and looked in my direction. I froze, trying to fade deeper into the darkness, but she'd spotted me. She nudged her companion, who looked over, her eyes opening wide with surprise.

"Hey there, boy," the one I'd been staring at sang out, in this deep, soft whiskey-voice, a voice like the woman's on the jukebox, "what're you doing in here?"

I didn't answer, pretending like she hadn't actually seen me and was talking to someone else. The bartender, who had looked up at the sound of her voice, spotted me as well.

"What the fuck," he said, mostly to himself, like he wasn't believing what he was seeing. "What the fuck you doing in here?" he called over to me. He could see I was white but he couldn't see my face clear enough to tell how old I was.

I licked my lips and shrugged, but I didn't say anything.

The woman stared at me through the haze of her cigarette smoke.

"Hey, you, come over here, where I can see you," she commanded.

Slowly, reluctantly, I pushed off from the wall and nervously shuffled towards her.

"Oh, shit," the bartender moaned, "it's a goddamn kid. A white underage kid. Do me a favor, kid," he said, "get the fuck out of here and do it fast."

"Hold your goddamn horses," the woman told him. "I want to get a look at this boy."

"So I can get my store shut down?" the bartender asked her. "No thank you, I take enough chances serving black kids whiskey. Get his paddy ass out of here."

What he meant when he said "black kids" was that in Washington you can drink beer and wine when you're eighteen, but you've got to be twenty-one to drink the hard stuff. Everyone I know who's older, like my sister's friends, start when they're sixteen; the girls change their driver's licenses and the boys cop an older buddy's draft card. I know my sister does, I've heard her brag about drinking in this bar or that, pulling the wool over some bartender's eyes. Like any bartender gives a shit, all he wants is to be able to tell a cop he saw ID, in case he ever gets busted.

The woman stared at my face, ignoring the bartender. I stared right back at her. She was pretty, for a colored woman. Not that I don't think colored women aren't pretty or anything, it's just that they have a different look from white ones.

"Are you deaf or something?" the bartender asked me.

He was a big sonofabitch and built like a lumberjack. One thing I didn't want was trouble with him. I turned and started to leave.

"Ease up, Deuce," the woman told him, flashing him a smile, "it's raining out there. How'd you like to be standing out in that slop getting your ass all wet?"

"Ain't none of my never-mind if his honky ass gets wet," the bartender shot back at her.

She exhaled her smoke in his face. "What're you, prejudice or something? You got something against white people?" She turned and smiled at me. I was liking her immediately—besides being sexy, she was friendly to me, and anybody that was friendly to me I had to like, especially now.

Other people in the bar were watching us, though, and that was making me nervous. If one of the men in here took it in his head to beat up on me there wouldn't be a damn thing I could do about it.

But no one seemed inclined to, I realized as I stood there near the woman. Everyone was sitting with their drinks, watching me with baleful expressions, like I was an animal in a cage at the zoo. They weren't welcoming me with open arms—you could cut the hostility with a knife it was so thick—but they didn't have blood-kill in their eyes, either. I thought about what would happen if things were reversed, if it was a colored kid walked in the Dixie by accident when it was raining. They'd be carrying out what was left of him in a matchbox, more'n likely.

"Fuck yes, I'm prejudice," the bartender answered her. "They don't want me drinking they water, I don't want 'em drinking mine."

She ignored him and turned back to me.

"Hey, boy."

"Yes, ma'am?" That sounded weird, calling her "ma'am," seeing's how she was colored, but I felt insecure, and she was a grown woman.

"What you doing 'round here? You lost?"

"Yes," I said. "I mean no, I know where I am." What I meant was, I knew where I was, but it wasn't where I wanted to be. But I didn't feel like explaining all that to her.

"So how'd you wind up in this neighborhood?"

"I was over at the Smithsonian with my class on a field trip," I explained, "and they took off and I got left." Taking a risk, I moved closer to her. "Can I borrow one of your smokes?" I asked, pointing to the pack on the bar.

"You old enough?" she said, sort of kidding me.

"I smoke all the time," I boasted, "I've been smoking since third grade."

She smiled at that and pushed the pack over to me. I fired one up and took a deep drag. The bartender leaned over towards me. He really was a big motherfucker, he could've squeezed my head like a grape. "Let me give you a piece of advice, white boy," he said in this low but very threatening voice, emphasizing the word "white." "Walk your ass over to New York Avenue, set it down on a bus seat, and go back to wherever the hell you come from."

"I can't," I told him honestly, "the last bus already left, otherwise I'd be on it."

When she heard that the woman got in the barman's face. "It don't make a bit of difference what color he is, even a blind man can see this boy is hungry. Now make yourself useful and fetch him a bowl of that stew you've got on the stove out back."

"I can pay," I kicked in hopefully, quickly, "I've got money."

The woman stopped nagging on him. She turned and gave me a sharp look. "How much?"

"Five bucks." Actually I had ten, but something told me not to tell her the whole amount.

"Five dollars?" she asked me. "You really carrying five dollars on you, boy?"

"Ruby, you ain't gonna," her friend said.

"Money's money," Ruby said to the other woman. She turned back to me. "Lemme see it."

I took my wallet out of my pocket and pulled out five singles, making sure she didn't see the five-dollar bill I had next to them.

"Boy tells the truth," she said.

"This is bullshit," the bartender said. "You want him fed, you feed him." He turned away. "I ain't feeding no white kid."

"Maybe I just will," she told him to his back.

"He's a juvenile, you fool," her friend warned her. "Don't go asking for trouble, you got enough already."

"I got rent due and it's raining out, that's my trouble," Ruby told her. She grabbed her purse and jacket off the barstool next to her. "He walked in here and copped a butt off me. He's old enough."

R uby's apartment was down the block, on the second floor of one of the old brownstones.

"You drink coffee?" she asked me, as soon as we were inside.

"Yes . . ." I started to say "ma'am" again, but caught my tongue.

"I got some from this morning I can heat up. It'll take the chill off till I can fix something up for you."

"Thank you."

"Can't leave somebody just standing out there in the rain," she said. "It ain't your fault you're white." She laughed. "Some of my best friends are white. My man friends, that is."

Her apartment was little, but nice and cozy. One room and a pullman kitchen, her bed in a corner, covered with a chenille spread, the same kind my grandmother has.

"Where you from?" she asked, shaking the water off her coat before hanging it on a floor lamp that had some other clothes on it. She felt my jacket. "Take that off and let it dry. Here, give me it."

I took it off and handed it to her. "Dumb white kid, doesn't have the sense to get in out of the rain."

She shook it, water spraying onto the carpet. " 'Ravens-burg,' " she read off the jacket. "You from there? Out to Prince Georges?"

"Uh-huh."

"You're a distance from home, ain't you." She put my jacket on a wooden hanger and hung it from the windowsill. "You want another cigarette?" she asked, offering me the pack from her purse.

"Sure. Thanks."

She shook two out and handed me one, along with the pack of matches. She stuck hers in her mouth and waited for me to light it for her. When I did she touched my hand, holding the match steady to the end of her butt. I got a funny feeling when her hand touched mine. She definitely was sexy, especially with the fake-satin dress, dark stockings and high heels, and all the makeup.

"You take milk and sugar in your coffee?" she asked.

"That's how I like it," I told her. I thought of saying "I like my coffee black and strong, like my women," which is something guys say all the time for a joke, but I wouldn't have said that to her in a million years. I was already nervous enough, alone with some colored woman in the middle of Washington, D.C., who had her own apartment.

She grabbed a handful of my shirtsleeve when she handed me the coffee.

"You're wet as a hound dog," she said. "How long were you out in that?"

"Since it started. I was trying to hitch a ride but I couldn't get one."

"You better take 'em off. Here, give 'em to me."

I stared at her, wide-eyed I'm sure, feeling goofy. She wanted me to take my clothes off in front of her? Shit I reckon, she wouldn't have to tell me twice. She was close to my mom's age, but she was still sexy. I started stripping down lickety-split.

She opened a closet door and rummaged around. "The bathroom's down the hall. You can put this on." She handed me a man's old flannel robe. "Better take it all off."

"That's a nice dress you're wearing," I complimented her.

"Thank you." She smiled in a kind of a smirk as she inhaled mightily from her cig.

I was eating what she'd cooked up—greasy red beans and rice and moldy cornbread she'd had left over in her icebox. She wasn't much of a cook, judging by the quality of this food, she looked like the kind of person who hardly ever eats in, but I was hungry, and beggars can't be choosers, as they say. She herself wasn't eating anything, just smoking and watching me.

My clothes were drying off in her oven. I'd stuck them in there when I came back from changing, it's a trick I learned from my grandma out in the country. They'd be wrinkled when I took them out but at least they'd be warm and dry.

"Can I have some more?" I asked, my hunger overriding the crumminess of the taste. She gave me a sour look before picking my plate up and carrying it to the stove, where she scooped up a spoonful of seconds and dropped it down in front of me.

"Thank you," I said, even though I could tell she'd wanted me to do it myself.

She took a sip from her glass of wine. When we'd sat down she had poured herself some wine into a jelly glass, then looked at me.

"You want some?" she'd asked.

"Okay," I'd said.

"Can you handle it?"

"Oh, yeah, I drink it all the time. I don't mean all the time, but I drink it."

I drank some from my glass.

"Hey, take it easy with that," she cautioned me, "that ain't Coke you're drinking."

She butt-lit another cigarette and watched me eat, squinting through the smoke.

"You don't know how lucky you are," she proclaimed, "ain't many men get me cooking dinner for them."

Good, 'cause you'd kill them, I thought. "It's real good," I told her out loud, being polite, even though we both knew it was about half a cut above canned dog food, "thanks a lot." I finished off the wine in my glass and reached across the table for the bottle to pour myself another.

"You better watch how you drink that wine, it'll knock you flat on your ass."

"That's okay," I assured her, "I'm used to it."

"Yeah," she snorted, "you look like it."

"I am," I protested, "I drink wine all the time. Beer, too."

I took a swallow to show her how natural I was at it. It felt good going down. I was feeling good all around, sitting there with her in her cozy warm room, eating the heavy, greasy food and drinking the wine.

"That's a pretty dress you're wearing," I told her again.

"You already done told me that, Roy." She knew my name, I'd given it to her when she'd asked, it seemed like the polite thing to do, since I knew hers.

"How come you're all dressed up?" I asked. "Are you going to a party?" The wine was making me a little lightheaded, but nothing I couldn't handle.

Her laugh was really deep, like it was coming from her toes.

"I wish," she said. "Ain't no partyin' tonight for me. Not with this damn rain."

"Is that what you wear to work?" I asked. I don't know why I asked that, since it wasn't any of my business, but I was curious and the wine had loosened my tongue. "What kind of work do you do?" I knew she wasn't some white lady's maid, not dressed up like that. She was too restless for that kind of drudgery work, plus she had an uppity attitude no white woman would tolerate for five seconds, but I didn't know what other kinds of jobs colored people did.

"You joking?"

"No," I said, cautiously, her tone of voice informing me that had been the wrong question to ask.

"For real?"

"Why? Should I?" I felt stupid, because it was obvious from her question that I should know what she did, and I didn't.

"I'm a prostitute, boy. Didn't you know that? This here's my working clothes," she said, fingering her dress.

"A prostitute?" It came out dumb, slurred.

"Hooker? Whore? Prostitute? You never heard those words?" She exhaled a big puff of smoke at my face. I couldn't tell if she was smiling at me friendly-like, or putting me down.

"I know what a prostitute is," I said, defensively. What did she think I was, ten years old? "I just didn't think that's what you were, that's all."

She smiled again and sipped some wine. "I see."

"It's just . . . I've never known a prostitute. A real one."

"Now you do."

"Yeah." I thought about that for a minute. "You really are one?"

"I wouldn't lie about something like that," she said.

"No, I guess not."

I lit up a cigarette to cover my awkward feeling. Leaning back in my chair, I squinted against the smoke, looking around the room.

"This is a very nice apartment, Ruby," I exclaimed, trying to change the subject. I was nervous as hell. Here I was, in a colored prostitute's apartment, wearing nothing but an old flannel bathrobe, and getting high on wine. It was the dream me and every teenage boy I knew had ever had, and it was scaring the shit out of me.

"I'm glad you like it," she said. She slipped her shoes off and spread her legs out, her dress riding up on her thighs. I couldn't help but see where her stockings were attached to her panty girdle. I don't know if she knew I could see that far up her dress, but she probably didn't care. I did, though. She was making me hard.

I took a nervous drag off my cigarette. "How come you brought me over here and all?"

"My plans for the night, such as they were, were shot down because of the goddamn rain outside, and you looked like you could use a meal and a friend."

"It's a nice place," I said again.

She sipped her wine, staring hard at me.

"I ain't never been in a Negro's house before," I went on, "we got lots of y'all living nearby us but I don't know any, personally that is." I knew I was talking way too much but I couldn't shut up.

"Different worlds," she commented, saying it like she could give a shit.

"It ain't that I don't want to, I just don't. I'd like to, though, I don't have nothing against anybody, personally."

"I'm glad to hear that."

There was an awkward silence; awkward for me. To fill it I asked, "Are you married?"

She put out her cigarette. "Hell no! Marriage is for suckers. I tried it once, that cured me for good." She stared at me. "You all right?"

"Sure, I'm fine."

"I shouldn't have given you that wine." She stood up and took my hand. "Sit down here, you'll be more comfortable."

She pushed me down on her couch by the shoulders. Then she sat down next to me, put an arm around me, and kissed me, a good full kiss on the mouth. She had very soft lips, and her breath tasted good from the wine.

My cock was sticking straight up under the old flannel robe.

It felt really good, kissing her, but this was all happening too fast, especially when she reached under the robe and grabbed onto my pecker, which was as hard as a turbine.

"My, my, my," she said then. "You certainly are old enough. Yes you are."

I was scared shitless. Partly because I was afraid I might catch some disease, which you hear about people catching from whores all the time, but mostly because I wasn't ready for this, not with some colored prostitute who was almost as old as my mother. Not with a woman who'd know right away I was a virgin and didn't know jack-shit about what I was doing.

"Hey," she said, looking me in the eyes, "you don't have to worry about a thing. I'll take care of it."

I wet my lips, trying to get the cotton out of my mouth. "How much do you cost?"

"I'm usually fifteen a pop," she told me, "but for you, this first time, since I like you so much, I'll just charge the five you got, and throw in that fine home-cooked dinner, too." She started stroking my dick, real gentle-like. She sure as hell knew what she was doing, she had the expert touch. It set me on fire—I started moaning despite myself.

"The boy likes it," she laughed. She pulled me to my feet. "The man."

"You ain't using that on me, no way!"

We were lying in her bed together, the one that had the chenille bedspread like my grandmother's. I'd carefully taken the rubber out of my wallet, unwrapping the foil package like it was some kind of religious icon. It had been in there so long it had made an impression in the leather, perfectly round.

"How long you been carrying that relic around?"

"About . . . a year, I guess." It was almost two years; I'd swiped it from Doc Goldberg's the beginning of eighth grade.

"Shit, these things don't last forever, don't you know that?

It'd turn to dust soon's you put it on, and then I'd be in the family way, and we don't want that." She chucked it in the wastebasket. "I got goods we can use. Part of my job."

With her clothes off she wasn't built all that good. Pretty lumpy, to be honest. Her tits were saggy and so was her ass, and she had a roll of fat around her waist. It didn't matter, though; I was in bed with a naked woman, a naked colored hooker no less.

We kind of shuffled our bodies around each other. I felt awkward, not knowing what to do. As our bodies touched in different places her pussy hair rubbed up against my pecker. I'd never seen a woman with that much pussy hair. She had a muff on her that was football-sized, no exaggeration, a mass of hair thick and large and black, with the consistency of bailing wire, that practically came up to her bellybutton. What I'd seen of naked girls was strictly the white variety, and I knew none of them would ever have this much hair on their privates, even when they were grown women. Peg in my dad's car hadn't had half this much.

"How old are you?" she asked. She was stroking me lightly on the dick some more, the most incredible feeling I've ever had; it felt like I was about to explode and shoot a gallon of come clear to the ceiling. Nothing I'd ever done to myself could compare to what she was doing to me.

"Fifteen," I bleated in answer to her question. I cleared my throat. "I just had my birthday."

"Yeah, you're old enough," she said. Her fingers kept fondling my cock. I was squirming around; I couldn't help it. "Old enough to be a man."

"Thank you," I said. I didn't know why I said that, I knew how much like a kid it sounded, but I was nervous as hell.

"This is your first time, isn't it?"

I thought about lying; but that would've been stupid, and anyway she knew.

"Yes."

"Good. That's good." She looked me square in the face. "Do you think you know how to give a woman pleasure?"

"I don't know," I answered honestly. I knew with teenage white girls that wouldn't go all the way, but I didn't know about real women who did.

"You've got to have a slow hand," she told me, sounding more sexy and mysterious than she looked or felt. "Yes," she said, as my hand started stroking her nipple: "like that."

We wound up not using a rubber after all. Since it was my first time, she informed me, I should do it right, nothing in between—and she was clean, she told me that, too, she swore it, hand in the air and everything, she'd been to the doctor that very afternoon. Clean bill of health. She couldn't afford catching a disease, not in her line of work. She normally made her customers use rubbers, but because I was popping my cherry, she went on, playing with my cock the whole time she was telling me this stuff, she couldn't catch anything from me, so it was cool.

The truth was, she didn't have one. She must've run out or something, because I'd spied on her as she rummaged around in the medicine chest in her bathroom, while she was "getting ready for me," as she'd put it. I didn't complain; she could've told me she had a dose of the clap and I still would've fucked her anyway, hot as I was.

One thing she wouldn't let me do, once we got down to business, was kiss her on the mouth, like we'd been doing on the couch. ("You ain't paying for kissing, boy, kissing's for lovers, not customers," she'd said, pushing me away roughly.) Actually, we didn't do too much of any kind of making out at all, once we got going. She played with my dick for a little while, rubbing it kind of mechanically. I got the impression she wasn't feeling all that romantic, that it was part of the job, which it was, her being a prostitute and having lost business because of the rain and everything. None of that mattered, though, because just being in bed with a naked woman and having my cock rubbed was almost more stimulation than I could handle.

After a little bit of that she rolled over on her back and I climbed aboard. Almost as soon as she put me inside of her I shot the mightiest load of my career, I kept coming and coming, for a whole minute it seemed, it was like everything inside me was coming out of the tip of my cock.

"Damn, Ruby," I gasped, "that was fantastic. Really." I knew she didn't want me to but I tried to kiss her anyway.

"Glad you enjoyed it," she answered curtly, avoiding my lips while rolling me off her and climbing out of bed almost before I was finished spasming out the last squirts.

It should've felt more romantic, I thought as I lay there on the soiled sheets, sweating like a race horse. But maybe it wasn't supposed to with a whore.

"Your clothes should be dry by now," she said.

"Well, looky here," Ruby said, pulling the five-dollar bill out of my billfold, where I'd hidden it under my student bus pass. "You forget something?" she taunted, holding it up in front of my face.

"You can't go into somebody's wallet, that's thieving!" I yelped, grabbing for it. I was almost dressed, putting on my last sock and shoe. Almost home free; but not quite. "Gimme my money."

"No way, sweetheart. This be mine."

"You said five." I needed that money, for cab fare home.

" 'Cause that's all you had—so you said. I took pity on you and you lied to me. That ain't nice, Roy," she teased, pointing an inch-long red nail at me, "to lie to a woman and then fuck her. My price is normally fifteen, remember?"

"I need it to get home on," I whined.

"And what's wrong with your thumb?"

"Around here?"

Her eyes narrowed like a cat's. "What's that mean?"

What a dumb fuck—I shouldn't have said that, I'd known it as soon as the words came out of my big mouth.

"It's dark, there ain't gonna be hardly any cars on the road. Not any that'll pick me up," I added. Hell, it was the truth, speak it.

"Be grateful for what I gave you, boy. It was still a cut-rate price. Now beat it out of here, I've got to get my beauty sleep."

She opened the door to her apartment. "Feel free to come back any time, and bring your friends. Ruby does not discriminate who she fucks, either by race, creed, or size of dick." She laughed. I didn't.

"I could send it to you," I offered, grasping for straws. "I could send you the whole ten."

"A bird in the hand's worth two in the bush. Or in your case, vice versa." She stopped smiling. "Now get out, or there'll be trouble."

I didn't know what kind of trouble she was talking about, but I wasn't going to test her and find out. She could have some monster pimp with a twelve-inch switchblade waiting around the corner, I've heard all kinds of shit around that.

"See you around, Ruby," I told her as I walked out, trying to affect a swagger.

"Bring money." The door almost hit me on the ass as she slammed it.

I had no choice but to thumb it. Luck was with me; a taxicab deadheading to Mt. Rainier to pick up a fare stopped for me within five minutes. A nice guy, too, even if he was colored.

Even with that free ride I barely caught the last county bus home, with hardly a minute to spare. At least Ruby had left me my bus pass. The bus dropped me off on Defense Highway. I didn't even want to think what would've happened to me if I'd missed it and had to hitchhike the rest of the way home, because by this time there were absolutely no cars on the road.

As I got near my house, I heard the town clock tolling midnight. All the lights were out. I tried the front door, which was locked, naturally. I could have opened it with my key, but then I remembered my old man might be zonked out on the couch, sleeping off a night of drinking. If I woke him up this late I'd be road kill tomorrow, so I went around to the back, climbed up to my window on the second floor, and let myself in.

I sat on the edge of my bed and took off my wrinkled clothes, double-checking in my wallet to make sure I had her address, which I'd copied down on the sly while she was in the bathroom doing what it is women do after they've fucked. Even though she'd copped my remaining money I figured I should send her a couple bucks; I had lied to her, for one thing, and she deserved it, for standing up for me in the bar and feeding me dinner and cutting her price to fuck me.

Lying under the covers, I thought about her. I had her address, I could go back down there again. I could use my slow hand. I liked using it on myself, but I liked using it on a woman better.

TEN

My alarm didn't go off, since I'd been so wound up when I went to bed I'd forgotten to set it, which made me late getting up, getting dressed, having breakfast, getting out of the house. I got lucky for once—my folks didn't say a word about my coming home after midnight. My mom must've gone to bed early, like she usually does, and my old man was either sleeping off a pint of Four Buds or didn't give a shit, or both.

The last warning bells were already ringing as I grabbed my books out of my locker and took off down the hall for homeroom. I was on a roll, starting to do good in school, I didn't need another detention slip for being tardy.

So guess who I almost knocked over as I barrel-assed around the corridor?

"Roy!" Darlene meowed, smiling up at me like butter wouldn't melt in her lying mouth. "You almost knocked me right off my feet."

"Sorry," I said, real brusquely, picking up her books, which I'd knocked over. "I've got to get a move on, I don't want to be late, I've already seen Mr. Boyle too many times this year," I told her impatiently, as I shoved the books into her arms.

I started off down the hall but she grabbed me by the elbow, stopping me.

"Roy, are you mad at me?"

"Who said I was?"

"You never met me at the fountain after lunch even though I waited for almost half an hour and I didn't see you at all on the bus and you didn't call me last night and now you're not being very nice to me and I'd like to know why."

Her lip was shaking like she was about to cry. Girls can do that, cry at the drop of a hat, even when they don't mean it. Yesterday, I would've been all over her like a lovesick puppy dog, but today I was a new man, in more ways than one.

"Why don't you ask Danny Detweiler why?"

"Why should I ask him? I don't even like . . ." Her big baby-blues suddenly got real wide.

"Did you . . . were you *watching* us . . . that wasn't even . . ."

I was already walking away, I didn't need to hear any more.

"Roy, that wasn't nothing!" she called after me. "I didn't want to. He *forced* me to . . ."

Tell me another one, I muttered under my breath as I reached my homeroom door.

"Roy, he forced me! I swear he did!"

I turned back to her. She looked pathetic as hell, standing there in the empty corridor. She really was crying, too, I could see her mascara running down her cheeks. Tough titty for her; she'd had her chance, it wasn't my fault she'd blown it. Fool me once, that's life. Anybody can rise to the bait one time. But do it twice, I'm a prime asshole, and my mama didn't raise no fools.

I flat-out wasn't interested in Darlene anymore—I had bigger and better plans for my future.

Even in the gloom of winter, when the trees are bare, the branches black and spindly, the trunks frozen, when the air is wet with foggy air rolling in from the Chesapeake Bay, Annapolis is a beautiful place, all over the town, especially the Academy; the snow is on the ground, the birds that stay here all year 'round are circling high above the stone buildings. In some ways I like it more then, because there aren't as many people around, especially on weekdays, it's only midshipmen and other Navy people, and me. Still, when spring comes, which it's done this past week, overnight it seemed, everything suddenly turns green— the trees, the lawns and fields; the sky is blue instead of dull white like cataracts on old people's eyes, the water in the bay and on the Severn River lightens up, the dark green-black foamy waves become more turquoise, and everything smells like an explosion of blooming. Then it's incredible, it's my favorite time of year.

When I was little this is when I would come. My mom and dad would bring me and Ruthie. We'd make a day of it, walking around the campus, at lunchtime eating ham-and-cheese sandwiches down by the water that my mom had brought from home, then at night feasting on crab at one of the restaurants in town, smashing the shells open at long tables covered with butcher paper, having a good old time, all of us. My old man wasn't the asshole then that he is now—he still liked the idea of being a father, of having kids. We were little, we did what he told us, no lip, whatever he and my mom said was great. I remember this one time he bought a kite in Annapolis, a real box kite, and me and him spent a whole afternoon building it together and then we flew it out over all the boats in the harbor. It was only later that he became the sorry prick that we all know today, that my mom started jumping at his shadow, that Ruthie ignored him, that I both turned my back on him and did everything I could think of to piss him off.

It's been a long time since things were good. We haven't come up here as a family since I was nine. Now I come alone, and when it's beautiful like this it makes me sad for the good old days.

I ran the course three times. It's my marker, I have to do it a little bit, even when I don't feel all that much like it. A ritual, like a dog pissing on a tree, to let other dogs know it's his, keep away.

Something was different today. It was me—I had changed. The change had come fast, over the last couple months, since I'd met Admiral Wells and he'd taken me under his wing and talked to me about my future, going to Farrington Academy and then here. Before, even though I knew every nook and cranny of this place, I'd always felt like an outsider, an intruder—which I was —because I wasn't a part of it, I was only here on a pass, I always knew my time would be up and I'd have to leave. Now I felt like I was part of it, that it was mine, waiting for me.

Melanie's recital was set for Sunday afternoon at four o'clock. She had mailed my invitation to me at Admiral Wells's house, since she didn't know my address and I wasn't about to give it to her. I hadn't even given it to the admiral, or my phone number either, even though he'd hinted a few times it would be nice to be able to get in touch with me, in case something came up. I gave him a story about how my parents don't like me using the phone, which is true enough, since my old man (my "father" to the admiral) uses the home phone a lot for his business, which is total bullshit. He could look it up, I guess, but there's several families named Poole in Ravensburg, he's too dignified to cold-call them one by one. I call the admiral every weekend before

I'm scheduled to come over, and if he's got other plans I move on, it's no skin off my ass if I don't go over there, it's more of a habit than anything. Especially since I found out how much Mrs. Wells doesn't like me, although she's always nice to me in the flesh. People are like that, they'll smile to your face, then they'll knife you in the back when you aren't looking.

One thing I've got to say about Admiral Wells—he was still on my side as much as ever, even after Mrs. Wells had put the kibosh on me. He and I had spent a Saturday afternoon filling out the Farrington application together, fudging it a little to make me look better. Instead of giving him my grades to send in, which would have been the kiss of death, I gave him a couple of my recent test papers, a math one and an essay I'd written in history class about the building of the Panama Canal. I'd gotten A's on both, the first A's I'd ever scored in my entire junior-high tenure. The admiral had especially liked the Panama Canal paper. I didn't tell him it was mostly from a book I'd found in the county library. I put it in my own words, though, it wasn't like I copied it out of the book line for line. Anyway, I'd gone all the way to Hyattsville to do it and it had taken me most of an entire day, so I figured I'd earned that A.

Melanie had written a note on my invitation: "I'm *really, really*"—she'd underlined both *really*s—"looking forward to your coming, Roy. Every day when I practice I pretend I'm playing just for you. Melanie. P.S. I'll be wearing a new dress. It won't be like the one you saw me in last time. Wait and see."

I folded it up and put it in my pocket, so the admiral wouldn't see her handwriting on it. I didn't want him to get the wrong idea about her and me. Melanie was a nice girl. Too nice. I wasn't in love with Darlene anymore, but I was way past girls like Melanie in experience, especially now, after that time I'd spent with Ruby. Anyway, I could see me bringing her around to Ravensburg for my friends to meet. They'd laugh my ass out of town, even if she did have knockers as big as grapefruits.

It hadn't turned noon when I showed up at Admiral Wells's house with the new clothes he'd bought me (that I'd had to sneak out of my own house). I was nervous about going to this concert. That's one thing about being around Admiral Wells and Mrs. Wells, I'm always seeing stuff I've never seen or imagined before, and I always feel like I have to be on guard so I don't fuck up. It makes me so nervous I get a headache sometimes when I come home from being with them. There are often guests at their house, I meet them and talk to them and act nice and normal, but inside it feels weird, like I'm not really there, just part of me is, the other part's standing outside of me like a ghost, watching. No one seems to notice this, they all treat me okay, but I feel it. What happens when I'm feeling particularly uneasy is the admiral will put his hand on my shoulder, or ask me if I want a Coke, or say it's time him and me worked on our models, and we'll go downstairs by ourselves. It's like he's reading my mind.

"Pretty stuffy up there," he'll say, working on his model, standing at the bench next to me.

"It didn't seem too bad."

"Cooler down here."

Then we'd just work. We can go an hour without saying anything, it doesn't bother me and I can tell it doesn't bother him. Maybe that's one of the reasons he likes having me over, so he can get away from what's going on in his own house.

The day before, yesterday afternoon, I'd gotten a fresh haircut. I didn't go to Ernie's, my usual place, where everybody I know goes. I went across town, to a barbershop where they didn't know me and where none of my friends get their ears lowered. Only old guys get their hair cut in this place, it's so square even kids like Sarkind don't go to it.

"Give me a regular haircut," I told the barber, scrunching down in the chair. I felt like I was going to the dentist.

"A trim?" He was a short little guy who sported a pencil mustache and wore too much after-shave.

"Just a regular cut," I said. "Don't scalp me or anything, but shorter." I pointed to a picture on his wall, one of those Wildroot ads. "Like that."

"Robert Taylor," he said. "Without the wave," he added, pushing his fingers around on my skull like it was a bowling ball, "you don't have the body for it, your hair's straight as a string. But I'll make you look good."

It didn't turn out as bad as I'd dreaded. It was pretty square, but I could still comb the sides back. What they call the Ivy League look, like kids in Catholic schools have to wear. I felt kind of naked, as the skin around my ears and the back of my neck was pale and stubbly, it was much more military than my old style, more like Annapolis. They'd rib me at school, but I could handle that. I wanted to look right for this recital, so the admiral wouldn't be embarrassed by me, not that he'd ever said anything. It just felt like it was time for a change.

"Got a haircut," the admiral declared when he opened the door for me. "Looks good on you."

That was all, but I knew I'd scored one.

"Try these on for size," he said. I'd gone upstairs to change, in his dressing room. He handed me a new pair of shoes in a box, the tissue still wrapped around them. Wingtip oxfords, in cordovan, the same kind he wore when he dressed up.

"They'll go better with what you're wearing. You don't want to stick out."

He gave me a shoehorn, and I slipped them on. They fit me like a glove.

"How are they?"

"Good. They're really nice. Thanks." I don't argue with him anymore when he gives me stuff, he can afford it and it makes him feel good.

"It was Mrs. Wells's idea. She had me check your shoe size the last time you slept over."

That was a crock of shit, but I let it pass.

"I'll have to thank her," I said, "when she gets home from church."

"I've already done so on your behalf." He smiled. "You can be extra attentive to her today. She'll appreciate that."

He was trying to get her to like me. Like if I fell all over her she'd change her mind. I wanted to tell him it doesn't work that way, but I didn't. If that's what he wanted, fine. After all he'd done for me, I'd have kissed her ass in broad daylight in the window of Woodward & Lothrop's if he'd asked me to.

We heard Mrs. Wells's car pull into the garage.

"Let's surprise her," he said.

We walked downstairs together. I was all dressed up, except for my tie. I hate wearing it, it makes me feel like I'm in a vise, so I don't put it on until the last moment. The admiral feels the same way; he told me that one day when he was getting dressed to go out to some shindig. That was one of his secrets, to put your tie on at the last minute.

"Hello, boys," Mrs. Wells greeted us, coming in the kitchen door. She had a bag of groceries in her arms. I grabbed them away from her right away.

"Thank you, Roy. There's another one in the back seat of my car, would you . . ." She stopped and took a better look at me.

"What happened to all your hair?"

"Cut it off," I told her, like it was no big deal.

"Hmmm." She cocked her head, looking at it. "I like it," she said. "You look like a regular boy now, instead of a juvenile delinquent."

"Yes, ma'am." I didn't like being thought of as a hood, but she'd meant it as a compliment, so I let it pass.

"You're shaping up, Roy, you're shaping up. We might make a proper boy of you yet."

She came over and gave me a kiss on the cheek. Her lips were dry, so light it was like a butterfly's kiss.

"New shoes, too, I see," she said, noticing them. "Smart idea. Yes, Roy, you are definitely changing for the better."

She went upstairs. The admiral watched her go.

"She means well," he said, reading my mind again.

"It *was* a kind of hoody haircut," I said. I could have told him every kid in my school wore his hair that way, but I didn't. "Anyway, it feels cooler." I rubbed my hand over it. Any shorter and it would be a Marine Corps special.

A few minutes before it was time to go to the Prescotts', Admiral Wells asked me to come into his study for a minute. Mrs. Wells was already there. She was wearing an emerald-green cocktail dress and dark-green satin heels. As usual, she was a knockout.

"This came for you," the admiral said, handing me a thick envelope. "Yesterday."

I turned it over in my hands. The return address read "Admiral Farrington Academy."

"Go ahead, open it up," he urged me impatiently, like a kid waiting on his Christmas presents. He and Mrs. Wells exchanged a smile. "Go ahead," she echoed.

I ripped it open. There were several pages stapled together, folded over to fit inside the envelope, with a single-page letter paper-clipped on top.

"Read it," Admiral Wells commanded. "Out loud."

"Dear Mr. Poole," I read. No one had ever called me "mister" before. I started over: "Dear Mr. Poole. This is to inform you that you have been accepted into Admiral Farrington Academy for the scholastic year 1957–1958 . . ."

I stopped and looked up. They were beaming at me, smiling the two biggest shit-eating grins I'd ever seen.

"I . . ." I looked down at the letter, but everything was a blur.

Admiral Wells took the pages from my hand before I dropped them. I was shaking, I hadn't realized it until my hand was empty.

"Congratulations," he said softly.

"Yes, congratulations," Mrs. Wells added. She came over

and kissed me again, then hugged me. Admiral Wells shook my hand.

"I . . . I can't believe it." I couldn't, I'd never expected this, even with the admiral behind me. It didn't seem real, like I was watching a movie of myself.

"Well, I can," Admiral Wells told me. His hand was on my shoulder, gripping me hard. "I knew you would do it, Roy. I knew it from the day I met you."

"It's true, he did," Mrs. Wells confirmed. "He told me that first day he brought you over, after you'd left. He said 'that boy reminds me of myself at that age.' "

"You didn't believe me," he said, turning to her.

Her face clouded for a moment.

"Yes," she said softly, almost whispering. "I didn't. I couldn't see beyond your background, to who you truly were."

"That's okay," I told her. I was numb; if I moved a muscle I'd shatter into a million pieces.

"No," she corrected me, "it isn't. I shortchanged you. And I shortchanged my husband." She looked at me with those incredibly green eyes of hers, piercing me right through to my heart. "I apologize."

She said it to me, but she really meant it for the admiral. It didn't matter; either way, it still made me feel good.

"That's nonsense," the admiral said to her, jollying her up. "What counts is this letter," he crowed, brandishing it. "You're in! And in three or four more years, you'll be going to Annapolis. That's all that counts now." He glanced at his watch. "We'll celebrate properly tonight," he said, "after Melanie's recital. Speaking of which, we'd better get moving. The Prescotts are bears for punctuality."

I helped Mrs. Wells on with her coat, a thick mink coat that hung all the way to the floor, which she was wearing even though spring had come and it was warm out. Whatever Mrs. Wells had was the best, whether it was her coat or her car or her house. It was who she was—it was why she had to have everything around her, including people, be perfect. I wasn't perfect, not by a long shot, but I was closer to whatever perfect was for her than I used to be.

As we were walking out the door, the admiral stopped me, letting her get ahead of us.

"We'll have to tell your parents," he said, quietly, so she wouldn't overhear.

"Yes, sir." That was the one thing I was dreading. They didn't know about any of this—not the admiral, Farrington, anything. I didn't know precisely how my old man would react, but I had a good idea and I wasn't looking forward to it.

"We'll tell them together," he informed me, not giving me an option. "Tomorrow." He paused. "When I drive you home."

That's the way it had to be, I'd known it all along. It was okay now, he knew me, who I was. What I had been, where I came from, who my family was—none of that mattered anymore.

Since Melanie lived most of the time with her grandparents the recital was being held at their house, off Foxhall Road, a few miles away. We took Mrs. Wells's Lincoln. Sitting in that car was cherry to the core, the leather was so soft it felt like a baby's ass. I thought about how when I turned sixteen I could hit on Mrs. Wells to let me borrow it for dates, when I'm home on vacation from Farrington. If you can't get laid driving wheels like these, you're hopeless.

The Prescotts' house was huge, much bigger than Admiral Wells's house. The thing that impressed me the most was that the entire back of the first floor was an honest-to-God ballroom, at least sixty feet long. It had polished hardwood floors and floor-to-ceiling French doors and windows opening onto the back yard, which had to be a good acre of green, rolling lawn. Melanie was a rich girl, plain and simple.

There looked to be a hundred people there, maybe more. Almost all were grownups—the few kids besides me were all girls

Melanie's age, obviously from her school. Some were dogs, but a couple were pretty good-looking, wearing stylish dresses and makeup like the girls at my school wear. The difference was that their dresses were expensive, you could tell just looking at them, they had to cost more money than any dress my mother owned.

They all checked me over as I walked through the door. I was looking good in my nice sports coat and my new shoes and my new haircut, but a blind man could see what kind of boy I was: the kind girls like this wanted, and their parents didn't. I knew one thing that was definitely going on in their little minds—how did a loser like Melanie Prescott ever meet a cool boy like me?

"You're here. I was getting worried," Melanie said in a low whisper, popping up at my elbow like she'd been lurking near the doorway, waiting for me. "Hi, Mrs. Wells, Admiral Wells," she sang out. "Thanks for coming."

Admiral and Mrs. Wells said hello back to her and then immediately walked halfway across the room to talk to her grandparents, leaving me by myself with Melanie. Part of the plan, no doubt. This time, though, I didn't mind.

"Sure I'm here," I said. "I told you I'd be."

She was looking at me with a funny expression on her face, and it took me a moment to realize that I was staring at her with my mouth open. That's because while I may have been somewhat different-looking from the me I'd been before, Melanie was completely changed from the semi-pathetic girl I'd met that night at the admiral's house. She was still a porker, 'cause that's the way she's built, she can't do anything about that, but it was as if she had come out of a cocoon. She was wearing a tight midnight-blue dress that wrapped around her ass like an Ace bandage, bright red lipstick delicately painted on her mouth kewpie-doll style, a touch of eyeshadow, the works. Her hair was pulled back in a ponytail, she was wearing sheer stockings, and shoes with heels a good three inches high.

"Do you like my dress?" she asked, clearly nervous about my reaction.

"Does a bear shit in the woods? I like it a lot, it makes you look . . ." I was thinking *sexy,* but I didn't say it.

"What?" She wanted me to.

"Good. Pretty. You know."

She smiled, like she knew what I really wanted to say. "My mom didn't want me to, she said it makes me look like a . . . I'm not going to say, but you know what I mean . . . the makeup, too, she's not crazy about that, either."

"Yeah," I said, "I know what you mean." I winked at her, like we were sharing a dirty secret. She looked sexy as hell, this shy girl who'd come on before like something out of *Little Women.*

"I'm glad you like it," she said. She wet her lips nervously. "That's why I bought it."

"Well, I do."

"You have to meet my mother." She took my arm. "I can hardly walk in these heels, I feel like I'm going to fall on my face. I'll have to play in my stockings, I don't know how women walk around in shoes like these."

She led me towards the center of the room, where a bunch of grownups were standing around talking. One of the women in the group looked over at us, saw me, and smiled. Melanie's mother—a blind man could've seen how much they looked alike, at least in the face. From the neck down she was different, thinner than Melanie, she actually had a very good figure, especially her legs. She was a few years older than my mom, I could tell that, but from where I was standing she looked younger, even though she had a ton of makeup on. Maybe because she had so much makeup on. The real reason, I knew as I looked, was that she didn't have a look on her face like a dog about to be kicked, the way my mom mostly does. Melanie's mom was dressed up like the Queen of Sheba, wearing a silk dress that had to cost a shit-load of money, and flat-out dripping in jewelry; a necklace that looked like it had rubies and emeralds in it, bracelets with diamonds, long diamond earrings. The woman was a walking jewelry store—if I hocked what she was wearing on her body I'd be set for life.

"Mother, this is Roy Poole," Melanie said, introducing me. "The boy I've told you about." She was shifting her weight from one foot to the other, nervous as hell.

"So." Melanie's mom looked me over like I was a prize heifer at a 4-H fair. "This is the boy."

Melanie turned red as a beet.

Her mom kept looking me over. Melanie still had her hand on my arm. She was squeezing so tight I thought she'd tear the material. The way her mom was looking at me, it was like she wanted to make Melanie uncomfortable.

"It's nice to meet you, Miz Prescott," I said. I held out my hand. She looked at it for a moment, like she was expecting dirt under my fingernails. Then she shook it, and held on longer than she needed to. Quite a bit longer.

"It's nice to meet you, too, Roy." She looked me over again, then turned to her daughter. "You weren't exaggerating," she said, flashing me this flirting kind of look.

Melanie blushed even worse at that. I felt my face getting a little red, too. What the hell had she been saying about me, and what was the deal with her mother?

"Are you a classical music aficionado, Roy?" Mrs. Prescott asked me. She smiled when she said it. She had a mouthful of big white teeth.

"Roy likes all kinds of music, mother," Melanie answered for me, saving my bacon, 'cause she had to know I didn't know jack-shit about classical music, seeing's how I'm from Ravensburg.

"I like anything Melanie plays," I added. I'd especially like it if she played skin flute, I thought.

Melanie moved closer to me, giving my arm a little squeeze. I was figuring out what was putting me off about Mrs. Prescott —it was as if she was in a contest with Melanie, and didn't want to lose. She was an old woman trying to look young, trying to beat out her own daughter.

"That's very gallant," she said to me. "I can see why my daughter is so taken with you."

"Mother!" Melanie squealed.

"I'm teasing you," Mrs. Prescott told her. "Now I think you need to get ready." She took my hand again. "I'll make sure Roy is properly attended to."

Melanie reluctantly let go of my arm. "Sit in the first row," she asked me, her eyes pleading.

"He'll be sitting right next to me," her mother assured me. "Now go on. Your girlfriends are dying to help you with the last-minute details."

"See you later," Melanie told me. She walked away from us, tottering on her high heels. A couple of her girlfriends gathered around and followed her out, their heads together, jabbering away. I knew what they were talking about.

"A big day, Chloe. You must be proud." Admiral Wells had joined us. He put a hand on my shoulder. It made me feel a lot more comfortable.

"Yes," Mrs. Prescott answered. "Melanie's worked very hard."

"You've met Roy, I see," the admiral said.

"Oh, yes. Melanie has talked of nothing else all week. One would have thought this entire affair had been arranged solely for his benefit."

Man, did my ears burn at that. She smiled at me, about the phoniest smile I've ever seen in my life.

"I don't see Horace," Admiral Wells said to her.

The smile vanished from Mrs. Prescott's lips. "He wasn't invited. He doesn't even know his daughter *plays* the goddamn piano."

"He's Melanie's father, Chloe. You can't arbitrarily cut him out of her life."

"Sorry," she said, "but he's a lousy father. I'm not going to gild the lily on his behalf. He cut himself out."

Boy, you could see how bitter she was.

"I'm going to borrow Roy for a minute," the admiral said. He wanted to get away from her as much as I did, I knew him well enough by now to know that.

"As long as you promise to return him," Mrs. Prescott said, turning her smile back on. It was like a skeleton smiling. She gave me the chills, this lady. I was going to have to be careful around her.

"Surviving?" Admiral Wells asked as we walked away.

I shrugged. I can survive most anything, including Melanie's mother.

"God didn't intend for every woman to be a mother, and Chloe Prescott is living proof. Thank heavens Melanie has her grandparents. They've raised her almost from infancy. Salt of the earth, those two."

He really liked old Admiral Prescott and Mrs. Prescott, I could tell, not just because Admiral Prescott had helped him out early in his career, but because of who they were as people, the way they were with their granddaughter.

We walked around the room, Admiral Wells introducing me to some of the other guests—he knew just about everyone there. It was an important group of people, and not because some ninth-grade girl was going to show off her stuff on the piano. For one thing, Melanie's piano teacher was famous. She was a tiny old lady with a thick German accent, dressed all in black with two bright red rouge spots on her sunken cheeks. She had one of those faces that looks like she's sucked lemons all her life.

But the main reason for all these important people being here was that Melanie's grandfather was a big deal in Washington, even though he was an old retired guy now. A rich big deal. One thing I do understand—even though I don't know much about the life people like this live—once you're a wheel it stays with you for life, and if you're rich to boot everyone wants to kiss your ass.

"What was the Prescotts' gift to the symphony this year?" I overheard one old biddy ask another as the admiral worked the crowd, with me in tow.

"Ten thousand," was the reply.

Shit! Melanie's grandparents had donated ten grand to an orchestra! No wonder it was a star-studded recital. Even the conductor of the National Symphony Orchestra, a slick-looking gray-haired man named Howard Mitchell, who rambled on to me for about three minutes about my own upcoming piano recital, which he unfortunately wouldn't be able to attend because he would be in New York at a recording session—he'd obviously mistaken me for another student of the old piano teacher's, and Admiral Wells didn't correct him, either because he thought it was funny or he didn't want to insult the guy, or both—was here to pay his respects, like he didn't have anything better to do on a Sunday afternoon.

A bunch of colored servants came out and set up folding chairs in rows. The shiny black piano was in front of the French windows, facing the room and catching the rays off the afternoon sun. It was the biggest piano I've ever seen, even bigger than the one Liberace plays on television.

I sat in the front row. Melanie's mother was on one side of me and the Wellses were on the other. Then Melanie walked out, and everybody got quiet as she sat down to play.

She was good. I don't know fuck-all about this kind of music, but a deaf man could tell she was playing the shit out of that piano.

You could have heard a pin drop. Nobody even coughed. She sat straight as an arrow at that piano. Her shoes were kicked off like she'd told me she was going to, her stockinged feet pumping the pedals in rhythm to the notes and chords she was playing.

I glanced over at her mother, sitting next to me. Mrs. Prescott was sitting rigid in her chair, not moving a muscle. She was actually holding her breath, she was so tensed up. I could feel her tension in my own body.

I turned my attention back to Melanie. Her eyes were half closed now as she swayed to the rhythms she was creating. An older woman was sitting next to her, flipping the pages of music as Melanie played, but it was as if Melanie wasn't even looking at the music, she was playing it from some place inside of her, like it was a part of her that was coming out the ends of her fingers. I closed my eyes, too, just listening to the music. It was like her body was coming into my body through the music, from her heart to her fingers to my ears to my heart. It was what her note on the invitation had said: she was playing this music for me alone.

It was a great feeling, knowing that. I opened my eyes and watched her.

A thin line of sweat had formed on her upper lip, making the red lipstick glow. It was a turn-on. Everything about this was turning me on. Melanie was playing this beautiful music just for me and using it to tell me she wanted to fuck me. And it was working, because I wanted to fuck her back.

I closed my eyes again and it was like I was alone, just her and me in this big room together, her playing and me listening. I could feel my heart beating in time to the music, and I knew her heart was beating at the same time, the same way.

She played three pieces. The last one was real long, a good fifteen minutes. After she finished, there was a moment of silence, then the whole place started applauding, people yelling "bravo, bravo," standing up, everything. I was, too, not yelling "bravo," but standing and clapping.

Melanie looked around the room. Her face was flushed and wet, and she was panting to beat the band. It's tough work, playing that stuff, I could tell. I was smiling like an idiot I was so proud of her.

Then our eyes met, and it was like it had been while she was playing—just her and me, alone in this big room by ourselves. She smiled hard at me, as if she was saying "what do you think of me now, I'll bet I look pretty damn good to you now." She did, too. She'd already been looking good, but now she was pure beauty. I smiled back at her. I knew she felt better and prouder than anyone else in the room, but I had to feel second-most proud.

W e were making out like bandits, like there was no tomorrow. Melanie and me, alone.

Everybody had milled around after she finished—congratulating her, congratulating her teacher, her mother, her grandparents, the works. The colored helpers moved through the crowd, carrying silver trays of caviar on crackers and other kinds of stuff like that, a whole mess of strange things I've never eaten in my life, and serving punch out of a big cut-glass bowl that probably cost as much as my old man's car. It was a real party atmosphere, with Melanie the center of all the attention, it was probably the most attention she'd ever gotten in her entire life. I hung around on the sidelines, taking it all in, feeling happy for her.

Some of her girlfriends, the cuter ones, came over and talked to me a little. What my name was, what their names were, what schools we went to, the usual shit. When I said "Ravensburg" they gave me the once-over, like I'd said "Mars." A couple, the ones that'd had some experience, came on to me like girls will, as if they couldn't believe I was there for Melanie. I let them know right off that I was, though, and made sure that if Melanie was looking in my direction I had my attention on her, not one of her friends, especially not one of the pretty ones.

"They all want to know . . ." She squirmed around a little, giving out a low moan. We were in her bedroom. Everybody had cleared out except for her grandparents and the Wellses and a few others, who were downstairs.

"I'm going to show Roy my room," she'd told her mother. She had her own room at her grandparents' she was there so much of the time.

Her mother didn't care. Now that the recital was over she

didn't have to play-act around Melanie anymore. If anybody noticed they didn't let on when I followed Melanie up the stairs to the third floor and into her room.

I was sitting on her bed while she laid in my lap. Our mouths were all over each other, my free hand working its way up the side of her leg, along her stocking. When I got to her bare leg and started for her underpants, she grabbed my hand.

"No," she said, "that's too fast. I've never done this before. Here, up here." She put my hand on her tit, over her bra. The front of her dress was down and her bra was out, a dark-blue bra like her dress. It was stiff and shiny, I knew she'd never worn it before, like everything else she was wearing. Even though she was sucking on my tongue like a fiend, I also knew that she'd never had a boy put his hand on her tit either. She sure was liking it, though, she was squirming all over me, I could feel her ass pressing down on my dick through the material. This girl was hot as a pistol, it was like she had an entire life of stored-up sexual desire inside of her and now it was exploding out.

"They all want to know what?" I asked.

She kissed me some more, her hands all over my neck, my hair, inside my shirt. Her mouth was soft—big soft lips, soft tongue. A born makeout queen, breaking free from inside that prissy old-fashioned life she'd been living for fourteen years.

"Know what?" I repeated. I worked my hand under her bra, onto her bare tit, onto her nipple, which was standing up erect. I started massaging it gently and that really got her moving all over me, her legs sliding around, her toes curling and uncurling in her stockings.

"Know what?"

"How I . . . oh God, oh God, I've never felt anything like this before!" She grabbed me by the hair and looked me serious in the face. She had a wild look in her eye.

"How I got you!"

I sat back, my hand resting on her breast. Jesus, what a bitch! Here she was, the nicest girl I'd ever met, definitely the *hottest* girl I'd ever been with, in ten minutes I'd be finger-fucking her, she'd stop me and stop me and then she'd let me because she wanted to all along but had to play the game, here all this was happening and she was feeling shitty about herself. I hate that kind of garbage, it made me think about poor old Vernice and other kids I know, boys too, who think that because they're a little bit fat or not so pretty in the face they're doomed forever.

"Roy," she said, putting her hand on top of mine and moving it around on her tit again, "don't stop."

I started up again, real gentle. Her eyes closed and she started moaning softly.

"That's their problem," I told her. Theirs and her mother's and everybody else who only saw what she looked like on the surface.

She smiled up at me, her eyes still closed.

"I love you, Roy." She pulled my mouth down to hers and frenched me so deep I could practically feel her tongue stroking my tonsils. "You're the best thing that ever happened to me."

I kissed her back and slid my hand inside her panties. She didn't even mock-protest that she was trying to stop me.

"I have to go to the bathroom."

"Me, too," Melanie said. "I'm sticky all over from you." She was grinning like crazy, like Eve must have the first time she ate the forbidden fruit.

"Where'd you learn to talk that kind of trash?" I teased her.

"Other girls. But I know it's mostly lies, I know that much."

No shit, I thought. Ninth-grade girls are just like ninth-grade boys.

I'd been finger-fucking her for about ten minutes. She had sucked her breath in hard when I first put a finger in, just one index finger, she was plenty wet but she was tight as a drum, obviously she was a virgin, she probably had never had anything in there in her life, not even her own fingers. It took me a good five minutes to squeeze a second one in there, but that's all she was going to take. I thought about Ruby, my colored hooker. I could've put my whole fist inside of her if I'd wanted to. Forget that shit now, this girl was going to give me all the loving I could handle and then some, she'd do anything I wanted.

"Next time," she'd said breathlessly. "You can come to my house, my mother's hardly ever there."

"When?" I had panted, so horny I thought I'd shoot my load right in my drawers.

"Next weekend?"

"Yeah." I'd do it on my way over to the admiral's, and on my way home, too. I thought about Burt and all those guys who were always talking about getting it. The difference was, they all *talked* about it, while I was *going* to, the real thing, and for free, not with some hooker, although I'd liked it fine with Ruby, she'd taught me more that one time than I could've learned from doing it a thousand times with girls my age. The only problem was, I wouldn't be able to tell them about Melanie, not her actual name. She was too nice a girl; I could never do that to her. They wouldn't understand anyway, if they saw her they'd just think she was a plain girl, certainly not worth writing home about.

The only thing was, which I have to admit was eating at me even as I was thinking about it, was that I didn't know if I actually would fuck Melanie next weekend, even if she let me. It didn't feel right somehow—she was too inexperienced, she'd never even kissed a boy, practically. Fucking Melanie this early on would be like taking candy from a baby.

Maybe I'd change my mind when the time actually came, but next week seemed too early. We could make out like crazy for a whole bunch of times, until I was sure in my own mind I wasn't going to do a wham-bam-thank-you-ma'am on her and then never see her again. Once I was sure of that, then we could fuck all day and night and I wouldn't have any guilty pangs about it.

We got off the bed. She looked at herself in the dresser mirror.

"Oh, God! If anyone sees me like this I'll die!"

She did look pretty raggedy. Her lipstick was smeared over half her face, her hair was a mess, her clothes were all wrinkled and undone.

"I've got to clean up," she told me. "You, too."

I looked at myself in the mirror, next to her. It was the usual look you get after you've been making out hot and heavy for a half-hour. She didn't know the look, never having done this before.

"You can use the guest bathroom at the end of the hall, on the floor below," she said. "My grandparents' bedrooms are on that floor, so be careful they don't hear you, my grandmother might be old but she's got ears like a hawk. Just don't let anyone see you, especially my mother, that's all I need. I'll meet you downstairs in ten minutes," she added in this real flirty tone of voice, giving me one last soul kiss and pushing me out of her room. We'd been together two times and she'd gone from being a shy wallflower to a red-hot makeout artist. It's incredible how easy that is once you know somebody wants it from you like you want it from them.

I tiptoed down to the second floor, making sure I wasn't spotted, not only because I had her makeup smeared all over me, but also because I had a hard-on like an elephant, even with my hand in my pocket it stuck out like I had a ruler in my pants. I didn't know what the admiral and Mrs. Wells would think, but I didn't want to take any chances. Melanie was this nice girl they liked, they didn't want her corrupted by some hood from the wrong side of the tracks—Mrs. Wells especially. Even though she was being much nicer to me, I remembered all too clearly the way she'd put me down when she thought I wasn't listening. I was doing good all around, I didn't need to fuck anything up.

Melanie had about creamed in her jeans when I'd told her I'd gotten into Farrington, up there in her bedroom before we'd started making out.

"Oh, Roy," she'd squealed, "that's *great*, that's so *great*, why didn't you tell me *earlier?*"

"It was your big day, I didn't want to steal your thunder."

"It's a big day for you, too, it's even bigger for you. Oh, Roy, I'm so proud of you." She'd given me a kiss on the mouth, the first of many. I knew she wanted to do it with me, she didn't need any excuses, but telling her about Farrington hadn't hurt.

"You'll look great in a uniform," she'd said.

I'd thought about that, how cool it would be. Their uniforms were modeled after the Naval Academy's; it would be like I was a midshipman-in-training.

"There's a great girls' school nearby, Agnes Walker," Melanie had told me. "Some of my friends have gone there, they say it's neat, you date boys from Farrington. I could transfer, we could both be there."

"Yeah," I'd said, "that would be great." I got a little uneasy when she'd said that, not that it wouldn't be great, hot and cold running pussy any time I felt like it the way this girl was going, but she was pushing mighty hard, pretty soon she'd be telling me what kind of engagement ring she wanted. It's like my sister, she's finishing eleventh grade and if the right boy comes along she'll get married the day she graduates. That's not a life for me, I've got a whole career ahead of me to worry about. Still, it's nice when someone wants you as much as Melanie wanted me.

After I finished washing Melanie off my face and combing my hair I took a look at myself in the bathroom mirror. It wasn't perfect—a trained eye could see what I'd been up to, but like my old man says, it was good enough for government work.

As I left the bathroom I could hear voices drifting up the staircase from downstairs—the admiral, Mrs. Wells, old Admiral Prescott and Melanie's grandmother, Melanie's mother. And Melanie, she was already down there, I must've been daydreaming in the bathroom, remembering her taste in my mouth. I felt kind of nervous as I walked down the long, musty hallway towards the staircase, because I wasn't comfortable up here by myself in old Admiral Prescott's house. I wasn't part of this house, part of the lives of these people. I was not here because of myself,

but because Admiral Wells had brought me into his home and
I'd met Melanie because of that, and she'd invited me to her
recital because she'd fallen for me, and for that reason they had
to be nice to me. And even though Melanie Prescott had just told
me that she loved me and had let me put my hand inside her
pussy and was ready and willing to give her cherry up to me next
week even though she was only in the ninth grade and hadn't
had a real date in her life didn't make up for my not being part
of this. I was an outsider to them, and I always would be. Even
if I married Melanie Prescott and lived in this very house, I still
wouldn't be one of them.

That was okay, though, because a lot of what they were was
bullshit to me. I didn't want to be like them, I wouldn't mind
being rich and shit like that, but not all the rest of it. Not the
boring parts.

Partway down the hallway was an open door leading into a
bedroom. As I walked by, I stopped for a second and glanced in.
I didn't have any reason, I was curious was all, maybe I wanted
to see how different it was from what I knew. Or maybe I was
just being my customary nosy self, which is closer to the truth.

There were the usual items, chests of drawers, lamps, a bed
—all the best quality, even my untrained eye could see that—
and clothes thrown on the bed. A woman's clothes, like whoever's
room it was had been trying different dresses on until she found
the one she liked. My sister's room is like that, half her clothes
are on her bed most of the time.

Melanie's mother was using this room, I realized, she would
sleep here overnight some of the time, the times when Melanie
was staying here with her grandparents, since she wouldn't want
to be alone in a big old house, especially if her daughter wasn't
there. She probably kept several changes of clothes here because
of all the fancy affairs they must've put on—I could see her lug-
ging out a bunch of dresses and trying them all on, one after
the other, deciding which one was best for the occasion. She
would've brought some from her own house, too. She was that

vain kind of woman, I could tell—she'd take forever figuring out what she should wear so people would look at her; especially men. Trying dresses on all day, putting on her makeup, all that vain shit women do. I'll bet she made Melanie help her, too, she'd tell her "I want to look good for you, darling," when what she really wanted was to look good for herself, and just as important, better than her daughter, even though it was her daughter's big day, not hers. I remembered her holding my hand before the recital, trying to flirt with me right in front of Melanie, to steal her daughter's thunder.

The thing is, she *was* kind of sexy, for an older woman. I'd noticed her figure when Melanie had introduced us, I couldn't deny that. She was the kind of woman who made you look at her, that was what she was all about. She had to be horny as hell, being divorced from Melanie's father (who had humiliated her by leaving her for a younger woman); she was probably on the make for every man around, even if he was only fifteen and her daughter's date. Of course, that could've been my own fantasy: guys're always fantasizing about fucking a mother-daughter combination, that's one of the ultimates—I'll bet some of Ruthie's boyfriends have even thought about fucking my mom. She probably would, too, if she thought she could get away with it, the way my old man treats her. Serve his ass right.

I shouldn't go in that room; I knew that. I should haul my young ass downstairs before they started wondering where I was. But now I'd built this fantasy in my brain about Melanie's mother, about the two of them naked together, with me in the middle. It was being with Ruby that did it; ever since then I'd been thinking about older women.

Melanie's mother's clothes were calling to me, lying there on the bed. I wanted to touch them, just for a moment. Maybe part of her smell would be on them. Something. I'd just take a quick look, pick up one dress.

That was bullshit: a pair of undies is what I wanted to pick up, a stocking. Something with the touch and smell of her sex on it. I still had this raging hard-on from having made out with Melanie, and sex was the only thing on my mind. What I really wanted to do—I hated to admit it but I had to—was jack off into a pair of Melanie's mother's panties. I'd do it real fast, be rid of my boner in thirty seconds, I'd stuff the panties in my pocket and nobody would ever know.

I picked up a pair. They were real silk, a light peach in color, they practically slipped out of my fingers they were so silky and slippery. I moved away from the bed, towards a corner of the room, turned my back to the door and reached for my fly.

Then I saw it, sitting on top of her chest of drawers, hidden behind a picture in a gold frame, a picture of a baby girl. Melanie as a baby, it was the same hair. If I hadn't been standing inside the room I wouldn't have seen it, because it couldn't be seen from the hallway.

The *it* I am referring to was Mrs. Wells's silver statuette, the one that had been stolen. The one I'd seen old Mrs. Prescott pick up. I'd known that old bitch had stolen the statuette from the giddyup, and now here it was.

Forget about beating off. My cock went limp so fast it was like it had never been erect at all. I tucked it back in and zipped up my fly.

I didn't know what the fuck to do. I could go downstairs and tell on her to the Wellses, but then I'd have to admit I was in her room, and what was I doing there? I was going to tell them I wanted to masturbate into a pair of Melanie's mother's under-pants? I couldn't say I'd seen it from the hallway as I just hap-pened to be strolling by, because that was impossible, even if it hadn't been hidden behind the picture frame it was too small to be seen from there, you'd have to have better eyesight than Superman.

Ratting on old Mrs. Prescott would cause a huge stink. Ev-erybody would be embarrassed as hell, Melanie most of all. She'd take it personally, like somehow it was her fault, like if I hadn't been up there corrupting her it would've all passed over. Today was her special day—first she'd knocked people over with her piano playing, and then she'd made out for the first time in her young, innocent life with the boy of her dreams. It would kill her, finding out that her grandmother, who took better care of her than her own mother, was not only a common thief, but had stolen from Beatrice Wells, her best friend.

I should never have gone in this room in the first place. I should've learned my lesson back there in the Smithsonian, with Darlene and Danny. But I had, and it was too late to turn back.

I picked it up, hefting it in my hand for a second. It was heavier than it looked, real silver. Mrs. Wells wouldn't have anything phony in her house, that I knew.

"What are you doing in here?"

I spun around. Old Mrs. Prescott was standing in the doorway, staring at me.

"I . . ."

"What are you doing in my guest bedroom, young man?" she demanded in a loud, harsh voice. She didn't sound like a singing little bird now, she was barking like a dog. Her face was all red and splotchy, the way people's faces get when they've had too much to drink or they're mad as hell.

"Nothing," I mumbled under my breath. I was holding the statuette in my fist. It felt like a burning rock.

"You thief!" she screamed at me.

"No, no, I'm not . . . you got it backwards, lady." I was fucked, now everybody would find out, Melanie's day would be ruined, I'd never see her again, Admiral and Mrs. Wells wouldn't be able to be friends with the Prescotts anymore. All because this old bitch had stolen from her friend, and I'd been a nosy asshole and found the fucking evidence. What pissed me off more than anything, besides getting caught where I shouldn't have been, was *her* calling *me* a thief, when I was holding onto the very thing she'd stolen.

"What's going on?" Admiral Wells was all of a sudden in the

doorway next to old Mrs. Prescott, and Mrs. Wells, and Admiral Prescott, and Melanie's mother, and Melanie. The whole shooting match, standing in the doorway, staring at me.

"I can explain," I told him, my eyes begging. I wanted to explain in private; I didn't want it all to come out in the wash here.

Admiral Wells looked at me with a questioning stare, like he didn't know what was going on, but didn't like whatever it was.

"What is it, Roy? What do you have?"

Slowly, I opened my hand and showed them the statuette.

"Oh." Mrs. Wells had her hand to her chest, like she'd had a heart attack.

"I didn't take it," I said, talking feverishly. "I didn't. I found it. Here," I pointed to the chest of drawers, "it was hidden behind this picture." I looked at the admiral, who stared back at me. Everyone else was staring daggers at me, all except Melanie, who had eyes as big as saucers.

"It's true, I swear to God!"

Melanie started hiccupping, like she couldn't breathe. Her mother put an arm around her shoulder, glaring at me with pure hatred in her face. If looks could kill I'd be a dead man already, the way she was looking at me.

"That's a disgusting lie," old Mrs. Prescott yelled, turning to Admiral Wells and Mrs. Wells. "He took it out of his pocket, I saw him do it. Look at him," she said, pointing a bony finger in my face, "he's trembling like a leaf, he's been caught red-handed and he'll say anything to get out of it." She was spitting she was so angry. It wasn't me she was angry at, though, it was herself for being found out, but me and her were the only ones that knew that.

Mrs. Wells looked at me. She had tears in her eyes.

"Roy, how could you?" she pleaded, in her soft, smoky voice. "After all we've done for you?"

"I didn't, Mrs. Wells, I swear to God! I would never steal

from you, you've been nicer to me than anybody in my whole life." I really was shaking, not only because I was scared shitless, but also because I was angry as hell. I hadn't done it; this was outrageously unfair. "Why would I steal something and then a month later bring it with me here? Nobody's that stupid, not even me!" I yelled.

"Give it to me," the admiral said, his voice flat and quiet. He stood there, his hand out.

I walked over to him and placed it in his hand.

"Go to the car," he ordered me. It was the way you would talk to a dog.

I pushed past them and ran down the stairs and out the door. The only thing I remember was the look on Melanie's face. It was a look of pure pain, and I knew that even though I'd never see her again it was hurting her as much as me.

W e sat in the admiral's study. Me and him. Mrs. Wells had gone up to her bedroom as soon as we'd gotten back. All the time we'd driven to their house in her car she hadn't said one word, she'd just sat by herself in the back seat, stone-faced.

I was wearing the clothes Admiral Wells had bought me; my own were bundled up in a sack, at my feet. The little silver statuette was in its place of honor with the others, in Mrs. Wells's drawing room.

"Do you believe me?" I asked him. I knew everything was fucked, that it had all fallen apart, but at least I hoped he knew the truth of it—that I would never steal from them in a million years.

He looked away for a minute, then looked back at me. I tried to read him behind his glasses, but I couldn't—he was a Navy admiral, he knew how to play poker.

"Why would I?" I pressed on. I had to convince him, if I did nothing else I had to do that. "Why would I want something like that anyway? If I was going to steal anything I'd steal some tools or something I could really use. But I didn't," I added quickly, "and you know it."

He got up and walked across the room, stopping by a shelf that held some of his model collection, including a couple we'd built together. He picked one up, an early Civil War Union fighting yawl. We'd celebrated the day it was finished—the first of many, he'd promised me then.

He looked at it sorrowfully, then carefully put it back.

"That doesn't matter, Roy," he said, turning to face me. "Not now."

"It does to me!"

He shook his head sadly. "You shouldn't have been in that room. You shouldn't have touched it."

"I know," I told him, "but that doesn't mean I stole it."

"It was in your hand. Helene Prescott saw you take it out of your coat pocket."

"She's a liar! You know she is!" I was crying now, I couldn't help it.

"That's not the point!" He took his glasses off and rubbed his hand across his face. "That's not the point," he said again, this time quietly, almost a whisper, like he was trying to convince himself it really wasn't the point.

"The Prescotts are our oldest and most cherished friends," he went on in this real earnest tone, like he was explaining something important to me; or more accurately, convincing himself of the honesty of what he was saying. "I served under Sherman as a young man; I rose under his tutelage. If it hadn't been for his guidance and support I might never have achieved what I did." He paused for a moment, looking at me to make sure I was taking this in.

"It doesn't matter who's lying," he continued, "you or she. What matters is our lives, and our friendships. Regardless of what I feel personally, I can't take a position against a dear friend. I can't, Roy." He paused again. "And even if I could," he said, "I wouldn't."

"But that's unfair! That's totally unfair!"

"Perhaps it is. But that is the way it is."

He walked over to his desk and picked up the letter I'd gotten from Farrington earlier in the afternoon, the letter that had promised me that my life was going to change. He held it up to the light, looking it over.

"When I decided to sponsor your application to Farrington," he said, "knowing that if you did apply you would be accepted —let's put all our cards on the table, what military academy is going to say no to me, or to Admiral Prescott—I knew what kind of person I was recommending. I knew where you came from, I knew what your background was."

"You did?" I asked dumbly.

"Of course. I checked up on you. Thoroughly. I looked into your school, your grades, your attitude in class. The reports I got back weren't very good, Roy. In fact, they were awful, across the board. A bad student; a nonstudent would be a better description, a disciplinary problem, an all-around troublemaker. The last person one would associate with achievement of any kind." He paused, looking down at the letter again.

"But I saw something in you that perhaps—no, obviously, others had not. I saw intelligence, I saw perseverance, I saw commitment. I saw *you*, Roy, I saw you better than anyone has ever seen you. And that's why I stuck by you, that's why I pushed you, that's why I made my own commitment to you. And it paid off. This letter says it paid off. And I knew that in the future it would pay off a hundredfold more."

He dropped the letter back on the desk, as if it suddenly didn't exist, as if what the words on the page said didn't exist anymore.

"I can't stand behind that commitment now. I wish I could, because there's promise in you, real potential. But if I were to stand up for you against her, that poor old lady, I would be doing more harm to my family, to my friends, to my own life, than I'm willing to. I feel like a coward in saying this, but that's how it is."

"That stinks," I spat out.

He picked the letter back up again.

"I'm forced to withdraw my recommendation," he said. "It's out of my hands."

He looked at the letter for a minute, then back at me. "Why did you go in that room?" he cried out. "For God's sakes, why?"

I was staring at the floor. I had no answer, because there was no answer, none that had any sense to it. I just shook my head, like a dumb dog.

"I should never have pushed you this fast," he went on in a rush. "You're a boy, you don't know these things, you have no experience."

"I know more than you think," I told him, darkly, under my breath. I knew about lying, I'd gone to school on that today for sure, all the little lies I'd told over the years were peanuts compared to him and his bullshit society friends. And I knew about women, something about them, anyway, I knew that Melanie Prescott, his friends' precious granddaughter, wanted to fuck me more than anything in the world. Maybe I still would, I thought, one time, a revenge fuck, just to teach them all a lesson.

"You think you do," he said, sadly. "That's the most regrettable aspect of it all." He buried his head in his hands for a minute. "I have to take the blame for this. You're the one who's going to suffer the consequences, but the blame is mine, mine alone. I refused to acknowledge what a huge change this would be for you. I didn't give you the time you needed to digest it. You trusted in me, and I didn't protect you the way I should have. I should have taken better care of you, Roy."

The way he was talking, it was like it was me that should be feeling sorry for him, not the other way around. But I didn't. He'd fucked me over, plain and simple, and no amount of him feeling sorry for himself was going to change that.

"Sometimes the only course of action is no action," he said finally, exhaling his breath. "That's the lesson we learned today, you and I, and a bitter way to learn it it was."

I looked up at him. "That's not what I learned." I stood up to face him. I was almost as tall as he was. I'd never realized that before.

"You want to know what I learned today, Admiral Wells? I learned that kids like me get screwed by people like you. That's what I learned."

He turned away.

"I was right back there, and you knew it, and you chickened out on me. All that bullshit you laid on me, about the code you live your life by, how you're judged by your actions, not on who you are or who you know. It was all bullshit, wasn't it? The Naval Academy code—what a joke! Just a fucking pack of lies," I was really crying now, crying like a baby, I didn't give a shit either, I couldn't help it, it wasn't my fault. Who I was, that was my only fault.

"I wanted to help you," he said. "That's not a lie."

"Big fucking deal."

I had run out of steam.

"Say goodbye to Mrs. Wells for me," I told him, my voice flat, empty. "I guess she feels good now, knowing she was right about me all along."

"If it's of any consequence, she doesn't."

"Well, tough titty," I said. I knew I sounded like a kid when I said that, but I didn't care anymore. I just wanted to get the fuck out of there.

"Roy."

I was at the front door, holding my sack of clothes.

"What about your models?"

"I don't want those fucking models. You keep 'em."

He winced at that. For a split second, that made me feel good.

"They belong to you. You made them."

"You touched them, so I don't want them anymore. I wasn't lying!" I yelled at him, starting to cry again. "Can't you even say that? Can't you even live up to your own fucking code?"

He didn't say a word: he just stood there. I slammed the door behind me on my way out.

I stood on the bridge that crosses into Ravensburg, looking down at the Anacostia River. It was dark out; I couldn't see the water very well. I was stripped down to my shorts and socks. The clothes the admiral had bought me lay in a pile at my feet. It was warm out, I didn't feel the cold at all.

He had used me, plain and simple. He'd wanted somebody to follow in his footsteps and he'd decided that was going to be me, to replace the son his wife had never let him have. All that garbage about helping me out, getting me into Farrington Academy, changing my life—it was a crock of shit. Maybe he had really wanted to help me, but to make himself feel good, not because of me, Roy Poole. He didn't know Roy Poole from a fucking hole in the ground.

I had been right. Earlier, in the Prescotts' house, when I was thinking about it all, after being with Melanie, when I was thinking about how I didn't fit in there. I had always known it, but like a dumb asshole I'd thought it could change.

It couldn't, now I knew.

I put on my own clothes. They felt good, right. The only thing that still pissed me off was the haircut—it would take at least a month to grow out, I'd look like a pussy for a month.

I wadded the fancy clothes the admiral had bought me into a ball, and wrapped the sports coat around them. Then I went to the railing and tossed them over, like Burt's brother had done with his high school ring. I heard them hit the water, but I don't know if they floated away or sank. Either way, I didn't give a shit.

ELEVEN

Palm Sunday, a week after my catastrophe, was for me just another fucked day. We'd been on school vacation—we get two weeks' vacation, the same as Christmas. It had been a total waste of a week. My friends and I hadn't done anything with it—we'd fucked off as usual, going down to the bowling alley and shit like that. Another boring week in Ravensburg, Maryland, the excitement capital of the world.

Most kids I know go to church with their families on Sunday morning, then have a big early-afternoon dinner with all the relatives. Ravensburg's a churchgoing community—for a small town it's got a shitload of churches. At Easter-time people parade up and down the streets in their new fancy outfits, the girls especially. Not my family, though; my old man is not a churchgoer, to put it mildly. He hates anyone telling him what to do, so he hates preachers with a purple passion; church for him is one more scam for someone to take your money. He belongs to the church of Four Roses, that's the only church he's willing to attend, and he does it faithfully, every day of the week practically. Of all the crappy deals in our family that pisses my mom off, not going to church is at the top of the list, because she grew up in a strict Methodist family where going to Sunday school and church was as much a part of her life as eating or breathing. It wasn't a major issue when they were courting because he let it go then, he knows to lay low when the tide is running against him; one thing he knew with certainty was that my mom's parents would've made her break off their engagement if they'd realized how he felt about religion in general and churchgoing in particular, so he kept his mouth shut about it until they were clear of my grandparents; after they got married and the old folks didn't have any say in the matter my old man showed his true colors: he put his size-eleven down hard. My mom's too scared to cross him on it, like everything else in her sorry life. Once in a blue moon, if he's not around on a Sunday morning, she'll sneak out and go to service at First Methodist. Their minister is Reverend Boyer, and Mrs. Boyer is one of my mom's best friends. She drags Ruthie and me to church with her sometimes, but the strain of doing it on a regular basis isn't worth the wear and tear on her nerves. She prays privately, though; I've seen her sitting alone, studying on the Bible when she thinks no one's watching. It helps her keep going through all her daily bullshit.

Ruthie likes going to church with mom, 'cause she gets to dress up and mingle with her friends, but I find it boring, personally. All that fear talk about hell, damnation, and doom. To hear Reverend Boyer preach it, God hates a good time worse than anything. Since I love a good time, that shit don't wash with me.

I had planned on thumbing a ride to Annapolis this morning,

but at the last minute I changed my mind. I didn't feel like going to Annapolis today—I don't feel like being anywhere near the Naval Academy, not right now.

So I moped around most of the morning, finally meandering over to Joe's house. His family lives down the block from St. Aloysius Catholic Church, which is where they go. Joe's family is fish-eaters from way back, to Lord Baltimore practically the way they tell it. One of Joe's uncles is a Jesuit priest, Father Martin, I've met him a couple times, he used to teach at Catholic University in Washington. He's a pretty cool guy, he plays touch football and drinks beer just like any other of Joe's uncles, but he's a priest deep down, he's committed. He can't ever get married, he can't even jack off, at least he's not supposed to, although Joe says he bets he does, his uncle, since he's such a regular guy otherwise.

A lot of my friends are Catholics; around here you're either a Catholic or a Methodist. There's some Holy Rollers and Jehovah's Witnesses and weird shit like that, but most people take their religion straight. Even when it comes to religion Ravensburg's a square, old-fashioned, boring town.

The other drawback about going to church, at least on a regular basis, is that if I did I couldn't spend my Sundays at the Academy. Sometimes, though, I wish we did, just a little bit more, despite the phony piety, because sometimes you feel like you've got to pray for something. I know I can do it without going to church and I do sometimes, but I don't feel I deserve to get what I'm praying for, since I'm not putting in the time. I could've prayed about getting into Farrington, for instance, but it wouldn't have counted as much as if I'd done it regular, in a church. Anyway, being at the Naval Academy on a sunny Sunday morning beats the shit out of sitting in a hot, dark church any day.

Joe and his family were just coming back from church service. He spotted me and came trotting over, running his finger under his shirt collar. He was dressed up, wearing a coat and tie, looking like a monkey and feeling like one, I'm sure. Like all the boys I know, Joe owns one crappy sports coat, from Robert Hall or Sears, which he wears every Sunday to church or any other special occasion, summer or winter. It's dog shit compared to the expensive one I'd had from Saltz, the tweed the admiral had bought me. Even though I was pissed as hell at the admiral and didn't want anything around that reminded me of him, I wish I hadn't thrown that sports coat away. I'd looked good in it, it made me feel like I had class. No point in crying over spilled milk, though, that's one of my mottos.

"How's Jesus?" I asked.

Joe laughed: "Man, you are one blasphemous motherfucker."

We walked over to where his family was congregating outside his house, trading lies, gossip, and bullshit. Spring had truly arrived, the surprise nighttime cold snaps were no longer a worry, people were dressing lighter, the women more than the men, putting their heavy winter coats and wool dresses in mothballs and breaking out the lighter cotton ones. Some of Joe's girl cousins, the ones in high school and a few years older, working girls now, looked mighty fine; I checked out their asses, which I couldn't help but notice, seeing how tight their dresses were. They still treat Joe and me and all his buddies like we're kids, even though we're taller now than some of them. Little do they know how we think about them when we're in bed under the sheets.

"Roy, you are getting bigger by the minute," Joe's mom joshed me, running her hand through my stupid short haircut. She's a nice lady, Mrs. Matthews, she's always laughing and smiling about something, always looking on the bright side of things, as she says. She's also a great cook, so I spend a lot of time over there, anytime I'm there at dinnertime she just sets an extra plate for me, no questions asked.

"That is pure baloney!" I heard a voice exclaim. I turned to look at Joe's dad, who was doing his usual friendly pontificating. "You think Jim Lemon's a bad outfielder?" he snorted. "You never saw Carlos Paula play, then. He made Lemon look like

Mickey Mantle out there." Joe's father and uncles were gathered around the front porch, their jackets off, arguing baseball—the Senators, of course. The Senators are the worst team in baseball, they always have been ever since I was a kid. "Ball's hit to right, routine line-drive single," Joe's dad went on, working up a good head of steam, the Senators'll do that to you, you start discussing them in a quiet kind of voice and pretty soon you're ranting and raving, "runner's on first, going to third, Paula scoops it up on the run, fires the ball to third, *misses* the cutoff man, *misses* Yost"—Eddie Yost has been the Senators' third baseman all the years I've been following them—"*misses* the pitcher backing up, I think it was Connie Marrero but it could've been the other Cuban, the fat one . . ."

"Ramos," one of Joe's uncles cut in. "Anyway, Marrero was the fat one."

"No, not him, the other one, maybe it was Bob Porterfield, it doesn't matter, Paula throws the ball into the *second* deck behind third, not the first deck, the *second*. He almost threw it into Virginia. It was Al Rosen got the hit, now I remember, '53, when him and Mickey Vernon were fighting out the batting title."

"Cuban ballplayers," one of the uncles pronounced. "They'll do it every time. Clark Griffith, that cheap SOB."

Not only were the Senators the worst team in baseball, they were the cheapest by a long shot. They had more Cuban ballplayers than any other team in baseball, because they could pay them less than Americans.

Joe's mom called over to one of the other women, "Do me a favor and fix up lunch for mine, I'm behind on sewing my Easter outfit and I haven't even started in on Julia's." Julia is Joe's little sister, the one in seventh grade. He's got three other sisters and two brothers; typical Ravensburg Catholic family.

"Don't fix me up none," Joe called out real fast, "I'm eating at Roy's house."

That was news to me, but I didn't give him away. He wanted

to get shed of his family for a while, that's all, sometimes they get to be a handful, all those aunts and uncles and cousins, especially the girls with their gossiping and giggling.

"Wait up," he said, "I'll be right out." He ran inside to change.

I waited on the sidewalk. Even though I'm almost like another son to them, at times like these I feel a little out of it, being as how they were all dressed up, coming from church, and all together, one big family, and I was by myself in my usual jeans and T-shirt. I was glad when Joe came back out, dressed like me, and we could take off down the street.

We dropped by Burt's and picked up his ass, then headed out, the three of us. One for all and all for one. Burt was glad we pulled him away, otherwise he'd be working. Burt's folks are okay, but they're not as nice as Joe's. His old man's straight as a country preacher, always on him for chores, Burt's got a million and one items he's expected to do around the house before he can go out and just fuck around, it's like his family's getting a handyman for free the way they treat him. Not that they're mean or anything, but Burt's father's a hard-working man and he expects his son to be the same way. At least he's got expectations for his son, which is more than I can say about mine.

We drifted through town, doing nothing. It's easy to do that with someone you're as close to as brothers, twins almost, I think of us as brothers sometimes, we're the same age, the same grade, we think the same about almost everything. Me and Joe and Burt, the Three Musketeers. There are times when I wish we were brothers, all living together, in a happy family, a family like Joe's, the father cracking jokes and carving up everybody's portion at dinner, the mother like Mrs. Matthews, cooking for everyone and doing their laundry, three sets of boys' clothes, all the same size. We're not exactly the same size, I'm the biggest and Burt's the smallest, but we're close enough. Sometimes I think these guys are more my family than my real one. I know it's a lot easier to be with them than with my family, even when I'm really liking Ruthie or my mom, loving my mom, there's always something else, some pressure, something to be scared of coming through the door.

At least I've got them. Ruthie has her girlfriends, too, and boys, she could have more of them if she wanted, girls built like her are the most popular. It's my mom that needs more in her life; that's why, I've been realizing lately, she gets all dolled up to see Mr. Boyle, that moron. At least he pays her attention; maybe a lot more. Maybe I'm doing her a favor by being such a fuckup, it gives her an excuse to get out, to be around people.

Without knowing how we'd gotten there we wound up down by the junkyard. Something must've pulled us, something dangerous. I sure as shit didn't have any eyes for being around there, not after the incident with the dog that night, but all of a sudden I looked up and there we were, walking across the railroad trestle a hundred feet above the river, coming up the backside of the junkyard.

Burt and Joe are almost as good at walking the trestle as I am, those boys have no fear in their bodies, it's one of the things that makes us close—guts to spare. We tightrope-walked the outside track single file, feeling the wind in our faces, even looking down once in a while to the riverbed, which you're not supposed to do, it's supposed to scare you, since you're seeing how high up you are, but it doesn't scare us. We're not reckless about it, you fall over the side and you're dead meat, we all know that, but we feel comfortable in being able to do it. Anyway, live fast, die young, that's one of my mottos. Like James Dean, that guy was as cool as they come, I could picture him up here with us walking the tracks, squinting against the sun and having fun.

We fired up cigs when we got to the other side, hunkering back on our heels and staring down at all the junk clustered around the river on both sides. At night it's kind of pretty here, mostly because you can't see much of anything, but in the day-

light all the junk and shit is right in your face, not only seeing
the shit but smelling it, all that old crappy junk from years and
years.

"What a dump," Burt drawled.

"The genius speaks," I countered, flicking a rock against the
side of the embankment and watching it bounce down and splash
into the river. My eyes were watching the rock, but my main
focus was keeping my ears open for that scum-sucking dog, even
though he normally would be chained up, being's how it was
daytime. I didn't want any more encounters with that motherfucker—he'd know my scent in a heartbeat and come for my
throat, I was sure of it.

I hadn't told anyone about that night and I didn't feature
doing it now, even though I could score points for having been
in there alone; being there alone at night would be double points.
But there were things about that night, things that happened, that
I wanted for myself; sharing it would've made it less important,
less special, so I'd kept my mouth shut about it and didn't see
any reason to change now, just because we were here, close to it.
They're my best friends, Burt and Joe, but I'm not going to tell
them everything about me. I never once mentioned the admiral
or any of that, that's a secret I'll take with me to the grave. What
they don't know can't hurt them.

Can't hurt me.

We wandered away from the tracks and snuck into the junkyard proper, the back part. I hadn't heard the dog, so I was comfortable with that; he had to be chained up, people come in and
out of the yard all the time on business, one dog bite and they'd
get their ass sued for a million bucks, they don't need that. We
kept a wary eye out for the watchman, but he's usually up towards the front, hanging around the guard shack near the entrance where the highway passes by, listening to the radio and
drinking bad pint-bottle whiskey, more'n likely Four Buds, like
my old man drinks. That would be a good joke on my old man,

finding out him and some nigger junkyard watchman drink the same rotgut.

It's a big yard, acres and acres of shit, we've found over the years if you stay in back you're okay. The important thing is to keep out of sight—if they see you they've got to chase you, whether they want to or not.

We ambled around the place, finding small objects of interest, like old spinners off steering wheels with half-naked ladies in the inset, fake gold-plated cigarette cases, stuffing things into our pockets even though it was all worthless junk which we didn't want anyway. Stuff you wouldn't look at twice in a store becomes valuable when you find it in a junkyard.

After picking the back area clean we walked over to the south end of the yard. It's mostly automobile parts in this section. In the middle there's a small mountain of tires, piled high on top of each other. I climbed up and looked around. All the way at the other end I could see smoke coming from the guard shack, but no sign of any guards, so I sprawled out in the center of the pile and with a shove of my foot sent one of the tires down the side of the pile, where it bounced along the dry bedside and then into the river where it floated slowly away from us and out of sight under the railroad trestle. Far off in the distance I heard a slow freight approaching from the north, a couple miles away at least.

Burt and Joe climbed up the pile of tires and joined me at the top. Burt grabbed one, took careful aim, and rolled it down the side, narrowly missing a telephone pole at the edge of the riverbed.

"You missed, ace," Joe dug at him.

"Let's see you do better," Burt challenged.

Joe took careful aim and sent a tire rolling down the side, the tire bouncing crazily when it hit the bottom, missing the phone pole and drifting off down the river in search of its brothers. I lay back on the pile, lazily smoking. It was hot on these tires; I was tempted to just lie back and fall asleep.

"You pussies can't do anything worth a shit unless I take you by the hand and show you," I commented in my usual helpful style, eyes half-open, watching them.

"Shit, you couldn't hit that if your life depended on it," Burt threw in my face. He'll get in your face in a heartbeat, that boy, no stone gets left unturned around Burt.

No way was I going to let that pass. "How much?"

"A quarter."

I stood a tire on edge and took careful aim, sighting over the top at the phone pole, and rolled it down the slope. It was heading straight for the pole, so straight I started to turn to him and put out my palm, when it hit a rut and bounced away, barely missing the pole and floating down the river.

"Pay up, sucker."

"Double or nothing," I countered.

"Shit, yes." He smiled, thinking he was going to pick my pocket. No way I was going to let that happen, my youthful pride was at stake.

I carefully sighted another tire and sent it down, this time allowing for the rut. If it missed by an inch I'd be surprised—but it missed, that it did.

"Pay up."

"One more. Double down." I had to hit one, I'm a near-genius at this.

"Shit," Burt complained, "you're bound to hit one sooner or later."

But I'd already lined up another tire. All three of us watched intently as it rolled down.

It hit, dead square in the center.

Joe yelled out at the same time: "Jesus Christ, look out!"

We'd been so intent on our tire rolling that we'd neglected the first rule of junkyard cruising—don't ever forget to keep an eye on the guard shack. Bearing down on us like a runaway freight train was a colored man at least 6'6" tall, with blood in his eye and a big mother .44 in his hand, less than a hundred feet away and closing fast.

We scattered down the other side of that pile like our asses were on fire.

"We're even!" I yelled at Burt, as we tumbled down like three Humpty Dumptys.

We started running for the railroad tracks, which are the junkyard boundary. Once we got past them, he couldn't follow us.

"Stop, you sonsofbitches!" he hollered at us. "I'll shoot, I mean it!"

We kept going like bats out of hell. He fired a shot into the air. I took a peek at Burt and Joe. Their eyes rolled clear to the backs of their heads when that shot went off.

"Keep running," I yelled at them, "no nigger's ever gonna shoot a white boy."

He fired again, lower this time, the bullet ricocheting off the ground five feet away.

"Talk louder, genius," Burt yelled back at me, "he can't hear you tell him what he ain't gonna do."

"Shut up and keep running," I yelled back, "we're almost there." I could feel my lungs burning, my heart pounding. I'd been scared that time the dog came after me, but that was nothing compared to this.

We could hear his heavy footsteps pounding behind us, gaining with every step. Then Joe, like a fool, turned and looked back to see how far from him we were, and his foot caught a battery cable. He fell heavily into the dirt, landing right on his chest.

I could tell in a flash the wind had been knocked out of him. Burt hesitated a moment, not sure what to do, but I grabbed him and pulled him along.

"He's fucked," I said, knowing it was true but feeling like shit anyway, "we've got to get out of this yard and then figure out how to break him loose."

The tracks were close now, less than a hundred yards away,

but as we approached them, almost running faster than a speeding bullet we were so pumped up from fright, we realized that the freight, even going as slow as it was on its approach to the trestle, was going to beat us to the crossing. We were trapped like rats between the train and the junkyard watchman.

"Son of a fucking bitch!" I exhaled.

We stood at the edge of the track as the train slowly rolled by. It was a long one, hundreds of cars, I couldn't even see the end around the bend. The big Negro had Joe by the arm and was dragging him towards the tracks, right at us, figuring he had us pinned, getting close enough for us to see the big shit-eating grin on his face. He looked like the goddamn dog, except he wasn't drooling as much.

I looked around, desperate.

"Let's jump it," I said to Burt, not even knowing I was going to until the words popped out of my mouth.

"Are you crazy?"

"Shit, it ain't going more'n five miles an hour, we can jump off soon's it clears that field over there," I said, pointing to a field on the other side of the ravine, about half a mile away. "Come on!"

I started running parallel to the freight. Burt hesitated a moment, then took off running with me. I grabbed the side of an open freight car and swung aboard. It wasn't that hard—the movement of the train slingshotted me right in, then I reached down and grabbed Burt by the arm and pulled him up alongside me.

From the safety of the moving train we watched the watchman run up too late, pure anger on his dark, sweaty face as he watched us. He had a good solid grip on Joe, who looked as miserable as any human being I've ever seen. Two hours earlier he'd been on his knees praying in church and now he was in the clutches of a junkyard nigger who would be doubly pissed, first because of us sneaking in and rolling the tires down the river, then because of me and Burt getting away. Joe was going to pay the price for all three of us. All for one and one for all, this time it would be only one poor sorry bastard for all.

At least he hadn't gotten Burt and me. As the train pulled away from the junkyard I gave the watchman the finger.

"Shit, I reckon," I said. I was smiling, I couldn't help it, I knew Joe's ass was in a sling but I'd hopped a freight, the first time in my life, something I'd always wanted to do.

"Poor Joe," Burt sighed.

"Poor bastard is right," I said.

"Better him than me!" Burt cracked, laughing I did, too. I couldn't help it, we weren't laughing at Joe, we were laughing because we were scared, we were laughing because we'd made it.

We stood in the doorway as the freight train lumbered across the trestle, waiting for it to hit the field on the other side, so we could jump off.

"Fun fun fun!" I yelled. I was feeling lightheaded, from the excitement and the experience of hopping the freight. "Get ready now, we're almost there."

Right as I said that, the train started picking up speed, almost like the engineer a hundred cars to the front had heard me and was going to prove to me who was running this show.

"What the fuck?"

I leaned out the open boxcar door. The last of the cars had cleared the trestle—we were going straight again, on solid ground, and as it straightened out the train started moving faster and faster. Too fast for us to jump off.

"Now what, genius?" Burt turned to me, scared and angry.

I looked down at the ground moving under us. No way could we jump this train.

"We'll have to ride it into Washington and hitchhike home. It's better'n getting caught by some coon with a .44 in his hand, ain't it?"

"I guess so," Burt said, nervously.

We sat on the edge of the boxcar and watched the scenery roll by. The tracks run alongside the Washington–Baltimore

Parkway. As we moved along we waved to people in cars driving alongside us, especially a load of high school girls, who waved back. From this distance they would've thought we were men, or at least boys their age. They would've wanted to meet us, since we were brave enough to pull a dangerous stunt like this.

"I do believe I'll get me a little pussy tonight," I said, lying back like a rajah. I was thinking of Ruby, we could swing by her place. Maybe her friend would be there, too. Burt's eyes would pop out of his head when I sauntered in there real casual-like.

"I reckon I will, too," Burt said. In his dreams, I thought, this time I'd call his bluff. The pro. If any of us was the pro now, it was me.

Suddenly I started laughing, giggling like one of the girls at school.

"Did you see old Joe's face when we pulled out of there?"

"I'll bet he damn near shit his pants."

We laughed as we lit up cigarettes, hunching over against the wind, watching the world pass us by.

The afternoon sun moved across the sky as we crossed into the outskirts of Washington. More and more tracks started joining ours, crisscrossing each other, electric wires buzzing overhead. Afar off to the right, in the hazy, smoky distance, we saw the tail end of the long lines of passenger cars docked in Union Station. We stood in the doorway watching as the train started to slow down.

"Does it look like we're turning off?" Burt asked uneasily.

I took a quick glance at where he was looking. "Hell no, what're you talking about, we're going right into the station."

"Well, how come then the station's over to the right there and we're peeling off to the left?"

"That's just the main building," I told him, feeling confident, "the freight yards're spread out all over."

"I guess so," he answered, not sounding very sure about it.

We stood and watched as the train slid by the station, passing it on the right, watched as the station slowly passed completely out of view, the train still on the move, heading down towards southeast Washington. Although it wasn't moving with any real speed the train was moving too fast for us to jump.

"She must be going on down to the Navy Yard," I said, cogitating on it.

Burt looked over at me. I was worried and I couldn't help but show it, and that scared him even more.

We sat in the boxcar as the train rolled through the Virginia countryside, not looking at each other, glum and angry and nervous. Burt was more than nervous; scared's more like it. I was scared, too, but not as much, I've hitchhiked more places than him: what goes out must come back, that's one thing you learn being on the road. It was beautiful; rolling country, green hills and leafy trees, horses running behind white fences, like out of a storybook, very pretty to look at if you're not concerned with getting the hell out of it. Neither of us had a watch, so we didn't know how long we'd been riding. A couple of hours, anyway.

Needless to say, the train hadn't been going to the Navy Yard. It bypassed Washington completely, going east of Union Station and then dropping right into Virginia, through Arlington, Fairfax; from the way the sun was dropping it looked to me like it was heading southwest. For all I knew it could be going clear to New Orleans, or Mexico for that matter, I know about hitchhiking but I don't know jack-shit about trains, I've always wanted to, though, like I've always wanted to get away and be on my own for real. It's just that this wasn't the time and place to do it, but beggars can't be choosers. Anyway, we'd have to stop sooner or later.

"Now what, genius?" Burt asked again, staring out the open boxcar door. He's like a stuck needle in a record with that expression. He was freaked out, not even trying to hide it. He may be the pro on the Ravensburg Junior High playground, but out here he was just another scared kid, scared of not knowing where we were going, scared of what would happen to him when he finally got home. I was scared of that, too, but there wasn't anything I could do about it, so I just watched the scenery.

"It's got to stop pretty soon," I told him, like I knew all there was to know about riding freight trains, "we ain't that far out of D.C."

"You don't even know where we're at," he said, totally disgusted.

"The hell I don't."

"Where are we?"

"Somewheres in Virginia."

"Shit." He hocked a big lugy out the door. "That could be anyfuckingwhere."

This was true, so I kept my mouth shut. One thing we had to do was stick together, if we got at each other's throats we'd be doubly fucked.

As we moved south the sun moved west, almost to the ridge of the mountains. I looked out the door. Up about a mile I could see a small switchyard, some boxcars sitting on a side track. Our train started slowing down.

I pointed out the door to Burt, who looked.

"We'll be off this mother in two seconds flat," I told him, feeling pretty smug after all that nervousness. I knew I'd fucked up, kind of anyway, but we could get off now, hitch a ride home, and it would still be better than having got caught back there at the junkyard.

The switchyard was coming up fast now. We stood in the doorway in anticipation. Another minute and it would be going slow enough for us to jump off.

As the train approached the yard (coming to a stop now, in five seconds I was going to yell at Burt to jump), a bum suddenly appeared out of the weeds at the side of the tracks and jumped into our car, moving with an agility that came from years of jumping trains, like the way I move over the obstacles at the Academy. He skittered into our car and gave us a wild look.

"Don't stand in that doorway like that," he yelled urgently, his voice hoarse and shot, "you're a goddamn three-alarm fire with cowbells!"

As we looked at him in puzzlement, frozen for a moment at his unexpected entrance, he grabbed us roughly and hauled us into a dark corner of the boxcar. I turned away from him in disgust as I got hit with a blast of his foul whiskey breath, right in my face. The guy stunk like a pigsty, he probably hadn't taken a bath or brushed his teeth in a month.

I twisted my arm out of his grasp. "Let go, goddamnit, we're getting off here!"

"Are you shitting me?" He pointed outside.

A few cars away, we saw a railroad detective pacing down the line.

"You see that sum'bitch out there?" the bum told us in a deep southern accent, his vocal cords almost shot from all the booze he must've drunk over the years. "They's three of them in this here yard, they'd as soon break your goddamn head as scratch their ass they catch you riding one of their cars. You jump off in this here yard, son, you're committing suicide."

Burt exchanged a fearful glance with me.

"Duck down now and don't breathe," the bum commanded, pulling us further into the car.

We hid behind some crates as the detective peered into the car for a minute before moving on, not seeing us. Almost immediately, the train jerked and started moving again.

Burt turned to me, his eyes as big as dinner plates.

"How the hell are we supposed to get off now?" he cried. He was really shook, beyond normal scared.

"You'll have to wait till she pulls out of the yard before you can jump," the bum told us, leaning back against the wall of the car and sliding down to a comfortable sitting position. He was home, like he was sitting in his living room. In less than thirty seconds, he was fast asleep.

We crabbed to the edge of the car and stood in the doorway. The train was clearing the yard, moving fast, too fast for us to jump out. I turned to look at Burt. He turned away.

We watched the yard vanish in the distance.

It was getting late in the day, the sun sitting on top of the mountains in the west, which I figured to be the Blue Ridge Mountains. I've been here before, with Joe and his folks, to Luray Caverns, it was beautiful up there, we went in the fall when all the leaves were turning, like in a postcard. We'd gone down into the caverns, seen thousands of stalactites and stalagmites, plus the added attraction of about a ton of bat shit on the walls and floors. No bats, though, they only come out at night is what the guide told us.

"You ever been to Luray Caverns?" I asked Burt.

"What kind of stupid question is that?" He was so mad at me he liked to have killed me.

"Just asking. I have, with Joe."

"Big fucking deal." We were sitting on the other side of the boxcar from the bum, who seemed to be sleeping.

"If you'd ever been there you'd know it was a big deal. Miles and miles of caves, really cool ones, you could spend days in there exploring them." I was trying to cheer him up, get his mind off our problem.

"The answer is no."

"Just wondered," I said.

"Just shut the fuck up, Roy, okay?"

"Excuse me for living," I said. He was scared shitless, that's why he was acting so dumb. Like it was all my fault. Nobody made him jump on the train, he could've stayed back there with Joe and taken his medicine. I knew that if he had stayed back there instead of jumping on with me he'd have thought differently, but it wasn't the time to remind him of that.

"Shit," Burt said, looking out the doorway again, "we'll never get off this fucking train."

He was close to breaking down, I could hear it in his voice. That's all I needed, being on a freight train in the middle of nowhere, in the same boxcar with a drunken bum, and my best friend starts crying like a baby.

The bum woke up, glanced over at us, pulled a half-pint from his back pocket, and took a healthy swig. Then he held the bottle up to us, offering it.

I shook my head and turned away. The thought of sharing anything that bum had put his mouth on was enough to almost make me puke my insides out. Burt was turning yellow from the thought.

"Suit yourselfs," he croaked, grinning at us. His teeth, the ones he had left, were coated with years of tobacco-juice stains. He took one last hit and tossed his empty bottle out the car.

"Listen, boy," he told Burt, "this here's the best education money can buy, so you might as well enjoy it while you can; 'cause right now, you ain't goin' nowheres."

Burt and I slumped against the side of the car, as the truth of what he'd said sunk in. Outside, as the night closed in on us, the train continued traveling south into uncharted territory.

TWELVE

The train creaked to a halt, the wheels throwing metal-on-metal sparks as they ground against the tracks. Even before it had stopped completely the bum was wide awake and on his feet. Standing in the doorway, he took one look around outside, threw a hurried "see you in hell, boys," over his shoulder, and jumped to the ground, hitting and rolling heavily. He was probably so drunk from that cheap booze he'd been drinking he hadn't felt a thing.

It was night. The moon was down and the stars lay buried under a thick layer of fog. We didn't know where we were, or what time it was. We'd been lying on our backs, strung-out in the boxcar, for hours.

I walked to the open door and looked out. The train was resting in a small freight depot, on a siding. Up ahead, near the front of the train, there was a water tower standing tall against the darkness, the kind you see in every southern town. I could read the name "Staunton" painted in black paint on the white tank.

We were about one hundred and fifty miles from Washington as the crow flies, which I knew for a fact, because Staunton is the town where Staunton Military Academy, Admiral Farrington's archrival, is located. The catalogues from Farrington had stories and pictures about football and basketball games between the two, because theirs was as intense a rivalry as between Annapolis and West Point, since Farrington is a Navy prep school and Staunton does the same thing for the Army. I'd dreamt of being here, but not under these circumstances.

My mouth tasted like shit. Neither of us had had anything to drink or eat, since we were prisoners on this fucking train, and I was thirsty as hell. My tongue felt like a caterpillar, I was so thirsty. Sometimes the most important thing in your life is something real trivial; right now the most important thing in my life was to have a glass of water.

Burt joined me at the door. He was still pale as a ghost, hardly able to stay on his feet without holding onto the side of the boxcar.

"Let's go," he said, super-anxious. He was as thirsty as me, maybe more, he looked about one heartbeat away from losing it completely, breaking down and bawling like an infant; probably thinking he'd never get home again, see his family, all that shit. I knew I would, and wasn't looking forward to it.

Burt stood in the doorway, ready to jump.

Even though I was thirsty as a motherfucker and wanted off this train, I wasn't leaving. I sat down in a corner, leaning back against the wall.

"What's the matter?" Burt looked back at me, anxiously.

"I ain't going."

"Why not?" I could hear the crying in his voice, it was right under the surface.

"You go ahead if you want to. I'm staying in here."

"What for?" He sounded like he was in second grade.

"I ain't jumping off this train in the middle of the night, for all we know there might be one of those railroad detectives around the corner, waiting to nab our ass."

"That's a bunch of bull," he cried, "that prick was full of shit. Anyway, he jumped out and nothing happened. Jesus Christ, Roy," he whimpered, his voice rising about two octaves, "we can't stay here, what the fuck's wrong with you?"

He was losing it, losing it completely, and it was pissing me off. Being around somebody that scared is like looking in a gas tank with a lighted match to see if there's any fuel inside.

"You're crazy, Roy," he continued. "You've gone plumb loco." He was beaten down completely—his voice sounded like air coming out of an old balloon.

I felt shitty. Burt was my best friend and we were at each other's throats, like we wanted to kill each other. Being on the run like a couple of gypsies can do that to you. But I didn't have a choice—my destiny was ahead of me, down this railroad line.

"I ain't moving until I can see that the coast's clear," I told him in the toughest voice I could muster, trying to stay cool and collected, which wasn't at all the way I felt.

"Well, shit," he moaned. He stood in the doorway, looking out; then he turned back, looking at me like I might change my mind.

"You want to go, go ahead," I told him. I wasn't changing it.

Burt wasn't going anywhere without me, I knew that for sure, and I wasn't leaving this boxcar, not now. As soon as I'd seen that sign on the water tower that read "Staunton" I knew exactly why I was on this train, and where it was taking me. It wasn't an accident, the result of some normal teenage fucking up back there at the junkyard. This was a twist of fate that I had to follow.

It took a while for the train to get moving again. We rode it through the night into the following day without one stop, the two of us not talking to each other the whole time, just sitting in the hot, smelly boxcar. Occasionally one or the other of us would drift off into a troubled sleep and then jerk awake, hot and sweaty with fear. Burt was feeling sorry for himself, wishing he'd never jumped this stupid train, maybe even wishing he'd never met me. I had a feeling that when all this was over it would be the end of the Three Musketeers. Every man for himself, and fuck all the rest.

Finally, around dusk, the train started slowing down. We were coming to a town. I looked out the door to see if there was a water tower. There was: "Randolph" was written on the side in bold letters.

"Goddamn, I'm starving," Burt said, coming up next to me.

I hardly heard him, because my heart was beating a mile a minute. Randolph was the town where Farrington Academy was located.

The train was making for the yard, the middle of it, not a siding. There were quite a few trains parked in it, it must've been a crossroads of some kind.

"My old lady must be worried sick," Burt said.

"She'll get over it," I told him. I knew that was cold, but I couldn't help it. I had more important things on my mind than his mother's feelings.

"Jesus," he said, looking at me, like I looked different somehow, like he didn't know me.

The train ground to a stop, the cars banging against each other. I looked outside. No one seemed to be around.

"See anyone?" Burt asked, trying to be sarcastic, like he could give a shit less; but I knew he was shaking in his boots.

"Don't matter," I told him, "I'm out of here." I dropped to the ground and started running for the edge of the yard.

"Hey, wait up!" he called, more scared that I was going to leave him than he was of any railroad detective who might be lurking in the weeds. He jumped out, hitting the ground hard, and chased after me.

Randolph was one of those picture-postcard southern towns, sleepy and old-fashioned, like it hadn't seen any progress at all for at least fifty years and would be just as happy if it never did.

We passed by a Mobil station a couple blocks down from the train yard and washed up as best we could, first drinking a gallon of water apiece and gargling the puke taste out of our mouths, then checking ourselves out in the grimy mirror over the sink—two road-dirty kids who looked like runaways from reform school.

"We'd better lay low," Burt said, trying to comb his hair with his fingers, which just made it look worse, his cowlick stood up like a rooster's tail, "cop sees us, our ass'll be in the clink." He had his shirt off and was giving himself a sponge bath with some wadded-up paper towels.

"Can't throw you in jail for being dirty," I said. I knew they would, though, they'll do that to kids; they don't like the way you look they'll kick your ass good, just because they feel like it. I'd stripped all the way down to my drawers and was washing myself off from head to toe. It didn't make me look much better, but at least I felt cleaner.

"How much money you got on you?" Burt asked me after I'd dried off and put my clothes back on.

I checked my pockets—a quarter, two dimes, two pennies. He had three dimes.

"We're fucking millionaires," he said, real sarcastic.

I thought on that for a second. "Maybe we could find us some washing machines in some little apartment house," I came up with.

"No fucking way!" he protested, backing away from me. "That's all we need, get arrested in some cracker town, we'd be in jail the rest of our natural lives. You're crazy, Roy."

"Don't get your bowels in an uproar," I told him. "Anyway, we don't have a screwdriver."

"I wouldn't give a shit if we had a stick of dynamite, I ain't breaking the law, not after everything else we've been through." He picked his sticky shirt away from his body. "I sure as hell wish I had me some clean clothes, I feel like I've fallen into a barrel of piss."

We were standing outside the filling station. Even though the sun was almost down it was still hot and humid, as bad as Washington in August.

"Say no more," I told him, coming up with one of my brainstorms.

"Say no more what?"

"See that nice big tree over there?" I asked, pointing across the street to a little park, that had a big white oak in the center and some old wrought-iron benches set out under its shade, "you park your weary ass under that tree and think sweet thoughts until I come back."

"Hey, wait a minute, where're you going?" he asked, his voice all high and scared.

"I ain't gonna leave you, don't worry," I assured him. "Just sit down and rest. What you don't know ain't gonna hurt you." I wasn't going to do anything bad, not really, but I didn't want somebody panicky around me for what I was contemplating— he'd go crazy on me and then we would be up shit's creek without a paddle. "Cool your heels and I'll be back lickety-split," I promised.

He didn't feature letting me out of his sight, but he knew I was going to try something hairy, something he didn't want to be a part of, so he walked across the street and slumped down on one of the benches.

I strolled down the street, turning the corner, looking back one time at Burt, who was staring at me. Even from a distance I could see sorrow written all over his face. That boy was learning a lesson he'd thought he'd wanted but didn't, and he was paying a heavy price for it.

I, on the other hand, was feeling all right. I was on my own, really on my own for the first time in my life, and even though it was tough, scary, and could turn to shit any moment, I was surviving. I was making it in the world.

The block I was walking down was houses, two-story wood, with nice green lawns and well-tended flower beds. A few people were sitting out on their porches, drinking lemonade and watching the world pass by. I waved to them, and they waved back to me. Another neighborhood boy on his way home.

After about two blocks, I saw what I'd been looking for. I glanced around to make sure nobody was watching me suspiciously; but like I said, I was just another kid, invisible. I circled around the side of one of the houses and peeked over the fence, into the back yard.

There wasn't anybody there. More importantly, there wasn't a dog. Nothing but a freshly mowed back yard, some lawn furniture, and a full clothesline, shirts and pants and socks and dresses hanging from it, flapping in the breeze.

I didn't waste any time counting back from a number. I hopped the fence and crabbed over to the clothesline, keeping low to the ground like an Indian scout so if anybody was looking out a window they wouldn't see me. I checked out the man's clothing; it all belonged to a grownup, a few sizes too big for Burt and me, but passable, much better than the grubby rags we were wearing, and anyway beggars can't be choosers.

One more look at the windows. No shadows moving in them, no face looking down. I'm good at telling if someone's spying on me, it's something I've learned over the years from pocketing shit from the dime store. Faster than a speeding bullet I snagged two shirts, two pairs of pants, four socks, and two pair of drawers, boxers, the big billowy kind, which I normally hate like the plague, but this was no time to be choosy. I wrapped everything in a bundle and was back over the fence and down the block like a bat out of hell.

"What'cha got?" Burt asked, sitting up as he saw me strutting towards him, my booty tucked under my arm.

"Your wardrobe, sire," I grinned, unwrapping my package and spreading the clothing out on the grass.

"Where the fuck'd you get this shit?"

"Ask me no questions, I'll tell you no lies."

We ducked under some nearby bushes and changed into our new clothes. They fit us pretty well; the guy who owned them must not have been too tall. Nice stuff, nothing fancy, just right.

"Shit I reckon."

"You trust me now?" I challenged.

"I never said I didn't trust you," he said, trying not to sound defensive.

"But you acted it."

"Do you blame me?"

"Naw, I didn't hardly trust myself," I confessed.

We threw our old, dirty clothes into somebody's trash barrel and headed towards the center of town. I was on a mission, but Burt didn't know it, and it wasn't something I could share with him.

Admiral Farrington Academy was exactly the way it looked in the pictures. Like the Naval Academy, which it had been modeled on over fifty years ago, only smaller. I knew there was a river nearby, because sailing was a big part of what they did—there were sailing photos all over their catalogue. We weren't near that area. We were standing outside the main gate, looking past the stone walls to the dormitories and buildings inside.

"What the fuck is this?" Burt said in this real derisive voice, "one of those stupid military schools my old man's always threatening to send me to if I fuck up too much?"

Parents are always telling their kids that if they fuck up they'll ship their ass to military school. It's like a running joke because nobody I know has the money to go to one even if their parents wanted them to.

"You've got to be pretty smart to go here," I told Burt. I was checking the place out, peering inside. The sun was almost down: I had this strong feeling in my guts that I had to go inside the gates. I had to see it for real, one time.

"Shit. Pretty smart." He hocked a major lugy onto the grass. "Anybody'd want to go to some shithole like this would have to be pretty *dumb,* in my opinion."

"Well, you're entitled to your opinion," I said.

"What, you'd want to go here?" he laughed. "I can just see you in some pissass place like this, you'd walk your ass out in about two seconds flat if they didn't kick you out first. This is a school for losers, man, not guys like us."

I didn't answer that. I kept looking in.

"Come on, let's get the fuck out of here. We need to figure how to get home." He turned away, expecting me to follow.

Instead, I walked through the gates and into the school.

"Where the fuck are you going?" he called when he realized I wasn't right behind his ass.

I wasn't paying him any attention. I kept walking in.

"Oh man. What the fuck!" He hurried in after me, like a puppy dog following his master. Right about now I wished I'd ditched him back there when I'd had the chance. Not forever, just while I was here. I needed something from this place, what it was I didn't know, but I did know I didn't need Burt Kellogg tagging after me like some lost puppy dog, while at the same time putting Farrington down with every single sentence.

"Why don't you wait outside?" I told him.

"What, are you crazy?" He was practically stepping on my heels he was so close behind me.

"Maybe."

"We've got to find something to eat, and we've got to call home," he wailed. "We're in deep shit, Roy, we can't be fucking around some stupid military school."

I turned to him. "Go ahead."

"What?"

"Go find something to eat. I'll catch up to you later."

"Sure, yeah, where?" He was talking fast and high again—just the thought of us separating was giving him a huge case of hemorrhoids.

I was looking from building to building. I knew every one of them, every dorm and classroom, all their names. I knew them like the back of my hand, I'd memorized them while I was looking over the catalogue, studying up for the stuff I had to send them. I hadn't even realized I was doing it until right this second.

I had been accepted to come here in the fall. To be part of it. To have a chance in life, for a change.

Two students came walking towards us. Older guys, seniors or juniors. They were in uniform, their hair cut extra short, their brass so shined-up you could see your face in it. They weren't that much older than Burt and me, just a couple years, if they hadn't been in uniform you couldn't have told the difference between us. Being in uniform made them look older somehow, more grownup, like they had something going in life, a purpose.

As they walked by us they took a look-see at who we were, since we could be two other students who happened to be out of uniform, as it was Easter vacation; a couple of younger Farrington boys, brothers all. One look, though, and they knew we weren't. They bent towards each other and talked, too low for us to hear.

Then they laughed.

My face was burning; I could feel it. They had laughed because they had seen us and knew we weren't from there, we weren't one of them. Definitely not Burt, and not me, either. We were two hicks from the sticks, permanent outcasts.

"God, what a couple of assholes," Burt said, looking at the

two Farrington men as they walked away into the twilight gloom. "Can you imagine having to dress up like that every day and live in a place like this?"

"No," I told him. "I can't imagine that."

It was dark. We had to do something, at least get some food in our bellies before we fainted from starvation, so we headed towards the center of town, which was laid out around a town square, the grass cut as short and precise as a putting green on a golf course, some weather-beaten wood benches clustered around, and the obligatory statue of a Confederate soldier in the center, covered from head to toe with years of bird shit. Every southern town I've ever been in seems to have this same Confederate statue, somebody must've made a thousand of them and gone around the south selling one to a town, so they'd always remember how badly they'd been beaten.

Around the square, on all four sides, were stores, offices, a few restaurants. The commercial section of town spread two blocks in each direction before it petered out into houses. It was the kind of sleepy old town that except for the famous Admiral Farrington Academy, home of future Naval Academy midshipmen—big fucking deal—you could drive through in two minutes flat and hardly know it was there at all.

The first thing I noticed was there was no Little Tavern, no White Palace, no place to eat cheap. The second thing I noticed was that the only grocery store in town was already closed for the day, so we couldn't buy a loaf of bread and some cheap lunchmeat.

Burt wasn't looking at any of that stuff. He hasn't been out on the road like me, he doesn't think about important things like that. As soon as he saw a phone booth he ducked into it and pulled one of our precious dimes out of his pocket.

"What're you doing?" I demanded.

"Calling home."

He dropped the dime. I reached over and jerked down on the cradle.

"You can call home later. Let's get something to eat first." My heart was beating faster than it should have been.

"Listen, my mother'll be worried sick by now," he pleaded. "She can't eat when she's worried."

"She's gone this long without eating," I said firmly. "Another hour ain't gonna make any difference."

I took off down the street, walking fast. Burt followed after me, like I knew he would. He didn't want to, but I wasn't cutting him any slack. I had places to go and things to do before I could even think of going back to my real life.

W e stood outside the larger of the two restaurants, the one that was doing all the business. People came in and out; some families, a lot of old people. It was that kind of town, an old-people kind. Kids hate towns like this, it was even worse than Ravensburg, judging from the little I'd seen of it in the few hours we'd been there. Any kid worth a shit would leave this town in a cloud of dust and a hearty you-know-what about five minutes after graduating high school.

"How about them?" Burt asked, the two of us loitering on the sidewalk, checking out the action, which in this case was a family coming out the restaurant door: mother, father, two little snotnoses, a boy and a girl. The man was connected with Farrington, he had Marine Corps written all over him. A hard-ass to the core, probably sang a chorus of "The Marine's Hymn" after his mandatory once-a-month fuck with the old lady.

I shook my head: "No."

"Why not?"

"Trust me, I know what I'm doing."

A moment later: "Them?"

"I promise, you'll be the first to know."

We hung around. I bummed a couple weeds from a kid our

age who looked like Elmer Fudd; I had to give him a pretty tough look before he'd give them up, but I needed a cig-fix bad, and anyway what's two lousy cigarettes? I'd have done it if he'd asked me and it was in my own town. A kid like that would last about one hour at Ravensburg Junior High, he was lamer even than Sarkind, and he was smoking Old Golds to boot, my least favorite brand, but beggars can't be choosers, definitely not at this point.

An old couple came out of the restaurant. No kids, grandkids, nothing. Just the two of them, almost leaning on each other. Nice clean people, like everyone's favorite grandfolks. I smiled at Burt, flicked my butt into the gutter, and walked over to them.

"Excuse me, ma'am," I said. You talk to them both but you always address the woman.

They turned to me, kind of squinting up their eyes to see if I was someone they knew. They both wore glasses, the kind with the big thick lenses, like after a cataract operation. They probably couldn't see their hands in front of them very good even with those glasses.

"Me and my brother here are on our way to Texas on account of our grandma's dying of cancer and we were robbed of all our money on the train and we haven't had anything to eat for two days now and I was wondering if maybe you could loan us a quarter so's we could buy a loaf of bread to take with us on the train." It came out in one rush, without my even pausing to take a breath.

Burt stared at me, glassy-eyed. He was watching the master at work, he'd never known this kind of stuff about me until now.

"That's terrible," the old lady said, in one of those slow southern-molasses voices. There was a lot of quiver to her voice; they were really old, both of them. "Have y'all informed the police?"

"No, ma'am," I explained, "because it happened yesterday and they'd make us hang around while they looked for the men that robbed us and we've got to get on down to Texas to see our grandmother one last time before she dies which could be any minute now." I was out of breath, they probably took my deep inhale for worry about my poor dying grandmother. They were somebody's grandparents themselves, someday they might be dying and their own grandson could be in this very same predicament.

I heard a noise like somebody choking. It was Burt, who was fighting like a son of a bitch to keep a straight face.

"What about your parents?" the old woman asked. "Aren't they along with you?" She was the talker in the family, that was obvious, the old man could've been deaf and dumb for all I knew.

"No, ma'am, you see our mother's got to stay home and watch our younger brothers and sisters, besides she's got a job which they won't let her out of and they won't give her any time off either, and our father's dead, he died in Korea four years ago, he was a fighter pilot in the Navy, he was shot down on a mission." Butter wouldn't melt in my mouth, I said all this with such a straight face.

The old lady started quivering like a violin. I thought she was going to break down and cry right there on the spot.

"That's terrible," she told us, patting us both on our heads like we were cocker spaniels. "You poor, poor boys."

We ate everything except the tail and the hoofs, I mean we chowed down royally. The old couple sat at the table watching us, beaming like a pair of cats that ate the canary. I finished my apple pie a la mode and burped into my napkin so's not to offend the old folks. Burt was still finishing up, fighting like crazy to keep up with me, even though he was stuffed to the gills. Nobody can keep up with me when it comes to eating, I've got the original hollow leg.

"Oh, man," I sighed, "that's about the best meal I've ever eaten in my whole life." As I reached over for the last of my milk, my third glass, the waitress turned up with another piece of pie and plunked it down in front of me.

"Now don't you be telling me you can't eat one more piece," the old lady scolded in advance, seeing the bloated expression on my face, "this restaurant bakes their pastries fresh every morning, even Sunday."

What was I going to tell her? I picked up my fork and dove in.

We stood outside the restaurant. I felt like I had three bowling balls in my stomach—if I'd even looked at one more of anything I'd have barfed my whole dinner up on the sidewalk. Burt was actually green, leaning up against a lamp pole.

It was kind of awkward, standing there, us and the old folks. They had to go, it was way past their bedtime, but here we were, two kids out in the world on our own, taking the long train ride to our dying grandma's house all the way down in Texas. They were feeling guilty about leaving us alone; if we weren't careful they'd be bringing us home and putting us in a nice warm bath and a soft feather bed and the first thing out of the box they'd be wanting to adopt us.

Finally the old lady cut the cord.

"Y'all better be getting back to the station, you don't want to be missing your train," she counseled us.

"Yes, ma'am," I agreed quickly; now that they'd fed us they were getting on my nerves, being so grandparently and all, you can only take so much of that shit, "and thank you ever so much."

"Thank you, ma'am, and you too, sir," Burt chimed in.

The old man nodded his head in thanks. It was about the first gesture he'd made that showed he actually was aware that we were there.

"Good luck, boys, and God bless you," the old lady said.

They started to walk away, arm in arm, as if they might fall down otherwise.

"Wait a second," I called out.

They turned back to us. I ran over to them.

"Excuse me, ma'am, do you have a pencil and a piece of paper?"

"I believe so," she said, fishing both out of her purse.

"If you would please write down your name and address, ma'am," I told her, "so we can pay you back when we get home."

"There's no need for that," she said, clearly taken aback. I guess she wasn't used to politeness from teenagers.

"Please, ma'am," I told her, "we don't take no handouts in our family."

"I understand," she said, scrawling her name and address down on the paper and handing it to me. I glanced at it—chicken scratches even the FBI wouldn't be able to make out. I put it in my pocket.

"Thanks again, ma'am, it was a pleasure making your acquaintance."

She was beaming like a kid on Christmas morning. She came over to me and gave me a big hug and a kiss, just like a grandmother does. She gave Burt one, too.

"Now you boys hurry along," she told us.

She took the old man's arm. They walked down the sidewalk away from us. They were feeling good, you could see it radiating off them, they'd done their Christian duty and a little bit of the world was better off for it.

Burt and I watched them go.

"So long, suckers," I said, after they were out of earshot. Being as old as they were, that wasn't far.

"Hey, they were real nice," Burt protested.

He was right, but it didn't matter. I didn't want anybody taking care of me, not like that, getting all grandmotherly over me just because they bought me a meal. It makes me too beholden, and I don't want to be obligated to anyone—I already have enough shit to deal with without adding any more to it.

I crumpled up the paper with their name and address on it and threw it away.

"Big fucking deal," I told Burt. "I guess you're going to call your mommy now and tell her how much you miss her and what a bad boy you've been." I was in a foul mood, that's all there was to it.

"Damn, Roy, what's got into you?"

I turned and walked down the street at a fast pace. Burt immediately caught up with me.

"Come on, Roy, what's eating you?"

I spun on him.

"You fucking crybaby, you're gone from home two goddamn days and you're crying for your mother. You know how many guys would love to be in your shoes? About the whole damn school, that's all. Shit, Burt, you've lived your whole life at home. How often do you get to ride around the country on a freight and have to make it on your own?" I spat onto the sidewalk. "You go ahead and call if you want, but I ain't about to hang around this pathetic excuse for a town."

I turned and walked away, heading in the direction of the train station. Burt hesitated for a moment—I could almost hear his brain working, even though my back was to him—then he caught up with me, like I knew he would.

"Hell, this is the life, ain't it?" he sang out.

The train rambled through the Tennessee countryside. We'd gone back to the yards and found the same train we'd been on, the same boxcar even. This boxcar was something we knew, I can't explain the feeling, but we felt safe there. The train was getting ready to leave—some men were in the process of checking it over, so we hid in the tall grass from them until they passed by. One of them definitely did look like a railroad detective, a mean-looking SOB, packing a gun on his hip. Dodging the railroad workers gave our journey a greater sense of adventure, like we truly were runaway boys, heading out into the great unknown.

I stood in the door of the boxcar, looking out upon the rolling hills, which were green with spring and clustered with wildflowers of every color you could imagine, so inviting you wanted to dive into it like a swimming pool. The weather was hot and humid already, barely eight in the morning from what I could tell looking at the position of the sun in the sky. By noon the boxcar would be a furnace. I still didn't know what it was exactly that I was looking for, but hopefully I'd find it sooner than later and we'd be off the train for good.

Way off in the distance I saw a rider on a beautiful horse, dark brown with a white star between his eyes and white stockings on all four legs, a racehorse like the kind they have in the Kentucky Derby. The rider was a boy, teenaged and buck-naked, urging on the horse as it galloped along parallel to the tracks, as if they were racing the train. As I watched, I could see that I was the rider, galloping along with the wind. Behind me on the horse, holding on tight to my waist, her head pressed against my back, was Melanie, also naked, holding onto me tight, her titties pressed hard against my back, her long girlish hair strung out behind her like fire burning in the wind.

The sight of this dream, so real in front of my eyes, caught my breath and held it trapped in my throat; staring out at the passing fields as I was, it felt as if I was seeing my life passing before me, not as a dream, but for real. I blinked and looked again, and as I did the image started fading, becoming less and less concrete, the colors turning to smoke, so transparent I could see through all three of them, rider and passenger and horse, all of it fading and fading like a rising mist, until the two riders galloped off into the hills; and as they rode out of sight they completely faded away.

I watched the mirage disappear, for a while staring out at the countryside going by; then I turned and looked back at Burt. He was sleeping the sleep of the dead, he hadn't seen any of it, neither the dream or the reality of the dream. I *had* seen myself out there, it may have all been in my head but that didn't make it one heartbeat less real.

I slumped down against the side of the door and closed my eyes, listening to the music of the train as it kept moving on down the tracks.

THIRTEEN

When the train stopped again we were in Chattanooga, Tennessee, a big old city, the smokestacks blasting away a mile a minute. The freight yard was huge, the biggest one I'd ever seen, even bigger than the one in Washington. They would have railroad bulls here for sure, so we jumped the train before it came to a complete stop and hopped the tracks that crisscrossed the acres and acres of cars that were sitting on sidings, waiting to be loaded up and sent back out.

Dusk in the south: the sun a huge orange ball hanging over the city, slowly sinking down like it was falling into tar. We drank out of a water bucket from a common ladle that was used by railyard workers, maybe even colored as well as white, there weren't any White Only signs on it like we'd seen in other places, bathrooms and drinking fountains and things like that, and anyway beggars can't be you-know-whats—the two of us gulping down the cool flinty spring water and dumping ladlefuls over our heads to cut the heat, picking the grunge out of our teeth with matches, then strolling into town, looking for a mark. We had the hang of it now, we were starting to believe we were seasoned veterans, not just me but Burt, too, he had the traveling strut, the don't-fuck-with-me swagger you get when you know you can outwit the local yokels with one hand tied behind your back.

Getting into town was no problem; finding the kind of people we could hit on comfortably took some time. Finally, we found a restaurant that suited our needs—family-style, good but not fancy, lots of traffic going in and coming out.

". . . and our grandmother's dying in Texas and we've got to get down there as soon as we can," I told our "prospects." They were another old couple like the ones we'd conned back in Randolph, clean and neat but not rich-looking, the kind of people that'll go to a restaurant and order the same chicken-fried steak in country gravy, mashed potatoes, and wax beans that they could make for themselves at home.

The old man looked Burt and me up and down. We'd been extra-polite, calling them "sir" and "ma'am," shucking and jiving them like a couple of field hands asking the massa for an extra hunk of salt pork.

"That's a crying shame, boys," the old fellow told us. He reached into his pocket and nonchalantly pulled out a roll that could choke a steer—he must've had a couple hundred bucks on him, easy. He might've looked like a farmer and dressed like one, him and the missus both, but he wasn't any hayseed, not with a wad of cash on him like that.

He wet his thumb and forefinger and started peeling off a couple fives; then hesitated.

"Whereabouts in Texas did you say your ol' granny lives?"

he asked, staring at Burt, like he wanted Burt to answer instead of me, since as usual I'd been doing all the talking.

"She lives down by . . ." I started to say, but he cut me off with an upraised palm.

"Where was that?" he asked Burt, shooting me a look that said "keep it shut."

"Um . . ." Burt was sweating; he was okay hanging with me, but since we'd been on the road, talking to strangers made him uncomfortable. At home he had a mouth on him big as a manhole cover, but we were a long ways from home.

The old man stood there waiting, the two fives sticking up out of his fingers the way you'd hold a smoke.

"New Orleans. That's it, she lives in New Orleans," Burt sang out, "just outside," he added, in an attempt to be casual.

One thing I know is geography, from reading all the encyclopedias, and I don't remember New Orleans ever being in Texas.

The old man nodded and smiled.

"I think I can help you boys. Wait right here a minute."

He walked away from us, heading in the direction of a policeman who was walking his beat down the block.

"Hey, where're you going?" I called.

The old man stopped the policeman and said something to him.

That's all I needed. "Move it!" I yelled at Burt, pushing past him so fast I almost knocked him ass over teakettle as I hightailed it down the street in the opposite direction, bumping into passersby as I barrel-assed away from the cop.

Burt was right on my tail, breathing like a racehorse. Behind us I heard the policeman blowing his whistle, but by then we were around the corner, and we didn't stop running until we'd skedaddled half-a-dozen blocks and were way out of that section of town.

"New Orleans," I gasped, holding my side as I braced myself against the side of a building. "New fucking Orleans is in Louisiana, you dumb shit," I railed at him, "don't you know anything? We had U.S. geography last year, for Chrissakes."

"So I'm not a genius at geography," Burt wheezed back. He was breathing harder than I was, bent over double, like he was coming on to a heart attack, which he might have been, with all the running and the fear.

"Now what, genius?" he panted.

"I'll figure something out." I was getting sick of this "genius" bullshit he was laying on me, especially since compared to him I really was a genius. "Let's went, there's too many cops around here."

We padded off down the street like a couple of beat dogs with their tails dragging between their legs. That was us, two beaten dogs looking for a hole to hide in.

We had no money, and we were hungry, really hungry. And to make matters even worse, we had somehow managed to stumble into the colored section of town.

At least it was warm. That was the only saving grace. The weather had brought many of the locals out—big old fat women wearing print dresses and carpet slippers, reclining in the windows of their houses looking out at the passing scene, raggedy-assed kids playing stickball and hopscotch in the streets, groups of tired-looking men sitting on stoops and slouched in doorways, drinking and talking.

We ambled on down the street, trying to look casual, like walking in a colored district was no big thing to us. Burt was hugging my ass like he was my shadow; I could feel he thought that if we got two feet apart he'd get snatched up and spirited away for one of those voodoo rites his brother was always jawing about.

"I don't like it around here," he said in a hoarse whisper, "let's go someplace else."

I glanced over at him. He was sweating bullets.

"In a while," I told him.

"Jesus, Roy, there's a million of 'em here."

"Don't get your bowels in an uproar. They don't give a shit about you."

"Fuck," he muttered under his breath, tagging after me.

I knew what he was thinking. He was thinking I was a goddamned bastard is what was in his teenage mind—thinking that jumping that freight train was the biggest mistake of his young life and that once he got home he'd never pull another stunt like that again, that facing the junkyard watchman, especially since he was a white boy and the watchman was a nigger, wouldn't have been anything compared to the ordeal he was going through now.

He was right—for him. I wasn't doing a very good job of taking care of him, which I should have been, because I was the one with the experience and I was the one who'd gotten us into this mess in the first place. The problem was, I had more important things on my mind than wiping his sorry ass. There was something about being in the midst of all these colored folk that was intriguing to me, beyond my understanding. I *wanted* to be here, plain and simple. I didn't know why, but at this moment in my life it felt like the right place to be. So I pretended like I didn't hear his mutterings, and kept on walking.

"Let's get out of here, Roy!" Burt hissed in my ear. If nothing else, he certainly was persistent. "These coons make me nervous."

"You're scared of your own shadow, nothing's going to happen."

"I've heard stories."

"Like what?"

I was actually having a good time, considering. I was peering into stores, even "howdying" people on the street. Some people looked at me kind of strange, some people said "hello" back. I felt the same way I'd felt in the bar back in D.C., when I'd met Ruby; on guard, but no real fear.

Burt obviously didn't share my good feelings.

"All kinds of stuff," he whimpered, "you know what I'm talking about." He was sticking to me like glue, not even Superman could've pulled us apart.

"That's all bullshit," I scoffed.

"Yeah, well I've heard some pretty weird shit."

"Uh-huh, and you still believe in Santa Claus too, don't you?" I was taunting him, I didn't mean to, I knew he was scared shitless, but I couldn't help it, the way he was bugging me and carrying on like a crybaby, like Sarkind would do. Burt was my friend, he was supposed to have balls, and here he was pussying out on me.

"Well, I'm getting out of here."

"Go ahead," I challenged him, walking right along, "I ain't stopping you." This was getting old already; if he was going to do it, he should fucking do it. "Be a man," I wanted to tell him, I wanted to shake it into him, "be in charge of your life, even if you're a kid you can be in charge of your life."

He didn't leave my side. Being separated from me was scarier for him than staying here, even though he really does believe all that voodoo shit his brother's laid on him.

Down the block, isolated between two vacant lots overgrown with weeds, stood a big old wooden church, built on concrete blocks like they build them in the south, the paint peeling and cracking, the front steps sagging. It definitely had seen better days, but it was solid and impressive despite the wear and tear; the kind of building you knew would tell a lot of interesting stories if only it could talk.

People were coming to the church from all directions; men, women, and children, from babes-in-arms to great-grandfolks tottering along on their canes, all dressed in their Sunday-go-to-meeting dress-ups. They came walking down the sidewalks, meeting and greeting each other outside on the cracked pavement before going into the church. All of them colored folks, of course. Most of the women were carrying dishes of food, covered platters and bowls—meats, casseroles, salads, everything.

My mouth got to watering, smelling all that good country cooking. These may have been city colored people, but you could tell they'd come from the country, not only in how they dressed, but in the smell of their cooking. I've smelled cooking like that all my life, it's the best kind, especially when you're almost dying of starvation.

"Goddamn, that smells so good," Burt moaned.

"Tell me about it." My stomach was twisted up in knots, so powerful were the aromas wafting off that food. Then a brainstorm hit me. "What's today?"

"I don't know," came his surly reply. "Why?"

"I'll bet you it's Good Friday!" I yelped, suddenly excited. If it was, it meant we'd been gone from home for six whole days, a week almost. By now there were probably sheriffs looking for us all up and down the Eastern Seaboard. For the first time since we'd jumped that train, what we had done hit me like a ton of bricks.

It scared me, to tell you the truth. There was going to be hell to pay on the day of reckoning, of that I had no doubt. Thinking back on it, the bright move would've been to have gotten off the train back in Staunton, when we had the chance; but none of it had seemed real then, not *real* real like now. And anyway, I was on my mission—what I *should* have done and what I *had* to do were two very separate and different things.

Burt broke my daydream: "So what?"

"Come on," I urged, grabbing him and pulling him along.

I ran towards the church, clutching Burt by the collar. A few of the parishioners glanced at us, but nobody paid any special attention. We'd seen a few other white people on the streets—it wasn't like nobody with white skin ever came down here. All the turmoil was inside our own heads, it was our *fears* about being around colored people, the *fear* more than the *reality*, that was the real problem.

We cut around the side, out of sight from people on the sidewalk. The weeds were almost over our heads and full of trash: the locals used this lot for a dump.

"You smell what I smell?" I asked. We were parked under an open window—the evening breeze was carrying the commingling smells of the food out of the church, right by our twitching nostrils.

"Yeah, I smell it, so what?"

"That's our dinner you're smelling is what."

That stopped Burt cold in his tracks. "Oh no. Not me."

"Ain't you hungry?"

"Not hungry enough to try and steal food off a nigger church. Never in a million years."

"I'll do it myself then," I informed him. "Give me a boost."

Burt looked around furtively, like he was expecting some heavy black hand to come down on his shoulder any second and carry him away to depths unknown.

"Come on," I snapped my fingers, "time's awasting."

He made a stirrup with his hands. I stepped in, and he hiked me up. Real carefully, I lifted my head up over the sill to eyeball height and looked in the window.

Several long tables were stretched out right near the window, groaning under the weight of the food laid out on them. It was so appetizing it brought drool to my mouth. I tried leaning in to snatch one of the dishes, but they were tantalizingly out of reach—so near and yet so far.

I dropped to the ground, licking my chops.

"Take a look," I said.

"Roy . . ."

"Come on, you can look at least."

"Fuck. All right," saying it like I was pointing a gun at his head and commanding him to pull the trigger.

I cupped my hands together. Burt stepped on and I lifted him up.

"Jesus Christ!" he exclaimed as soon as he looked in.

"Keep it down," I instructed him, giving him another second to whet his appetite before dropping him to the ground beside me.

"That's more good-looking grub than I've ever seen in my life," he whispered, the saliva drooling out of his mouth like mine had, his hunger beginning to overcome his fear.

"No shit, Sherlock."

"What if we get caught?" he asked, still scared. He didn't know whether he was more scared or hungry, but he was willing for me to talk him into being more hungry.

I had a plan. "We'll wait out here till their service starts, then sneak a couple plates out the back door. They'll never notice a couple less plates with all that food."

He nodded—the hunger had won out over the fear. We hunched down in the weeds, waiting to hear voices in prayer, our own silent prayers already repeating in our heads.

It seemed like an eternity before the congregation started their service but in truth it couldn't have been more than twenty minutes; it just felt like it was taking so long because we were famished out of our gourds. I didn't know what exactly was going on in there, but it sounded like they were having a good old time with their worshiping.

None of these happy sounds were doing anything for Burt. He was a hungry and scared white boy who wanted to fill his belly and get the fuck out of here.

"Come on, man," he implored me, "let's do it and bail."

"Don't get your bowels in an uproar," I soothed him. I was starving as bad as him, but I was enjoying listening to the singing too much to get the deed over and done with lickety-split. "Couple more minutes," I cautioned, "so we're sure it's safe."

He muttered some pissed-off lament and slumped against the side of the church.

There was a momentary break in the service; then the singing started up again, and I knew we couldn't postpone making our move any longer. I counted backwards from a hundred, then from fifty, then from twenty.

"Let's went," I whispered, nudging Burt out of his stupor.

Real quietly, like two Indian scouts, we crept around to the front of the church, checking up and down the street to make sure nobody was watching us suspiciously. Satisfied that the coast was clear, we each took a deep breath, I cracked the door, and we snuck inside.

The church was packed to the rafters. From the looks of it every colored person from this part of town was present and accounted for, singing and clapping and shouting hallelujah to the Lord. Even some of the old drunks who had been loitering out on the sidewalk earlier, drinking Country Club malt liquor and Thunderbird wine, were here now, praising Jesus and testifying.

I double-checked the situation one last time, to make sure the coast was clear. Everyone's back was to us. Tiptoeing as quietly as we could, we approached the table that was groaning under the weight of the food.

Burt grabbed the nearest platter and turned to run, but after all this time of going without I wanted to make sure we selected the cream of the crop. I started lifting lids off the various covered dishes, checking them out.

"Come on," Burt hissed, holding his plate of whatever. He was about to piss his pants with fear and here I was, fussing over the menu.

"Roy, come on," he hissed again in a fierce whisper. I could almost hear the tears in his voice.

"Just a sec," I whispered back, waving him off. There were so many good dishes in front of me I was having a hard time making up my mind: fried okra, fried catfish, pork chops in country gravy (one of my very personal favorites), scalloped potatoes, slow-cured baked ham: I was getting delirious just being close to all this good food. What I really wanted was to take some of this and some of this and some of this; but this time beggars had to choose. I finally settled on the pork chops and the okra, because I love them both, although I was leaving plenty of dishes I love about as much.

We turned to go—and we froze. Standing in front of us, square in the middle of the doorway, no more than ten feet away, blocking any chance of escape, was a large, middle-aged colored man, dressed all in black except for his starched white shirt.

I didn't know whether to shit or go blind. The way Burt was trembling, standing next to me, he was likely to do both.

Real slowly, I turned and looked behind me. Everybody in the church was staring at us.

"Whatever you do, boys," the man told us in this deep, melodious voice that sounded like it was coming from the bottom of a barrel, "don't be dropping those plates. Those are offerings to the Lord you're bearing."

Reverend Williams—he was the actual preacher, the boss-man himself—*assisted* us (as he called it; he could've called it something else but he was a preacher and must've been practicing turning the other cheek) in putting the food back from where we'd taken it. The good reverend stood tall in the pulpit. Really tall, he must've gone six-four, two-fifty; he would've been a great defensive end for the Redskins, who could use some help. Burt and I stood on either side of him, his heavy arms on our shoulders framing each of our bodies. He was being a shepherd, holding us tight—he was also insuring that we didn't take off like two bats out of hell, which I have to admit had crossed my mind.

Burt was scared so bad I wouldn't have been surprised to see some wet Tootsie Rolls oozing out the bottoms of his pant legs. This was his worst nightmare come true: a captive in a nigger church, waiting to have the voodoo put on him, to be drawn and quartered, his heart torn out and eaten raw, his blood drunk in some kind of sacrificial native ritual.

I, on the other hand, wasn't all that scared; I mean I was scared, I'm not going to bullshit and say I wasn't scared, I was damn scared, but I was scared a lot less than I'd thought I would be, which came as a surprise. I had been scared; my heart had practically jumped out of my throat when I'd seen that big motherfucker preacher. After all, we'd been caught red-handed stealing food from them, not only from them but from their *church*, stealing from God, the way Reverend Williams had put it. And even though I'd started being around colored people more, up in The Heights that time I'd been chased over the tracks by the junkyard dog, and at the bar with Ruby (not to mention her bed), I was ignorant of their lives—for all I knew they hated white boys as much as most white boys I knew hated them, that they, meaning the entire congregation, not only the men but the women and children, too, would be more than happy to have an excuse to tear us limb from limb.

It sure would've happened if the situation was reversed. Somebody colored wandering into a church in Ravensburg, any church, would've been courting a shitload of pain. Being in God's house wouldn't have made one tiny bit of difference, because that was on everybody's minds—the fear that had been festering for centuries, since before America was founded, probably, but the last couple of years that fear had really flamed up, ever since the schools in D.C. had integrated—that after the schools it would be the churches, and after that it would be one small step to coloreds wanting to marry whites, because everybody knows the one thing colored men want more than anything in the world is white pussy: to a nigger, possessing a white woman is the ultimate, even better than driving a tricked-out Cadillac.

Everybody knows that. The southern white boys' catechism.

But none of that happened—the tearing-limb-from-limb shit or any kind of blood rituals, either. We were strangers in their church; even though we had been caught red-handed stealing from them, we were still two boys who were scared and hungry and needed a helping hand.

That was the official line, anyway. Reverend Williams's words.

Unofficially, we were getting some mighty dirty looks. Everyone was eyeballing us with great intensity, and nobody was smiling—there wasn't a friendly look out there. Some of the younger men were looking downright unhappy about the whole affair; but at least they weren't beating our tails from here till next Tuesday, which they had every right to do.

"We are blessed this night," Reverend Williams boomed out to the throng, "with two young visitors come all the way from Washington, D.C. . . ."

There was a chorus of "amens" and "wells" on that; Washington is the promised land to a lot of colored people from the south; many of these folks staring at us would have friends and relatives who had migrated up there.

". . . come all the way from Washington," he repeated in his rich, heavy voice, "on their way to Texas, who have stopped here at our humble church to share our worship with us. So let us welcome them with open arms and open hearts."

"Get rid of 'em!" came a yell from the middle of the room —a man's voice. "This ain't no white man's church!"

There followed a low undercurrent of mutterings, agreements. This could get ugly fast, I realized. Maybe Burt had been right all along.

That got me to shaking. I looked over at Burt, behind Reverend Williams's back. He was flat scared to death. Then I felt the reverend's hand clutch my shoulder, hard.

"Let he who is without sin cast the first stone," he thundered.

He glared out at his congregation. The mutterings settled down. It became very quiet, very fast.

"Is that the best we can do?" Reverend Willams implored his people. "Cast them out into the streets, hungry and alone, because of the injustices others have done unto us?"

I could hear people's voices, their low breathing, the uncomfortable shifting in their seats.

"Because we have been beaten low, must we do the same? Must we stoop to the same depths as the whites who beat us do? Or should we remember that this is the day Our Lord was crucified for our sins, and raise ourselves to His standards?"

A whole bunch of "amens" answered that.

I took a deep breath. It wasn't going to turn ugly. This man lived what he preached—I could feel the goodness flowing from his touch into me. We had been saved.

Reverend Williams turned to Burt and me and gave us each a smile. It was a nice, warm smile, a smile that said "it's okay, boys, you're safe here now"; but it also said "I know this game, so don't for a minute think you've pulled the wool over my eyes."

Watching these folks pray was better than going to the movies. We stood off to the side, staring wide-eyed as the church rocked with singing, praying, and witnessing, people jumping up and yelling how they'd found Jesus, how Jesus had cured them of every ailment under the sun, what a friend they had in Jesus, all that good shit. They had a whole rhythm 'n' blues band up there along with the choir; not only an organ, but drums, too, played by a young guy who looked like he'd be comfortable sitting on stage with Fats Domino, also a woman wearing a washboard on her chest who played it Cajun-style with a couple of spoons, keeping time with the drummer, plus an electric guitar and bass. I mean it was rocking, if my sister had been here she'd have jumped up and commenced to dancing.

After awhile Reverend Williams delivered his sermon and it was powerful, about prodigal sons and living by the golden rule and how all men are brothers, which, he reminded the congregation, was especially important to remember during this holiday season when we celebrate that Jesus Christ died for our sins, *all* of us, he emphasized; I knew he'd thrown those lines in to cover me and Burt being there among them. He just didn't talk his sermon, either, he sang some of it, he'd be preaching his lungs out and then all of a sudden he'd break out into song for several lines. He had a terrific voice, like that singer from "Ol' Man River." It gave me goose bumps listening to him preaching and singing, you almost felt Jesus in the room with us.

As I said, I've never had much truck with religion; it's one of the few areas where me and my old man are in agreement, that old gloom and doom stuff they cram down your throat. Standing in this colored church, though, listening to the preaching and singing and testifying, I didn't feel doomed. I felt good, like life wasn't so bad, not if people like this, who one way or the other got the shit kicked out of them every day of their lives, could be happy, even if for just these moments.

"This is great, ain't it?" I smiled at Burt, nudging him with my elbow, trying to get him to shed that black cloud he was carrying around with him.

"So niggers got rhythm," he spat at me in a whisper so no one would hear, not buying into any of this, "big fucking deal."

"Jesus, man," I implored him, "where's your sense of fun?"

"You call this fun?" he asked, talking low out the side of his mouth so no one else would hear, not that they could, they were raising the rafters, their singing was so loud. "Being held captive in a nigger church?"

"Looks like fun to me."

"You've always been weird, Roy," he said, glancing at me sideways, making sure he kept his eye on things, in case one of them got it in his head to jump him with a knife or something, like anyone would do that in a church, "but back home it was funny-weird. Now it's scary-weird."

"Hey, fuck you, too," I told him, moving away slightly.

"They're niggers, Roy," he said, his voice flat.

"You're gonna eat their food, ain't you?"

"Only 'cause I'm starving and don't got a choice."

I shook my head sadly. He hadn't gotten it, not at all. Not the train jumping, the adventure of almost getting caught, even the getting caught. We'd been gone a week and I was changed forever; I didn't know how or why, but it was inside me, moving and growing like something alive.

All this experience had been for Burt had been six days of fear and homesickness.

I felt sorry for him. We'd paid a shitload of dues these past six days. You want to get something for your money when you go through that kind of hell, and he hadn't.

Chow time. They sat us smack in the middle of one of the long tables that had been set up down in the basement, our plates filled with more food than either of us, even me, the kid with the hollow leg, could possibly eat. I was in hog heaven—I'd basically forgotten that I was surrounded by a sea of black faces, because I was digging in with both hands, barely chewing a mouthful before shoveling in the next, dipping my bread in the gravy, forking up huge portions of mashed potatoes, pork chop, chicken-fried steak, catfish, two or three other kinds of fish I'd never seen but tasted delicious, vegetables by the dozens, it went on and on.

Burt sat next to me, of course. He'd have sat on my lap if I'd let him. Despite his feelings, he was eating as hard and fast as I was, matching me forkful for forkful. All around us people were talking, laughing, gossiping, passing plates of food back and forth, having a high time.

"You ain't eaten none of my sweet-potato casserole," a huge lady said, standing behind me with a big bowl of candied yams in her monstrous arms, "I'm famous for this and you're passing it by," then immediately, without waiting for me to tell her I just hadn't gotten around to it yet (because I couldn't talk with a mouthful of food, it wouldn't have been polite), dumping a huge portion of the stuff right on top of everything else on my plate.

"You eat every bite now," she smiled, showing a whole set of gold false teeth, "it's guaranteed to grow hair on your chest." She was laughing her big old head off to beat the band. Everybody around us was laughing with her, people looking at us to see what was so funny. I would've laughed, too, except I would have sprayed a mouthful of food all over the room. "You, too," she commanded Burt, giving him an equal portion.

The women, in general, were being nicer to us than the men were. I could understand that—they were mothers, they had kids. There were boys here Burt's and my age. Some of these women probably worked for white families and were around white children.

Women are nicer than men generally, anyway. I know my mom would've treated a colored kid a lot nicer than my old man would.

"Beats hell out of Ravensburg, don't it?" I nudged Burt.

He didn't answer; just grunted and kept on eating, like it was his last meal on earth. After they stuffed him like a Christmas goose they'd cook him up was the way he was imagining it. I wanted to shake him, to say "goddamn, man, it's only people," but that would've scared him even more, so I left him alone and let the tide of good feeling carry me along.

That was it—I was sitting in this Negro church, surrounded by two hundred colored people, and I was happy. I felt good around these people, like I belonged, as much as I belong anywhere. I could see there were a lot of things about colored people that were good, maybe even better than some things about white people.

And that got me to thinking, pretty deep. I don't want to be colored, not even for an instant. I wouldn't wish being a nigger on my worst enemy, not even Danny Detweiler, but I felt comfortable here, in a weird way better than I sometimes do back home, with all the crap going on there. What I realized was, all the bullshit I'd heard all my life about Negroes was just that: bullshit.

Even though it was night there was still some pink in the sky from the factory smokestacks that pump twenty-four hours a day. Everything was finished now—the service, the singing and testifying, the incredible meal, then more singing after the meal, which had been as much fun as any of the other stuff, they sang all those old Negro gospel songs, and then while they were cleaning up the remains of the dinner everybody socialized with everybody else, old folks with kids, men with women, friends greeting friends.

People headed home toting their empty plates, drifting off in groups into the darkness. Reverend Williams stood in the doorway, saying "Praise Jesus" and "God bless" to each of his parishioners as they left.

Then only a few churchwomen were still there, doing the last of the cleanup. I helped out some; I ain't too proud to sweep a floor or wash some dishes. It seemed the least I could do, after eating that bodacious meal. Burt was antsy, hopping from one foot to the other, wanting to get out of there; he'd had his fill of food and then some, he hadn't been killed or any of that gruesome stuff he'd imagined, he wanted to be gone, right now.

I hung back. I still wasn't ready to leave.

Reverend Williams said his last good-nights and walked over to us.

"I trust you young men enjoyed yourselves, spending a few hours in the Lord's company."

"Yeah," I told him enthusiastically, "it was great, the churches we got at home you can't even scratch yourself even if you've got an itch."

That tickled him. He smiled like I'd cracked a good joke.

"Thanks, it was really nice," Burt added dutifully. He turned to me. "We got to be going."

"Naw, there ain't no hurry."

"We've got to be moving on, Roy, they'll be expecting us."

The whimper was strong in his voice again, I could almost hear the tears.

"Who's expecting us?" I asked him innocent-like. I didn't want to be this way with him, I knew I shouldn't be, he was looking to me for protection, and I was fucking him over. I didn't want to, I really didn't, but I couldn't help myself.

Nervously he replied, shooting the reverend a look: "You know, down in Texas and all."

I scratched my nose—I had come to a decision. "Why don't you go on ahead?"

He didn't understand what was happening. Reverend Williams looked at us, from Burt to me and back.

"Go on," I told Burt, "I'll catch up with you later."

I wasn't leaving. That's the way it was.

Burt looked like he might cry.

"Go ahead if you're going," I told him irritably.

Burt looked at me like he'd never seen me before; then he started down the sidewalk, his head hanging low like he was on his way to the electric chair.

Reverend Williams stood over me. "Shouldn't you be joining your brother?" he asked with concern. He placed his big hand on my shoulder.

"He's not my brother." I had to tell someone the truth, I'd been living in this bullshit too long, I had to get rid of it. "We don't have a grandmother in Texas, either. I made all that up."

"I know that," he said. He did, too, he'd known it from the get-go, I knew it now; I knew everything. "But still," he continued, "you don't want to be leaving him."

"Yes I do, too. All he wants is to go home."

"You should go home with him," he instructed me.

"I don't feel like going home," I pleaded. "Why can't I stay here with y'all, just for a few days? Then I'll go home. They don't care anyway, I won't be no trouble to you, I promise." I was begging as hard as a puppy in a pound but I didn't care, I didn't want to leave—I couldn't, I wasn't ready.

Reverend Williams regarded me for a minute.

"You can't stay here any longer, son."

That was that. We stared at each other in silence for a moment—then he ushered me out the door and closed it firmly behind me.

I slowly walked down the steps. About a block away I saw Burt, waiting for me.

We walked down a residential street like the one we lived on back in Ravensburg; white, working-class, common. It was after midnight. The street was dark, empty, lifeless.

"I'm tired of all this walking," Burt said. He was tired of everything, all he wanted was to be home, safe in his own bed.

"Yeah," I answered by rote. I didn't care anymore.

"Niggers," he muttered.

"What about 'em?"

He gave me a look, like "you've got to ask?"

"What about 'em?" I asked again. "You didn't like that church service? You didn't like that food? Shit, I thought it was great," I went on, getting excited again, remembering it.

"Yeah, you would," he shot back.

"How could you not've liked that?" I didn't get it, I knew he was tired and scared, but he wasn't brain-dead.

"I hated it, okay?" He was almost yelling. "I hated being in that church, I hated eating that shitty food, the only reason I did was because I was starving to death and if I hadn't it would've pissed them off and I sure wasn't about to do that. Nigger food, I feel like barfing it all up, I wouldn't give a shit if they fed me T-bones from now till Christmas, it would still be nigger food. I hate niggers, you know that, I've hated 'em all my life with a passion and I always will."

"You're nuts," I told him.

"Not me, man. Not me."

I was tired of arguing with him. I was tired of all his bullshit completely. I was flat-out tired.

"Have it your way," I said.

He spat on the sidewalk and didn't reply.

There was a big Buick sedan parked at the curb. I walked over to it and tried a door. It was unlocked.

"What're you doing?" Burt asked in alarm.

"Come on," I told him, "get in."

"You're crazy."

I climbed in and stretched out on the front seat.

"We'll be gone as soon as the sun comes up. Get in. I'm giving you the back, it's roomier."

He didn't have a choice; it was my way or the highway, and the highway wasn't for him. Reluctantly, he climbed into the back seat and stretched out. I fidgeted around for a minute, trying to find a comfortable position. Just before I fell asleep I thought I heard a door opening somewhere, but my fatigue overwhelmed me, and within a minute I was dead to the world.

I came awake with a start.

The front door of the Buick had been yanked open. I looked around, squinting against the morning sun that was shining on my sleep-smooth face. Half a dozen cops were ringing the car. Burt hung behind them, unable to look me in the eye.

"I couldn't help it, Roy," he whimpered, pleading for forgiveness, "I'm sorry."

It was over.

"That's okay."

I had no malice towards him. He'd done what he had to do.

FOURTEEN

The ride home on Trailways took twenty-three hours. Burt's folks wired us the money. We didn't say one word to each other the whole trip.

Mr. and Mrs. Kellogg were waiting at the bus station, which is downtown near the cheap bars and girlie shows, where Burt, this sniveling mama's boy standing next to me, and I would sneak in to look at magazine pictures of big-titted women.

What the fuck, I thought. He's just a kid, like me. He showed his emotions more is all. Years of bitter lessons had taught me to bottle mine up. That was the only real difference between us.

Mr. and Mrs. Kellogg stood back from the bus ramp, holding

hands and looking anxious. Burt started towards them, dragging his ass, afraid to look them in the eye, figuring his old man would take half his ass off for openers, but they didn't have that angry look in their eyes; they looked real happy and relieved to see him. Mrs. Kellogg was crying, you could tell from clear across the floor. As soon as he saw the tears in his mom's eyes Burt ran over to them. She snatched him up like he was a baby and gave him a big hug. His old man patted him on the head awkwardly, like he wanted to hug Burt, too, but was embarrassed about doing it in public.

My folks weren't there. I didn't figure they'd be.

"We told your mom we'd give you a lift home," Mrs. Kellogg told me, looking at me with an awkward stare while at the same time wiping her face with a handkerchief, like she didn't know how she should be with me. They were all teary-eyed, even Mr. Kellogg, who's normally a pretty tough customer.

I nodded. I was acting nonchalant about the whole thing. I wasn't looking forward to being home. The trip had been incomplete for me, unfinished. And I wasn't much looking forward to my encounter with my old man, either.

We walked out of the bus station to their car. I lagged behind, feeling out of it, wishing we'd taken separate busses so I wouldn't have to watch their mushy shit.

Mrs. Kellogg turned back to me. She gave me this lame smile.

"I almost forgot. Your mother asked me to tell you they went over to the Eastern Shore to visit Easter with your grandparents."

She was embarrassed, telling me. I'd been gone for more than a week, the whole world had probably figured I was dead, and my parents hadn't even waited for me to come home, they'd just carried on with their lives as if I didn't exist.

The Kelloggs dropped me off in front of my house. I got out of the car.

"You're welcome to stay with us, Roy," Mrs. Kellogg offered. She said it because she had to.

I looked in at Burt, sitting by himself in the back seat. He was staring out the far window.

"No thank you, ma'am." I slammed the door shut. "See you around, Burt," I told him through the open window.

"Okay." He didn't turn to look at me.

They drove away. I watched until they were gone, then I walked up the front sidewalk and let myself in.

It was hot inside; the windows had been shut and locked, the curtains drawn. The air was heavy and still, like in a funeral home.

A note from my mom was propped up on the kitchen table with a ten-dollar bill attached to it: *"We have gone to Grandma's for Easter vacation. Here is money for you to take the bus there."*

I stuck the money in my pocket and threw the note in the trash.

There were odds and ends of food in the fridge. I was hungry as a bear—me and Burt hadn't eaten anything but a Clark bar apiece on our bus trip, because the money his folks had wired had barely covered the fare. I fixed myself a four-egg western omelette and fried up a couple pork chops to go with it, along with half a loaf of toast. I was starving; as I scarfed down the food I thought of the meal we'd eaten in that church down in Chattanooga. The last supper, before it all ended.

I cleaned the kitchen, washed and wiped the dishes and pans, put everything away. I hate a dirty kitchen, if I was going to be on my own for a few days until they got back I could at least live in a clean house, for a change.

What I needed more than anything was a hot bath, something to soak all that road dirt and fear off my body and out of my mind. I walked upstairs, stripping my filthy clothes as I went, balling everything up to chuck in the hamper.

I opened the door to my room.

It was a shambles. If the worst tornado in the world had gone through it, the damage couldn't have been worse. All my models, every single one, lay scattered all over the floor, smashed to bits.

The only things I cared about in the world had been destroyed. My father's work.

I was numb as I stood there, surveying the carnage. Then I turned and walked out, closing the door behind me.

May

FIFTEEN

I wore a T-shirt to school. T-shirts are supposed to be against the rules, along with tight-fitting jeans, pegged pants, full-on duck's-ass haircuts, and about a million other petty rules. They'd been pretty lax about enforcing the rules this late in the year, though, especially with ninth-graders—the teachers were all looking forward to graduating our disruptive behinds and moving on with next year's class, which had a bigger share of pussies and not as many bad-asses. It's a bitch, what things are coming to; Ravensburg has always been known as the baddest of the bad, the end of the line, so to speak, but pretty soon it's going to be just another sorry junior high, no tougher or ornerier than a junior high in Montgomery County or Virginia.

To really flout authority, I had my smokes rolled up in the left sleeve of my shirt, which is strictly verboten, getting caught with a pack of cigs in your sleeve is automatic detention or worse, which it would be in my case, given my history of behavior, and it could even award me a trip to Boyle's inner sanctum, if I was super-lucky I might wind up with another paddling. Give my old lady a chance to doll up and come down, flash some thigh at Boyle like last time. The least I could do for her; to say we weren't getting along very well, after my trip down south and all, would be the understatement of the century. At this point I didn't give a shit about any of it, I just wanted the year to end, to be shed of all this crap, take it easy over the summer and have a fresh start in senior high.

I wasn't going to be a complete asshole about it, though; when I got inside I'd stash the Marlboros in my locker. But I was in a dark mood, that was for shit-sure, if there was a teacher outside who spotted me, I'd pay the price. You pays your money and you takes your chance, as I always say.

"You're taking your life in your hands, Poole, wearing that stuff," Mary Jackson, a charter member of the big-tit contingent, cat-called at me as I strolled up the front steps.

"Like I could give a shit."

"Tough guy," she said, smiling uncertainly at me. She's not much in the looks department, Mary, but big tits cover a lot of sins, as my old man likes to point out. Big tits, a tight pussy, and her own bottle of Four Roses, that's his ideal kind of woman.

Speaking of my old man, we haven't. They came home a few days later, he cracked "look what the cat drug in," like nothing in the world had happened, and left it at that. No ass-whipping, no threats, nothing. He'd already done the damage and he knew it, anything more would tarnish the deed.

My mom and Ruthie had been pretty shook up, asking me a

million questions, wanting to know why it'd happened, trying to
get a handle on it, like was I kidnapped against my will or something, to explain away why I had left, and more importantly, why
I hadn't called all that time. I didn't give them any satisfaction,
it was something that happened was the way I put it, now it's
over. My lips were sealed, which was the only way to get through
it, because if I'd told them the truth, that I wanted out of the
family, and why, it would've at first hurt their feelings something
awful, and then they might've found a way to accommodate
me, send me away for good, and not to anyplace I'd be wanting
to go.

So I kept my big trap shut for once, and after a few days the
incident faded. But since then they've treated me differently, like
I was some alien creature from outer space. That was fine by me;
the more space they gave me the better I liked it. I was living in
the house, but for all intents and purposes I was on my own.
Training for the future.

There were a whole bunch of kids milling around the front,
talking and arguing. Burt and Joe were two of them. I nodded to
them, they nodded back. Nothing more. Things are different
now, we don't have that same old relationship we did before, no
more Three Musketeers. That had ended back in the junkyard,
when Burt and I had abandoned Joe. The real bitch of that affair
had been that after the junkyard watchman had caught Joe he
had threatened him all kinds of ways, scaring Joe so bad he liked
to piss his pants, so he told it, but then the guy just kicked Joe's
ass out of the yard and told him to keep out, permanently, which
Joe was more than happy to do. When Burt heard that story from
Joe he about had a heart attack, 'cause if he had stuck with Joe
back there like he'd thought of doing that's all would've happened to him. It was another reason for him to have a hard-on
against me, for putting him through a bunch of needless and scary
shit—needless and scary for him, not for me of course. I was glad
of what had happened, every bit of it.

It was a shame, the three of us breaking up, but that was

water under the bridge. Maybe we'd get back tight again, maybe we wouldn't. I wasn't going to lose any sleep over it.

"What's going on?" I asked nobody in particular.

Stevie Worrell, this small, nervous redheaded twerp who has more energy than any other kid in the school, jumped up, practically in my face. There's something about teensy redheaded kids with freckles that makes them hop around like Mexican jumping beans. He's been that way since first grade, and his sister, who's in seventh grade, is just like him.

"Ain't you heard the news?" he shouted, right into my ear. "It's been all over!"

"What news?" I asked.

Mary was standing next to me. Her tits, stuck in one of those wired-up bras that push them up to a girl's chin, poked me in the side. Not much of a feel, but better than nothing.

"Don't you watch TV? It was all over the TV last night." She was right in front of me, practically using her tits as a battering ram. Her face was all flushed, like she was excited. Maybe she liked me, I thought, I'd hardly noticed her before, even though we'd been in class together for three years. Could do worse—not as anything steady, of course, but for one or two dates it might be fun, those big squishy titties.

"Naw, I wasn't watching TV last night," I said. My old man had been parked in front of the tube from right after dinner until bedtime, no way I was going to sit in the same room with him. "So what's the big deal's got everybody's bowels in an uproar?"

"We've got to go to school with niggers next year!" Stevie shouted, not wanting anyone else to pass on the news, like he owned it.

I laughed in his face: what a crock of shit. "You're crazy. Who told you that?"

"It was on TV last night," he answered hotly, like I was calling him a liar to his face, which I wasn't, I couldn't believe it, was all. "It's all over the newspapers this morning, too, you're the one that's crazy, you don't even watch TV."

"The Supreme Court said it," Mary added.

"The Supreme Court said that shit three years ago," I told her. "That's old news."

"They said it about Maryland this time," Stevie said. "About us."

Burt joined the group, throwing me a dirty look.

"I don't give a shit what the Supreme Court said," he told everyone, but looking at me, "I ain't about to go to school with no niggers. I'll quit first."

As soon as he said that several others kicked in their sentiments, which were all the same.

"My old man said we'd move to Australia before he'll ever let me go to school with coons," Burt went on.

"I'll believe that one when I see it," I said.

He stared at me, hard and cold.

"Well, I reckon you don't give a shit if you go to school with niggers or not."

"It ain't happened yet," I answered, shrugging him off, "so I ain't gonna get my bowels in an uproar about it."

Joe slid over next to Burt. "When your sister starts dating them you won't talk so free like that," he said.

Whoa. I could feel the hairs starting to rise up the back of my neck.

"I wouldn't talk like that if I were you, Joe," I warned him, making sure he heard the threat.

He hocked a pearl onto the sidewalk between our feet. "What are you, some kind of goddamn nigger lover?"

Everybody went quiet.

I couldn't believe my ears. "What'd you say?" I slowly asked him.

"You heard me."

"Say it again. One time."

"Nig-ger lo-ver," he threw in my face, enunciating every syllable clearly.

I was on him before the words were out of his mouth, throwing him to the ground, throwing punches immediately, hard punches, no holding back. I was beside myself with fury—this motherfucker had been one of my best friends my whole life and now he was laying this kind of shit on me.

We went around and around, the others cheering us on; everybody likes a good fight, what they want is to see someone kick the living shit out of someone else. Joe's a tough guy and he's big, like me, but I was fighting way beyond normal, Superman couldn't have beaten me the way I was feeling. I got the upper hand on Joe and started beating the shit out of him, really pounding his ass. I was going to knock every tooth out of his pissant mouth, that's how enraged I was.

The others weren't going to let that happen, though, especially Burt. He and some of the other boys jumped me and started wailing away, really beating up on me. I fought like a banshee, I was crazed, it was like they'd been thrown in a sack with a panther, the way I was fighting.

All the shouting and commotion brought the teachers out, Mr. Boyle being the first, pulling them off me, then jerking me to my feet, his hand holding me tight by the front of my T-shirt.

My clothes were torn, shirt and pants both. My face was cut, too, I could taste a trickle of blood in my mouth. I looked over at Joe and Burt. If looks could kill I'd be a dead man several times over. They were as bad off as I was, Joe had blood all over his mouth from where I'd knocked some teeth loose, and Burt was going to have a mighty shiner on his right eye before sundown.

Boyle jerked me to my tiptoes.

"Go to my office, Poole," he ordered. "Every goddamn time—won't you ever learn?"

He shook his head, almost like he was sad about it. Whatever he and my mom had talked about or done the last time, he was feeling some kind of sympathy for me, it seemed. But not enough to let me go.

That was all right. I'd made my point and then some.

"Go," he said, pushing me towards the front door.

I scooped up my crushed pack of Marlboros and stuffed them in the pocket of my jeans. As I started up the steps, I turned back to Joe.

"I'd rather go to school with niggers than you any day," I spat out defiantly.

I turned my back on them and walked to the front door.

"Nigger lover!" Burt yelled at my retreating back.

Some of the girls giggled. Fuck 'em if they can't take a joke, I thought, not turning to look, I was tougher than all of them put together, when they were crying for their mamas I'd be out in the big wide world making my mark.

I didn't break stride as I flashed my former best friend the finger and marched into the building, head held high.

The rest of the week went by, more or less without incident. I was being shunned by practically everybody, but that was no big thing. I was counting down the days until summer, when I could start all over again.

There were several other students already waiting in the guidance counselors' outer office when I walked in. They do it by alphabetical order—in front of me were O'Hara, Pam, one of those invisible kids you go to school your whole life with and never know anything about; Palmer, Teddy, another asshole of the first order, I've realized recently how many of them there are in this stupid school; Parker, Lisa, another member of the big-tits-no-brains group; Petty, Mike, a pretty good guy, especially in baseball, he's been starting second baseman for the school all three years; and Pillsbury, Leonard, a complete loser, Sarkind without brains.

"Yo, Roy Poole."

"Yo, Mike Petty."

"Hi, Roy." This from Lisa, smiling at me. What is there about me that's making all these chicks with big tits come onto me this year all of a sudden? I'm not even a tit man, I'm much more interested in a pretty face. I don't mean I'd kick her out of bed for eating crackers or anything, but she's not my style.

"Looking good, Lisa." I winked at her, gave her a friendly smile. You never know, I might run across her some dark and stormy night, I wouldn't want her to be turned off on me, it doesn't cost anything to smile at someone, especially when they have big tits and a friendly attitude.

I flopped down next to Mike.

"What's the problem between you and Burt and Joe?" he asked.

Everybody'd heard about the fight, like it was still front-page news, even though it had happened a week ago.

"No big deal," I assured him. "Everything's copacetic."

That wasn't true. We weren't talking. It was the Two Musketeers now.

"Four more weeks," he said.

"No shit, Sherlock," I said back.

"I'm counting the days."

"Everybody is." This from Lisa, who wanted to be included in. She leaned across Mike to face me. "What're you doing this summer, Roy?"

"I'm sailing my dad's boat to Hawaii," I told her, straight-faced.

"You're kidding! I didn't even know your father had a boat."

Like I said, no brains at all.

"Just kidding. I don't know, hang out, whatever. The usual." The thought of hanging out in Ravensburg all summer long was enough to give me the hives. "Go to Ocean City, maybe, try to get a job there."

I wasn't about to tell her my real plans—to go up to Annapolis and find a boat to crew on for the summer. That was *my* secret, which I wasn't about to share with any of these morons.

"My folks joined the club," she volunteered, "Claymore. I'll be at the pool every day. My mom said I could bring guests."

Claymore Country Club is the rattiest country club in the world, but it's the only one around. Anybody whose parents are hot shit is a member. I've been a few times to the pool; it's not bad, keeps you cool at least, and there's a lot of cute girls parading their stuff.

"Sounds like fun," I said.

"Maybe we could go sometime," she offered.

"Yeah, that would be nice."

The two guidance counselors' doors opened at the same time. Two kids came out. They must time them, I thought. The secretary called out the next two names.

Kids came and went, every couple of minutes. The doors opened again, and Mike and Pillsbury came out. Mike gave me a wink, moved out. The secretary called the next two names.

"Roy Poole," pointing to one office, "Tony Quarles," showing the Q-man the other.

Real nonchalant, like it was no big deal, I pushed up from my chair and went in, closing the door behind me.

Miss Tayman was the guidance counselor I got. She's middle-aged, older than my mom I'd guess, it's hard to tell with these old maids. They always look old and dry, although this one made an effort—she dressed nicely, wore perfume, curled her hair. Kind of sad when you think about it, she probably doesn't have anybody in her life. Maybe a cat.

She sat across the desk from me, gave me a friendly smile, one of those smiles that says "I'm a nice person, I'm fair, on your side." Guidance counselors have to be able to smile like that, it's part of their job. They want you to think they understand kids in a way regular teachers don't. The truth is, they don't understand shit, no more than any other teacher.

Miss Tayman scanned through my file, looking up at me once with another quick smile. It wasn't particularly reassuring; this was something every kid had to do, like going to the dentist.

She laid the file aside.

"Well, how are we doing today, Paul?"

"Roy, ma'am," I corrected her.

It took a moment. She opened the file again for a quick look.

"Roy. Of course." She nodded her head vigorously a couple of times. It's an assembly line: in two days two guidance counselors would be seeing every ninth-grader in the school. Names were a distraction that only took time.

"Well, then. You know why you're here."

Before I could attempt to answer she continued on—a canned speech. "You have to decide . . . you need to make certain judgments about what you plan to do that will affect the rest of your life . . . what kind of job you plan to have someday. Do you understand?"

"Yes, ma'am."

"Good, good." She gave me that bullshit smile again. She gives it to every kid, whether she likes them or not. The woman doesn't even know me, I've never been in her office before. Wait, technically that's not true, I was once, back in seventh grade. She passed me on to Mr. Boyle right away, she could tell from the get-go I wasn't a kid she wanted to deal with.

She doesn't remember.

"There are several types of curriculums you can take, Roy," making sure she said my name, trying to convince me the mistake about it before was a fluke, like I could give a shit, as soon as I walked out of this office I'd never see this lady again for the rest of my life. "Several types, depending on what line of work you want to get into. There's the academic, and the general, academic of course is if you think you want to go to college, and the general is kind of all-around, so to speak, and then of course there's commercial and vocational."

"Yes, ma'am. I know."

"Good!" she said energetically. I could see the relief on her face—some kids wouldn't know academic from commercial from a hole in the wall, and then she'd have to go through this lengthy explanation of each, and it would fuck her schedule all to hell.

"Have you ever given any thought to what you might like to be? When you finish school? What kind of job you would like?"

She smiled at me again, but she wasn't seeing me.

I took a deep breath. This was it—I had to make a commitment, I had to say it to someone from Ravensburg out loud.

Admiral Wells was wrong about me. I'd show him. I'd show everybody.

"I want to go to the Naval Academy in Annapolis and be a Navy officer for my career."

Real slow: "I see."

It was very quiet. The air hung still, warm with the hint of summer.

She took my file up again and leafed through it. "You know, Roy, to pursue that you would have to take the academic course . . ."

"Yes, ma'am. I know."

She looked away. I don't know who felt more awkward, her or me.

". . . and you would have to maintain high grades in difficult subjects, like trigonometry and chemistry and a foreign language . . ."

"Yes."

She laid the file back down, squared it up on her desk.

"Well . . . up to now your grades haven't been all so good." She took a peek inside the file again. "I see there has been some recent improvement, but . . ."

"I know," I interrupted, "but they'll get better, I promise."

"I certainly hope so. And your conduct as well. Still and all . . ."

She thought hard for a moment, then flashed me a sympathetic smile.

"I have an idea, which I think is a pretty good one. Let me tell it to you and you tell me what you think. Instead of academic why don't we put you down for vocational for a start . . ."

"But . . ." I started to protest.

She put her hand up to stop me.

"Please let me finish. We'll put you down for vocational, but we'll also include a foreign language. French would be nice, *parlez-vous français?,* and that way you could see if you liked it and how well you did and if your grades are good you could switch curriculums if you felt like it, all right?"

Without waiting for me to answer, she started to fill in some cards.

"So that'll be English, shop math, gym, French, I'm sure they'll let you take French instead of U.S. history although history *is* required, wood shop, and let's see, how about engine shop, that's real interesting."

She finished filling the cards out and pushed them across the desk. I'd been blind-sided—it had happened so fast I was too discombobulated to protest.

"You know, Roy, you could always enlist in the Navy after you graduate high school, that's a good career and your vocational training will be of great use to you then."

She stood up: the interview was over.

I stumbled to my feet. She'd planned my whole life out for me in less than five minutes.

"Yes, ma'am," I said numbly, "I reckon that's what I'll wind up doing."

I shuffled the cards in my hands. They felt hot.

"You may leave."

I walked out of her office.

"Academic," I heard her mutter to herself, even before I was out the door. "What'll they think of next?"

The blood rushed to my face. I looked around quickly, to make sure no one was watching.

June

SIXTEEN

"Oh, lover boy. How you call your lover boy?" Ruthie sang out.

"Shut the fuck up." I snatched the phone out of her hand.

"Well, excuse me for living." She danced around me. "Baby, oh, oh, ba-aby . . ."

I motioned for her to go away. I hate that calypso shit, that's all they ever play on "Bandstand" nowadays.

"Hello?" I said into the phone.

"Baby, oh, oh, ba-aby," Ruthie sang into my ear with a whisper. Ever since her last boyfriend dumped her, she's been a real pain. It was like I was the big brother and she was the little sister, not the other way around.

"You're the one," she sang, actually sticking her tongue in my ear.

"Cut it out, goddamnit!" I yelled at her. Then quickly into the phone, "not you." I didn't know who it was, but you don't yell at somebody like that over the phone.

"Who is that, Roy?" came the voice over the wire.

I felt like I'd had an electric wire jammed up my ass.

"Melanie?"

"Hi, Roy." Her voice was kind of quiet, tentative, like she wasn't sure she should be talking to me.

"It's my sister," I told her after I recovered, "my stupid, dumb, ugly, stupid sister."

"Ugly?" Ruthie pouted, hands on hips facing me.

"Wait a second, will you, Melanie?"

I cupped the receiver and turned to Ruthie. "I don't do this to you."

"Baby," she sang, wiggling her hips like a hula dancer, "oh, oh, ba-aby . . ." She stopped. "Who is she?"

"A friend. From school." I still had my hand over the phone.

"I never heard you talk about any girl called Melanie before."

"She's new. She just transferred."

"Two weeks before school's ended?"

"Her dad's in the Navy. He got transferred here." It wasn't a complete lie, it's her grandfather, not her dad, and they've lived here a long time, but no way was I going to tell Ruthie about Melanie.

I don't like lying anymore. Ever since the incident in that colored church down in Chattanooga, talking straight to preacher Williams about Texas and all, I haven't wanted to do it. Sometimes you have to, like now, but it wasn't as much fun as it used to be.

"Come on, Ruthie, no shit now."

"All right, all right. If you think you have to keep secrets from your own sister, who's the only person left in the world who cares about you . . ."

This was true. As far as my old man was concerned, I didn't exist. We'd never said one word about what he'd done to my model collection; we hadn't said anything to each other at all. My mom was all fucked up about me; sometimes she was all weepy, "what am I going to do with you?," that kind of shit, other times she was mad as hell, threatening to kick me out for good, send me to military school, the usual list. Mostly she was bewildered, and that scared her, which made me feel like shit; but there wasn't anything I could do about it, not for now.

"I'm gonna want details," Ruthie bargained.

"Okay, okay," I said. Anything to get her to leave me alone with the phone.

"I'm holding you to it." She danced away.

I scrunched down in the corner against the wall, my back to the room, the most privacy I could manage. "Hi. You still there?"

"Yes."

She was quiet. I could hear her breathing.

"How'd you get my number?"

"I started calling Pooles in Ravensburg. This was the fifth one."

I smiled; she didn't give up easy. "Smart thinking."

"I've been wanting to talk to you," she said.

"Me, too."

"I felt awful about what happened."

I didn't say anything to that. She had something to say, and it was her nickel.

"I still like you, Roy."

I could hear her breathing. The kind of breathing where she would've heard it, too.

"Aren't you going to say anything?" she asked finally.

"Yeah, well, I like you, too, but, you know . . ."

"Yes."

There was a pause.

"I'd like to see you again, Roy. I'd really like to."

Now I could hear my own breathing. This girl was so uncool it was great.

"Yeah, well, me too, but you know . . ."

Down the hall I could hear my sister still singing that bullshit song. I stuck a finger in my ear so I wouldn't be distracted.

"My grandmother was lying, Roy."

"What?"

"She took that statue, not you."

Oh, Jesus. I had an immediate case of cottonmouth, I had to lick my lips to speak. "How do you know?"

"You said so."

"You didn't believe me. Nobody did."

"I did. Really. I did, but I was afraid to say anything." She started crying, I could hear her sobs coming over the phone. "I wanted to."

"Yeah, well . . ." I didn't know what to say. "Come on, don't cry. Stop crying."

"I'm sorry. I don't mean to." She kept sniffling. "Give me a second, okay?"

"Sure."

I heard a loud "honk," right in my ear, then the kind of breathing you do when you're trying to control your breathing.

"I'm all right now."

"Good. I don't want you crying, especially over me."

"We caught her."

"You what?"

"Stealing something. From another house." I could hear the tears starting to come again. "She's been doing it for years and nobody knew. My own grandmother!"

The faucet was on now, full blast.

"Melanie. Melanie, come on."

"And you got blamed and nobody believed you and everything got so messed up!"

No shit, baby.

"Roy." The sobs were slowing down, coming in gasps; I

could imagine her face, all red and teary and blotchy. "Roy?"

"Yeah, I'm here."

"I want to see you again. I mean really."

"Yeah, me too. Really." It wasn't bullshit, I did want to see her. There wasn't anything phony about her, not a thing.

"You do? Really?"

"Yeah."

"Oh, God, I'm so glad, I thought you'd tell me to . . . go jump in a lake."

"No, I do."

She stopped crying. "Roy?"

"Yeah?"

"Admiral Wells knows."

My chest got tight, hearing his name.

"Knows what?"

"About my grandmother."

Fuck. "So?"

"He feels terrible about it. I heard him talking to my grandfather."

Big fucking deal, now. Like he hadn't known before.

"I think he'd like to see you again," she said. "To apologize."

I slumped deeper against the wall. "I don't think that's a good idea. Anyway, I'm not building models anymore."

"They were talking about seeing if they could still get you into Farrington. Admiral Wells and Grandfather. They know they did badly by you. I'm sure they'd like to make it up to you, Admiral Wells especially."

Now it was my own breathing I was hearing.

"Roy?"

"Yeah, I'm still here."

"Did you hear me?"

"Yeah."

"Don't you think that's great?"

My mind was racing, going in a million different directions.

"I don't know," I answered truthfully. Make it up to me. The way to make it up to me would've been to stand up for me then when it was hard, not now when it was easy.

"If you went to Farrington I could go to Agnes Walker," she said, her voice full of excitement. She didn't have a clue to where I was inside my head, all she knew was she might see me again. It made me feel good in one way, but shitty in another. "I've already filled out an application."

"Yeah?" I was numb, I had no answers.

"Roy?" she asked again.

"Yeah, Melanie?"

"Do you really want to see me?"

"I said it, didn't I?"

"You're not just saying it to be polite?"

She was starting to piss me off a little. Calling me out of the blue, the stuff about her grandmother, then the admiral. It was too much to handle all at once.

"No." I separated the being pissed-off from how I felt. "I really want to see you."

"Will you take me to my prom, then?"

"What . . ." Jesus, what was going on?

"It's next week. I know it's short notice but say you will, please, there's no other boy I want to go with."

Like every boy in the world was dying to take her. I didn't say that. What the hell, she was a nice girl and next time she was going to go all the way with me, if I could get past my goddamn conscience.

"Well . . ."

I drew it out a little, to tease her. She'd just put me though a ton of shit, I deserved five seconds of payback.

"Yeah. Okay."

"Oh, God!" she screamed over the phone, so loud I had to pull it away from my ear. "That's great!"

"When is it?" This was happening awfully fast.

"Next week. Saturday night. It's at the Shoreham."

The Shoreham's the fanciest hotel in Washington. I've driven by it, but I've never been inside.

"The Shoreham. Saturday night. Okay." Everything was going so fast, my head felt like it was spinning. "Listen, what do you wear?"

"It's formal."

"Formal?"

"You know, a tuxedo."

I almost laughed out loud. One of those monkey suits, like the admiral wore. She really thought I had those kind of clothes? She probably thought the clothes I'd worn to the party had been my own, not something the admiral had bought for me for the occasion.

"You rent it," she giggled, reading my thoughts. "No boy owns one, not even the morons I know. They're stupid, but you have to wear it. I'll rent it for you," she went on before I could protest, assuming I would, "I'll pay for everything, it's my prom, I'm doing the asking, all you have to do is come."

My heart was pounding like a tom-tom. That part of my life was over, finished, I'd put it behind me—now here it was again, right in my face.

"Roy?"

"Yeah, Melanie?"

"You're not thinking of changing your mind, are you?" Her voice was quivering.

I didn't answer right off.

"I mean . . . I know you just said you would but you have every right to back out. I would have understood if you hadn't even talked to me, after what happened."

"Yeah, I know, I mean this is a lot . . ." "to ask," I left unsaid, "of someone all of you fucked over." She must've realized that, so she was giving me a chance to back out. Maybe I'd better take it, I thought, I don't need getting my teeth kicked in again by those assholes.

"Oh please, Roy, please!" She had felt what I was thinking, it was coming over the wire, as clear as if I'd actually said it. She hadn't meant it, she didn't want me to say "no" to the prom. Say "no" to her.

She had no shame. She wanted me and she wasn't embarrassed to admit it. I pictured her in that big house of hers, all alone. Any second now the tears would be starting up again, I could hear it in her voice. Goddamn, but I felt sorry for this poor girl.

It wasn't her fault, what had happened.

"I love you, Roy," she whispered, barely loud enough for me to hear.

You don't hurt a girl this innocent.

"Sure, Melanie," I promised, hearing the words come out of my mouth, how calm I sounded. "I'll come."

Friday night. Date night at the Ravensburg Fire House, except I wasn't dating. It's always packed, mostly with high school kids, but some junior high kids come, too, ninth-graders, the cooler ones. They've got a good band, the Key-Tones, a bunch of guys from Ravensburg High who play rock 'n' roll to knock your socks off, which is what everybody wears; you check your shoes at the door, so the firehouse floor doesn't get all scuffed up. That's why they call it a sock hop, although a lot of the girls wear stockings—they get all dolled up, putting on stuff they're not allowed to wear to school, heavy makeup and perfume, pushup bras and falsies, skirts so tight on their asses you can see the line of their panty girdles. Lots of close dancing, dry-fucking right out on the floor.

I moped around, sticking to the sidelines. My sister was dancing her ass off, drawing plenty of attention. She's a great dancer, Ruthie, she knows how to shake that thing and she does it with any boy that'll ask her, any cool one, that is. I watched her slow-dance a couple with Rufus Marlowe, a senior who was captain of the football team, this year's rock supreme. He's a smart guy, too, he's going to Duke on a football scholarship. They moved around the floor to "The Great Pretender," grinding each other's pelvis against the other. I could see she was all hot and flushed. She probably dreams of him at night, Mrs. Rufus Marlowe, that kind of shit. The sad truth is, the day ol' Rufus graduates RHS is the last day Ruthie'll ever see him, unless they run across each other accidentally. Guys like Rufus aren't interested in girls like my sister, girls with no ambition beyond marriage and babies.

Right now, though, she's in heaven. She can still dream.

Tomorrow at eleven in the morning I had an appointment to meet Melanie at Shapiro's Tux Shoppe on 8th Street in Washington, to get my tuxedo. I knew exactly the kind of jacket I wanted—a blue-green-black plaid with peaked satin lapels. All the neat guys in high school had worn that style to their prom this spring. If they didn't have one of those left I'd go for a straight white dinner jacket and black pants. Melanie would cream in her jeans and so would her stuck-up girlfriends.

None of my friends came near me. Former friends. I was an outcast, starting from the day I'd gotten into the fight with Burt out front of the school. It bugged me, I can't say it didn't, you don't run with a bunch of guys your whole life and then stop without feeling left out. But that's the way it had to be; for now. Tomorrow, as the saying goes, was another day, and I'd be spending it with a rich girl at her fancy prom, and then screwing her afterwards. And who knew, maybe it would lead to other things, maybe I'd see her regularly, maybe I'd even run across Admiral Wells, and he'd apologize for being a chickenshit, and I'd wind up at Farrington after all.

The band struck up another slow tune, "My Prayer," one of the all-time greats as far as I'm concerned. For that one brief moment when me and Darlene were secret boyfriend-girlfriend that was our song; we'd heard it on the radio and she'd claimed it for us.

Now she was dancing to it—with Burt. They slow-danced

around the floor cheek to cheek, his chest to her titties, his leg between hers, flattening her skirt tight against her body. As they did a turn Burt caught me staring, and he looked at me for a moment, then smiled smugly, look what I've got, the smile said. He knew how I felt about her, the bastard, and she'd undoubtedly filled in the blanks for the rest of it.

I couldn't stand the sight of the two of them together. I turned away and walked to the back, where they sell the Cokes.

"Want to dance, Roy?"

I turned. Ginger Huntwell had come up from behind. She'd been dancing with different high school boys, pushing up against them, letting them rub their hands all over her ass. She looked up at me, a thin line of sweat on her top lip, her lipstick glowing brightly.

Nothing wrong with a free feel. You dance with Ginger, you've got her titties right up against you, no extra charge.

"Sure, Ginger. Come on."

She didn't waste a second, she grabbed my hand and led me onto the dance floor, pulled me into a super-tight embrace, and started grinding away at me while we shuffled our feet, her head resting on my shoulder. I could smell her cheap perfume mixed with her shampoo mixed with her own bodily smells, it almost seemed like I could smell her pussy, the smells of her sexuality were that strong.

Burt wasn't with Darlene now, she'd left him for a high-schooler. He and Joe stood on the sidelines with their Cokes, watching Ginger and me. I flashed them a wicked grin as I slid my hand down to Ginger's ass. It was nice and soft, kind of squishy.

"You dance real nice, Roy," she said, snuggling even closer.

"So do you, Ginger."

We danced like that for a little while. Her hand went to my neck, stroking it softly.

"How come you've never asked me to go out with you?" she asked, out of the blue.

"I don't know."

"Somebody told me you were going with Darlene Mast," she said, shifting her weight slightly so her pussy was pressed right up against my leg through her skirt.

"Somebody was wrong," I told her. "She's too stuck-up, I wouldn't touch her with a ten-foot pole."

"Good," she whispered, her hand still stroking my neck. I was getting the feeling-up of my life as we ground it out to the beat.

"Hey, Roy?"

"What, Ginger?"

"Do you have a hard-on?"

I almost choked. "How'd you guess?"

"I can feel it. It sure feels good. And big."

"That's what my nigger-whore girlfriend down in the District tells me," I boasted.

As soon as the words popped out of my mouth I was mad at myself for having said them. I'd only done it to boast, which was petty and chickenshit. Ruby had kept me from having my ass tossed out of that bar into the pouring rain, taken me home and fed me dinner, and most important of all, popped my cherry. And here I was saying she was just another nigger. I didn't even like hearing that word anymore, not after what they'd done for me down in Chattanooga.

"Have you screwed a colored person?" Ginger asked, wide-eyed.

"Sure, lots of times," I lied. I was in the shit now, I might as well make it a whopper.

"Is it true they're better than white girls?" she asked.

"I don't know," I replied casually, like it was no big thing. "It depends."

"Well, I bet she ain't as good as me," Ginger informed me defiantly.

That tore it. We were still out there on the dance floor, cheek to cheek, chest to tits, cock to pussy. My shirt was stained clear through with sweat I was so hot for her.

"Well, Ginger, there's only one way to find out."

She smiled up at me. "Guess so."

Home run.

I led her off the dance floor towards the exit. Out of the corner of my eye I saw Burt and Joe watching me, the envy burning in their eyes. Serves them right, I thought, feeling as smug as the cat that ate the canary.

As she was standing by the door, holding onto my arm for balance while she slipped into her moccasins, she turned to face me. "Listen, Roy, you got any money?"

I had less than a buck left in my wallet. "Not on me. Why?"

"Well damn, Roy, you don't think I give it away for free, do you?"

"Shit, Ginger, I didn't think you were a whore." Nobody will ever accuse this girl of beating around the bush.

"I'm not." A practiced pout. "But I like to go out and get a hamburger and a milkshake afterwards."

"Oh yeah, that's right." Women always want something— money, love, whatever, there's no such thing as plain, regular fucking.

"Could you get any money? I sure would like to." She bit on a fingernail, looking at me sideways. "Five dollars would be enough."

I thought about where I could get five bucks. I still had eight or ten dollars in my jar in the closet, but if I went home my old man might decide to not let me back out, just to be a perverse prick. I wasn't grounded or anything, he'd been pretty low-key about the entire affair, it had been so past his understanding, all that I'd done, that he basically made out like I didn't exist— which suited me fine.

Besides, what little cash was left I was saving to use tomorrow night. Even with Melanie covering the expenses, paying for going to eat afterwards and anything else, I still had to get her a nice corsage and have some walking-around money.

All in all, it would be easier to go straight to the bank and make a withdrawal.

"Wait here," I told Ginger, "I'll be back in a half-hour. Less."

She wet her lips. "Make sure you've got a rubber."

Talk about luck. I'd bought a pack this very afternoon, for tomorrow night with Melanie.

"I've always got one," I boasted.

It was darker than I remembered down in the basement, under the apartments. Some of the bulbs were burned out and hadn't been replaced. That was fine with me—the darker the safer.

I hadn't been back here since the time we'd almost been caught. We'd laid low after that, figuring the manager would have somebody patrolling for a couple weeks; you get extra-cautious after an incident like that. By the time it was safe to go back into business I'd met the admiral, and boosting coin boxes seemed like petty shit. Anyway, if I was going to Annapolis I needed a clean record.

But—one last time wouldn't be any skin off somebody's ass. Not when a piece of prime teenage pussy was on the line.

For one moment, right after I left the firehouse, I'd had a guilty conscience about fucking Ginger the night before doing it with Melanie, but I'd decided fucking Ginger would be good practice for Melanie, it would make me better. I wanted Melanie's first time to be special, as good as I could make it. Ginger was doing both of us a favor, was the way I looked at it.

It was taking longer than usual to crack the coin boxes. I was sweating, nervous, because of what had happened the last time, and because I was alone. It had felt safer when it was the Three Musketeers, all of us in it together. Of course, we'd had to divvy it up three ways—this time I'd get to keep it all to myself.

I kept hearing noises. Not having Burt and Joe for lookouts was making me nervous. I kept stopping and listening to every creak and rat-scratching. But it was all in my head; the machines were empty, nobody was going to come down. Still, the sooner I could get out, the better my peace of mind.

Three boxes down. I counted the change: four bucks, one more dollar to go. I went to work on the next box. The fucker didn't come easy, I was cursing it under my breath, jamming my pocketknife against the catch; a knife doesn't work as well as a screwdriver, but it was all I had on me.

It popped open, scattering coins all over the floor.

"Son of a bitch!" I scurried around on my hands and knees, picking them up. This box was fuller than the others had been. This would do it.

The sound of heavy footsteps came charging down the stairs.

I looked up, petrified. Some people came storming into the laundry area from the far door. I grabbed as many coins as I could and took off like a bat out of hell in the opposite direction.

"Stop, you thieving bastard!" A woman's voice, full of outrage and self-righteousness, rang out.

Over my dead body, I thought, going as hard as I could for the darkness.

The roar was deafening, an explosion of shotgun blast, both barrels, echoing and echoing in the corridor.

I felt a sudden sharp stab of fire, like someone sticking a hot poker into my calf, bringing a cry of pain I was unable to stifle. The entire bottom half of my right pant leg, below the knee, had been blown off, completely shredded, the jagged remains flapping like pennants. Hobbling as best I could I reached down and felt the wound. Blood was starting to ooze out from the half-dozen pellets of birdshot that had found its mark.

But I was lucky, if you can call getting shot at and hit lucky: most of the charge had missed me. Barely, by less than a foot. The paint on the wall alongside me was pocked with the full impact of the discharge, a spray pattern almost a yard wide, I saw it clear as day even though I was running like an Olympic sprinter: a limping, wounded Olympic sprinter. If whoever had fired the shotgun had aimed one foot to the left I would have been hamburger from the waist down.

I was running on adrenaline, on instinct. Around the corners I sped, hearing my pursuers closing behind me. They were grownups, not in as good shape as me, but they hadn't taken a fistful of #8 shot in the leg, either, and they had the advantage of pure hatred fueling them. If they caught me they'd kill me, or give it a damn good try.

Around the last corner. I pushed the fire door open in passing but didn't go through, running instead for my safety valve, the side corridor Burt and Joe and I had used as an escape the last time we'd almost been caught.

Behind me, I heard the fire door slam hard as it rebounded from my push.

"Up here, he went through here!"

"We've got him now, the bastard, that front door's locked upstairs!"

Voices rich in gloating, a pack of dogs cornering the fox, they took the bait, rushing through the door and up into the hallway.

Finally: the safety, at least temporarily, of the unused corridor. I pried open the trap door. My leg was killing me—I was afraid I'd pass out before I could pull myself in. Pretty soon they would realize they'd been tricked and would be back down here, searching for hidden nooks and crannies. They might come down this way.

I pulled with all my might, painfully hauling myself up into the crawlspace, reaching back down for the panel to seal me in.

Then I collapsed. Around me, hundreds of beady red eyes glowed in the dark, approaching as they smelled the blood, squealing like a banshee orchestra. I picked up a clod of dirt and flung it, so they'd know I was alive, dangerous to them. I'd crush the fuckers in my bare hands if they tried to get to my wound. They kept their distance. They were patient; they could wait. So could I.

I don't know how long I waited there, in the low crawlspace, surrounded by darkness. An hour, two, I didn't have a watch, I had no idea of time. More than long enough to smell the stink of the mustiness and the rat shit, of the rats who might've died in here from rabies or anything. You see them sometimes when you overturn a pile of garbage, rabid little creatures running around and around in crazy circles, dabs of foam at their mouths. Sometimes, when we're especially bored, we'll cherry-bomb the garbage piles behind the grocery store. Hundreds of rats will come pouring out, like in those old-time cartoons you see on Saturday-morning television. If we're feeling particularly adventuresome we'll try to beat them to a pulp with baseball bats and shovels. The only good rat's a dead rat, that's my motto.

I hoped none of their relatives were in here with me now. That would really be the shits—to escape being shot by some pissed-off humans only to be mortally wounded by a bite from a sick rat.

But I didn't get bitten; not once. They must've sensed they were in here with a madman, someone who would sink as low as them. I may be sharing your space, you assholes, I said to myself, but I'm not one of you. They understood that, somehow, and kept their distance, watching and squealing, hoping for a long slow slide into blackness.

Tough shit for them. I was as aware as I'd ever been my whole life. I was the rat in the garbage dump that got away.

At one point I thought I heard voices, from some distant corridor. Or maybe I was imagining it, a fear-induced nightmare, except I was awake. But they faded away, and for a long time there was silence.

The fresh air hit me with a blast as I crawled through the opening where I'd pushed out the grate. Sticking my head out cautiously, I looked around. The coast was clear. I squirmed through the hole, wincing as I scraped my bad leg on the asphalt.

It was dark out, but I could see the injury. Not too bad, considering. Only a few pellets had actually been embedded— most had grazed me. I'd be black and blue the length of my leg for a week, but it didn't feel like there was any permanent damage.

The leg loosened up as I made my way through the dark, empty streets. Keep moving, I told myself, keep moving, don't stop. Don't give in to it. That's how they get you. I wonder if this is how a deer feels, I thought, when it's limping through the woods after being shot. Do they die or do they live?

SEVENTEEN

Tecumseh felt cool against my back. I stretched, coming awake, and as I did the pain from my leg shot clear through my body, taking my breath away.

Motherfucker, that hurt. Slowly, I got to my feet, gingerly rubbing my wounded leg. It was throbbing, all the way from my waist to my toes, like a horrible toothache.

I braced myself against the stone Indian, waiting for the dizziness to clear my head. It was barely coming dawn; way to the east, over the Chesapeake Bay, the first tentative yellow-pink rays were breaking through. It would be hot today and humid to boot, the beginning of another steamy Maryland summer, months of miscry, as soon as you put on a fresh shirt it's wet with sweat, and there's no such thing as straight hair.

The leg was tightening up, almost like I was wearing a cast. By nightfall it would be stiff as a board if I didn't keep moving it. I'd torn off the other pant leg to make a raggedy-assed pair of shorts.

I could've gone to Prince Georges County hospital, down the road in Cheverly, last night, but they would've called the cops, and reform school was not in my plans. Later in the day I'd find someplace where I could get my leg looked after; maybe the infirmary here, I'd give them some cock-and-bull story about how I'd been out hunting with my friends or some such shit. They might not believe me, but they wouldn't let a kid walk around with a bum leg, either. Then I'd clean and wash the wound every day until it healed. Right under my parents' noses, too. What they didn't know wouldn't hurt them. By now they saw so little of me I could be gone for another week and they probably wouldn't notice.

Slowly, step by painful step, I hobbled across the campus in the direction of the obstacle course. I wanted to get there before the sun was up, before anyone could see me and try to help. A limping kid draws attention, and I needed to be invisible.

In a few hours, a lot of things would be happening. Melanie would be showing up at the tuxedo shop, waiting for me with great expectation, her little heart pounding in her chest. When at first I didn't show she'd be peeved, then impatient, then pissed-off, then she'd get worried—maybe I'd been in an accident, the boy of her dreams had been hit by a car on his way there, because she knew I was coming, I had to be, there was no other way. It was the most important day of her life, even more important than her recital: I'd be there, I had to be there.

Then panic would set in, and she'd call my house, and whoever got on the phone with her wouldn't know jack-shit about her or what she was talking about—what prom, who the fuck was she, where had we met? The way my luck was running she'd spill the beans on me, the whole shooting match. The admiral and Farrington and everything. My old man would kill me if he ever found all that out, I knew that for shit-sure.

Or maybe she'd ask for me, shyly, and they'd tell her (Ruthie I hoped, there'd be some dim understanding from her, not much but maybe just enough to let it slide by) that I wasn't there, my room was empty, they had no idea where I was, they never had any idea of where I was or what I did anymore. I was lost to them, whoever it was would tell her, and they didn't give much of a fuck about that, either.

She'd wait at the tux shop for a long time, well into the afternoon. Hoping against hope that I'd show with some acceptable excuse; my dog had been run over by a car, my grandmother had to go to the hospital. Anything—she'd believe anything, as long as I showed up.

But I wasn't going to. I wasn't going to see Melanie Prescott again—not ever. I wasn't going to see Admiral Wells or Mrs. Wells or any of them, not even if they called and begged me to —not that they would, but I wasn't. And I wasn't going to go to Farrington Academy, either. Not if they called me up tomorrow and offered me the biggest scholarship in the world.

It wasn't for me; it wasn't me. Not Melanie, although she really and truly was a nice girl and I could have her cherry if I wanted it. Not Admiral Wells, either. None of it. I was a kid from Ravensburg, Maryland, a kid with lousy grades and a shitty attitude, who was going to start Ravensburg High School in the fall and take the vocational course.

That was me.

And this. This was me, too. I hadn't been coming here all these years, dreaming about it all these years, to just throw it away. Not for any of them, or my teachers, or my friends. Or my sister or my parents. None of them could stop me from this.

The obstacle course was empty. It always is early in the morning, that's why I like it this time of day: when I have it all to myself, when I can own it.

I took my usual slow, deep breaths, clenching and unclenching my hands as I always do, shaking my fingers, rocking back and forth a few times, trying to get loose, free up my leg. The leg wasn't cooperating; it was as tight as a steel rod, and it hurt badly.

Only one thought was going through my mind: if you finish, you get in. If you finish you will come here, you will be a midshipman at the United States Naval Academy, one of the long blue line. And if you don't, you won't come here. You'll be what you've been your whole life until now—nothing.

If you want to be in the Navy you have to learn to live with pain. I counted backwards from a hundred, then from fifty, then from ten.

Then I started running.

It hurt like hell. Every time I came down on my wounded leg I could feel the pain shooting up, all the way through my body. I did the best I could to concentrate on the first obstacle in front of me. That was all—one step, then another, then up and over.

The pain was like a fire in my body. I collapsed to the ground, unable to stop tears from forming at the corners of my eyes.

"Get up, asshole."

I looked around for the voice. There was no one in the area, only me.

I limped towards the next obstacle. One step at a time, one foot in front of the other. Up and over and down, landing on one leg this time, my good leg, hopping a few steps on it until I felt I could put weight on my bum leg again, almost collapsing when I did, but managing to go on. Another obstacle—a rope-climb, no wrapping legs around this time for momentum, all arms. Lifting slowly, up, higher, feeling the rope starting to burn my hands. One hand over the other, finally reaching the top, swinging over, dropping down twelve feet, landing on both legs this time, the pain so intense I had to scream, I couldn't help it.

No one was there to hear me. I pushed myself to my feet and hobbled along the path towards the next obstacle.

Push, up, over. Land, collapse, scream. By now I *wanted* to scream, I wanted to scream my lungs out, until my throat was raw and I couldn't scream anymore. I would scream until I either passed out or my leg fell off. One or the other, that was all that could stop me.

One obstacle was overcome; then another; then another. Finally I was on the last straightaway; the last three barriers. I didn't know how long I'd been on the course. It could have been an hour or more, easy. It had been a long time, that much I knew: the sun was up now, full into the sky, the day was already hot and muggy, as hot as a steam bath. Sweat was pouring off my body—my shirt was soaked clear through with it, my armpits were dripping wet, my face was so wet I could hardly see past the salty water dripping off my hair and forehead and eyelashes.

One leaden, painful step at a time.

That kept me going. Nothing else could have.

And then, I had done it; I had arrived at the final set of jumps: a very high wooden barrier I had to climb, hand over hand, and then a rope swing, hanging in space, that I had to dive for, which would carry me over the last expanse of water to safety.

I stood at the bottom for a moment, taking in air. The top of the barrier looked like it was in the clouds, it was so high, like you could climb all day and never reach the top. By now my hands were raw from rope burns, strands of torn skin lining both palms. It would hurt to pull myself up, it would hurt like hell.

My climb began. Hand over hand, the pain searing through me, the rope cutting into the flesh, it felt like it was cutting me to the bone. Drop, my body screamed, let it go, you'll get in anyway, this doesn't matter, you've already proven yourself. Let it go.

Another handhold. Hanging there. My hands in more pain than my leg, my entire body on fire with pain.

Another hand up. One more; and then another. Until finally,

I had done it: I had reached the top. I sat there for a moment, looking at the rope hanging in space in front of me; and as I looked at that rope, which looked impossibly far away for me to reach, my eyes changed focus and I saw beyond it, I saw the rest of the Academy in the distance: Bancroft, Dahlgren, the library, the dorms, I saw the boats on the river, the birds wheeling overhead. I saw the whole world.

I gathered up the last bit of strength I had left in me; and as I did, crouching there on top of the last barrier, the pain in my leg and hands miraculously went away. I took one last, cleansing breath; then, diving as high into the air as I could, I reached with all my might towards the last obstacle.

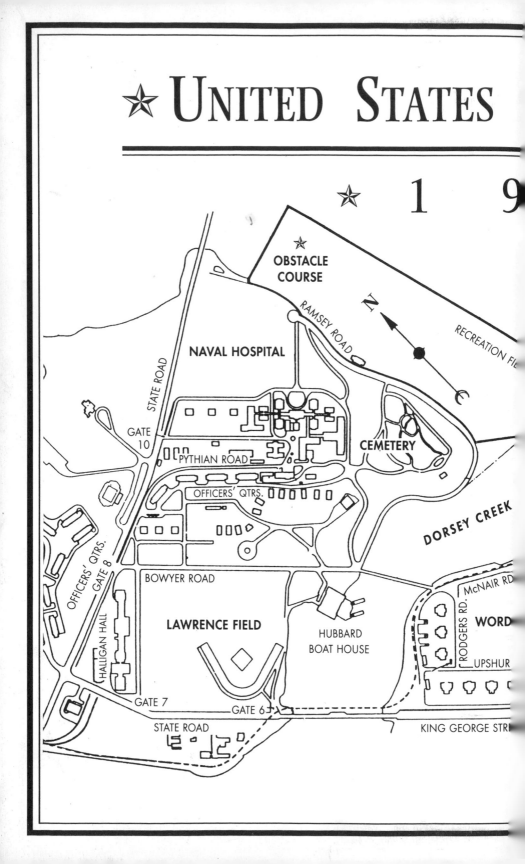

★ UNITED STATES

★ 1 9

OBSTACLE
COURSE

RAMSEY ROAD

N

RECREATION FIE

NAVAL HOSPITAL

STATE ROAD

GATE
10

PYTHIAN ROAD

CEMETERY

OFFICERS' QTRS.

DORSEY CREEK

OFFICERS' QTRS.

GATE 8

BOWYER ROAD

McNAIR RD

RODGERS RD.

WORD

LAWRENCE FIELD

HUBBARD
BOAT HOUSE

HALLIGAN HALL

UPSHUR

GATE 7

GATE 6

STATE ROAD

KING GEORGE STR